HAPPINESS IS BLUE AND GOLD

By Beryl Dyson

Published by

MELROSE BOOKS

An Imprint of Melrose Press Limited
St Thomas Place, Ely
Cambridgeshire
CB7 4GG, UK
www.melrosebooks.co.uk

FIRST EDITION

Cover by Melrose Books

ISBN 978-1-910792-58-2
epub 978-1-910792-59-9
mobi 978-1-910792-60-5

Printed and bound in Great Britain by:
TJ International Ltd, Padstow, Cornwall

To Skipper

All names of characters are fictitious.

Chapter 1

'Blue', namely Bryan Leslie Unwin Everest, was born in Australia in the late 1800s. With his father, Duke, a doctor, and his mother, Martha, a teacher, they travelled with horse and wagon, tending the sick, getting a living wherever possible. Not all folks could pay with cash, and some would settle debts with various items and commodities. Some of Duke's patients had nothing to give, having spent their all on a fruitless claim in search of wealth. Whichever way, the doctor was a good, kind man, dedicated to healing the sick. Both the doctor and his wife had no desire to settle and were constantly on the move.

Blue was well educated, having been taught by his mother. As he grew up, he often assisted his father treating patients, especially those with broken limbs, although he had no wish to follow in his father's footsteps.

At a very early age, after a party of entertainers had stopped at a small township seeking the help of the doctor, Blue, fascinated by the clown, immediately declared he would become a clown and travel the world. His Ma and Pa thought this a nine-day wonder but, with this aim in life and with great determination, he practised juggling and became adept at walking on stilts made from crude pieces of wood. Perfecting his balance on the two poles, he jumped, danced, twisted and twirled as if he was born with them.

He made friends easily and the first true and long-lasting friend Blue ever had, by sheer coincidence, was one of his father's patients.

Now, their wagon loaded, the doctor and his family were ready to leave the small dusty town that had been their home for over a year.

Many friends gathered to wish them well, very sad they were moving on.

Blades of green grass became more visible, leaving behind barren wastes, as the Everests moved further into the countryside.

Duke Everest sang as the wheels turned and, glancing at his wife, saw she had a happy smile on her face, enjoying the new scenery and the feel of freedom again while Blue, who was whittling a large piece of wood with his knife, was whistling.

Duke noticed a freshness in the air. Soon they must look for a place to spend the night.

They came upon a waterhole quite by accident. The wagon trail had branched off to the right, near some large boulders, which Duke decided to follow.

His luck was in, for around the corner, some way along the track, was an open space with fresh grass for the horse, trees for shade, and a waterhole.

He pulled up some way away from the well-trodden bank of the waterhole, watching as a party of brightly coloured birds took flight.

No one moved far from the camp fire as it seemed a popular drinking spot for animals, according to the many footprints.

A few days later they were on the move again, intending to make good progress before the sun became too hot. At noon, as Duke was about to call a halt, Blue shouted, "Pa! A ranch-house! Look!" pointing in the direction of some far distant trees.

Coaxing the horse on, they saw to their delight a long low building surrounded by fences and trees, set in a green pasture, looking neat and clean and so inviting. A long wide veranda alongside the now shuttered windows stretched the whole length of the wooden building, dotted here and there with cane chairs.

The place seemed deserted. Usually the doctor was met by a hubbub of children, dogs and chickens. Here, none, not even a stockman. Suddenly a door opened, there were voices. A tall, well-dressed man in his late forties appeared, looking surprised at the trio on the wagon seat.

Duke lifted his hat.

"Good day, Sir," he said, jumping from the wagon, holding out his hand as the man was about to turn on his heel and go back inside. Ignoring the proffered hand, the man said, almost inaudibly, "No time for traders today. I thought you were the doctor."

"I am a doctor, Sir, my name is Duke Everest and this is my wife, Martha, and son, Blue. I have credentials," replied Duke, pulling a leather case from his pocket.

Ben Dere looked at this stranger in disbelief.

"You – a doctor? It's my son, Matthew, an accident, his leg and foot, terrible." His voice faltered. "My man has gone to fetch a doctor. The waiting is unbearable. My wife, Beth, is with the boy. Come in."

By now Martha had moved to Duke's side, leaving Blue to care for the horse.

Ben called out. A young girl, about seventeen years of age, quickly appeared. Her eyes were very red from crying and her face ashen.

"My daughter, Rebekah. Look after Mrs Everest." Having made the introductions, he quickly showed the doctor to the boy's room.

The room was in semi-darkness. The doctor passed a greeting to the boy's mother, crossed the room and opened one of the shutters. Light fell upon the dark-haired boy. He seemed to be in a coma. Removing his coat, the doctor washed and dried his hands; thoughtfully someone had prepared the room. Duke lifted the boy's eyelids, then gently removed the light covering off the damaged leg. His sharp intake of breath said everything to the two onlookers. There was no time to lose.

Duke, taking Ben outside with him, said as he did so, "I must fetch my bag."

After closing the bedroom door he added, "Your wife must

leave the bedside, I'm afraid there is no alternative but amputation," trying to comfort the man as he spoke. "You knew, didn't you? You do not know me. Will you trust me to go ahead? No time must be wasted."

The man nodded his agreement, too full of emotion to speak.

Martha joined them, her neat clean clothes covered now by a large white apron. She had brought clean linen for her husband to wear. The look on her husband's face told her things were not good. Ben returned to his son's bedroom and gently told his wife what was about to happen and the urgency. With one last look at their son, they quietly left the room.

Chapter 2

Blue wandered into the bungalow. He was hungry. The smell of cooking lured him in the direction of the kitchen. Hat in hand, he pushed open the kitchen door. Beth had to keep busy. The aroma from the freshly baked cakes, mingling with a large pot of brown stew simmering on the big cooking range, was delicious.

"How-do Ma'am, smells lovely in here, Mrs ...?" He paused shyly a moment. "Sorry, I don't know your name, but mine is Blue Everest."

The boy looked at the kind, rather flushed face of a short, plump lady, who had been moving pans of boiling water to new positions on the hot stove.

"Our name is Dere."

Blue looked as she pointed to a man in a rocking chair with a Bible resting on his knees.

"My husband, Benjamin, and mine is Beth."

Benjamin, sitting with eyes closed, gently rocking the chair, made no sound. Beth continued, noticing how clean the boy had made himself, "Will you take hot water to your father, please?"

The boy nodded, dropped his hat onto a chair, lifted a large pan of boiling water from the stove and followed Mrs Dere from the room. She tapped lightly on the bedroom door. Leaving the hot water, they made their way back to the kitchen. Ladling stew into a large serving bowl, she said, "I expect you are hungry. Blue, the table is laid in the next room. Shall we go? Come along Ben. I don't think you have met our girls yet, have you?"

Blue shook his head.

As if in a daze, Benjamin followed.

At the long, polished table three girls were sitting waiting. Their ages varied from seventeen down to about twelve, at a rough guess, thought Blue. Beth placed the stew at the head of the table for Ben to serve, and introduced each girl separately.

"Our eldest daughter, Rebekah. Next is Abigail and our youngest, Ruth. Meet the doctor's son, Blue Everest. Take a seat, Blue."

Looking at her family, she said, "I think we should all try to eat something. I know Blue is hungry."

Benjamin nodded. "Yes, my dear, we must try. Let us say grace. For what we are about to receive, may the Lord make us truly thankful, Amen."

Blue cleared his plate, enjoying the stew and large pieces of freshly baked, crusty bread. The others merely picked, having no appetite, occasionally talking, each wondering what progress, if any, the doctor was making.

Blue rose from his chair.

"Please, Sir, Ma'am, thank you for the food. May I leave? My father or mother may need something." Ben nodded.

On his way, Blue took more boiling water from the kitchen, sure the other would have been used. 'Cleanliness and good manners'. He could hear his father's words echoing in his brain.

It was now late afternoon. Surely they would know soon. A noise outside attracted his attention. A wagon and riders. Could be the other doctor had arrived.

A man came bustling up the veranda steps, bag in hand.

Mr Dere, also hearing the wagon, met the doctor at the front door, and quickly ushered him into his study.

Blue was about to leave more hot water when the bedroom door opened.

"Thank you, son," said his very tired father. "I have done my best. We still have a long way to go, but there's hope."

When Blue told him the other doctor had just arrived, Duke Everest, heaving a sigh of relief, immediately made for the study.

Not knowing exactly what to do, Blue ambled outside to their wagon, made himself comfortable, and promptly fell asleep.

Doctor Everest knocked on the study door and gently opened it.

"Excuse me, I heard voices. I understand your family doctor has arrived."

Ben Dere quickly came forward.

"Yes. He was about to come to you. What news? I must know. My boy … Matthew?"

Duke held his arm and gently persuaded Ben to take a seat, quietly saying as he did so, "I have done my best. Matthew is a strong young man. The next three days are crucial. Unfortunately, he has lost the lower part of his left leg. I had no choice … I'm sorry."

Ben whispered, "Yes, you've done your best, I'm sure. I'm truly grateful. Doctor Everest, meet our doctor, Edward Jackson. I must go now to my son."

Hearing the name, Duke turned and saw for the first time Edward Jackson.

"Eddy! It really is?"

"Duke! It can't be?"

Both men spoke simultaneously, shaking one another by the hand.

"Duke … Ed," Ben gasped. "You two know each other?"

"We sure do, Ben, let me tell you, if miracles happen, you have experienced one this day. You see here one of our finest young doctors."

Ed repeated the words Ben had greeted him with, 'And he just happened to come our way!' Then, solemnly, he said, "Shall we go to Matthew? I have no doubt in my mind whatsoever that your son has had the best surgery possible."

Martha turned up the lamp to give more light as the three men entered. She had been watching the still boy for any sign of movement. She knew Matthew was lucky to be alive. An axle had snapped on a wagon loaded with fencing posts, falling on him, crushing his foot and leg. A post had hit his head, rendering him unconscious.

"Martha," Duke said in a quiet voice, "meet Doctor Ed Jackson. We studied together. Ed, meet my wife; she helps me often."

Martha smiled at Ed. "Pleased to see you."

Taking his outstretched hand, but only seeing the distress on Ben Dere's face, Martha gently touched his arm, saying, "Mr Dere, I'm really in need of some refreshment. Shall we find your wife?"

Duke nodded to her.

They found Beth and the three girls in the parlour.

"Papa!" Ruth cried, running to him and enfolding him in her arms.

Beth, looking at Martha, said, "Mrs Everest, we have a room prepared for you and your husband. Rebekah will show you. You must be totally exhausted. When you are ready, we have some supper prepared. Will you join us?"

"Thank you, Mrs Dere. Please call me Martha."

"I am Beth," came the quick reply.

On their way to the room, Rebekah asked after her brother. Martha explained as tactfully as she could, saying a lot of nursing would be needed, night and day. The young girl told her she was nearly eighteen years old and wanted to help, promising she wouldn't be a nuisance. Sensing the young woman needed something to occupy her mind, Martha thought this a wonderful idea and told her so.

"I must find Mother. Should you need anything else, please call," she said, placing the lighted lamp on the small bedside table.

Martha found Beth and Rebekah in the warm kitchen; she had heard their voices as she walked down the passage.

"I hope I'm not intruding?" asked Martha, entering quietly.

The forlorn look on Beth's face spoke a million words. How it happened neither of them quite knew; both women became locked in each other's arms, sobs wracking their bodies, one

8

trying to give comfort, thinking it could have been her son, Blue; the other wondering, not knowing what the future, if any, might hold for her precious Matthew, sharing her grief with this kind, understanding woman.

Rebekah watched and waited quietly before pouring the tea, realising the necessity for her mother to give vent to her pent-up emotions. Placing the tea tray, fresh scones and cakes on the table, Rebekah quietly left, taking another laden tray to the study.

Chapter 3

A chink of light through the wagon cover told Blue it was morning. As usual he was hungry. Wondering how Matthew was, he looked out. All seemed very quiet, but he could see a man sitting, propped up against a post on the veranda. It was Jake, the yard hand. Jake had seen the movement in the wagon, he missed nothing.

"Hi, Blue, I told your father I'd keep an eye on ya. Come on in. Breakfast soon."

"Any news yet, Jake?" Blue asked before going inside.

Jake shook his head, popped something into his mouth and started chewing. He had been sitting out there for most of the night, whilst young Matthew's Ma and the new lady had taken it in turns to watch over the young lad.

Jake looked around. It was a beaut of a morning. The Dere Sheep Station, close to the Darling River, had been his home for many years. Anyone lucky enough to work for the boss knew they would never find another place in the area equal to this. He wasn't married, never had been. He had his own living quarters a short distance from the bungalow, with everything he needed, not that his needs were great, because he was looked after like one of the family. Bless 'em. The married fellas did quite well; fine new quarters alongside the new barn. On the whole everyone seemed happy. Until this accident happened.

The station was big and ran several thousand sheep. Casual labour came at the peak of the season, joining the regular hands, working from daylight until dark, which he enjoyed, listening to the gossip and news from surrounding homesteads. He watched two of the wives walking towards him. Coming to help Boss' wife no doubt, mused Jake.

Two days passed before Matthew opened his eyes. His mother was with him. Her call brought the two doctors to the bedside.

Matthew took a small sip of cool water, giving his mother a wan smile, before closing his eyes and dropping off into a natural sleep. To everyone's relief it marked the beginning of his slow recovery.

Doctor Everest insisted it was his duty to tell Matthew of his disability; also some of the many problems to be endured. It was possible that Matthew would blame him, the doctor, for the amputation. He had to be convinced there was no alternative, and Duke felt it was his responsibility to do just that.

Duke Everest sat beside the bed. Rebekah, who had been a tower of strength, was also there. Matthew, awake, was feeling stronger and had taken a light broth, and begun asking questions. The doctor felt now was the right time to tell him, and began explaining.

Rebekah found and held her brother's hand under the cover, quietly thinking what an honest, kind man this doctor was. They hadn't known or heard of the Everest family until some days ago, yet she knew in her heart they would remain friends forever.

Rebekah watched as Matthew's face blanched; she thought he would pass out again. He couldn't believe it.

"It's not true?" he cried, looking at Rebekah. "I'll never be able to walk again or ride my horse?" The despair in his voice was tragic.

"Yes, you will, on my heart, I promise," replied the doctor. "You are young and strong. Your father assures me you have a great determination. He's relying on you."

At that moment both parents came into the room. Leaving the family together, with a heavy heart, Duke went in search of his wife.

He found her sitting on the veranda surrounded by books; on the table were glasses and fruit juice in a covered jug. He took some.

Abigail, Beth's second daughter, and Ruth, the younger one, sitting next to Blue were chattering away nineteen to the dozen. Duke nodded to Martha. Oh, so he has told Matthew, she thought, looking into her husband's sad eyes.

Duke then turned his attention to the young ones, saying "Lessons or pleasure?"

"The way Martha teaches," Abigail answered, "it's a pleasure."

Martha laughingly said, "But you said your teacher, Mr Bantok, was a dear. Your mother can be very strict, can't she, Blue?"

He nodded agreement, pulling a funny face at the girls, then asked, "It's Abigail's birthday soon, she's having a party, do you think we'll still be here, Dad?"

"Hard to say, son. Doctor Jackson could take care of Matthew now."

Changing the subject, Duke asked, "Have you looked to the horse, son?"

"Jake has."

Satisfied, the doctor went inside.

Many weeks were to pass before the Everest wagon left the Homestead. Some were very enjoyable for Blue, after his meeting with Matthew.

"I'm sure Matthew would like your company, Blue."

Looking at his Ma, he hesitated before answering her. "What could I say to him?"

"I'm sure you'd think of something, he does need cheering up." Her mind was dwelling on Matthew's pale, sad face; no incentive to move, or say or do anything.

She carried on, "I seem to remember your one and only ambition, Blue, is to be a clown, to make unhappy people laugh, to forget their troubles for a while. Have you forgotten, or have you changed your mind?"

"No! My mind's made up. I'm determined to be a clown," came his quick reply, "but Jake has promised to teach me to ride, he taught Matt! Said Matt was good."

He sat quietly for a moment. "OK," he agreed. "I'll try."

Martha sent up a quiet prayer. If Blue couldn't do it, no one could.

The bedroom door was ajar. Blue peered around to make sure Matthew was alone. Gee, he did look sick. Blue hadn't met him before. He must be fourteen or more, his age. He thought, no one told me how old he was.

Sensing someone had come in, Matthew had opened his eyes and stared at his visitor.

"Hi Matthew, I'm Blue, the doctor's son. Mind if I come in?"

Matthew closed his eyes.

Blue looked around the room.

"No books, Matthew?" he queried.

"Don't want any," came the dull reply.

"I'll fetch my treasure box from our wagon. Would you like to see our treasures? Some may interest you. My father has numerous things given to him. So do I," went on Blue.

Before Matthew could say 'no', Blue had made for the door. Returning, he drew up a chair beside the bed and opened a carved wooden box. Matthew couldn't resist looking.

"This," said Blue, holding a long musical instrument, "an Irish man gave to Father for making him feel well again. He hadn't any money, but he insisted Father took it."

He placed the instrument on the bed. "Dad said he earned his money playing in bars."

Matthew looked at it. "It's a flute," he said.

Blue turned out more pieces, pleased to know Matthew had taken an interest in the flute. It was a start. He watched as Matthew picked it up from the bed. He turned it over and over then placed it to his lips with the kind of reverence known only to musicians. Blue sat transfixed as Matthew played. Only once had he heard the flute played by the Irishman, a completely different melody to this.

Matthew loved music. He delighted in composing melodies on his harmonium, and would sit for hours. In no time he was in complete command of the flute, the room filled with its melodious sound.

Matthew stopped for breath, he was smiling.

"I didn't think …"

Then he remembered, and the smile left his face.

"I'll never play my harmonium again. I need both feet for the pedals."

He was silent, putting the flute back on the bed.

"The flute is yours," said Blue quickly. "When you are ready to play your harmonium again, someone will work the pedals. Here and now I volunteer, I am your slave, Sire," he mimicked, giving a most lowly bow. "Now, most noble lord, I would like more music. Play on."

Picking up the flute, Matthew played again, a lively tune.

Blue began juggling anything from within the box that came to hand, catching, balancing, twisting and jumping. Matthew had seen nothing like it before. They both stopped, breathless.

"Wow. Matt, with a bit of practice, we would make a good double act," Blue gasped, flat out on the floor.

"Who taught you juggling, Blue?"

"Same person who taught you, I expect," came Blue's quick rejoinder. "I remember when the Irish fella played, people sang and danced. Wonder who taught him? I'm no musician, Matt," he said while replacing his treasures to the box, "but one day I hope to be a clown or juggler in a circus."

He finished with a determined flourish.

"What about your father, Blue, doesn't he assume you should follow in his footsteps? My dad expects me to take over the ranch," Matthew said, matter-of-factly.

"No," replied Blue. "His philosophy, is that one must choose for one's self. He believes happiness is a great thing in life, as is love. My parents have given me both. My future will be up to me."

The boys chatted together like the brothers neither of them had had. Blue's opinions and outlook were far more advanced than Matthew's, because of his vast experience due to constant travel.

Neither Beth, nor Martha, could stand the suspense any longer, and nor could Jake, for that matter. The three of them peered through the open window.

"No need to ask if you've enjoyed yourselves. The look on your faces alone is enough," said Martha.

For an answer Matt lifted the flute and began to play. Tears rolled down his mother's cheeks. As she dabbed at them, Matthew stopped playing.

"No need to cry, Ma, everything's going to be hunky-dory!" he cried, and continued playing. It wasn't long before Matthew had progressed to spending his time on a divan on the veranda with Blue close at hand.

Jake, with Duke's help, had made the lad a pair of crutches. With a little practice, he would soon be on the move again. The leg was healing nicely. There were no after effects from his head wound, so Matthew's own Doctor Jackson decided not to call again for a while, leaving Duke Everest in charge, much to Beth's delight, as Martha and Beth had become bosom pals.

Everyone was taking it easy on the veranda. Ed Jackson, about to leave, enquired of Duke if he was interested in joining him at his practice.

"I need some help, what with the railway coming through, the general run-o'-the mill ailments, I have very little spare time. We could do with a nurse, Martha, or a teacher maybe. Think about it folks. There's a house close by, a school and a store. The town is really growing."

Rebekah listened intently to him, her heartbeat quickening. Perhaps this was the chance she had been waiting for. She had no intention of settling down with Mark Weston, son of their nearest neighbour. She knew that would delight her Papa, who had encouraged that young man to visit the homestead often. He was not her idea of a husband; in fact, she had no wish at all to become a wife on a homestead, living a humdrum existence. Helping to nurse her brother had given her a real purpose in life. Now, with great determination she spoke out.

"I'd love to train as a nurse. Doctor Jackson, do you think it at all possible?"

"Oh no! Rebekah, you're far too young to leave home. Isn't she, Ben?" her mother intervened quickly.

Ben looked at his daughter. "Well, we had hoped ..." He stopped talking as Rebekah shook her head.

Her mother continued, "I think you are far too young to be on your own, even if Martha and Duke were there, and perhaps they wouldn't like the responsibility. It would not be fair to ask."

Rebekah continued to argue, but both parents were adamant.

It was Ed Jackson who suggested a solution. Providing Rebekah's parents agreed, she would be quite welcome to live with him and Mrs Jackson, at Justville, returning home to her family as and when she pleased. Beth said she would need some time to think and talk it over with her husband. Rebekah decided she had said enough for the time being.

Chapter 4

At first Matthew felt very self-conscious when, with the help of his crutches, he ventured outside. Everyone was so delighted to see him out and about again, encouraging him, giving him the confidence he needed, it was not long before he moved with great speed.

For some while now, Blue had experimented with his stilts, gradually extending their length, making balancing more difficult. He then challenged Matthew to race, crutches versus stilts. Blue towered over Matthew.

"Must be all of twelve feet up there," Matthew said, looking skywards.

"What you need now are a pair of long billowy trousers. Shall we ask my sister Abby to make you a pair?" he suggested.

"Do you suppose she would? I would like white ones with blue stripes, circles or stars on them or something like that. Race you to the house, Matt!" Blue laughingly challenged him.

Jake, watching the two boys loop along, took off his hat, scratched his head, laughed out loud and said, "Blue, the Kangaroo Clown." A name which stuck and became Blue's nickname.

They shouted for Abby. When she appeared on the veranda, she saw two breathless boys.

"Abby," asked Matthew, "could you make Blue some long baggy trousers?" Blue hopped on the stilts again, puffing and wobbling about.

"I could try, I would need some measurements."

Abigail, Ben and Beth's second daughter, loved sewing, spending hours painstakingly embroidering covers for the cushions and backs of chairs, exquisitely smocking bodices and night garments, never wasting the smallest piece of material.

The trio searched trunks and boxes in the sewing room, only finding worn cotton and linen sheets.

"Suppose we paint blue stars and stripes on the linen, we have some blue ink," suggested Matthew.

Measurements taken, the boys left Abigail full of enthusiasm. She planned, snipped and sewed, having great fun. She even fashioned a shirt with a deep frilled collar and cuffs. Carefully she painted on dots and stars.

The garments were wonderful and fitted perfectly. Blue, showing off the suit, paraded and pranced about on his stilts for all to see, tormenting Ruth, Matthew's younger sister, mercilessly. She thought it was a fuss about nothing. He was just a show-off. For some strange reason she and Blue always aggravated each other. He did things to annoy her, like quietly tying her hair ribbons to the chair back. The worst possible thing, for which she never forgave him, was the time he sent her to Jake, the head stockman, and others present, for a tin of elbow grease. No doubt her time for revenge would come: until then she avoided him as much as possible.

Ruth, the youngest member of the Dere family, had long, flaming red hair and a temper to match. She adored her father and her greatest pleasure was riding the ranch with him, talking about cattle or sheep or discussing the number of men required for the shearing, as each year the ranch grew more and more prosperous. Her great grandfather had settled here on this piece of land, seeing the potential future of stock-raising, and turning his back on the improbability of becoming rich through gold-mining.

Soon it would be shearing time. Ruth, almost in her teens, loved the hustle and bustle, loved the homestead and everything connected with it. From the time she was knee high, she had crazed her father to let her ride. Why 'Bekah wanted to leave was impossible for her to understand.

The morning of Abigail's birthday was perfect, and for her

special treat, a trip of some miles through the grass pastures to the Darling River, was all she asked.

With freshly baked pies, cakes and cooked meats, the two families set off for the river for a picnic. This was the first time the Everests had visited the river. A small log cabin, set some distance from the river bank, well equipped with chairs and tables, looked idyllic. Soon the tables were laid. Everyone was hungry. The girls wandered off to the wide, sparkling river, where a sandy area had been cut out from the bank to make crossing easier. Rocks made ideal seats on which to sit and dangle one's feet in the cool, clear water.

Duke and Ben walked the bank, occasionally stopping to look towards the other side of the river.

"It's my ambition to own land on that side of the river, taking us near the edge of the range you can see in the distance."

Ben pointed to the green grass scrub-covered land shimmering in the heat haze.

"There is some good grazing, bit more rocky though. Grandfather had this in mind when he staked his claim."

Duke looked towards the rocky range.

"I agree and you would be ideally placed here, if the railroad were extended in this direction. Selling your livestock would be much easier."

Looking about him, Duke felt a sudden urge to put down roots. Never before had he seen a place inviting enough to settle in. He quietly wondered if Martha felt the same way.

"Supposing Martha agreed, what would you say if we invested in a small patch over there? This is the loveliest spot I have seen in all my travels. If you don't mind, would you look into it for us?"

Ben took Duke by the hand. "Nothing I would like better to have you both for neighbours."

Smiling, he slapped Duke on the shoulder.

The two of them stood quietly listening as the sweet sound

19

of the flute filled the air. Overcome with emotion, with tears trickling down his cheeks, Ben turned to Duke.

"How can I ever repay you? But for you, we would have lost him ..."

In silence they returned to the party.

Jake, who had been left in charge of the homestead for the day, met them as they arrived back.

"We've had a lovely day, Jake, we didn't want to return home," chorused the girls.

"Good thing you did," Jake replied. "Doc Jackson sent a message, he wants some help. I've sent his man down to the bunk-house for a clean-up and eats. Says there's been a fall. Blasting brought a slide. Several casualties."

Chewing and lifting some baskets from the wagon, depositing them on the veranda, Jake took charge of the horse.

Matthew's leg had now healed enough and could be tended by his mother. Duke felt he should give help to his friend, Ed Jackson.

"It will be dark soon, I think I will go back to Justville with Ed's man. Martha, you could pack and come first thing in the morning with Blue. What do you say?"

Martha was in agreement. "I'll pack your bag, dear."

"What a sad end to our party," declared Beth, collecting bits and pieces, calling to her daughter. "Here, take this basket, 'Bekah. What's the matter with you?" she said, looking at Rebekah standing motionless.

"Mother, I want to go with them."

"There's no place for you at Justville," said her mother, bustling towards the door. "Anyway, Mrs Jackson will have enough on her hands taking care of others, without you in her way."

"I won't get in her way, Mother. I'm determined to go, nothing will stop me. Matthew is better, and I would rather go with Duke and Martha than by myself," she added, knowing this would add weight to the argument.

"I think we'd best discuss this inside," Ben said calmly.

As they went in Blue was heard to say, "I'll miss you, Matt. Our expedition to Puttock's Pool, which Jake promised us, will have to wait."

Leaving the family to talk things over, Duke and Martha started to pack. Blue ambled in, looking very dejected. "Do you think we'll come back here again, Dad?"

Duke ceased packing and gazed out of the window.

"Perhaps! Who knows! Would you like to come back?"

"Wish I wasn't going really," replied Blue, sadly.

Rebekah came rushing down the passage, her face aglow.

"They said I can come if you agree. Do! Please! I promise I'll do my best." She eagerly looked from one to the other.

The doctor held out his hand and she placed hers in his strong grasp.

"It won't be easy for you Rebekah, often very disheartening. That so, Martha?"

"Yes, sometimes very sad, you'll have to harden your heart, but I'm sure you'll make a good nurse," she agreed, giving the girl a hug. "It will be wonderful for me to have female company."

Rebekah was overjoyed.

Blue had a sudden thought.

"If 'Bekah comes with you, why can't I stay here? I could help Matt and Mr Dere around the homestead."

Excitedly he looked at Rebekah. "Do you think your Ma would agree?"

"You bet she would! But have you thought about your own family. Won't they mind?" Rebekah enquired, looking at his parents.

Duke laughed. "You seem to have it buttoned-up," he said, looking at the two beaming faces. "Come, let's ask your Ma," said Blue and the pair disappeared.

So it was arranged. Duke left with Doctor Jackson's man.

Martha and Rebekah would leave with Jake at first light next morning, Jake returning on Duke's borrowed horse.

After their departure, Beth went about her business, feeling sad at the sudden upheaval and her firstborn leaving the family home. Although with Blue and his joviality, her sadness became less apparent.

Blue learned from Jake very fast, always willing to help, thoroughly enjoying the thrills and spills of ranch life. Best of all, he felt as if he were one of the family, the Dere family. He stayed behind with Matt, who was unable to ride yet, helping to tend the large vegetable patch and was delighted to see how quickly the vegetables flourished, never before having had a garden. They set a variety of plants and vegetables and had a very important task keeping the vermin from eating the young, tender shoots.

Blue had one great problem on his mind. He wished Matt could throw away his crutches. Something must be done. An artificial aid, perhaps? He had seen some being worn. An idea began to form; he would consult Jake.

Blue excitedly told Jake of his idea. A strong cup-shaped frame with leather straps attached to secure to Matthew's upper limb or waist, with room to pad the inside with material or sheep wool, into which Matthew could place his damaged leg. It could have a clamp-like fitting, perhaps, to take a strong wooden peg for height adjustment, on which Matthew could balance. Of course, it must not be too heavy. Jake listened intently. The travelling blacksmith was due to call at the home-stead shortly, he informed Blue, and would stay for some time. Maybe he would have some ideas. They agreed to say nothing of this to Matthew in case of disappointment.

The more Blue thought, other ideas came to mind: if something could be fitted to a stirrup, Matty could ride again, once he obtained his confidence. He looked Heavenwards.

"Oh! Please! Please!" he begged, "let it work."

Impatient to know if his idea would work, Blue hurried to the forge. The blacksmith had arrived and was busy hammering a red-hot horseshoe into shape on the anvil. Sparks of iron showered everywhere. After punching the holes, he picked up the hot shoe with his tongs and plunged it into the cold water tank. Blue waited until the hissing had ceased, then told his story to the blacksmith. Nodding, and drawing with a piece of white chalk, and occasionally wiping the perspiration from his nose, the kindly 'smith made a pattern as if this request was not new to him.

"Must have his measurements, need time to think," the blacksmith grinned, showing brown uneven teeth. "Come again and bring Matthew. Good lad!" He slapped a delighted Blue on the back.

Back at the bungalow, Beth, Matthew and Abigail were lazing in chairs on the veranda. Ruth was out with her father. Accepting the drink that Beth held out, he asked, "Expect you've wondered where I've been?"

His face flushed with excitement, Blue told his story.

"I hope it will work. Abby, we'll need your help for the padding ... then after a time, with practice ... Matthew, what do you think?"

Matthew could only stare, he was lost for words.

"You'll be measured? Give it a chance?" Blue asked.

"Sure I will. Sounds like a good idea," he said, his face beginning to light up.

When his father and sister returned, they were told immediately. Everyone hoped it would work.

Ruth said very little. It would be excellent if it worked. Of course it had to be that big-headed Blue's idea, pest! He even had Abby falling over herself stitching coloured material, making balls of sawdust for his stupid juggling.

News of the blacksmith's task spread around the quarters like wildfire and, one by one, folks dropped by to see what progress had been made, each in turn offering suggestions and ideas.

The day arrived for the last fitting. Being very careful with the seams, one of the stockmen had stitched the leathers. Tom, the blacksmith, felt pleased with their efforts, as he drove along the track to the bungalow, the special package safely beside him.

The boss called him inside to where the family were gathered. Kneeling in front of Matthew, Tom gently pushed the appliance into position, explaining as he did so how this or that strap fitted and where to make an adjustment at his waist for comfort.

"Does it feel comfortable?" Tom asked, helping him to stand, holding out the crutch. "Dare say you'll need this for a while. It will seem strange at first," he added, seeing Matthew wobble.

Beth had tears in her eyes as she watched her son take a few nervous steps. Tom declined Beth's offer of tea, accepting her thanks and gratitude.

"He will soon master it, Ma'am."

Replacing his hat, Tom followed Matthew to the veranda with words of encouragement as he tottered along like a newly born calf, pleased with every step the boy took.

The family were delighted with Matthew's progress. Every day there was further improvement, until eventually he cast away his second crutch, using only a walking stick to help him balance and ease pressure off the still tender flesh.

Tom knew the stockmen were waiting to see Matthew, so he asked Jake to bring him to the stockmen's quarters.

The married stockmen's quarters were situated a half mile or so from the main bungalow. A large building built of timber and galvanised sheet designed to house six families. A large oblong building, suitably partitioned, sheltered single men and casual workers when required. Abigail and Blue accompanied

Jake, giving Matthew a helping hand. Sure enough, as soon as the party reached the living quarters, a group came to greet them, watching quietly as Tom helped Matthew to alight.

When the lad walked towards them unaided, they were overjoyed. The men tossed their hats in the air, giving whoops of delight.

Abigail thanked them for their help and a smiling Matthew shook each one by the hand. "Soon be riding with you again," he told them, full of confidence. Taking his flute from his pocket, be began to play the polka.

They clapped and danced and stamped their feet – a most joyous occasion.

Before Tom moved on, unknown to the boys, he fashioned an iron which could be fitted to Matthew's stirrup. This he entrusted to Jake, saying, "You'll know when the lad is ready. Best not to raise his hopes too high for a start."

Jake gave Tom a mighty pat on the back. "I've been headman here many years, Tom, old pal. I can't thank you enough for what you've done. You've given us all a new lease of life."

Blue was pleased to see Doctor Jackson, who called at the homestead, checking on Matthew, and to have news of his parents. All was well with them. They missed him, but were very busy.

The doctor told the family that Rebekah was a born nurse. She also had countless admirers but was not interested. Inspecting Matthew's artificial limb, praising Tom's work and satisfied with the patient's progress, he continued on his journey.

The ranch continued to prosper. A dutiful Jake watched as Matthew moved around with ease, eventually suggesting to him he should ride again, showing the two lads Tom's aid for clipping on the stirrup. Blue was ecstatic, while a serious Matthew inspected the piece of metal.

Matthew rode again. He felt he had a great deal to live for, now he was becoming accustomed to his disability.

Teaching Matthew the accounting side of the homestead, his father explained to him some business matters needed attention and thought it a good idea if he and Blue accompanied him on a trip to their Adelaide solicitor.

To Beth and his daughters, he thought it an opportunity for them to spend time with Martha, Duke and Rebekah in Justville for a holiday. They were overjoyed.

"When? How soon?" They demanded.

"We must leave that for Martha to decide," he replied, nearly deafened by the barrage of questions.

Martha hastily replied to their message, "Come as soon as possible."

There was sheer pandemonium in the Dere household. Boxes and trunks were assembled, clothes pressed and packed and, last but not least, a special batch of baking had to be done. Departure time came, leaving Jake in charge of the homestead.

Chapter 5

Duke and Martha were fortunate to acquire a large house in Justville, a small township with a wide drovers track running through its centre. A number of new houses had been built and the town's population was growing fast. New roads were being made and the promise of a railway, close to the mining area, brought settlers and prospectors needing medical attention.

The doctor's house was a large wooden structure, a two-storey dwelling consisting of ten rooms. Designed by a French architect, it was one of the oldest houses in town. Five wide steps and carved wooden handrails led up to the main entrance, with more railings continuing along a balcony on either side of the front door, the door centred between four large sash windows and neatly carved shutters.

Upstairs, French windows opened onto a similar balcony, giving a general appearance of a well-to-do establishment.

Inside, the rooms were sparsely furnished, just enough for their immediate needs. Duke used a small downstairs room for his visiting patients and in a long, light sitting room were arranged three single beds, a table and three comfortable chairs. This room was always ready for any emergency, and its cleanliness was now Rebekah's responsibility, as she had made her home with Duke and Martha.

Satisfied everywhere was neat and tidy, Martha and Rebekah decided they needed a rest and took their tea into the parlour. It would have been nice sitting on the balcony, but the wind whipped the dust from the road into clouds. Rebekah sat very quietly. Martha looked at 'Bekah as if through her mother's eyes. Dark brown hair platted and pinned neatly on top of her head, almost the same colour as her honest, velvet brown eyes, enhanced by her cream and gold linen dress, making her look neat and slim.

Rebekah had matured and blossomed as the two women worked together, Martha finding her a tower of strength.

"What will your mother say?" she pondered. "She hasn't seen you for so long. You are so grown up. I expect Blue has grown beyond all recognition."

Then she added wistfully, "I have missed him."

Duke joined them, bringing his tea. "Ed is taking care of things this evening. I've missed Blue, be good to see him."

In silence he drank his tea. Martha took the cup and saucer lovingly, looking at his handsome face. In a matter of moments he had fallen asleep. The two women left quietly.

From the time of taking up residence, in partnership with Doctor Jackson, Duke had been in great demand, working round the clock, as the saying goes, with either Martha or 'Bekah by his side, never sparing himself, only satisfied by the complete recovery of his patient, sadly disheartened with failure, always thinking he could have done more.

Much later, Martha stood by the front balcony. A horse and rider pulled in near her.

"Mrs Duke, ma'am," the rider said removing his hat. "Just passed a wagon heading this way, must be your folks, miniature edition of Doctor Duke driving. Be about half an hour I'd say." Replacing his hat he rode on.

It was no secret the family were coming to stay. Martha rushed inside and gave them the message. Kettle boiling, everything ready, they could hardly contain themselves, and for no apparent reason Martha wanted to cry.

All three were waiting and waving at the doorway as the wagon approached. Duke called his helpman, Brin, to come and hold the horses. A great surge of pride shot through him when he saw his tall, healthy looking son. Blue, acknowledging his salute with his mischievous grin, cried "Hi Dad, hi Ma."

Talk, hugs and kisses, laughter and tears, all mingled unashamedly as they greeted one another.

The boxes and packages were deposited on the veranda. Martha ushered them inside. Inquisitively, they toured the house, Rebekah eventually showing them their respective rooms. Delighted, they opened the French windows and walked onto the balcony. It was quite an experience to have a two-storey house.

"We have a store that way," said Rebekah, pointing to the right. "Close by is the saloon and barber shop and Mrs McBean, our dressmaker, stitches in her parlour. You must meet her, Abby," she said, beaming at her two sisters. They chatted happily.

"Did you notice how well Matthew walks now, 'Bekah? Tom made him a fine frame. He can even ride his horse," declared Ruth.

Abby chipped in, "You didn't say it was Blue's great idea."

"No! It's Blue does this and Blue does that," said Ruth sarcastically. "If it wasn't for him, I could have gone on a trip to Adelaide with Father."

"You know that's not true," contradicted Abby.

Eventually Rebekah left them to clean themselves, as it had been a very hot and dusty ride. The meal was a happy occasion and they could have sat all night, everyone having so much to say. 'Bekah, excusing herself, left the table and walked to an enormous pile of something, covered with a pretty cloth, which she removed, revealing wrapped parcels. Reading the names, she handed the parcels around.

Martha said, "We were bringing them home with us, but you beat us to it."

'Bekah was surprised when she found one for herself – from Martha and Duke. Rebekah acknowledged the gift, smiling at them.

Ruth, the first to unwrap her parcel, gasped, "How lovely." She held up a suede riding skirt and jacket, the jacket emblazoned with bright stitching and long trimmings from the sleeves. The jacket fitted perfectly. She paraded around and gave 'Bekah and Martha a hug. Duke and Ben, sporting hand-sewn waistcoats of the latest fashion, watched as Beth and Abigail held, to their delight, hand-woven dress lengths.

Serviceable black leather boots for Rebekah and Martha were revealed, while Blue opened a portable wooden case on which were carved his initials. Inside it contained various compartments filled with theatrical make-up, a mirror, wig, gloves and a blue and white cone-shaped hat. The temptation was too great, Blue started to paint his face. In the box he also found an imitation red nose.

"Where on earth did you find this?" he asked, donning the cap, advancing towards Rebekah, who backed away to avoid a 'paint kiss' which he promptly plopped on his mother's face, to her shouts of mock dismay.

Meanwhile, Matthew, who had been struggling with quite a large box, exclaimed in astonishment, "A concertina!"

Ruth, earnestly watching her brother, did not notice Blue until he bent and placed a beautiful kiss on her cheek, mocking and laughing at her crimson blushes but moving away quickly to avoid a slap.

"You horror! Nincompoop!" she yelled at him, rubbing her face, trying to remove the paint. "Just you wait, Blue Everest. Just you wait!"

Matthew began to play, at first unable to coordinate the notes, then gradually picking out the tune of 'Auld Lang Syne'. The music filled the room and Duke began to sing, then everyone sang with gusto.

After this, goodnights were said and Ben and Duke adjourned to another room to discuss Ben's proposed trip to Adelaide.

* * *

Morning saw them all about early, Martha and Duke to attend the surgery, leaving Rebekah to look after her family.

Taking a walk to the store, they passed Mrs McBean's sewing parlour. Abigail pressed her nose to the large, bow-fronted window showing a display of haberdashery, and saw the lady busy sewing. She also spotted a spinning wheel in the corner of the room.

"I'd love to learn to spin. Shall we call in on the way back?" Abby smiled and waved to the dress-maker.

The store, an Aladdin's Cave, was filled to capacity with every conceivable item. As they picked up their purchases, plump Mr Dobson leaned on his counter and whispered to Rebekah, "Did the boots fit?"

"Oh! So you were in on the secret," she said, smiling and nodding her head.

Ruth and Abigail were looking for a present for Jake. "What should we get him, Rebekah?"

"Oh, you'll think of something. Father and the boys expect to be away for a while. There'll be lots of time," she told them while making for the door, just as a tall, suntanned fellow came barging in.

"Pardon me," he said, lifting his hat. Seeing it was Rebekah, he stopped. "Thank the doctor for me, he did a grand job. By the way, Seth sends you his love," and in a most sarcastic tone of voice he added, "No doubt, another string to your bow!"

He turned abruptly away as Rebekah's face paled.

"Who on earth was that rude fellow?" demanded her sisters. "Who is Seth? You didn't let on you had someone calling."

"I haven't," exclaimed 'Bekah. "That man, Brent Gordon, is Seth's brother. Seth had his appendix removed. Martha and I nursed him. Brent is in charge of drilling operations at the mine. We heard he doesn't approve of women, and thinks Martha and I shouldn't be doing our kind of work."

Rebekah remembered the look of disgust on Brent's face as

he stood leaning against the doorpost of Seth's room. Martha had left the room for a moment, leaving her to straighten his bed, when Seth, seizing the opportunity, grabbed her by the arms, pulled her to him, and kissed her. Laughing, she had managed to release herself. It was then she saw Brent. Shrugging her shoulders, she muttered, "Let's forget him. We will call on Mrs McBean."

The room in Mrs McBean's house was stacked with bundles of materials, all colours and various thickness, silks, organza, satin and linens. Abigail had seen nothing like it before.

"These are my sisters, Mrs McBean. Abigail would like to spin. Does it take long to learn?"

Answering Rebekah, she said, "Some it does, some it doesn't, depends." Looking at Abby, she asked, "Have ye time?"

"Now?" Abby questioned.

"If ye'd care to? My next customer will-na be here for a while."

Leaving Abigail with Mrs McBean, Ruth and Rebekah found Mrs Jackson taking tea with their mother. Mrs Jackson had called to meet Beth and her family, hoping also to see Martha to tell her their news. Edward and James, their two sons, were coming home from Sydney any day now.

"Isn't that wonderful news?" she said, her face beaming. "I wonder if they have passed their examinations. Fancy, could be three doctors in the family." Turning to Beth, she continued, "They made their home with my sister in Sydney when we came here."

"We both missed them tremendously."

"Yes, I bet you did," sighed Beth, looking at her Rebekah.

Duke and Martha arrived home. They had been to the Big 'C' cattle ranch to visit a patient of Duke's, taking Blue and Matthew with them. Beth offered them tea and fruit juice as they trouped in.

Mrs Jackson, so excited, immediately told them their two

boys would soon be coming home.

"Emily! How wonderful! Do you think they have qualified? You said both were in their early twenties and very studious."

Martha continued, "The Carters have given all of us an invitation to their place next week, for the betrothal of Katrina and Paul. Wouldn't it be great if your boys were home?"

Ruth gave a whoop of delight. "How lovely! A party!"

Matthew chipped in, "It's a beaut of a place."

Ruth, looking at Blue and clapping her hands said, "You two won't be here."

"Where is Abigail?" intervened Beth, just noticing her absence. Rebekah answered, "Having a spinning lesson with Mrs McBean."

"Oh, so soon?" she exclaimed.

"I think it's about time to eat, I expect Blue is hungry as usual!" Rebekah declared, clearing the cups and glasses.

Chapter 6

Ben Dere and the lads started their journey to Adelaide early the following morning. Beth and Ruth had spent much of the previous day making certain they had all they required for the two-day journey to the railhead.

"It's sure good to be travelling again, Mr Dere."

"I expect it is, Blue," he replied. "The time spent with us has been your longest stay ever, I suppose?"

Blue agreed as Ben continued, "When I was your age, I had never been away from the homestead. We worked very hard. My father trusted one special drover to do the selling and buying for him. The man was honest. He and my father became great friends."

The three of them chattered away. Matthew learned more of his grandfather's hardships, pleasures and plans than he had ever known. The journey became a pleasure.

By nightfall they had reached the outskirts of a small town where they planned to stay the night. Soon a small fire was burning on which they brewed some tea.

"Blue, this pack is yours, it has your name on. This is yours, Dad," said Matthew, handing out the packages.

"Good, Ruth has packed one of her special treacle cakes, mmh!" said Matthew, taking an enormous bite. His father undid his pack saying, "I have two in my pack. Lovely, she must have thought I'd be hungrier than you two."

Blue looked at his cake and took a large bite. The next moment he was dancing and hopping about shouting, "Oh! Ah! Some water, quick! Help!"

Throwing the cake on the ground, rinsing his mouth, he spat two, three times.

"Whatever is it, Blue? What's the matter?" Both were very concerned.

"That Ruth," he blustered, "you said she made the cakes? She has filled mine with chilli paste!" He picked up and held out the offending cake. "Look!"

Both began to laugh and continued laughing as Blue rinsed his mouth again and again. Still laughing, Ben offered Blue his other cake.

"That is why I had two, no doubt."

Blue shook his head. "No thanks. I believe my mouth is on fire or blistered," he sulked, puffing and blowing, causing them both to laugh all the more.

The train journey was fantastic, if not comfortable. Distant mountain ranges, enormous gum trees and flocks of brightly coloured birds seemed to glide by ceaselessly. Gigantic waterfalls tumbled from rocks, making bright rainbows. Soon the lads settled themselves, reading and playing pocket solitaire, occasionally gazing out, until they reached their destination. A large gathering of people, standing well back, watched as the train arrived at Adelaide. Still very much a novelty, the hissing monster came thundering to a standstill.

Ben was quick to alight, his trained eyes searching a long line of cabs and horses. He spotted what he thought was a clean, healthy horse with a young and strong cabby. Ben had a theory that if the beast was well cared for, the man was genuine.

Beckoning the young man over, Ben rejoined the lads to help with the luggage.

"Where to, Sir?" asked the cabby, picking up some of the luggage and stacking it on the top of his carriage.

"If you know of a clean, well-kept boarding house, suitable for the lads and myself, I'd like you to take us to it."

The cab driver had taken an instant liking to this gentleman, and the boys seemed to be well mannered. Could be his and his mother's lucky day. He had noticed one was handicapped, but still helped to move the lightest luggage.

"My mother, I'm sure, would be delighted to take care of you. Her name is Mrs Harriet Green. My name is Albert, Sir."

Taking Albert's outstretched hand, Ben replied, "Good to meet you, Albert. I am Benjamin Dere. My son Matthew, and our great friend, Blue Everest."

They settled themselves comfortably in the cab and were soon away at a steady pace, joining the hurly-burly of horses, carts, carriages and people. Albert drew up outside a large three-storey house, jumped down from his seat and opened the cab door. Ben proceeded to the open front door and was met by a rosy-cheeked, rotund lady, neat and tidily dressed in a long black skirt, frilled blouse, enveloped in a large, snow white apron.

Albert, close behind, introduced them. Ben proffered his hand.

"Pleased to meet you. I would like to see your accommodation, Mrs Green, if I may?"

"Certainly, sir. Step inside," she replied, showing him the way to the upstairs rooms. The whole place was spotless and the furniture gleamed from regular polishing. The beds, also, were as clean as a new pin, and the linen had the aroma of a scented herb to which Ben couldn't put a name.

"Ideal," declared Ben, arranging with her the fee and length of stay. He signalled Albert to bring the luggage, thanking him at the same time.

"Albert, I have business affairs to attend to next week. Would your cab and your good self be available for hire?"

Without hesitation Albert agreed. "Sure, sir."

Ben and the boys cleaned and tidied themselves and strolled outside. The evening was pleasant. Mrs Green had promised an early evening meal and, true to her word, she soon sounded the gong.

The food was delicious and she evidently believed in large portions. Her ginger pudding was a real delight. It seemed an age since they had eaten so well and were completely satisfied. Talking among themselves, Ben reminded the boys it was the Sabbath on the 'morrow and that they should find the Chapel. Mrs Green, overhearing their conversation, enlightened them as to the whereabouts of the Wesleyan Hall.

"We have a large congregation, not very far to go, sir. I make a practice of going along myself. Service at ten, we have breakfast at eight. Would you care for anything more?" She started to clear away the dishes.

"No, thank you, Mrs Green. We will see you in the morning," Ben affirmed, kindly holding open the door.

Walking to the Hall the next morning, Matthew, thinking of the service at home taken by his father, remarked it would be a new experience for him.

"What about you, Blue? Have you been to a service like this before?"

"Once or twice, I can hardly remember," he answered. "In the larger settlements, I have listened to a Gospel Preacher."

They had almost reached their destination.

"Must be a large Hall, judging by the number of people heading this way," declared Blue, looking about him.

The people seemed very friendly. The Minister, who stood by the door to welcome his congregation as they entered, greeted each and every one by their names. He appeared rather agitated, as if he were looking for a particular person who hadn't yet arrived, but only gave the newcomers a brief, "Good morning".

The service commenced by the Minister saying how sorry he was that today they had no organist.

He had tried, at the last moment, to get someone else, but unfortunately he was otherwise engaged. Looking around his congregation he said, "If anyone could help I would be delighted."

There were audible murmurs and general glances, but no one seemed forthcoming. To Ben's delight, his son stood up.

Matthew had noticed the beautiful organ standing near the reading desk. "I would like to play for you, sir."

All eyes were centred on the young man. There was a hush in the congregation. The Minister cleared his throat, looked as if he offered up a small prayer, then smiled at Matthew, who, with Blue, was heading for the organ.

The Minister produced a large hymn book, as well as the hymn numbers for the service. He asked their names as Matthew seated himself at the organ, while Blue took charge of the bellow mechanism.

"Our organist today is Mr Matthew Dere, with his friend, Blue Everest. Our first hymn, 'Forth in thy Name'..."

Matthew played the first two introductory lines. The music flowed evenly, delightfully and the amazed congregation began to sing. Matthew gave his best, following the service and paying great attention to the Minister's words, duly rendering faultless music. The final prayer was said. Matthew played one of his favourite pieces, expecting the congregation to file out, but no one moved. They sat spellbound, recognising this young man was a genius.

Finally, Matthew closed the lid of the organ.

The Minister, standing close by, shook him by the hand, saying, "Wonderful! Wonderful!" over and over, again and again.

Ben and Blue waited together as Matthew received thanks from the congregation. Mrs Green, full of importance, informed her many friends they were her guests and she must hurry away to prepare the meal. Giving Ben a smile and having a final word with the Minister, she left.

Leaving Ben and the Minister talking, the two lads hurried away.

"Matt, you were really good, were you nervous?"

"Not one bit," he laughed, "I enjoyed it immensely."

Little groups of people, who stood around talking, smiled and spoke to the two lads as they made their way back to the guest house.

Albert was sitting in the shade when the two arrived. He called, "Come and look at the stables. Do you ride?" he asked Blue.

"Yes. Both of us. Matthew rides better than I."

Albert looked at Matthew unbelievingly.

"He has an adapted stirrup. Did you bring it with you, Matt?"

"Yes. I thought perhaps Father might ride out to a sheep sale, it's quicker on horseback."

They found the stables – four in all – immaculate, bridles and saddles all neatly hung on pegs in the tack room. Albert whistled from the paddock gate and four horses came trotting to him, blowing and nuzzling, expecting a tit-bit.

"My great grandfather, in England, was a keen horse-man, lived in Norfolk. Mother thinks that's why I love horses. Bred in me. A friend of mine has horses for riding should your father need one."

"What is that square patch and pole for, Albert?" Matthew asked, pointing to a raised earthen bed and well-worn patch, leading to it by the paddock fence.

"It's a Quoit bed. Popular in England. Father made this one and taught me to play before he died."

He then explained the game in detail, showing them the Quoits that were hanging in the stables. "Show you how to play tomorrow, that is, if there's time," he promised.

Albert was a likeable chap. In his twenties, he did all he could to help his mother, especially by keeping the house in good repair. He was very handy.

Ben was waiting for them when they all returned to the house. It was dinner time. He was very pleased.

"Mrs Green has told me the name of the sweet smelling herb she uses in her polish and linen. It's lavender. Said her relations brought some from Norfolk, England. Had you noticed it? I'm sure Abigail would love to make some lavender bags."

The lads hadn't noticed the perfume. They were full of stables and Quoits.

"Have you played Quoits, Father?"

Ben shook his head.

"Albert has promised to teach us tomorrow, if there's time."

"Business matters tomorrow, Matthew. I must remember to ask Albert if he can take us," Ben said, helping himself to more berry pie.

The morning saw everyone about early.

"First of all, the Government Office, Albert please, somewhere near the waterfront I think," explained Ben, checking he had his documents, as he followed the lads into the carriage.

The Gulf was alive with tall ships and boats of various size. Eagerly, Matthew and Blue viewed the great expanse of water and busy scene, for this was the first time they had been to the coast. The work of unloading and loading the ships looked tedious, involving many men and all types of goods. On the quayside, they found the government building.

As they stepped inside, a young man approached and enquired their names and business. In due course, he ushered them into a musty smelling room filled with ledgers and books where an elderly man, seated behind a very large wooden desk, bade them to take a seat.

"Mr Dere, pleased to meet you. How can I help you?"

Ben discussed his business and also that of Duke Everest, showing him the claim documents for transfer, which he had been given by Duke. These they left in the office to be dealt with. They would return in a few days' time.

The sunlight was very bright, enough to dazzle them, when they stepped from the office. "Now to find Albert," said Ben, looking around.

Albert had seen them and gently eased his way towards them.

"To the Apothecary, Albert please, and then to find our way to Blizzard and Company Solicitors," he said, giving Albert the two addresses.

The Chemist was in the wide, main street. On either side, the street was arrayed with multi-coloured stalls, with traders of all nationalities and every conceivable item for sale, leaving just enough room for vehicles to pass. The boys were fascinated, and would have liked to spend some time browsing through the market.

"Another day, when we collect our goods," declared Ben as he returned from leaving Duke's prescription with the chemist. The business with the solicitor was more complicated and took much longer, leaving little time to return home for lunch. Mrs Green had promised fish pie. They had been told not to be late.

True to his word, Albert taught the two lads the game of quoits. Ben joined them, making a happy foursome, during which time he outlined his plans for the next few days, depending on Albert's goodwill. It was decided to ride to the Sheep Breeding station on the 'morrow, and this they did on horses from Albert's friend and with food kindly packed by Mrs Green. As they were riding, Blue thought about his family and friends. Had they all enjoyed the party at the Carter ranch? A smile crossed his face as he remembered Ruth and the chilli paste.

"You look happy, Blue," observed Ben.

"Just thinking about the chilli paste," he replied. They all laughed. "Hope Mrs Green hasn't packed any for me."

Blue needn't have wondered if the Carter party was enjoyable. It had gone with a swing. Back home at Justville, as soon as Abigail was told about the forthcoming engagement party, dresses became the topic of conversation. The dressmaker's stock of material was turned over many times, until each girl had made her choice.

Gold taffeta for 'Bekah, fine blue linen for Abby, and white organza with blue stars and half-moons scattered all over it was Ruth's choice.

Martha fitted her grey lace dress and decided it would do

fine. Beth felt comfortable in a black taffeta skirt and frilled lace bodice, which was just as well, the two confided, as three dresses at such short notice was almost impossible.

"With Mrs McBean's stitching machine," declared Abby, "nothing is impossible."

The evening of the party arrived.

"My goodness! What a bevy of beauties I'm escorting this evening," said Duke, twirling them round and round one by one.

Beth and Martha looked at the girls in their exotic gowns, and beside them stood Mrs McBean with her needle and cottons in case anything had been missed.

"Oh, Mrs McBean, you are a clever person."

"It's not all due to me, Mrs Dere, you have a very talented daughter," the dressmaker told her, looking at Abby dressed in blue lace and linen. "Even Ruth, although she doesn't sew, did her share, she had the unenviable task of pressing."

Beth turned and looked at Ruth, young and beautiful, red hair gleaming. Her dress, neatly gathered at the waist, had a broad frill on the bodice front. Her collar and cuffs were frilled in pale blue and white. That's strange, thought Beth, where have I seen something like that before? Dismissing the thought from her mind she inspected Rebekah, who had on a plain but delightful gold taffeta dress with leg o'mutton sleeves, heart-shaped neckline, her appearance enhanced by her thick, neatly pinned coronet of dark brown hair.

"Who chose the designs?" Martha asked.

"We made our own choice," 'Bekah answered, handing her sisters warm wraps.

"Pity father isn't here," chipped in Ruth, taking a last long look in the mirror. The betrothal party at the Big 'C' ranch was in full swing when the Dere and Everest families arrived. A long, low shed had been converted and decorated with greenery and flowers, a small stage for the musicians erected at one end and wooden benches placed against the walls. Coloured lanterns suspended from the roof gave the whole place a mellow glow. Everyone looked relaxed and happy. Duke introduced Beth and her family to the Carters.

"We hope you enjoy yourselves. We'll talk again later," he said, taking leave of them as another party of guests arrived.

"Hi! 'Bekah, care to dance?" someone shouted loudly.

It was Seth.

"Hallo, Seth, may I introduce you to my family?" Flushing slightly, Rebekah made the introductions.

Dutifully he shook hands with Beth, smiled and bowed to her sisters, taking both by the hand on which he bestowed a kiss, giving them a most adorable smile, as if butter would not melt in his mouth.

"Hope to have the pleasure of your company later," he said wasting no time, whisking Rebekah off to the area set aside for dancing.

"Of course! The brother of the rude man in the store," said Ruth, giving details of the meeting with Brent Gordon to her mother.

Not many minutes passed before all three girls were dancing, returning to take a refreshing drink and get their breath back. Their partners came again, this time to make a set. Needing eight, another couple came along. 'Bekah heard Seth groan, it was his brother Brent, with a dark haired young woman, whom 'Bekah did not know.

She wondered if Brent was a good dancer. Having not noticed him before, somehow she did not associate him with dancing. It was her turn to partner him. They waltzed around the set in complete unison.

"How many more strings to your bow this evening?" he queried.

Whether deliberately or not, she trod on his foot. He held her tightly, making her breathing difficult. "Temper!" he whispered into her ear before relinquishing her to Seth.

Much later in the evening, Brent crossed the floor to Rebekah.

"May I have the pleasure?" he asked, giving a slightly mocking smile.

Unable to refuse in front of her mother and Martha without an inquisition, she accepted with good grace.

Following his steps perfectly, feeling the warmth and pressure of his hand upon her back, she thought it would be most pleasurable if this man was not so sarcastically rude, always suspecting that she and Martha were out to seduce every male patient. Just because he had seen his brother trying to steal a kiss!

The dance ended. Not a word spoken. Holding her arm, he propelled her to the buffet table, passing Seth, whose face was consumed with envy and anger.

The long tables were laden with delicious sweetmeats, cold lamb, beef and stuffed pork slices, with piles of spiced bread and numerous vegetables and salads in various flavoured sauces.

"May I serve you with some?" he inquired, deftly ladling food on two plates.

"Shall we join your party?" he asked quite naturally.

Duke had found the family a table. Rebekah introduced her companion, rather offhandedly, as Seth's brother, Brent. Beth acknowledged him politely, saying, "My husband, Ben, is away in Adelaide. Pity. It's such a lovely party. Let me see, is it mining you're in or road building?"

They chatted and laughed, sometimes drawing 'Bekah into the conversation. He was sweetness itself. What was he playing at, Rebekah wondered. Her sisters looked rather bewildered, he was supposed to be so rude. Ruth thought him rather handsome and hoped he would ask her to dance.

When the music began again, Duke asked, "Care to dance, 'Bekah?"

As they moved away, Rebekah heard Brent ask her mother if she would care to dance. The Dere girls were very much in demand. Seth managed to claim another dance with Rebekah, this time holding her very tightly. His breath smelled of alcohol and he was making an exhibition of himself. The dance ended. Very quickly she slipped from his embrace. Although she felt like running, she calmly walked to her mother and Martha, who were saying their goodbyes to Mr and Mrs Carter, Katrina and Paul.

Talking to Duke was Brent Gordon, who, without a doubt, had seen his brother's latest behaviour.

Before leaving, Brent took her hand and placed it to his lips, wishing her 'sweet dreams', his eyes mocking her blushes.

Journeying home, they were happy, snugly wrapped inside the wagon, talking about the party dresses, their likes and dislikes. Duke, sitting alone, reins in hand, felt the odd one out.

The moon was brilliant, casting eerie shadows, silver ghost-like trees stood out from the mallee scrub, and the slightest noise sent animals scurrying into the undergrowth. Now, if Blue were here, he thought wistfully, no matter what time of night they travelled, Blue and he would sit together, sometimes in companionable silence, at other times discussing trivialities, until the boy snuggled close and slept.

Dawn was practically breaking when they arrived home. Ed still had a light burning at his place. Hope nothing's wrong, he thought.

Ed Jackson, who had been listening for the sound of an approaching vehicle, opened the door and hailed Duke.

Martha and Beth, thinking something was wrong, peered around the corner of the wagon.

"Our boys have arrived home. Come in, Emily has hot drinks waiting for you," he said, quickly relieving Duke of the reins, tethering the horse to the rail, giving him no chance at all to refuse.

"Our dresses must be crumpled and creased. My hair is in disarray," complained Rebekah. All of them had fallen asleep.

"Do please come in," pleaded Emily from the doorway. "You can all sleep later."

Even at this late hour she was brimming with happiness. The thought of a hot drink sounded marvellous to Martha. It would have been too unkind to refuse.

Inside the house a log fire burned brightly. It was warm. A large jug of steaming cocoa on the table, surrounded by cups, smelled delicious and a variety of biscuits had been neatly arranged on plates. Two young men, one the image of his father, Ed, greeted them.

"It's a shame dragging you in to meet us, we did try to dissuade them both. You must be Rebekah, whom I've heard so much about."

His mother, her face beaming, carried on with the introductions ending proudly, "Meet Teddy and James. Guess what, both are doctors!"

"Well done! The pair of you," Duke said, and stepped forward, shaking each by the hand. Raising his cup of cocoa, he proposed a toast. "Good health and good luck to you both. I'm sure we all agree, we need help here. That's right isn't it, Ed?"

Their father agreed. "Us 'oldies' could do with a refresher course."

Emily, collecting the cups, said, "Thank you for coming in. I think your dresses are beautiful."

Taking Abby by the hand she turned to James.

"This young lady and our Mrs McBean made them. I didn't come to the party. I wanted to be here when the boys arrived."

Goodnights were said and the happy little party walked the remainder of the way home.

"Matt would have loved this evening's music," said Ruth. "Do you think they are enjoying themselves in Adelaide? It seems an age since they left."

"Ruth! You don't mean to say you're actually missing Blue?" Abby teased.

"I didn't mention his name," she replied heatedly as Abby continued to laugh and torment her.

Chapter 7

At the Adelaide Guest House, Harriet and Albert Green cared for their new guests as if they were members of their own family, finding them so pleasant and friendly. On their return from the sheep station, a most sumptuous meal awaited them. Ben Dere felt on top of the world. His various business deals looked promising, ensuring prosperity for his family. He then turned his thoughts to the 'morrow; a little sightseeing and an evening at the Variety Music Hall seemed to be in order. The excursion to the Music Hall came as a big surprise to both Blue and Matthew. A beautifully attired young woman, her face colourfully made-up, directed them to their seats. The inside of the theatre had been decorated in shades of pink, gold and blue, with gaudily painted gargoyles leering from odd corners. Long gold curtains, rather dusty, draped the stage. Musical instruments were arranged in front of the stage, beside them a short catwalk. Soon the hall was filled to capacity.

The musicians, who had taken up their positions, started to play with gusto. With a flourish the curtains went up and the lights were lowered. Some of the audience began singing the popular songs as one entertainer gave way to another on the small stage. The two lads were stage struck. Equally, Albert and Ben were enjoying the entertainment as much as the boys, although it wasn't a new experience for them. The highlight of the evening came. Stretched high above the stage was a tightrope. To the roll of drums, a tall thin man and a petite young girl rushed to the centre of the stage.

Expertly, he lifted the girl on to his shoulders. She stepped onto his uplifted hand, turned a somersault and landed on a board at the end of the rope.

Her name, Mitzi. Dressed in an abundance of tulle and a tight fitting glittering ensemble, gently she eased her way across the rope, perfectly balanced, carrying an open parasol. Once or twice she appeared to slip, which brought loud gasps from the crowd. Blue, holding his breath, could hardly watch. Reaching the other end, she turned and bowed to loud applause, then began the return journey. Halfway across, she lowered herself to a sitting position. The rope swayed slightly, more gasps from the audience, but with perfect grace and agility, she attained her former position, completing her journey, quickly sliding down a rope on to the floor to tremendous applause and whistles.

More music and entertainment. Then scantily clad dancing girls concluded the show. Clapping and whistling continued as the lights brightened. Joining the jostling crowd, Ben and his party made their way out. Albert had gone to collect his horse and carriage. Whilst they waited, they noticed the tall man and the small girl from the high-wire act. Most of the horse-drawn transport had left. The couple did not appear to be in a great hurry, as were the rest of the performers.

Ben stepped forward introducing himself, congratulating the girl and the man. Off stage, both looked very sad.

"Mitzi, my daughter and I ..." The tall man paused as if lost for words. "Thank you for your kind remarks, but we are both very sad. My wife, Mitzi's mother, died today." He placed an arm around his daughter's shoulders. "So we are in no hurry to return home," Ronald Gould concluded.

Ben offered his condolences and asked, "May we offer you both a lift?"

Ronald Gould accepted Ben's offer gratefully, giving him an address.

Albert had returned and overheard their conversation.

Sitting in the carriage, Mitzi remained very quiet while her father briefly explained their situation. Their stay in Adelaide was to have been short, as in most towns. Normally they worked with the circus. Unfortunately his wife had become ill, so they found rooms, seeking work at the Music Hall. Later they would catch up with the circus.

Reaching their destination, Mitzi and her father thanked them profusely.

"Don't mention it," countered Ben. "We wish you both good luck."

The visit to Adelaide was coming to an end. Ben collected Duke's medicines and medical stock while Albert took the boys around the market. They had decided to take home presents of perfume for the girls, having seen a man wearing a turban sitting cross-legged on the ground, surrounded by glass bottles, large and small. Each bottle, containing a clear liquid, had the name of a flower marked on it. Seeing the lads were genuinely interested, the man removed a glass stopper, dabbing the perfume onto Blue's hand.

"Smell pretty good, lovely flower, Gardenia."

The dark-skinned man opened more bottles for them to smell.

Matthew thought Abby should have Gardenia, and Rebekah, Rose.

"Poppy for Ruth, she has red hair," laughed Blue. "And how about Lily of the Valley for our mums and Mrs Jackson."

Leaving Blue to pay, Albert and Matthew moved to another stall.

"We thought you had got lost, Blue, you were a long time."

Blue made no comment and handed the parcel to Albert.

Walking on the other side of the wide, dusty, and in some parts, smelly street, looking at all the colourful displays of fruit, pottery, silks and spices, Blue spotted a basket.

In it were four small puppies with their mother.

The owner, partly Chinese, saw Blue looking.

"She not for sale, she my best friend," he said, speaking in broken English. "Puppy very good," he added, picking up a small, fluffy ball.

The only black puppy in the basket sensed something was happening, placed both his front paws on the edge of the basket and yawned. Blue couldn't resist picking it up. Sniffing Blue's hand the puppy started sneezing.

"California Poppy, Gardenia ..." laughed Matthew and Albert, turning away.

"Wait, I'm buying it," said Blue, turning to the owner. "How much?"

"You're not serious! What will you do with it?" they asked.

"Train him to do tricks," was his cool reply.

"Him very good fella, from classy family," declared the owner, quickly taking Blue's money.

Albert, noticing the number of stray dogs milling around, said nothing.

"What you going to name it? Dingo?" laughed Matthew.

"Him no Dingo. Him Prince of Dogs!" exclaimed the little man, very put out.

"Fair do!" said Blue, "Prince it shall be."

The Chinaman, placing both hands together and bowing reverently to Blue, said, "You very lucky fella. One day you bring great happiness to many people."

Blue patted the dog's mother, said "Good-day," then hurried away to catch up with the others.

"Better drop into that apothecary, get him to fix some powder," Albert advised.

Blue looked at him naively.

"For its coat. Doubt if Mother will appreciate too many guests. You'll also need a brush and comb."

Ben caught sight of them. What was Blue carrying? "Oh! No!" he groaned.

Harriet Green eyed the pup and was about to say something when she saw the pleading look Blue gave her. She was like putty in his hands. "See it's clean before it comes in," was all she could say.

The pup was quite content. It had been tempted with tit-bits and fallen asleep in a wooden box especially prepared in which it could travel. This was their last evening. Harriet and Albert were extremely sorry they were leaving, assuring them of a warm welcome should any of them pass this way again.

The morning of the departure arrived. Luggage was loaded and goodbyes were said. Prince in his box, complete with food and water, didn't bother at all, as he started his train journey to his new home.

Back at Justville, talk of the party soon ceased as patients arrived for treatment. James and Teddy Jackson divided their time between their father and Duke, each gaining from the other's experience, helped, of course, by Martha and Rebekah. Teddy and Rebekah liked each other's company and were happy together. That was all. Teddy, in confidence, had told her of his intended return to Sydney, where Alice, a most beautiful young lady schoolteacher waited for him. Given time, he would tell his parents his intention of marrying and living in Sydney.

'Bekah was pleased for him, confiding in him her secret dreams and ambitions to study nursing somewhere in a large hospital. He was sympathetic and understanding and asked various questions. No, she had not thought of marrying until she had qualified.

He then told her the practical experience which she had gained here in Justville would stand her in good stead. Of that he had no doubt.

Working beside her and Martha had proved that. Indeed, her nursing capabilities, in his estimation, were far more competent than some he had seen at his local hospital, although Teddy refrained from telling her so.

Young James Jackson had eyes for no one but Abby. Lost

in her world of spinning and sewing with Mrs McBean, she appeared quite oblivious to his attention.

"I have completed so much work since you came, Abby, and lots more work coming, it's a pity ye canna stay a while and help," Mrs McBean lapsed into her Scottish accent.

Abigail looked thoughtful. Did she want to leave home? she asked herself. Not particularly, came her answer. Not yet anyway, she told her.

"Father will be returning soon," commented Ruth, who had been chatting away to Martha.

"Yes, no doubt the boys have had the time of their lives. It will be good to see them again," Martha agreed. They were in the kitchen, busy preparing a midday meal. Rebekah had almost completed her task, thoroughly cleaning the Doctor's room, when a terrific noise of people shouting and horses neighing sent her hurrying outside into the street, calling to Martha as she went, that there had been an accident.

Out on the dusty road people made way for her.

"What's happened?" 'Bekah asked, looking around.

"Horses bolted with a wagon, fellow on horseback didn't stand a chance. Straight into him," answered an onlooker.

Rebekah took a quick look at the wagon driver, spotted the horse rider on the ground, blood pouring from an arm and a large cut on the back of his head.

She couldn't see his face. Tearing a large strip off her white petticoat, she quickly made a tourniquet tightly around his arm. By then Martha had arrived. Someone brought hurdles to carry the two injured men into the doctor's house.

'Bekah looked at her patient's face; it was Brent Gordon. He moaned, muttering, 'Maria'. They made the two men as comfortable as possible. Old Sam, the driver of the wagon, was badly bruised and appeared to have a broken leg.

Duke and James arrived almost simultaneously and worked side by side with the two women. Brent, luckily, had no broken bones, but stitches in his arm and head.

"Lucky to be alive, I should say, he lost a lot of blood," confided the two doctors, talking together afterwards. "Brent's head will be rather heavy for a day or so. Quite a gash. But somehow, I don't think we'll be able to keep him here long, unless we tie him to his bed," explained Duke.

Martha saw Brent wince as he tried to turn his head. He was muttering incoherently. Walking to his bedside, she quietly assured him everything would be fine, but "Try not to move your head," she advised. At once he relaxed, his breathing became even and he slept.

It was late evening when Seth arrived. Martha invited him to see his brother and left them together.

Sam's wife had hurried to the doctor's house the moment she heard the news and had been consoled by Ruth with endless cups of tea, until she was able to see her husband in bed and now fairly comfortable with his broken leg in plaster.

Brent was no model patient. Eager to be up and away, he called for his clothes. He had slept fitfully during the night, the two women taking turns to watch over both patients.

"Please stay. You're not fit to go yet," pleaded Martha. "You've had a great blood loss and you are very weak."

Rebekah, hearing Martha's call, dashed into the room in time to see Brent sway and collapse on the bed. He looked ghastly. 'Bekah cradled his shoulders while Martha gave him some water.

"Foolhardy, know-all man," chided 'Bekah, "hasn't the sense he was born with."

"Not exactly the way to speak to a patient," he retaliated, feeling a little better.

"It's the only way for such as you."

Martha couldn't believe it was Rebekah talking, but it did the trick. Without further protest he was put back to bed.

Brent didn't attempt to get out of bed again until he was

told. Feeling hungry, he had eaten the food brought to him. Duke allowed him to sit on the veranda the next morning. With help, he managed to walk; every step taken sent his senses reeling, but he said nothing, only too pleased when he reached the chaise-longue.

Teddy, as he was passing, called to Rebekah, "See you at noon. Do you need anything from the store?"

"Nothing, thank you. Anything for you, Brent?" she enquired.

"No," came his terse reply, looking at her through half-closed eyes. "Another string to your bow?"

"Of one thing I'm most certain, Mr Gordon, you are not suffering from loss of memory," came her reply as she gently placed a book and water within his reach. Rebekah was looking forward to her afternoon off with Teddy, James and her sisters. Her mother had wanted to visit Brent. This afternoon, as it turned out, suited everyone admirably.

Standing beside Brent, still comfortable on his chaise-longue, Beth waved her family off, giving a little sigh.

"You are proud of your family, Mrs Dere?" said her companion, who had also seen the happy party leave.

"Yes, Brent, the years pass by so quickly. The time will soon come for them to leave home." Quickly she changed the subject.

"Ben and the boys will be back soon from Adelaide. Have you met Blue and my Matthew?" From him a quiet "No."

She laughed. "They are inseparable, and usually up to some prank. If it wasn't for Duke, we could easily have lost our son."

He said nothing.

Looking at this man who had his eyes closed, as she sat quietly beside him, she thought how handsome he was, even with a bandage tied around his dark head. She tried to assess his age, maybe in his late twenties. Difficult to tell.

"Seth tells me your partner is able to take charge at the mine."

Her mention of Seth caused him to open his eyes suddenly.

"Has he been to see Rebekah and you?" he asked.

Giving him rather a vague answer, she replied, "He drops by occasionally. Is there anything I can get you before I go to Sam?"

"Nothing, thanks, Mrs Dere," he answered her rather vacantly.

After she had left, Brent let his mind dwell on his brother. All his life he had bailed Seth out of trouble, women, mostly. If Rebekah made a fool of herself over his wayward step-brother, why should he worry?

Brent stayed with the Everests a week. Never, in all his life, had he felt so helpless. Beginning to feel like a caged animal, he vented his feelings on Rebekah. But what angered him greatly, was the fact she took no notice.

He tried reasoning with himself. "Oh, Hell!" he exclaimed, slamming his fist down in anger. Why this feeling Rebekah should be protected from his brother? She was not his concern, or was she? Brent asked himself. Something stirred within his heart, a feeling he'd not encountered before. His pulses raced and he could hear his heart beat drumming in his ears. Perspiration stood on his forehead. Martha came bustling in.

"You called, Brent?" Noticing his flushed face she checked his pulse, and wiped his forehead, wondering at this sudden increase in his pulse rate. Should she call her husband? She stayed with him, encouraged him to have a cool drink, and opened another window. Taking his pulse again, she noticed it was getting back to normal.

A light 'tap-tap' and an inner door slowly opened and her son's curly, blonde head first appeared, announcing, "I'm Blue Everest. May I come in?"

Smiling, he went to his mother and gave her a big hug. "They told me you were improving, Mr Gordon. Good thing 'Bekah was around at the time. Just popped in to let Ma know we're back, see you again."

The sound of squeaks and scratches drew his attention, so he hurried out. "That was short and sweet. I didn't have time to say a word to your son," said Brent, who seemed to have regained his composure.

Everyone was talking when Martha went back to the parlour some time later.

"Mother," Blue proudly held the pup for her to see. "We have an addition to the family. Meet Prince."

"Oh! No! Blue, what does your father say?"

"Him very classy fella, most honourable prince of dogs," Blue mimicked the Oriental.

"I bet he didn't," she said, laughing, going over to Blue and relieving him of the pup, fondling it.

"What plans for this? I expect something's been ticking over in your brain."

"We are teaching him tricks, aren't we Matt? You'll see Ma, he will turn out to be a professional."

Duke and Ben came into the room, looking pleased with themselves. Ben asked for everyone's attention.

"Duke has elected me as spokesman. We have great news for you. The area of our Homestead will be extended to the other side of the river, as Grandfather wished. That's not all. In due course, next to the Dere Sheep Station, Duke and Martha plan to build a house of their own for their retirement. The two families have also taken shares in a shipping company based in Port Adelaide, carrying wool and other commodities. If we continue to prosper, and neither of us see any reason why not, Duke's idea is to build a hospital here in Justville."

Ben, observing the look on his daughter's face, said "You have something to ask, Rebekah?"

"Yes, if I may, I would like to spend a year training in a hospital in Sydney with Teddy. He thinks I stand a good chance to attain nursing qualifications. Perhaps the hospital will be ready when I return?"

To her amazement, without argument her father continued, "Why not, if that's what you want? Oh! I almost forgot, we have acquired a new breed of sheep which will be coming to the Homestead soon. Their wool is much thicker, of better quality for export. I feel this calls for a celebration drink."

He proposed a toast.

"To the memory and goodness of our forefathers and the prosperity of our children."

The babble of excitement grew. Matthew undid the parcel and he and Blue handed around the bottles of perfume.

"Perfume from Adelaide, how lovely!" the ladies exclaimed and began removing the stoppers.

Ruth placed her nose to the uncorked bottle and started to choke and her eyes began streaming. She looked in Blue's direction, unable to speak. Someone taking the bottle from her read the label:

"Californian Poppy. Hmm! Smells like smelling salts." Blue retrieved the unwanted bottle, his face the picture of innocence.

"I must have been given the wrong one," he said, producing an identical bottle from his pocket.

Ben was careful not to smile; thoughts of the chilli paste cake came to his mind. I must remember to tell that story to Beth, he thought.

It so happened when Ben visited the Justville store the next day, a smartly dressed, middle-aged man was speaking to Mr Dobson, the store owner.

"I am a photographer. Do you happen to know anyone who would like to have a family portrait?"

Mr Dobson shook his head. "Not many such folks about here, I guess," he replied, answering him politely.

Ben Dere couldn't help overhearing the conversation. He thought a bit. Sounds rather fun.

"Excuse me interrupting, I might be interested. My name is Ben Dere. I suppose you have some sample portraits?"

They walked together to the photographer's wagon. Ben liked what he saw and made arrangements for him to call at Dr Everest's house the next day.

At the appointed time the photographer arrived at the house. The ladies had chosen to wear their party dresses and looked delightful.

Mr Dean, the photographer, asked them to group together, sit or stand, arranging jackets and dresses to his satisfaction. After some considerable time the first picture was taken, followed by several others. Ben had persuaded the Everest family to join them. Many more portraits followed.

Eventually, when the photographic session was over, Blue said laughingly of Ruth in her blue and white gown: "I should have worn my blue and white clown suit, we would have made a perfect match."

Of course, thought Beth, that's why Ruth's gown had looked familiar.

Ruth's face turned a bright crimson as the fact dawned on her.

"I hate you, Blue Everest, I'll never wear this dress again." Angrily she rushed from the room, near to tears.

"I'm sorry, Mrs Dere," Blue apologised and left.

Preparations were underway for the Dere family to return home and Brent Gordon had recovered sufficiently to leave. Soon the house would be quiet. Martha would miss them all, especially Rebekah, who had decided to spend a short while at home with her parents before leaving for Sydney.

Teddy, having told his parents of his beloved Alice and his proposed marital plans, promised to escort Rebekah to Sydney, sure that their Aunt would be pleased to accommodate her. Impatient to return to the love of his life, they would leave for Sydney quite soon. Rebekah's stay at the Homestead passed very quickly. Abigail, helping her sort and repair her clothes, spoke of James.

"Every day he called to see me at Mrs McBean's shop. I thought it might anger her. That was why I didn't stay to help her."

"You like him, for all that, don't you?" said Rebekah, noticing Abby's flushed cheeks.

"Yes, but I hardly know him," confessed Abigail.

The conversation was cut short by their mother bringing in a pile of white, starched linen aprons.

"You'll need several of these, dear. Is it tomorrow Teddy should be arriving? Will you have finished?"

Eyeing all the garments strewn around and others in neat piles, she said, "Tea is ready, by the way," and bustled from the room.

The sun was low in the sky when Teddy Jackson arrived, accompanied by James. Apologising for their late arrival, they began unloading the wagon. The family gathered around, introducing the two young Jackson lads to Jake.

"Doctors, you say? This'll be one of the finest places around for miles to get sick."

Giving a chuckle and taking the reins, he meandered off with the wagon. He felt really good in his new suede jacket and multi-coloured 'kerchief knotted round his weathered neck, gifts from his young Deres.

The photographs, wrapped and parcelled in a large box, had been brought by the Jackson lads from Justville.

Ben carefully unwrapped and looked at each of them, placing them around his study, then called in the family to see them.

"This one is good," said Rebekah, looking at her own image, standing beside her seated father.

"The family group is nice as well, we all look terribly smart," Beth said proudly.

Everyone passed comments. Matthew, grinning with a hint of mischief, said he was disappointed, he thought he was better looking. Blue didn't say a word.

"Oh, by the way," said Teddy, looking at Beth and Rebekah. "Mother has decided to accompany us to Sydney. Father is as yet undecided; but she is determined to meet Alice and stay for our wedding. I know Alice will be delighted."

"It will do your mother good. Have you somewhere to live?" enquired Beth, still admiring the portraits.

"Alice has rooms with her Aunt, which is very convenient for the time being."

Prince, thinking it was time for some attention, gave a whimper. Blue called him; the fat little puppy followed him outside.

"My, the patience Blue has with that pup is remarkable. He can persuade it to do anything," Ben admitted to no one in particular. "The adoration and devotion in that animal's eyes! And it's so young, it's unbelievable!"

Blue took Prince everywhere he went, talking to him, as did Matthew. Even Matt had to admit he was very fond of the dog. But the pup knew Blue was Master.

In the morning, Beth watched the wagon taking Rebekah away, until only a cloud of dust could be seen; wiping away a tear, she told herself a year would soon pass. She had no wish to stand in her daughter's way, after all, she was almost twenty-one years of age, and Rebekah's year with Martha and Duke had flown by. She knew her daughter had set her heart on becoming a qualified nurse. If the hospital materialised, then she would not be so far away. With a sigh she made her way inside. Abigail was clearing the table.

"What shall we do today, Mum? It will be quiet without them." She gazed out of the window. "I could start on the material Duke and Martha gave us, but Blue wants me to design and make a hat for Prince." She laughed.

Her mother also laughed. "What shape can you make to stay on a dog's head? It's nearly impossible!" she said, answering her own question.

"Oh, Blue thinks something like Lord Nelson or the Duke

of Wellington wore, would suit him admirably. I brought a large bundle of remnants from Mrs McBean. I wonder if we've anything suitable in grandmother's box?"

Happily, the pair of them went in search of materials.

Edward Jackson decided he would accompany his wife and son to Sydney after all. He hadn't been away for many years and he felt sure Duke and James would cope. Soon he would be too old for travelling. Needless to say, his wife was thrilled, bubbling over with excitement.

The Everest house was empty when Rebekah returned. Teddy brought her trunks from the wagon and stayed talking with her until Martha and Duke arrived home. They were all very pleased his father was having a holiday and going with them. The following day, Brent Gordon called in at the Doctor's to have his arm dressed as the deepest gash was not healing to Duke's liking.

Rebekah began unwinding the bandage from Brent's arm in readiness for when the doctor arrived. Brent could feel her cool hands on his arm and noticed her soft, unobtrusive perfume. His sudden desire to gather her into his arms and tell her that he, of all people, who swore never to let a woman into his life, had become another string to her bow, was forestalled, as the doctor hurried into the room, apologising for keeping him waiting.

Brent swore under his breath. The moment passed. He heard Duke explaining in detail to Rebekah as he dressed the wound, "Of course, if you work with Teddy in Sydney, he may have a more modern technique."

Brent sat quiet, thinking what a fool he was. An idiotic fool!

"Well, Brent, certainly much better today. I expect you were working too hard. I must go. Rebekah will finish the bandaging."

Brent politely thanked the doctor. Waiting until she had finished her task, he suddenly turned on her.

"So, it is on Teddy Jackson you have bestowed your generous affections. Seth did not stand a chance in your little scheme!"

She looked at him in amazement, unable to pinpoint the start of his tirade. Words failed her.

"So, you've nothing to say. Quite unusual for you!"

His brown eyes seemed to take in every detail of her face as he towered over her.

"I did hear correctly. You are going to Sydney with the Doctor?"

At last she found her voice. "I don't know what business it is of yours," she declared angrily. "Yes, I am! And his father and mother are going to the wedding."

As she was about to turn away, he pulled her to him, pinning her arms closely to her sides, planting his lips firmly over hers in a long, hard, brutal kiss. She struggled. Finally he released her. Bringing her hand up, she rubbed her bruised mouth as if to erase the memory. Seeing her movement, he stepped back, anticipating a sharp slap.

"You beast," she hissed.

Watching her, he laughed, "No, just something to remember, when Doctor Teddy kisses you, Rebekah Dere."

Deliberately emphasising her surname, he collected his hat and walked from the room whistling, leaving her fuming.

Quickly she washed her face, trying not to remember the look in his dark eyes, pleased she had misled him about the wedding. It was hard to concentrate on her work. She tried to put all thought of him from her mind. Anyway, she wouldn't have to tolerate his sarcasm for much longer. She would soon be leaving.

One evening, after Rebekah had left for Sydney, the Everests were sitting quietly on the veranda. It was a rare occasion, as they were always so busy. Duke, looking very thoughtful, made Martha wonder if something was wrong. When asked, he mentioned he was very worried about James.

"No question whatsoever over his capabilities. It's just that he seems rather vacant, lost. He is much thinner. You cook well, so it isn't that. It's over two months or more since his parents left … I know we've been busy, but …"

Duke hesitated, looking at his smiling wife. "It isn't funny, I like the young man."

"Oh! You men! Some of you go about with your eyes closed!" she said, reaching out to hold her husband's hand. "Were you ever in love?" She looked into his eyes.

"You know I was, still am, if you must know," he impatiently answered her. "But what has that to do with James?"

"Same thing, darling, he is madly in love with Abigail. The symptoms are still the same. I am quite sure of it from the moment he set eyes on her, the night of the party. So you can stop worrying, my dearest."

With a look of disbelief on his face, he exclaimed, "I don't believe it!"

Martha looked into the Jackson's house, making sure everything was spick and span. James was always tidy and quite helpful, so nothing much needed attention. Tomorrow was the day his father and mother should return from their vacation. Martha would be pleased to see them and hear about the wedding and how Rebekah was settling in at the hospital.

Expecting Emily Jackson to be exhausted on her arrival, Martha had prepared a light meal. Contrary to expectations, Emily emerged from the wagon, light of step.

Fashionably dressed in a three-quarter silk coat and straight, matching full-length dress in pastel blue, she was smiling and full of health and happiness. Her husband also looked years younger.

James was there to give a helping hand to his mother.

Emily, taking note of his changed appearance, enquired, "Aren't you well, James?" in her forthright manner.

"Of course I am, Mother, don't fuss," he replied rather irritably.

Once inside, sitting down, eating their meal, Emily and Ed

spoke well of their daughter-in-law, Alice, and how happy the couple were. A marvellous wedding. A beautiful cream wedding gown and two maids in attendance, both dressed in pink satin. Many doctors and their wives and friends attended. The Chapel was full. It was truly a grand occasion and excellent wedding breakfast.

Rebekah looked a picture. Meeting Teddy's friends at the wedding helped her enormously.

The story unfolded with so much to tell, until Ed, realising the time, thanked them for relieving him of his duties and enabling him and Emily to have such a wonderful holiday.

Chapter 8

Someone in a deuce of a hurry, thought Jake, as he eyed the ball of dust moving towards the Homestead. He was sitting in his usual place on the veranda in the shade, watching the lads and the dog doing their tricks, again and again, laughing from time to time as the dog shook its head to remove the offending hat that Abby had made. That creature has sense, all right, thought Jake. When Blue gave him a tit-bit the hat stayed on; without a morsel he tossed off the hat, as simple as that. When Matthew took the bone from under its paw and made off, the dog chased him. Blue did the very same thing with the bone and the pup sat up and begged until Blue brought it back. As soon as Matthew played music, Prince began to howl and would not cease until he was rewarded. They had worked out a routine.

"It's James," the lads shouted, picking up Prince as the dust settled.

James, taking his saddlebags, let Jake lead his horse away, and the three of them went inside, happily talking.

They found Abigail sitting on the floor surrounded by pieces of material as usual. Blushing at the sight of him, Abigail said, "You look awfully dusty, James. Matt, be a darling and show James to the washroom, please."

James didn't take long to clean up and soon returned, looking for her. On the table stood a cool drink. Abby, kneeling on the floor, gathering her materials together, told him to help himself to a drink.

He took a drink and paced the floor, not quite knowing where to begin. Placing the glass back on the table, plucking up the courage, he knelt in front of her.

"Abby, have you thought about me these past months?" he

asked, looking into her brown eyes. "We hardly know each other, do you think ... could you care for me?"

He groaned. "We are so far apart. I have become desperate to see you." Holding her hand, he searched her face for a glimmer of hope.

She smiled bashfully, nodding her head. "Yes, I have thought of you, James."

He stood up, pulling her to her feet, putting his arms around her waist. Coyly sliding her arms around his neck, hearing the strong beat of his heart, they shared their first kiss. They heard voices and quickly drew apart. Beth entered the room. James gave her a letter from his mother.

"News of Rebekah, perhaps," she said. Thanking him, she took herself off to read it.

James' visits became more frequent. He and Abigail would wander in the garden, spending time sitting in a hammock suspended between the apple trees, or leisurely talking with the family, watching Prince's antics. Parting became more difficult. Clinging, lingering kisses tortured them, lifting them into the wondrous world of love. On one of James' visits, he brought a letter from Duke, to give to Abby's father, with a large bundle of documents about the proposed new hospital. Ben invited James into his study.

"'An anonymous benefactor has given a large piece of land. There is more if required, if the position is suitable'," Ben read aloud to James and asked, "Did you know of this?"

"Yes, it's all rather sudden. Duke wanted Father's and my opinion as we would both be involved."

James had been very pleased Duke had included him in their scheme.

"My father, Duke and I went to view. It's a marvellous site," ventured James eagerly. "I hope there are no undesirable clauses, like a ninety-nine year lease attached to this 'anonymous gift'."

Ben voiced his concerned opinion – "I must get that checked" – and began making notes. "I believe Duke has enclosed the Solicitor's letter," replied James, turning over a pile of documents.

"Would you like to live there, James?"

Caught unawares, James hesitantly told Ben that it rather depended on certain circumstances.

"Such as?" demanded Ben.

"Well, Sir …" James grasped this heaven-sent opportunity. "I would like to marry your daughter, Abigail; that is, if she will accept, and you agree, of course." Then, getting flustered, "I'm not sure if she would like to live close to a hospital."

"Very considerate of you, James."

He paused, looking James over. "Mrs Dere and I are delighted with Abigail's choice of beau." Very soberly he added, "Oh yes, we had noticed. I have no doubt she will accept your proposal. You have my blessing."

Seeing the tension leave James' face, smiling broadly, he said, "Go quickly and find her. We can sort these papers another time! Don't keep us in suspense!"

Ben watched from his study window as James jumped the small fence, two flower beds and headed straight for the hammock in the apple trees. Still smiling, he settled himself comfortably at his desk.

James swang Abigail in the hammock while she begged him to stop, clinging desperately to the sides. "What's the matter with you, James?" she yelled at the top of her voice.

"I'm in love!"

Laughing, he gave the hammock an extra push, catching her in his arms as she toppled out. "Abigail Dere, will you marry me?"

"Are you really serious?" she asked, looking into his eyes, her heart turning somersaults. She needed no answer as his long, lingering kiss told her all she needed to know.

Settling her back in the hammock, delving in his pocket, he produced a small jewel case.

"I'm afraid it's not new, I hope you won't mind," he said, taking a sapphire and diamond ring from its velvet holder. "It once belonged to my great grandmother. Darling Abigail, will you be my wife?"

"Oh … Yes … James," she gasped. "I love you dearly." Holding out her hand for the ring to be placed on her finger, she added, "It is beautiful, James."

The family were gathered in the parlour when Abigail and James strolled in. Ben rose to his feet.

"Well?" he asked.

Abigail looked at her father and said hesitantly, "James has asked me to marry him and I have accepted." She got no further.

"Wonderful! Wonderful!" her father declared, hugging his daughter. Ruth came to her sister's side. "Do you have a ring?" she enquired.

Abby held out her hand for all to see. "This ring once belonged to James' great grandmama."

Beth kissed her daughter, taking James by the hand. "I wish you both the greatest of happiness."

From then onwards conversation in the Dere household ranged from the new hospital to the couple's wedding arrangements. It would take time to complete the hospital and they had no wish to wait. Abby hoped her sister Rebekah would be able to attend the wedding at the Homestead.

Blue listened to all the plans. He had begun to give serious thought towards his lifetime ambition. After Abigail's wedding he would start organising. First he would need a wagon. His father and mother would undoubtedly be invited to the wedding, then he could enlist their help.

The routine with Prince was as near perfection as one could expect from an animal. He would have to forego the added attraction of Matt with his accordion or flute, as his friend had never expressed the desire to team up with him, even if his parents agreed.

Blue was sitting in the shade on the veranda steps writing his list, when Matt, looking over Blue's shoulder, blurted out, "I would love to come with you and Prince. Do you think I'd get Father to agree? Ruth would be the only one left … I should ask first, would you have me?"

"You know all right I would!" he grinned. "Didn't think you'd want to come. The three of us would make an excellent team."

Blue admitted chalking down another item on his list. "We must think about it. How best to approach your father."

The two of them then took themselves off into the garden.

It so happened it was Ruth who solved her brother's problem, quite unwittingly. She had been trying to tarnish Blue's reputation for some time. The day was heavenly. Casually she mentioned Blue's intention of leaving the Homestead to her father as they were inspecting the cattle fences.

"Blue soon wants to move on. I bet he has persuaded Matt to go with him. What would you say Father, if Matthew wants to leave here?"

"What makes you think that?" queried her father.

Ruth felt uncomfortable. Perhaps she shouldn't sneak on them.

"I overheard Blue's conversation. Big-headed Blue," she said very sarcastically, "thinks the three of them would make a good team. He couldn't do it without Matt's music, I bet!" This was said with such vehemence that her father looked at her in amazement, commenting: "Never could understand why you two failed to agree."

Ruth continued, "He's too big for his boots, knows the lot or think he does!"

Why she was so overcome by anger she had no explanation.

"He is a very knowledgeable young man," countered her father. "Having travelled the country from a very early age, experiencing other folks' hardships, he really knows what he's talking about. He is very kind, I would trust him to look after Matthew anywhere on earth."

He pulled up his horse and looked about him, thinking of the rugged life he himself had endured. The miraculous way his son had coped with his disability, knowing full well that Blue had been the kingpin. As far as he could foresee, his financial problems were nil. He had given a lot of thought to his son lately, praying for some kind of opening, a guidance. Matthew was a gifted musician. Why not let him spread his wings and develop the great talent he possessed? Perhaps ...

Suddenly, as if light had been cast on his dilemma, "It would be the very thing for Matthew. To travel with Blue. Yes! I believe it would!" he said aloud, triumphantly.

All the time Ruth had sat motionless on her horse, watching her father, not daring to speak, not believing what she was hearing. She felt very peeved. Since the episode of the dress, Blue hardly spoke to her, shunning her completely. But now, seeing the triumphant look on her father's face, she decided to say no more.

The very next morning Ben called his son to his study. "Tell me, are you happy here, Matthew? I have brought you up to be honest; I want the truth."

Matthew looked away from his father, wondering whether he should divulge what he had in mind. How would his father react?

"So, Blue has asked you to go away with him on his travels, eh?"

"No, Father," Matthew replied, honestly, "I asked Blue if I could join him." Looking at his father, he continued, "We both thought it would be out of the question. You wouldn't agree. You would need me here to take charge of the Homestead, eventually."

Ben placed an arm around his son's shoulders.

"We, your mother and I, think you need something more

than this kind of life. Providing, of course, you agree to return. We have no wish to part with you, but we give you our blessing to travel with Blue, if that is your wish."

"Father! Do you really mean it?" he gasped almost in disbelief, wondering if he had heard his father's words correctly.

"Thank you. You have my solemn promise to return."

Spoken with such sincerity, Ben, overcome by love and emotion welling within his being, could only whisper: "May the Lord go with you, my son."

From the veranda, a beaming Matthew gave a sharp whistle. Prince came bounding along, followed by his master.

Matthew formed his arms into a circle, whereupon the dog gave a leap through, sat himself down and lifted a paw.

Blue clapped. Prince wagged his tail, while Matthew delved into his pocket for a well-deserved tasty morsel for the dog.

"I have to tell you, Blue Everest," he said with mock severity, "You see here, before your very eyes, your travelling partner, Matt-the-Music!"

Blue threw his hat in the air and shouted "Wow-ee! Ya-Ho!"

Prince became excited, barked and wagged his tail. Matthew took his flute from his pocket and played the tune from the Music Hall venue, 'The Whistler and His Dog'.

Clapping and whistles from Ben, Jake and Beth. Ruth was nowhere to be seen.

Chapter 9

Rebekah's father, brother and Blue, waiting to take her home from the railway junction to Justville, could not believe the vast difference from the eager young woman, who, so full of vitality, now looked a shadow of her former self as she stepped from the train from Sydney. She stood, with hat in hand, and her lovely coronet of hair, which had lost its lustre, topped a bleak, white face.

"Rebekah, what have you done to yourself? Worked yourself nearly to death, I bet," scolded her father as he hugged her, wanting to pick her up and carry her to their wagon.

"Yes, I am exhausted," she admitted, placing her pretty bonnet on her head. "My goodness, you're both so grown-up," she added, giving her brother and Blue a half-hearted smile as they carried her luggage.

In the wagon, they made her as comfortable as possible, so sure she would sleep. Sleep she did, and only awoke to take a little light refreshment.

Her mother and Abigail were waiting at Justville for her return. Staying with Duke and Martha was an ideal arrangement for them as Abigail's wedding day was drawing close, enabling Abby to visit Mrs McBean for dress fittings and seeing her beloved James.

When Ben's wagon stopped in front of the Everest house, Beth watched, horrified, as her husband helped their daughter from the wagon. She looked appalling, finding it almost too much of an effort to smile.

"Don't fuss Mother, I shall be alright!" said Rebekah, seeing her mother's anxious look, after exchanging loving greetings.

As soon as Duke saw Rebekah, he ordered her straight to bed.

"Complete rest for several days for you, young woman," he said, very concerned.

Making no attempt to argue, instead she said quietly to her mother: "There's a package for Duke in my trunk, from Teddy, please get it for him."

Beth found and passed the package over.

"No need for me to tell you how to look after your daughter, Beth. Try to keep her in bed," was his admonishment, casting a professional eye over Rebekah before leaving.

As the days passed, Rebekah had no inclination to leave her bed. Although being waited on by all the family, she didn't feel well enough to enjoy the luxury. No wonder, thought Duke as he read the letter from Teddy Jackson. Rebekah had literally pushed herself to the extreme. Volunteering for one thing after another, passing each nursing grade with flying colours, leaving little time for rest or recreation.

'Aunt and my wife Alice have been so worried', he wrote.

After a while, Beth felt her daughter was on the mend, so decided to return to the Homestead with her husband, leaving Abigail behind to help Martha and also Mrs McBean.

James had chosen an excellent spot, a short distance from the main hospital area, on which to build their home, a bungalow. This was nearing completion and Rebekah had yet to see it. James, thinking it about time for Rebekah to venture out, suggested she should join them on a picnic, to which she agreed.

"What a lovely place you'll have and your own water-mill!" Rebekah said, admiring the site and looking at the turning wind-wheel. "Is it the same type of building as that being built for the hospital?" she also enquired.

"Work has begun on that, too. Shall we take a look?" suggested James, taking up the reins. They travelled further along the track.

Several buildings had been erected, perched on foundations of wood some feet off the ground. Inner doors leading to balconies from the many rooms and large windows gave the building a very airy look.

"This is a beautiful place. I wonder who is the benefactor? Have you any idea, James?" Rebekah asked, her heart pounding as she sat with Abby on some steps.

He shook his head. "The solicitor's letter came from Hobart."

After the picnic and discussion of the proposed further layout of the new hospital, they decided to call at the store for items for their new home. By the time they reached the Everest's place, Rebekah was ready to flop on the nearest lounger on the veranda. She must have dozed. The next she knew, Abby and Seth were standing in front of her with James at the rear holding a tray of tea.

Seth had called to tell her he was moving on. Giving Rebekah a sheepish look, he told them of his new love.

Rebekah laughed inwardly. No need for him to worry, she never had designs on him. Sure, he was a good-looking chap with a certain charm, and the audacity to think all women would fall for that charm. Smiling at him, she said, "I wish you the best of luck."

He sure needed it, he thought, but said to everyone, "I don't know what came over Brent. After his accident he was in a foul mood. For months he hadn't a polite word for anyone on the site, till eventually, Rip, his partner, suggested he took a break. Doing just that, he saddled-up and said he was off prospecting."

"Where is he now?" James asked.

"We haven't set eyes on him since. Someone said he had been seen near Alice Springs. Another said Sydney. Never known him to behave like it before. Could have been the result of his accident, I suppose," ventured Seth.

"Have you any relatives?" Rebekah asked tentatively, hoping to acquire insight into Brent's past life.

"Brent had some in Tasmania, some years back. I'm Brent's step-brother," he added. "My ... Brent's father married again after losing his wife. After a while my mother left us. I was about five years old.

"I hardly knew Brent because he lived in Hobart with his grandparents. I am several years younger than him and he loathed my mother. Only saw his father occasionally. Father eventually drank himself to death, leaving Brent to look after me."

"What was your mother's Christian name?" Rebekah quietly enquired.

"Maria. Brent searched all over, but never found her."

Eventually Seth rose to go, wishing the engaged couple all the best, saying to Rebekah, "I'm sure all the patients will be head-over-heels in love with you." Laughing, he kissed her cheek as he and James left.

Rebekah declared as Abby was leaving, "He's more manly. I suppose with Brent away, he has to stand on his own two feet."

So Rebekah thought Brent Gordon had kept his promise. Now, sitting quietly by herself, she relived her encounter and those unforgettable days in Sydney with Brent, remembering every word as if it had happened yesterday.

When walking towards the Sydney Hospital gate with another young student, on her way home, she saw the familiar figure of Brent Gordon coming towards them. Her immediate reaction had been; what was he doing here? What did he want? Politely she smiled, knowing her face had turned a shade of crimson, remembering his kiss. He had asked if she would talk with him, and, in his usual abrupt manner, gave her no choice. Leaving her friend, they entered a cafe close-by.

She could almost hear his voice this very moment.

"Rebekah, you want a hospital in Justville?"

"Yes, as much as Duke and Martha and the rest of folks. Why do you ask?"

"I am the benefactor," he stated categorically.

Looking at his face, "You?" she had replied incredulously. "But the benefactor lives in Hobart!"

"That's correct. My home town. Unless you agree to marry me, Rebekah, there'll be no hospital." He went on in a deadpan voice, "Of course you'll need time to consider my proposal. Our marriage would remain a secret between us, in name only. I will meet you here lunchtime tomorrow for your answer."

A waiter had by then appeared and stood hovering. Brent tossed a coin on the man's tray without ordering, then escorted her outside. He left her speechless. Lifting his hat, he said, "Till tomorrow then," and walked away.

She couldn't remember walking the short distance to her room. Letting herself in, she buried her face into her pillow and sobbed. How could she let Martha and Duke down? James and Abigail were relying on a place for their new home. What was she to do? Pacing the floor, her mind tortured by unanswered questions, she fell on her bed into an exhausted sleep, only to dream again of the brutal kiss he gave her in Justville.

Morning came, and foregoing breakfast, she prepared for her morning's work, still in a dilemma.

Teddy Jackson had been the first person she saw going into the hospital.

"Rebekah! You look exhausted. You're working too hard!"

"So are you!" she had replied as he hurried away.

Her timepiece reminded her she had exactly five minutes of the morning left to make her decision. "Yes!" she decided. "I will marry him. 'In name only,' he had said. I am of age and have nothing to lose. Somehow, sometime, I will get even with him."

Seeing him waiting at the café she had almost fled. Then summing up the courage, head held high, she greeted him.

Seated at the small round table, his eyes searching her face, he immediately asked, "What is your decision?"

Boldly she had replied, "I will marry you, on the terms you stated. In name only and I will continue with my nursing."

"That's fine by me. Next Wednesday?"

Rebekah, as she had listened to him, winced inwardly. He had it all mapped-out, as if he had known what her answer would be.

"I will send a cab; shall we say twelve noon as good a time as any, don't you think?"

Taking out his pocket-book, he said, "I have your address. I need your full name and date of birth. Shall we eat?"

Even now Rebekah couldn't for the life of her remember what she had eaten, if any, only that he had ordered a bottle of Champagne, and raised his glass and gave her a smile. His parting words were, "See you Wednesday? Nothing bridal, please."

Those few days had passed like a dream. On the morning of her wedding, choosing the lavender and grey silk dress and hat she wore for Teddy and Alice Jackson's wedding ceremony, she waited for the carriage to arrive.

Nothing about that drive registered in her mind until they stopped beside a tall, grey unimpressive building. Brent stepped forward and opened the carriage door. One thing she did notice was that he had looked immaculate and handsome, dressed in a fine grey linen suit and top hat.

Only then did she realise the sun was shining and it was a very hot day. Before she had time to think, the wedding ceremony, of which she remembered very little, except for the signing of her name, was over and the Registrar was wishing them future happiness. Looking down at her left hand she saw the wide band of gold on her finger, then fainted.

Regaining consciousness, she found herself on a sofa in a strange room with Brent looking extremely concerned, dabbing her forehead with a water-soaked handkerchief and the woman who had been a witness to their marriage, standing by holding a glass of water.

She remembered him saying, "Come, Rebekah my love, drink this," placing his arm around her shoulders, pulling her forward and raising the glass of water to her lips. Doing as she was told, she had begun to feel better.

Brent, gathering her in his arms, carried her into the waiting carriage, thanking the unknown woman as they left.

"When did you last eat?" he had asked, after making her comfortable. "You look half starved!"

She couldn't remember when and was unable to tell him. He also asked if she had enough money to buy food.

"Of course! I have an allowance from Father," was her response, indignant at his suggestion.

By then they had reached a large house overlooking the water. He must have noticed her look of panic.

"Rather a romantic place to have a meal, especially a wedding breakfast, don't you think? Can you walk or do I carry you?" he said with a mischievous smile, helping her from the cab. "I'm quite willing. I would love to carry my wife over the threshold in the traditional manner."

She had walked.

A man known to Brent ushered them to a secluded table. Dishes of food were placed before them. He encouraged her to eat and her trembling had eased. From time to time she had noticed his gaze resting on her face as she pecked at her food. At one moment she thought him about to reach out to touch her hand.

"Money," he said abruptly. "As you are now my wife, you will have an allowance."

In horror she almost shouted, "I don't want your money!"

"Rebekah Dere. Oh! I'm sorry, Rebekah Gordon,' he said, watching her closely. "It is my duty to support my wife!"

A waiter arrived, finally putting an end to this conversation. A large grandfather clock, standing in the comer of the room, chimed the hour. With great emphasis, she had reminded him of her need to be at the hospital for duty that evening.

In silence, Brent returned her home. Helping her from the carriage, he thrust an oblong leather box into her hand.

"For you, Mrs Gordon." And taking her free hand, he placed it to his lips while looking deep into her eyes. Quickly he jumped into the carriage and was gone.

In the solitude of her room, with trembling fingers she had opened the case, first taking out a gold and diamond eternity ring, next a gold, heart-shaped locket and chain, which she opened. Inside were two miniature photographs, one of herself and her father together on one side, Brent's handsome face on the other.

Unfolding a sheet of paper, she found the name of Brent's solicitor in Hobart. Holding the locket to her cheek, she had wept uncontrollably.

Removing her wedding ring, she had dropped it into the box with the other golden gifts and closed the lid. She had not seen or heard from him since.

Chapter 10

Abigail's and James' wedding ceremony was being held at the Dere Homestead. To take the service, Judge Becket and the Pastor had travelled from Justville, along with James' family and friends.

The parlour, bedecked with sweet-smelling flowers and herbs, was filled to capacity with family and friends waiting for Abigail to appear.

Making her entrance, she looked radiant on her father's arm, wearing a cream lace and satin long-sleeved gown, with a bustle of gathered lace over her long skirt. The fitted bodice fastened neatly with pearl buttons. On her head she had a dainty satin and lace cap and her grandmama's short, embroidered silk veil.

Ruth had picked fresh forget-me-nots and pink roses for her to carry.

Ruth and Rebekah followed, their blue satin gowns festooned with chains of pink satin roses, looped from tight-wasted bodices. Insets of blue and white lace decorated their full, long skirts. Rosebuds dotted on lace caps and long, blue silk gloves, made the two sisters look even more beautiful.

Rebekah's mind dwelt on Abigail's words as she repeated after Judge Becket, "'till death us do part," remembering that she had made that vow with no intention of keeping it. How could she? What would her father say if he knew? She felt sick. Matthew had found some sheet music in a musty store in Adelaide, and when both Judge and Pastor had completed the service and pronounced them 'Man and Wife', he began to play a wonderful version of the Wedding March, much to the delight of the guests.

A sumptuous meal had been prepared by Beth and her many helpers and arranged in the long shed. The stockmen and their wives were dressed in their Sunday best clothes and were waiting there for the wedding party. Blue and Matthew had promised to give a small impromptu show after the meal.

Cheers and more cheers greeted James as he led his bride into the decorated shed. The party was well underway when Matthew and Blue prepared themselves, and of course Prince, and made their way to the centre of the barn floor.

The children were at first afraid of the clowns, frightened by their painted faces, but when Prince joined in, their attitudes changed and the barn was filled with laughter, both children and adults enjoying the dexterity of the clowns.

Prince completed his tricks by pulling a long cord, thus releasing Blue's long, baggy trousers, causing much laughter, whistles and clapping.

Matthew began to play his accordion. Feet started tapping, and some could not resist dancing so took to the floor with a partner. It sure was a good do with food and drink in plentiful supply.

Showered with flower petals and rice, their wagon loaded, James and Abigail set off for the log cabin beside the Darling River, Abigail's favourite spot. There they would spend a few days on their honeymoon.

The wedding day had been perfect, the hot, dry weather enabling the family and guests to sit around and chat, others dwindling away home.

Quietness eventually settled over the bungalow for the night.

In the early hours of the morning Prince began scratching at the boys' bedroom door. Blue told him to lie down. Matthew roused and also tried to quieten the dog, all to no avail, after which Blue opened the door and to his horror saw a red glow in the sky.

"Matt, dress quickly," he shouted. Racing along to Mr Dere's bedroom door, he called urgently, "A fire, a bush fire!"

In no time, Ben, taking a hunting horn from the veranda wall, blew into it with all his might. In the silence of the night the sound seemed to echo for miles.

Within minutes, Jake and some of the stockmen arrived with spare saddled horses, shouting where they thought the fire could be and the direction of the wind. Without hesitation every man rode off into the night, aware of the many dangers. Trained to be alert the moment he awoke, James, at the cabin, listened. Something had disturbed him. Now, only hearing the gentle breathing of his lovely wife beside him, he moved. She stretched an arm across his body, murmuring incoherently. Then he understood what had awakened him – horses galloping, neighing. Something upsetting? Leaping from his bed, picking up his gun, he opened the cabin door. The whole area was illuminated with a sinister orange glow, and alive with the sound of animals heading for the river.

"A fire!" he shouted. "Abby, wake up! Dress and get some blankets, hurry!"

Quickly pulling on his trousers and boots, he unhitched a rope and bridle from the cabin wall and ran the short distance to the paddock, hoping to catch the two frightened horses.

He called. Luck was with him, the mare came to him. He slipped the rope over her head, saying, "Steady girl, dare say you've seen the likes of this before." Reassuringly he spoke to her.

One horse would be enough for Abby and him, perhaps the other would follow. No time to hitch the wagon. Must collect my bag and gun and cross the river. All these thoughts chased through his mind. They had no time to lose.

He could hear Abby calling. Leading the mare, he answered.

Wrapped in her cloak, she met him at the front of the cabin.

"I have your gun, bag, food, water and blankets."

Her teeth were chattering and she was unable to still her limbs.

"We must be sensible," said James. "The fire looks to be on our side of the river. Do you know the easiest place to cross?"

She thought hard. "Father always maintained firebreaks along the boundaries. Perhaps the fire won't reach us here!"

"We must be ready to cross, just in case, darling," insisted James, taking their belongings.

"It's shallow here and the water level has dropped. I heard Father and Ruth talking about it a few days ago. On Jake's advice, the flock have been moved to a new pasture. He said the other was tinder dry."

The loose horse trotted around the restless mare, as if to say 'hurry'.

"We must go." James quickly lifted Abby on to the mare's back, passing her their belongings. In the wind he caught the acrid smell of burning.

Leading the horse, he made their way to the river edge. They paused. The sky glowed a deeper red. Wasting no time, James immediately waded in, urging the mare to enter the water. Steadily, they made their way across, James clinging to the mare when the strong current, in the centre of the river, swept him off his feet.

The loose horse forged ahead when the riverbank was plainly visible, eventually scrambling on to the dry land. The mare followed.

James tied the mare to a nearby tree. Abigail slid from the horse to be enfolded in James' arms. Wrapped in blankets, the couple clung to each other, looking back across the river and watching in horror as fierce flames leapt from tree to tree.

"That must be as far as Marley's Point," she whispered. "The fire is getting much closer, it can't jump the river, can it, James?" He felt her shiver. The noise was deafening. They could do nothing but watch and wait.

At first it looked as if the cabin, standing in the clearing, would escape destruction. To their horror, the wind whipped a mass of burning debris into the sky and sparks and blazing branches cascaded on to the roof and woodwork, igniting it like matchsticks. Abby could not watch. Sobbing, she buried her face in her husband's chest. Kissing her, James soothingly reminded her they were quite safe. Then his lips found hers. Passion and love erupted like the raging fire and both became oblivious to their surroundings.

Daylight came. James opened his eyes; he must have dozed for a moment. His arm was numb from Abigail's weight. On the other side of the river, as far as he could see, charred vegetation lay on the blackened soil. Occasionally a glimmer of flame and smoke erupted and quickly died. The fire had burned itself out.

As they leaned against a boulder, James gazed at his beautiful, sleeping wife, love and adoration filling his whole body. He could hardly believe it was only yesterday they were married.

Abigail awoke, sensing someone was looking at her, and looked up into her husband's eyes. Smiling shyly she blushed, then turned her attention across the water.

The remnants of the cabin were still smouldering. Silently she offered a prayer of thanksgiving; they were both safe.

James decided to stay, for the time being, where they were. Taking food and water from the bag, he said they must eat. He felt certain some firefighters or search party would be coming this way fairly soon, travelling beside the riverbank.

Without doubt, soon, a party from the Homestead would come looking for them. Firefighters were the first to arrive. The strangers were practically exhausted themselves, and filthy with smoke and ash. After a few words shouted to each other across the wide expanse of water, James and Abigail gathered their few belongings. Using the mare again, letting the other horse find its way, they crossed the river. Reaching the strangers, James quickly enquired about the extent of the fire damage, while Abby gazed woefully at the burnt-out wagon and cabin.

The man who did the talking, the boss, enquired of their

destination. When they mentioned the Dere Homestead, the boss stated immediately they should be accompanied by one of his group. "It is still very dangerous," he said, eyeing the bedraggled young woman in her night attire and cloak.

James agreed. "But first, I think I should take a look at that burn, young man," he said, pointing to an enormous weal on the forearm of a young firefighter.

Deftly, James dressed the burn. The young man thanked him, smiled and said, "If you're agreeable, Boss, I'd sure be pleased to ride with them. Jason's the name," he said, lifting his dirty, battered hat, as his Boss nodded agreement. With that, the others left.

The aroma of burnt, charred wood and grass made Abby's nostrils smart and her body ached as the three made for the Homestead, keeping to the track as best they could, avoiding large devastated areas, stopping only to make mercy killings, leaving the dead animals by the wayside as rich pickings for the scavengers. She thought of the Homestead and her parents, with sudden fear prickling her spine. When voicing her fears to James, Jason answered by pointing to distant riders. Two men on horseback drew nearer; it was her father and Jake.

"Father! Jake!" Abigail yelled as they pulled beside them.

Relief showed through the grime and sweat on Ben's face, and unashamedly, tears of relief ran down his cheeks. Finding the cabin and wagon a pile of smouldering timbers, he had become distraught with fear, even though Jake had done his best to convince him they were both alive.

"What a night it has been! A night to remember! Seems an age since I gave my daughter to you to love and cherish, doesn't it? Thank you James, my boy,' said Ben wiping his eyes, then noticed the injured man. "I see you have a casualty."

"Yes. This is Jason, a firefighter. He volunteered to accompany us home. He'll need a clean-up and some food, like the rest of us," said James, turning to Jake, who was eyeing the young stranger up and down.

"I do hope Mama is safe and well. Come along, do hurry, I'm hot and hungry. I can't understand, at all, why my sister Ruth loves to ride horses. I don't," Abigail moaned as she tried to make herself comfortable, grimacing with every movement. "The agony!"

"Yes. Let's go home. I too, am exhausted," Her father agreed.

Chapter 11

James and Abigail spent the remainder of their honeymoon at the Homestead, their escape and the extent of the fire damage the main topic of conversation. Thanks to Jake's intuition, none of their flock suffered.

Order returned to the Dere household after the newlyweds' departure. Beth missed her daughter tremendously. Her bedroom was now empty, as all her prized pieces of furniture, bed and bed linen had been taken with them to their new home. So often her daughter would pop into a room, wherever she happened to be, to seek advice or show her a piece of sewing. She remembered the time when Abigail promised to make a suit for Matthew. "Gaudy and baggy," he had said. "Black, yellow, blue, green and pink, all stripes." Beth could almost hear Abigail's astonished voice saying, "Oh! Matthew! Whoever gave you that idea?"

He had answered, "A Bumble bee among the flowers."

"Goodness me. Matt, you are as big a fool as Blue!" said a laughing Abigail, who then went in search of materials to fulfil his request.

Suddenly Beth's nostalgic reminiscence was shattered as Matthew, Blue and the dog came bounding into the kitchen.

"Ma, come and look, our wagon has arrived."

Jake had returned from Justville, bringing the promised wagon.

Duke had spared no expense. Made with wooden sides and roof, small windows both front and back, it stood polished and gleaming, the large wheels painted to match the beautifully coloured lettering: 'Blue the Kangaroo Clown and Matt the Music Maker'. Climbing aboard, they opened the two outer doors, each with separate bolts and latches.

Inside were bunk beds, combined chest-of-drawers and table and many other useful fittings. A large lantern, securely fixed in its holder, hung from the roof. Duke had thought of everything.

Jake handed Blue a small key, showing him a well concealed drawer, and told him it was for their personal documents. Blue opened the drawer. Inside was an envelope marked 'Open in emergency,' in his father's handwriting.

Ben gave Matthew a list of names and addresses of people whom he knew in various parts of the country, also for the drawer. It also contained their birth certificates. Stocking up the wagon amounted to great fun and kept them very busy. Ruth even offered to help, checking the inventory, fetching and carrying this and that from the storehouse.

To join a circus troupe was Blue's ambition, hoping to travel with them along the coast. They had fixed their departure date for the following week.

To keep busy, Beth set herself the task of preserving and cooking.

"Enough to feed an army for a month," declared Ben, seeing the array of goodies on the kitchen table.

Blue, sitting on the veranda, was busy sorting over oddments from his travellers' box, deciding which items to leave behind, when Ruth stopped to look. She had been quite pleasant of late, maybe, he guessed, because he was leaving.

"Are those beads, Blue?" Ruth asked inquisitively.

Taking them from the box he held them for her to see. Various coloured woods, carved into peculiar shapes and sizes, were linked together with a leather thong, to form a necklace.

"My! They're beautifully carved, may I put them on?"

Blue shook his head.

"Oh, let me, please!" she pleaded.

"No. They are not for wearing," he said, quickly putting

them back in the box, starting to take out other items.

Ruth, not to be thwarted, leaned forward and pulled the beads from the box, slipped them over her head and ran to her room. Looking in her mirror, her eyes began playing peculiar tricks, seeing what she thought to be the figure of an Aborigine. He appeared to be leaning against her bedroom door-post. Who could it be? He was not at all like anyone she knew or had met and his eyes looked so strange, unreal in fact.

Suddenly she felt very frightened. Her head spun and she wanted to vomit. The figure at the door was joined by a younger person, whose face she could not see. With trembling hands, her eyes riveted on the weird apparitions, she quickly removed the beads, popped them into the top drawer of her dressing table and turned the key. Her heartbeat was erratic as she watched the visions vanish into thin air.

Much later, after recovering from her ordeal, Ruth returned to Blue who was still sitting on the veranda. Looking as if he were in a trance, Ruth spoke to him. He gave no answer, only turned his head and looked in her direction in a vacant fashion, holding out his hand for the return of the beads, his other hand placed over the area of his heart.

With a tormenting laugh, Ruth said, "No! I am keeping them until you return!" and rushed away.

Blue sat, shaking his head as if to still her tormenting laugh echoing in his brain. Matthew joined him. After looking at him he stated matter-of-factly, "You look sick, Blue. Don't you feel well? I'll fetch Ma."

"Don't worry," said Blue quietly, adding, "Only a little something with Ruth."

Matthew watched as Blue shrugged his shoulders and, holding onto the veranda woodwork, made an ungainly effort to stand up and walk down the veranda steps and across the yard to the wagon with his box, as his friend was saying, "You don't torment her now. You shouldn't take Ruth's words to heart, Blue. Sure you don't need my Ma?"

"I'll be in the orchard if anyone wants me," said Blue.

"But it's time for dinner, aren't you hungry?" Matthew asked, watching his friend disappear, the first time ever seeing Blue ill.

For three days Blue ate very little, lazing around in a lethargic manner, quite unwell. During the second night it became apparent Blue had been dreaming, shouting and waking Matthew.

Matthew immediately inquired if he needed something. Receiving no answer, he assumed him to be asleep.

In the morning he asked him about his dream. Blue could tell him nothing. He didn't remember dreaming, but he felt a little better.

On the fourth day, the strangeness had left Blue; he was more cheerful. Beth had been very concerned. When Blue mentioned they would leave as planned the next morning, Beth asked, with great concern, "Are you sure you feel well enough to travel? Wait another day or so, Blue dear."

"I feel better, thank you – Hunky Dory, Mrs Dere." Giving her a kiss on her cheek, he was his usual grinning self.

Next morning, the loaded wagon was ready and waiting.

"Your parents will be pleased to see you, Blue. I bet they wish they were going with you," said Beth. "Give them my love!"

"One day, I'm sure they'll be on the move again, Mrs Dere. They've stayed in Justville longer than anywhere I can remember," said Blue as he jumped on to the wagon, taking the reins.

Matthew gave his mother a kiss and shook his father by the hand, then sat himself beside Blue and Prince and waited for Jake to give the signal to be away.

Jake was accompanying the lads to Justville to collect some documents from Duke. Ben saluted them, wishing them a safe journey, as he put it, on their journey into manhood. Beth, beside him, dabbing her eyes as she watched her beloved son go off into the unknown, wondering if she would ever see him alive again.

Ruth came to the veranda steps. She waved. Blue noticed the bright red of her hair glinting in the early morning sunlight, a strange, beautiful look on her face. A sight that remained with him for some time.

Chapter 12

The two young men left Justville for a destination unknown, but heading for the Australian coast in search of circus folk and travellers.

They began their journey making a few calls at cattle stops, investigating the small wayside stores, and, as Matthew and Blue were friendly and talkative, enjoyed mixing with cattle-drovers and the like, listening with interest to their conversation.

At one large stop-over, they noticed a big poster pasted on the front of a building. It read: "Solomon, The Strongest Man Known. Test Your Strength. Many other interesting attractions … taking place this Saturday."

"I'll go and take a look while you get the shoes on the horse fixed," Blue said with excitement.

Pulling over to a smithy, Matthew asked the Blacksmith if he had the time to fit a couple of shoes to his horse.

"Sure," he agreed. "Fine wagon you have there," he said, looking over the intricate paintwork. "My elder brother down the track is a dab-hand signwriter, he sure would like to see this one. He paints other things, mind."

Expertly he fitted a shoe, tapping the ends off the nails.

"Where you from?" he asked, picking up the other foot to investigate.

Matthew told him, as well as their reason for travelling.

"You go and see my brother Hubert, have a word with him, he'll tell you where to make for. Yeah, he's well-in with the travellers," he said, continuing, after taking off his hat to swat flies, to complete his task.

Matthew paid and thanked him.

He watched Matthew hitch the wagon, and still interested in

the young man asked, "What can you do then? You can't get around too well," he said, pointing to Matthew's wooden leg.

"Oh! I play the music," Matthew explained very seriously, but with a twinkle in his eye, and took his flute from a pocket and played a jig.

The Blacksmith stood with an unbelievable look on his face at the expertise of this young man. Then, smiling broadly, he started tapping his feet in rhythm.

Matthew finished with a flourish, gave the Smith a bow, then climbed aboard the wagon.

The Blacksmith shouted, "Bravo! Good on you!" lifting his sweat-stained hat again as the wagon moved away.

Blue and Prince were waiting under a shady eucalyptus. They then went in search of Hubert, finding him sitting in a shady place, mixing paints. His smock showed signs of wear and was streaked with paint of all colours under the sun. He wore knee breeches and odd socks, also daubed with paint and dilapidated shoes definitely beyond repair. Dark, curly hair protruded from beneath a broad brimmed and battered straw hat, the hat secured by string. An unkempt beard, streaked with paint, appeared to get in the way of the mixing of his colours.

"Have you time to talk with us?" inquired Blue from his seat, preparing to jump down. "Your brother sent us."

Hubert stopped mixing and looked up, his eyes resting on the painted wagon.

"What is it you want? I haven't any money."

Blue thought a moment. "We need some information, Sir, if you please. We'll make it worth your while!"

Hubert nodded and grunted.

"Your brother mentioned to my pal here that you had friends in the traveller fraternity – show people," said Blue, who had by then descended from the wagon and walked over to the man. He began briefly to tell their story.

Hubert said nothing, although his squinting eyes never left

Blue's face, as if he was weighing him up.

Eventually, without utterance of a word, Hubert went into his dilapidated shack, returning with a faded piece of paper. He handed it to Blue, who read, "Madame Clare, Fortune Teller. Clairvoyant."

"The last place I saw her, some while since, was Greenhurst," Hubert said. "Said she was making for the coast." Moving close to their wagon to take a good look, rubbing his chin, putting more paint on his beard, he carried on: "Dare say you could catch up with her before then. Takes her time, she does. Dandy wagon you have here."

About to return to his paint pot, Hubert added as an after-thought, "Take no heed of Solomon's gang."

Blue thanked him, pressing a couple of coins into his hand.

From then on the going became much slower, with many stops. Replenishment of food and water. Large and small boulders were strewn around as they found their way along the Smokey Blue Mountains.

Again they chose a clearing by the river to spend the night. A cool and pleasant place. They had travelled many days, happily enjoying the fresh surroundings. After the horse had been fed and watered and a fire burned brightly, Matthew prepared and cooked a pan of meat, while Blue mixed flour and water to drop into the simmering pot. They were hungry.

Sitting enjoying their meal some time later, they heard a most blood-curdling noise echoing around the mountain range.

"Sounds like Kilkenny Cats," joked Blue.

The noise was heard again and again.

"It's a scale of notes someone is singing." Matthew, standing up and laughing, said, "Shall we investigate?"

"After I've finished my food. Prince has eaten his. Sit down and finish yours, Matt," Blue said, helping himself to another plateful.

Taking a small gun with them, quietly they picked their

way along the track. After a few hundred yards or so, another clearing came into view. There they saw a wagon and tethered horse, one person seated by the fireside, another, a woman, standing, singing scales with all her might.

Unexpectedly Prince began to howl, carolling and howling. The scales ceased but Prince carried on.

The man by the fire rose to his feet as the trio approached.

Blue spoke in a friendly manner, introducing them both, and the man answered, "I am Frederick and this is my wife, Madame Clare."

Blue couldn't believe their luck. Before them stood a stocky man, twirling his sharp pointed moustache with thumb and finger, his collarless striped shirt neat and clean, thick worsted trousers held at the waist by red braces, matching a neatly knotted kerchief around his neck. His wife, Madame Clare, was typically dressed as a fortune teller in a floral gown, with a soft woollen shawl around her shoulders.

She looked a true gypsy with her dark skin and jet-black hair and an abundance of bangles and baubles around her neck and wrists. Both appeared to be middle-aged.

"I love to sing, especially in the quiet of the mountains. It gives me great joy. I am sorry if I disturbed you. Come take some tea," the woman said, shrewdly assessing the two young men.

Seated around the fire on cushions provided by Frederick, Matthew and Blue gave their reason for travelling, and also told of their meeting with Hubert.

"Oh, Hubert is a fantastic artist. They must join us, eh, Freddy darling?"

Giving him no chance to answer, she chattered on. "Us travellers meet each year, same time and place, then travel along the coast."

The conversation turned to music. Madame Clare and Matthew spoke the same language. "Tomorrow you bring your wagon and we'll travel together."

Madame Clare clapped her hands. "It will be a pleasure to have you both. We stay here for a while yet, that's right? Eh, Freddy darling?"

After leaving them and talking it over, they wondered if they had chosen the right path. "Our fate is in her hands," quipped Blue.

They stayed there for several days, really enjoying each other's company. Finally Madame Clare announced, "We go in the morning. I feel so happy to have young friends with us this year. We know Rodrigo very well, eh, Freddy darling?"

Matthew and Blue knew by now Freddy had no say in the matter.

"Who is Rodrigo? Tell us a little about him, if you will?"

"He is terrific. So good and kind. Master of our group of entertainers," she enthused. "Keeps everyone in order. Most people along the coast know him. His acts are popular. He chooses his company well but you must be prepared to work hard."

Of this she had no doubt. During the short time she had known them, she had watched them most carefully, especially when practising their routine, and Hubert was a good judge of character.

The journey through the mountains took considerable time. Eventually, upon reaching open country, Madame Clare called them to a halt, pointing and saying, "Not far now".

A low plain lay ahead. "We get there tomorrow," she added, as Freddy began unloading his goods and chattels.

Excitement and wonder gripped the two lads as they began their chores. Blue sighed.

"I'm not hungry this evening, are you, Matt?"

Matthew shook his head. Freddy had his fire going and had started preparing a meal. He called the two over. Madame Clare emerged from her wagon, clean and neatly dressed.

"You join us for a meal tonight." It was more a command than an invitation. "The only hungry one in our party is Prince," Blue answered.

"Come! Come! You will feel better when the stomach is full. Bring the music, Matthew." Laughing at them, she settled herself by the fire.

Freddy, using small portions of salted pork, onions, rings of apples and herbs, all thrown into a large pan with some oil, deftly stirred the sizzling mass over the hot fire. It smelled delicious. Both lads forgot they were not hungry and watched as Freddy poured liquid into a measure from a glass bottle and added it to the hot pan. Flames and smoke erupted.

"Ready now," Freddy shouted, quickly extinguishing the flames, scooping hot pieces on to four plates.

Prince sat patiently waiting, wondering perhaps if a tasty morsel would come his way, saliva oozing from his jaw. He had already eaten his supper.

"Freddy, you certainly know how to cook. I've never tasted the likes before," acknowledged Blue, his plate empty.

"I'm full," agreed Matthew. "We sure appreciate your generosity, eh, Blue?"

They watched Freddy hold a large piece of cooked meat in front of Prince. The dog lifted a paw, automatically placing it into Freddy's outstretched hand, taking the offering most gracefully.

"Good boy!" said Freddy, giving Prince a pat.

Later that evening, Madame Clare started to hum a lullaby.

"It's my Freddy's favourite, that's right, eh, Freddy darling?" and began again to hum the lovely tune. Matthew, quietly at first, followed the tune on his accordion. She then began to sing the words. The lullaby told of a young maiden, desperately in love with her childhood sweetheart and he with her, but because her father had been convicted of poaching, the Justice of the Peace had sentenced the whole family to deportation along with many other so-called convicts, to Australia, leaving behind her lover.

Sea sickness on board ship takes its toll, but the young lass soon realises she is with child.

"The ocean is so wide, you're so many miles away, but the child within my side will forever with me stay. As the golden sun doth rise and the earth forever turn, as diamonds fill our skies, my love for you will burn, I will love you 'till I die, truly love you 'till I die."

Having several verses and a chorus, the tune gave Matthew an excellent opportunity to harmonize. Madame Clare was delighted with this accompaniment. Blue was amazed by her beautiful voice after hearing that banshee on their evening of meeting. She sang the haunting lullaby most beautifully and to perfection.

Matthew asked if she sang with the entertainers. They knew so little about her.

"Oh, no!" she said reprovingly. And then, "Of course, you wouldn't know, silly of me," she said repentantly. Then with great pride, "I am the great Madame Clare. Clairvoyant and Fortune Teller. As Rodrigo is known around the country, so am I! That is right, eh, Freddy darling?"

Not wanting to upset their newfound friends, Blue hastily said, "Matthew and I are delighted to have met you. You sing most beautifully." Then giving Freddy some praise: "The meal was delicious. Maybe we can return the compliment sometime soon?"

A few drops of rain made them gather their belongings together hurriedly and retire to their respective wagons.

"Early in the morning, remember!" Madame Clare called.

Chapter 13

A small gathering of travellers greeted Madame Clare and her party when they pulled onto a wide grassed area, evidently a meeting place used by them over the period of time. Everyone looked happy to be meeting again after their short break.

Matthew and Blue stood by, watching. To them it was like one large family greeting each other after a long separation. When Madame Clare introduced the two young men as her friends, they were accepted instantly and made to feel welcome.

Rodrigo was the last to arrive. Every detail about him and his entourage could be described as flamboyantly immaculate, and his eyes missed nothing.

He went immediately to Madame Clare and Freddy. This rotund man was dressed in a colourful silk shirt and voluminous trousers, his soft, pointed shoes up-turned. The only thing missing from his attire, thought Blue, was a turban.

After enveloping Madame Clare in a tremendous hug, he accompanied her and Freddy into their wagon.

Matthew and Blue, busying themselves with their chores, could hear voices and the fortune-teller's high-pitched laughter, mingling with the chink of glass.

Rodrigo emerged from the Clairvoyant's wagon looking very happy, and, calling to the two lads, said, "Sure do want to see your act. Must attend to my other affairs first."

Still smiling he moved among his other friends, talking to the children who clamoured around him, patting the little ones' heads.

Word quickly spread later that morning that Madame Clare's new friends were about to perform their act in front of the boss.

"Do or die!" joked Blue as they waited eagerly inside the wagon for the precise moment to emerge.

Rodrigo tapped the side of the wagon. Blue toppled out in true clown fashion with Prince beside him, both dog and clown looking a picture of happiness. Blue had dressed himself in his billowing blue and white suit and dunce's cap, his face painted white, with large blue circles around both eyes, and a painted, blue vertical line from each eyebrow to his cheeks. A large red nose and enormous red lips. His curly blonde hair was waxed, protruding from beneath the cap at his temples.

He juggled expertly with five balls, deliberately dropping one for Prince. The dog then chased away with it in his mouth, stopping at short intervals for Blue to retrieve it, but would race away again, retaining the ball. Finally, Blue gave up in mock despair, sat in the centre of the makeshift ring, looking pitiful, whereupon Prince trotted over and placed the ball at Blue's feet, causing much laughter and amazement from the onlookers.

This clowning over, Matthew joined them with his accordion and a paper-covered hoop, which he handed to Blue. Prince jumped through this with perfect precision. Matthew played his music. The dog howled, and so it continued, one trick after another. Their final trick ended with the dog pulling Blue's trouser cord with Blue showing off a most garish pair of underpants. Applause from those around. They liked the act.

Rodrigo shook them both by the hand, very pleased. Prince sat still until Rodrigo was about to move away, then the dog stood up and pulled at Rodrigo's pantaloons, lifting a paw. The boss stooped and shook the paw. Satisfied, Prince returned to Blue and Matthew. The onlookers watched their boss stare and smile at the dog unbelievingly, still laughing as he turned away.

The group of artistes and children gathered around, praising and patting the dog, asking how long it had taken to train Prince to give a performance of such a high standard. Clowns had joined them before, but never with a dog or with such a clever routine as theirs.

Very pleased with the artistes' praise, and thankful they had been accepted, they were aware that Madame Clare had surely been an instigator to their acceptance.

Gradually Blue and Matthew saw the amazing talents of Rodrigo's troupe. Rodrigo lived not far from this meeting place and was able to stable his horse, an Albino, at his home until their touring began. This being the case, the two clowns had no idea the Boss was a very competent equestrian showman.

Within the group was a snake charmer, magician and acrobats, plus various side-shows, managed by an entire family, both young and old.

Setting up the pitch to accommodate the various side-shows and centre ring took a great deal of time and was very hard work. But with a general plan to guide them, the young novices were quick to learn. In time, names began to fit faces.

Prince was now accustomed to being detained on a leash, as the baskets of Azil the snake charmer held too great a fascination for an inquisitive dog.

Entertaining, working their way along the coast, took a considerable time. Almost from the beginning Blue was called upon to give one person or another a helping hand, especially with the erection of the swing-boats and the steam carousel. Everyone soon came to realise Matthew was also robust. Friendly and good workers, they became well liked and trusted, and their act pulled in the crowds.

Their next stop would be for a week or even longer.

They were approaching a large town, popular with cattle-drovers, and people from the surrounding area holding rodeos and races. It was a form of holiday time for some. Two groups of entertainers converged for this event – Rodrigo and his entourage and Barney Crutch with his circus. Both knew each other well and had worked together many times.

Putting the two shows together meant a lot of work for everyone, but it was very rewarding. By nightfall, all were extremely tired. Because the two clowns had no one to prepare their meals, they were often asked to share in someone's evening meal.

"Variety is the spice of life," Matthew quoted after accepting and savouring many delicious traditional dishes.

Prior to the great opening day, Matthew and Blue wandered round the side-shows and then into the main circus ring. A canvas awning, erected over the sawdust ring, was securely held in place by thick, strong ropes. Looking up into the top, fragile-looking swings were suspended on wires and more ropes. A tall, thin man entered the ring, followed by a slip of a girl and a strong, muscular young man. Pulling at a long, loose rope, the younger man began to climb. Upon reaching the platform on the level of the swings, the others followed.

At precisely the same moment Matthew and Blue turned to each other and said, "Mitzy and her father from Adelaide!"

Enthralled, they watched as the trio worked through a tremendously thrilling routine, twisting, swinging and catching. It was breathtaking.

"Enough!" shouted Mitzy's father, slithering down one of the long ropes.

Blue clapped, he couldn't restrain himself. Mitzy curtsied and smiled from a ledge high in the roof.

"I don't think they will remember us. A lot of water has passed under the bridge since then," declared Matt. "And it was dark."

Walking back to their wagon, Madame Clare called them. "Rodrigo wants to see you both, at once."

"What for?"

"I don't exactly know," she said, waving them to go quickly, her bangles chinking on her wrist. Dressed immaculately in black and gold, she was holding a large crucifix, its thick gold chain matching her gold earrings. She smiled as they left.

Rodrigo saw the two coming.

"Blue, I've been looking all over for you. My friend Barney Crutch thinks your act would be fine in his circus ring, but he wants to see it first. Care to have a try?"

They stood gaping at him.

"Well, say something, one of you. Will you or won't you?" Rodrigo asked impatiently.

"Yes, sir! Whoopee!" said Blue, throwing his hat up high and yelling.

Rodrigo laughed.

"The young men of today … Meet Barney in the morning, eight o'clock sharp in the circus ring."

Then as an afterthought, "Good luck!"

Prince had positioned himself close to Rodrigo, giving him a nudge, then lifted his paw and wagged his tail.

"You old scrounger," the Boss chided, feeling in his pocket, finding and giving the dog a barley sugar.

Barney Crutch watched the new act like a cat watches a mouse. Blue walked on his stilts with perfect balance, head almost touching the lower trapeze swing, his endless practice at the Homestead paying off. Prince twisted in and out of the stilts waiting for the command to jump through four hoops held by Matthew. Proudly he jumped.

Matthew's accordion music and Blue's juggling was synchronised to perfection. Fool-like clowning finally completed their act.

Barney, pleased by what he had seen, called them over.

"Fine. Good timing. Just fine!"

Then he gave them the order of their appearance.

"You come in three times. Different act each time, of course. About the same length of time as this performance. You follow the opening parade, the axe thrower and the elephants and you wait in the ring for the acrobats and trapeze artists."

103

Showing them the list in his hand, they then realised all Rodrigo's group of entertainers would be performing.

"Be back at noon, I want everybody in the ring."

From that moment, Blue, Matthew and Prince joined in the hurly-burly of circus life, working among horses, elephants and the other artists.

Blue, in his element, attractively attired, his face painted, walking on stilts, enticed and cajoled folks outside the arena to come and see their great show. Even the fire-eater and axe-thrower gave demonstrations to allure the crowd inside.

Satisfied enough people had been admitted, Barney closed the entrance. The first show was about to begin.

Music, laughter, shouts, roars and whistles filled the Big Top, much to the delight of both Barney and Rodrigo.

The following days saw seats filled and everyone was happy.

Apparently Mitzy's father had the notion that high-wire trapeze artists were more sought after than mere tight-rope walkers like themselves, thus joining with Hans and combining their two acts, created a more tense performance.

Hans, of German origin and a professional trapeze performer, adored Mitzy, and was very protective towards her, hoping one day they would marry.

The two clowns became very friendly with them, because it was their duty, under Barney's orders, to hold a net for their safety – true the two clowned around as expected, but were always accurately placed.

Madame Clare asked them to bring their new friends to share a farewell supper the night before the show finished, as she simply loved having young folks around her. It also gave her the opportunity to hear what was happening in other parts of the country.

"I'd like some music at the supper. What will you bring? I like the accordion but you play the flute magnificently, Matthew, that's right, eh, Freddy? Bring both," she instructed, her irresistible smile coinciding with waving hands and jangling bangles, adding emphasis to her persuasive powers.

On the morning prior to the supper, Blue and Matthew wandered to the cattle stalls. Really they had seen very little of the Rodeo or races.

Suddenly they heard a shout: "Hey there, Matthew! Blue! Hey there!"

Who should it be but Tom the Blacksmith.

"Well, 'pon my word, Tom," said Blue, grasping his strong hand.

"How's that leg frame? Any trouble?" Tom enquired.

"None at all, thanks to you," Matthew laughed, so pleased to see him, slapping him on his back.

They asked Tom questions galore. Had he been to the Dere Homestead of late? Or to Justville? After answering their questions, he told them he was about to go to town to stock up with food and such like. He asked if they would care to join him, as that way they could talk some more, assuring them it wasn't far into town and they would be back easily in time for their performance.

During the journey they asked Tom not to reveal their identities, not wanting their travelling companions to know their parents were wealthy and that they had no need to work for a living. Tom agreed.

The store was situated on the outskirts of the town. The store-keeper, knowing Tom quite well, started a jovial conversation as he weighed and packed his purchases.

His companions also made some purchases; a whole cheese, bread and preserves, several smoked fish, fresh vegetables, local apples and other bits-and-bobs.

Watching for the two clowns' return, Madame Clare saw Tom.

"My friend! Tom-the-Smith. Welcome! Welcome! Fancy seeing you with my two protégés!"

"It's a small world, Ma'am." Tom smiled and asked, "How's Freddy?"

"Freddy's all right, that so, eh, my friends? So, you know these two?" Not giving him a chance to speak, she continued, "They look well? Yes? Come to our supper this evening, Tom. Then you can tell me your news!"

She was watching as Blue and Matthew unloaded their goods.

"Time you two made yourselves ready for the show."

Hurriedly, they picked out some of their purchases, giving them to her for the supper.

"Oh, Tom! They are the most thoughtful young men I have ever met. Come, Tom, and talk to Freddy." She led him towards her fortune telling booth.

Their final day at this stop, Prince, wearing his comic Admiral's hat and neck ruffle, made theirs a star turn.

Following the clown act came the trapeze artists. As usual, they had the rather crudely-made net in place, and to the horror of everyone, Mitzy missed Hans' hands, tumbling quickly into the net below. With sighs of relief from the audience, with true showmanship, she jumped from the net.

Mitzy, twisting herself up the rope, stopped at intervals to pose. The crowd expressed their relief with clapping, cheers and whistles as she continued her act as if nothing untoward had happened.

After the show, Rodrigo saw the large, friendly gathering seated round a fire outside Madame Clare's booth.

"Rodrigo!" she called, "you have time? Come take supper with us. We have much food. All right! Eh, Freddy?" She patted a place beside herself. One never quite knew where Freddy managed to acquire such delicious food, and with the added contributions from other families, Madame Clare's supper turned into a banquet, the makeshift tables almost groaning under the food's weight.

The conversation ranged from each other's acts, the country from which they came, and of course Mitzy's fall, which she passed off lightly with a shrug and a laugh.

Rodrigo asked Matthew, who was sitting beside him, if Barney had invited them to join his circus group. Matthew told him no.

"Come, Matt-the-Music, play us some music," ordered Madame Clare.

Taking his accordion be began a soothing lullaby, followed by a livelier melody.

Hans sat with eyes closed, lost in his own world, his right foot tapping in rhythm. Matthew, with sudden intuition, asked, "Hans, my friend, I have a feeling you are also a musician as well as a trapeze artist, am I correct?" not knowing from where this intuitiveness had sprung.

Hans' eyes flew open and he looked around as Matthew eased the straps from his shoulders, saying, "Care to play?"

"It was so long ago, I have not played for many years," Hans hesitantly told them.

"Play something for me, Hans dear," said Mitzy persuasively.

Taking the accordion, Hans fingered the keys, picking out a soft Bavarian tune. Then in earnest, pent up emotion unleashed, he began to play melody upon melody from his country.

"Wonderful, Hans! And you have never mentioned this before!" declared Mitzy. Hans shook his head. He was close to tears. "I have not played since I left my homeland and mother."

"Please play again," pleaded Blue, "Your melodies remind me of the mountains, that so, Madame Clare?"

Hans obliged. After a while, Matthew accompanied him, playing his flute. Their only problem, but making people laugh, was a howling Prince of Dogs!

Darkness had fallen. No one wanted to break up the party or leave the glowing fire. Tomorrow would be the parting of the ways. Blue, much concerned by Mitzy's fall, gave Hans a card with Dr Teddy Jackson's Sydney address.

"I hope we meet again, Hans. Contact this man should you ever need help, he's an excellent doctor and a great friend of ours."

Next morning, Matthew and Blue were busy helping dismantle cables and ropes when Barney Crutch looked in.

"Glad you get along so well together. How about joining my troupe?"

"Thanks, Mr Crutch, but no. We aim to move on around the coast, then maybe go abroad. We haven't decided yet, have we Matt?" Blue answered.

"Abroad, you say? England?" asked Barney, taking a book from his pocket and a newspaper cutting.

"My cousin, Leonardo Crutch, was an entertainer, still is, no doubt. It's a hard life but we don't give up, eh, Blue?"

Blue took the faded paper and read: 'Leonardo Crutch, Wethergate Goose Fair, Entertainer Extraordinaire,' asking, "What's your cousin's line?"

"Oh, a conjurer, magician if you like. Keep the paper. England's a small place, they say, you may come across him. Sure been dandy meeting you two. Good luck!"

Barney would have stayed longer but someone called him.

Rodrigo, pleased to think that all his performers preferred to stay with him and had not been enticed away by Barney, planned his itinerary for the months ahead with great precision, timing with luck, their arrival at Adelaide for the great sales.

"Adelaide, when we arrive there, is the ideal place for us, Matthew, to say 'Goodbye' to Rodrigo and our friends, then find a vessel leaving for England. We could ask Albert Green to stable our horse and take Prince and the wagon with us. Of course, Prince will have to stay in quarantine in England. What do you think, Matthew?"

"Fine. We could enlist help from the Government Officer and Father's solicitor," suggested Matthew.

Adelaide, when they eventually saw the town again, was much busier. Parts of the town were unrecognisable, although it still retained its wide street. Taking a chance, they found Albert at the railway station. Now young men, Albert only recognised Matthew by his disability. As for Blue and his dog, well!

"Circus clowns! I don't believe it!" Amazed, Albert stood looking, then told them he was married and had two children, Sammy and Pearl. He and his family lived with his mother in the same house. An extension had been built for more accommodation.

"Mother will be very pleased to see you again. She has never forgotten you."

Quickly giving Albert a run-down of their proposed trip to England, they arranged to meet again later, after they had left Rodrigo's group.

When Madame Clare learned of their impending trip to England, she immediately suggested a glance into her crystal ball. Blue had laughed.

"Mystery surrounds you both, I have yet to find the reason why!" she exclaimed in all seriousness as Blue laughed at her again.

"I think the yarns you spin those poor, unsuspecting cattle drovers, and what you would tell us, could be taken with a pinch of salt. That's right, eh, Freddy?"

Blue just stopped himself from saying 'darling'.

Freddy shook his head.

"There, you see, darling Freddy knows I speak the truth," she said, reaching up, trying to give Blue a box of the ears for tormenting her.

"Right, then," declared Blue giving a massive grin, "When we have made our final exit from the ring, your wish shall be granted, Madame Clare."

Hat in hand he gave a most solemn bow.

Matthew was not keen to have his fortune told and said so.

He thought it a load of old cod, but said of Madame Clare, "I like her and have a great deal to thank her for, but I have my doubts about her powers."

True to his promise, Blue entered Madame Clare's booth. Freddy was seated just inside the doorway.

"Always Freddy is with me. Sometimes we have aggressive customers, not nice, perhaps a little too much drink eh, Freddy?"

Madame Clare, dressed in her clairvoyant attire, beads and bangles chinking, sat at a table on which was placed a large crystal ball.

"Take a seat Blue, I am pleased you came. I knew Matthew would not, but we shall see, maybe you help him?"

Blue sat in front of the small table. Taking his outstretched hand, she turned it palm upwards. "So," she stated, sounding surprised, her eyes then searching his face.

"You are already be-spoken. Your heart is securely locked."

Placing her hands on the crystal ball she began a trance-like chant. This made Blue uneasy. "Your love is not over the sea. I see a large wheel. A wheel of fortune? No. It is not for you – perhaps your friend Matthew?"

Fumbling in a box, Madame Clare placed a wooden cube on the table. Blue couldn't take his eyes off it.

"You are surprised, yes? Perhaps you have seen something like it before?"

Blue didn't have to answer her.

"Part of a tribal love token."

More confusing words followed.

"I see your friend. You keep together. He will go through fire and water or perhaps danger. It will not be easy for him. You will know when to return to your home. You must not hesitate, it is very important you both return home quickly. You will be remembered, honoured and make people happy."

About to continue, then thinking otherwise, she took Blue's other hand only to exclaim, "You are rich!"

Freddy put a match to more candles. The session was over.

Blue rose to his feet, searching in his pocket for some coins. Madame Clare refused his money, insisted on giving him a lucky charm, a cube of intricately worked gold. He kissed her on both cheeks and shook Freddy by the hand, thanking them for their great help and felt sure they would meet again.

Early the next morning, with sad farewells, Rodrigo's troupe of entertainers moved on to their next venue, leaving Matthew and Blue in Adelaide to go their own way.

Albert Green was busy cleaning his stables when the two clowns arrived with their horse, wagon and of course Prince. He straightaway took them into the house to meet his wife, Lillian.

She was a small, plump, happy person, holding a little boy in her arms. Her dark hair was neatly pinned in a bun, her clothes spotless. Asking Albert to hold their son, Sammy, for a moment, she fetched Granny and their daughter, Pearl.

Granny, Harriet Green, struggled in with Lillian's help, delighted to see her fine young men, although they had grown beyond recognition.

"The best guests I ever had!" Harriet Green told her daughter-in-law. She asked after Matthew's father and told them how she had fallen and broken some bones. They had a few paying guests at times. With the children and herself to look after, Lillian had enough to do.

"Albert has much more work now, so it doesn't matter about guests."

They could tell she was very fond of Lillian and proud of their children.

Sitting in the front parlour, it was just as Blue remembered it, clean and smelling of lavender polish.

Discussing their proposed visit to England, Albert agreed to stable their horse for as long as was needed, and also take them to the shipping office and government building. They could stay with him and his family until they were ready to make their voyage.

"Albert, tomorrow is the Sabbath, I want to go to Church," Harriett Green said firmly.

"But, Mother, you're not fit. You know what the doctor told you," Albert said, trying to dissuade her.

His mother was adamant.

"I wish to go and hear Matthew play the organ once more. Surely you can't deny an old woman her last wish? We must all go, Lillian and the children."

"Mother, you are not sure if Matthew will be at Church," he questioned.

"He will be," she answered positively. "Please, Albert," she pleaded.

How could he refuse? He stooped and kissed her cheek.

Harriet Green and her family arrived at the Church. She asked the Minister if her friend, Matthew, could play the organ after morning service, reminding him of the time this young man had played before, and said with great authority, "Tell those present there will be a recital after the service."

Matthew, standing beside Mrs Green, felt quite embarrassed.

The Minister only smiled, saying, "I am pleased you have managed to get here. Your wish will be granted with pleasure. I must say, I like your bonnet," the Minister added. Harriet Green's cheeks coloured a little. It was her very best bonnet, only worn once before, when she married Albert's father.

The family seated themselves near the organ. Halfway through the service the Minister made the announcement: "After this service Mr Matthew Dere will give an organ recital. It has been especially requested by our 'dear sister and friend,' Mrs Harriet Green."

There were many murmurs and turning of heads.

When the time came for Matthew to take his seat at the organ, he began by playing one of his own compositions of church music, followed by well-loved hymns.

The voices of the congregation filled the room. Mrs Green had previously asked him to play her favourite hymn. Matthew saw her singing joyfully and she gave him a most beautiful smile. Then her singing ceased.

Little Pearl, sitting beside her, peeped under Granny's lovely bonnet, nudged her mother and said, "Mummy, Granny has gone to sleep. She isn't singing."

Lillian took one look. Her mother-in-law, Harriet Green, had passed away. With great sadness the congregation quietly left.

"It is the way she would have wished," many commented.

Matthew or Blue had never attended a funeral service. This was an especially sad occasion. Naturally, Matthew agreed to play the organ, listing Mrs Green's favourite hymns.

Packed to capacity, people of all ages were paying their last respects in the little church, hearing the Minister's kind tribute during the service and also the organ recital, which Matthew had put together, with respect, to a dear friend.

Days passed. Albert found the two young men a great help during their stay, doing various odd jobs around the place, neglected, due to the death of his mother.

He then conveyed them to Mr Dere's solicitor, Mr Blizzard.

The solicitor, choosing an enormous leather-covered ledger from one of many, selected a page, then gave them the name of the shipping line with whom their respective fathers had an interest.

Albert, knowing his way around the docks like the back of his hand, took them to one of the ships' offices, and shared their great disappointment when they were told the ship was fully laden. Finding room for the wagon was the difficulty.

Trying another ship, they found, to their great relief, one setting sail for England the following week with room for them and all their belongings.

Making necessary visits to obtain passports and other essential documents from various offices, their week positively flew by.

After recompensing Albert for all his kindness, it was time to leave Adelaide.

Their message of the proposed trip to England, which Mr Blizzard had kindly promised to send, had not reached Justville or the Dere Homestead by the time Tom the Blacksmith's visit was due. As Tom drew nearer to the Homestead, he wondered what Ben Dere would say about his lad leaving for England.

"A couple of real nice fellows, Blue and Matthew," said Tom to himself, thinking of his meeting with them. Tom stopped when he saw Jake by the veranda steps.

"How goes it, Jake?"

"Quiet, devilishly quiet, Tom. Been like this since the lads left," Jake, straightening his hat replied. "Haven't seen you for a long time, Tom. What's wrong, you getting too old?"

"Been busy. By the way, saw Matthew and Blue in a circus at the Rodeo a few months back. Shared a meal with them and Madame Clare and other folks, night before they moved on with their show. Sure was a happy party. Madame Clare has kept an eye on them."

Tom was pleased to tell Jake his news.

"Who? You said that Clare woman? Heaven forbid if she's filled their heads with twaddle. By jingo! What'll Boss say when he hears that?"

"Don't need to worry your head about that, Jake, the lads are in fine fettle. In England by now, shouldn't be surprised," said Tom as Ben and his daughter, Ruth, both on horseback, came trotting home. Tom touched his hat and wished both "Good-day".

"Boss," Jake said, "Reckon you'd better listen to what Tom has to say. I'll look after your horses."

Muttering as he took the reins, he said, "England, well, I'll be blowed!"

Chapter 14

So this is England. Blue felt excited as he watched from the deck as the ship was guided from the Solent up the busy river into port. It was a dismal day, weather wise, grey and overcast, but, with the promise of the coming spring, he felt elated.

Now securely tied alongside other vessels that were being unloaded, Blue felt the rise and fall of the ship as the Captain waited for the inspectors to come aboard.

No longer experiencing sea sickness, Blue leaned on the ship's rail, watching several men trundling full hessian sacks on barrows, while others lifted heavy boxes onto their shoulders and staggered towards the warehouse.

Gulls screeched, whirring overhead, as others landed on any suitable structure or dived into the river in search of food.

The ship's gangplank was lowered and two men came aboard to greet the Captain. Cargo, to be offloaded at this port, as well as their wagon, had to be checked. Wool, which was part of this shipment, would be taken to a more northern port.

Quite a time passed before any movement came from below, then suddenly orders were shouted to open the hatches. Bargaining began between a reasonably well-dressed man and the second-in-command on the ship. A quick shake of hands and a signal to a bunch of men waiting on the dockside, then unloading commenced. Blue felt cold and shivered as the miserable mist seeped into his bones, wishing he could do something to warm himself as he and Matthew stood waiting.

Eventually it was the wagon's turn to be hauled and swung ashore, then pushed into an area for collection later.

Matthew had agreed to take Prince to the Authorities to be quarantined.

Speaking to the dog, giving him a quick fondle, Blue picked up a bridle, slung it over his shoulder and left the ship hurriedly.

Handing his papers to the official, he asked where was the best place locally to buy a good horse. The man was very helpful.

The address he was given was some way out of town and he had difficulty hiring a conveyance. Eventually a cab-driver agreed to take him and they set off at a brisk pace, bumping over cobble stones, leaving ramshackle buildings and the smell of the dock far behind.

Soon they entered what he thought looked to be a better-class area, with avenues of trees and tall, grey brick buildings. Over a toll bridge and they were out in the open countryside. Blue liked what he saw. Pasture and clumps of tall trees and small houses close to the roadside.

Slowly the carriage came to a halt outside a quaint half-timbered, half-brick coaching house, surrounded by wooden outhouses or stables.

"This is it!" shouted the driver. Blue asked him to wait, inviting him inside to partake of a glass of ale.

Inside, seated at tables, some men were drinking and smoking and playing a board game using coins; others, standing beside the large wooden counter, seemed to be bargaining.

After ordering two glasses of ale from the portly figure behind the counter, Blue gave the reason for his visit.

The landlord shouted for someone to take charge of the business, then ushered Blue outside to look over some horses.

Blue looked at horses of various breeds and varying ages, then spotted a sturdy piebald horse in quite good condition. Giving him a 'going-over', Blue decided this was the horse for him. Without argument, he paid the amazed landlord the asking price, slipped the bridle over the horse's head, talking to it all the time in a friendly, persuasive manner and climbed on its back.

Hardly believing his eyes at seeing his customer astride the bare back of the horse, a now jocular cab driver agreed to escort him back to the docks.

Matthew was accepting clearance papers from an official when Blue introduced him to their new horse, saying, "I've named him 'Silver'. He's broken-in and ready for work."

"You're a dandy fella, aren't you?" Blue said to the horse, rubbing its nose. "We'll fit you with shoes soon, old boy."

With the wagon ready to be moved, Blue harnessed the horse and backed him into the shaft. "Made for him," he said, turning and about to whistle Prince, then suddenly remembered.

Matthew looked very downcast. "I left him behind bars. Almost broke my heart."

With Matthew in the driving seat, Blue led the horse away from the busy port, taking a road which followed the course of the river for a few miles.

Pear-tree Green, the landlord of the Inn had told Blue to make for, and if he had followed the man's directions correctly, they would soon be there. Darkness would descend soon, and they needed a place to rest.

Matthew gave a shout. In front of them was a large area of grass with several sheep grazing. It must be the Green.

From then onwards, the cold winter months while Prince was in quarantine seemed endless. Moving from one part of the forest to another, seeking shelter in any nook from the ice-cold rains, wind and snow, Matthew thought Blue's promise of spring would never arrive.

Suddenly the hedgerow flowers began to appear. With great joy and relief, the month of April came. Prince was released with a clean bill of health and the reunion was a sight never to be forgotten.

England in May was beautiful. Green shoots began to break on the trees with the help of the sun's warmth. More colourful wild flowers popped up overnight, or so it seemed, and the birdsong was a delight to hear. All so different from home. In no great hurry, just ambling along, stopping first at one town, then another, they found themselves travelling along a very busy highway.

Carriages of all shapes and sizes, the likes never seen by them before, passed them, their passengers within, smartly dressed ladies and gentlemen and the drivers shouting and sounding horns, telling them to move their horse and wagon from the highway.

"Not very friendly people, are they?" said Matthew, holding tightly to the reins as another coach with four horses charged by. "It isn't far to the next town. I think we should stay the night here. How about it?"

Pulling off the highway, they found a nice glade with enough grass for Silver. Leaving Blue to make a fire, Matthew walked a short distance to the end of the glade and saw they were on a hill overlooking heathland. Spread before him and in the distance, he could see horses and wagons. He hurried back to tell his friend, but he had disappeared.

Blue, hearing a terrific rumbling noise and horses neighing, had raced to the highway and discovered, to his horror, a carriage resting on its side, the coachman thrown from his seat onto the grass verge and his passengers trying to open the carriage door.

Blue, with finger and thumb, gave a loud whistle for Matthew's assistance, then grabbed the reins of the two frightened and neighing horses, pulling at their trace. Between them they quietened and tethered the horses. Matthew then opened the door of the carriage. A young woman tumbled out into his arms and fainted.

Another older lady waited until he had laid her companion on the grass, before being assisted from their conveyance.

Blue had gone to the groaning coachman. Removing his own jacket, he placed it under the man's head. Finding two blankets from inside the carriage, Blue passed one to Matthew for the young lady, taking the other to cover the moaning man.

The older lady was crying. "Oh, my poor Jacob! What can we do?"

Blue ran his fingers over Jacob's arms and legs. Finding no bones broken, he said thoughtfully, "It could be his ribs, we must get him to a doctor, Ma'am. Do you know where to find one?"

"In the next town, where we are going." Looking at the motionless young woman under the blanket and at the coach-man, she began again to weep.

The two young men discussed the situation and decided to take a chance and move the man. No one on this road seemed willing to help these people, so they decided to use their own wagon and take them to a doctor.

Very carefully, they lifted Jacob onto one of the beds in the wagon. Then they helped the young lady, who had revived sufficiently, to rest beside him. Blue remained close at hand to administer one of his potions for pain relief.

The older woman, who had pulled herself together, sat beside Matthew, giving him directions to the hospital.

From time to time Jacob fainted or moaned with pain, caused by the movement of the wagon, upsetting the young woman.

On arrival at the hospital, a doctor was called and after a brief examination, instructed two porters to carry Jacob on a stretcher to a hospital bed.

Blue promised the two ladies they would take care of their horses and luggage, until it was convenient for someone to collect them.

"My name is Miss Rachel Coleville-Grey; this is my special friend and maid, Kate Ellis. I do thank you both." Still in shock and spoken very quietly, she handed her card to Matthew.

It was only then that Rachel noticed the brightly painted

wagon. She gasped; what had she done!?

"Everything will be taken care of, Miss," Blue told her, doffing his hat. "Ready Matthew?" Jumping onto the wagon they were away.

Matthew spoke of what he had seen across the heathland.

"I think our luck's in. Maybe we'll get some information. A few circus venues or boss names, for instance."

Blue agreed, uttering a sigh of relief.

"Thank goodness! The carriage is still here."

The righting of the carriage was very difficult and took some time. Using the two horses, they managed to pull it into the glade. Finally, all horses were cared for and tethered securely. Blue declared, "What a day! I'm hungry." He began to re-kindle the fire.

Matthew gave a lengthy sigh.

Hearing the sigh, Blue asked, "What's come over you, Matt?"

"Wasn't she beautiful, Blue? Sure, bloomin' lovely!"

Matthew looked distant.

"Who was?" Blue asked needlessly, knowing quite well to whom he was referring. "I take it you're not hungry. Are you sickening for something?" he said, looking at his friend who was sitting with his eyes closed.

"Love!" said Matthew with a groan.

Blue laughed. Leaving, he collected the luggage from the carriage and stowed it away for safe keeping, then sat himself down with Prince to enjoy a meal.

Chapter 15

Leaving Jacob in hospital suffering from several broken ribs, Rachel ordered a carriage to take Kate and herself the remainder of their journey. Lucky for them, they had little damage, just a few minor bumps and bruises.

Their destination was a holiday villa on the other side of the town, rented by Rachel's cousin Neville, in a town where many of the landed gentry gathered every year for the benefit of their health.

Their cab stopped outside the large establishment. The front door opened and a woman stood in the open doorway with a young man beside her, ready to carry the luggage.

The woman, Mrs Crispe, was the housekeeper from Rachel's country estate, sent to take charge of the town villa for the holiday period.

"Where's your luggage?" the housekeeper asked loudly, almost uncouthly, seeing the two alight from the local conveyance.

Kate answered her politely. "We have had a bad accident, Mrs Crispe, Jacob is in hospital, it's a wonder we were not killed! Two very nice young gentlemen are taking care of our luggage, the broken carriage and the horses."

"Who are the nice young gentlemen?" queried Mrs Crispe with a leering smile, not in the least worried over Jacob's health.

Rachel, looking ghastly, spoke quietly, "Two from the fairground."

"Fairground? Scoundrels!" shrieked the housekeeper. "No doubt everything will have been sold by morning! What your cousin Neville will say when he arrives, I don't know."

"Mrs Crispe, please pay the cabby," said Rachel, walking past the housekeeper and going to her room.

Rachel Coleville-Grey owned a large estate and lived at Kiddsmere Hall in Suffolk, a very imposing house set in many acres of parkland. The arable land was let to individual farmers who supplied the Hall with various commodities, such as beef, poultry and fresh milk.

Rachel's father, Augustus Coleville-Grey, had been tragically killed in a shooting accident, and her mother, never fully recovering from the shock, died, leaving eight-year-old Rachel to be cared for by her most trusted servant, Kate Ellis.

Rachel's grandfather, Sir Augustus Coleville-Grey, having died before the tragedy of his son, had become responsible for, and befriended, a distant relative's son, namely Neville Coleville-Grey, whom Rachel referred to as her 'cousin'.

Neville was twenty years her senior. The small fortune, left to him by Sir Augustus, had been quickly squandered. After the death of Rachel's mother, Neville had taken upon himself the running of the estate to his own advantage, and to Rachel's detriment. Now, sitting in her room, thinking over the happenings of the day, nineteen-year-old Rachel felt quite sick. After the accident, she had been too upset to notice who it was who had come to their rescue. No doubt, if she had known they were gypsies, she would have refused their help. On the other hand, with poor Jacob in such pain on the roadside, she had no choice.

Kate entered the room, bringing a tray with tea.

"Honestly, Kate," Rachel blurted out, "I didn't know they were Gypsies until we reached the hospital."

"Both looked very clean and nice gentlemen. Did you notice one had an artificial leg?"

"No. I felt too ill," Rachel answered despondently. "Thank goodness I'm free from commitment. I shall retire early this evening."

The following day, Neville arrived at the villa, accompanied by his friend, Sir Chester Peggleton. Sir Chester, commonly known as 'Old Chessey', owned a stately home on the outskirts of the town.

Upon hearing the news of Rachel's mishap, and that her rescuers were indeed travellers, he immediately ordered his coachman and two of his heftiest staff to collect the carriage and belongings, 'if they were still at the place of the accident', had been his comments, and Kate was to go with them.

Tucked neatly within the shelter of the glade on the roadside stood the carriage. Kate gave a sigh of relief.

Recognising the woman, the two young men brought forward the two horses.

"Fine morning," Matthew greeted the coachman. "Your horses did themselves no harm, as far as we can see. 'Fraid a shaft is broken,' he said, watching the man looking the carriage over, while the others took charge of the horses.

It was Kate who spoke to Blue.

"We are so grateful to you, young man."

Then, turning to Matthew, "You also, Matthew. That is your name, isn't it?"

Lifting his hat, he replied, "Yes, Ma'am. How is the young lady this morning? No repercussions I hope?"

Disappointment showed on his face because she wasn't with them.

"Miss Rachel is well, thank you," answered Kate as she watched the luggage being loaded. "She will be very pleased you have taken good care of our belongings."

More than pleased, Kate thought, remembering Neville's outburst after Sir Chester had taken his leave.

"Thank you for your expert help for Jacob. He is as comfortable as can be expected. Several broken ribs," said Kate, shaking the two young men by the hand.

After fixing the carriage in a position to enable it to be towed away, the party left.

"Old Chessey will have the surprise of his life when we get back with this lot," one man said to the other. "Should have heard him and that Neville carrying on."

One of them then informed Kate, "That lot back there are circus folk, not Gypsies."

"No matter which, they are honest," Kate answered him firmly.

Later that same morning Blue decided it was time to go in search of the group of travellers assembled on the outskirts of the town.

They found a colourful fairground alive with show people, so went in search of the Master of the group.

He was busy tending his elephants. A large grey elephant was being very temperamental. For some time the two clowns watched the short, rotund man gently persuade the huge elephant to accept his grooming.

Seeing the man eyeing their painted wagon, they introduced themselves.

The Boss asked with suspicion, "I've heard tell, the pair of you've been in these parts for some time. What've you been up to?"

"We've come from abroad. Our dog's been in quarantine," explained Blue. "Oh. Yes … Well, what do you want from me?"

"Our last boss said to look up a cousin of his should we come to England."

Blue continued his story, mentioning the name Leonardo Crutch.

This information made the Circus Boss exclaim, "Well, I'll be blowed! You must have been with Old Barney Crutch!"

"You know Barney?" Blue asked.

"Of course I do. It's a long time since he left this country," he said, rubbing his chin, trying to remember. "Don't know the whereabouts of Leonardo."

The little man then asked, "Did Barney mention my name? Abdul!"

"No. Only Leonardo."

The fact they had worked with Barney Crutch worked wonders with Abdul, so he suggested they stayed and worked for him, if they were looking for work. He could use some extra hands. This place was good, busy, quite close to the Spa, some of the well-to-do strolled this way.

"They've plenty of cash," Abdul told them, grinning like a miser, pawing one hand over the other.

Thanking him, they agreed to stay as jobbers, after which they would find their way to the eastern side of the country, where Leonardo was last known to have worked.

Abdul issued the orders and he expected them to be obeyed. His elephants were his pride and joy and he soon had the two clowns working to a strict routine.

One morning, a day or so after Blue and Matt joined Abdul's set-up, Abdul was approached by an elderly, well-dressed gentleman. This man had arrived at the showground in an immaculate carriage. When Abdul saw him, his first thought was whether any of his gang had been up to mischief, because his visitor was none other than Sir Chester Peggleton, a local landowner.

Sir Chester asked Abdul if he had two men with a wagon entitled 'Blue the Kangaroo' in his entourage.

Abdul said he had and began cursing under his breath. He had taken a liking and trusted those two young men on sight. Now what?

"Good. Good. Where are they?" Sir Chester asked. "I would like to meet them."

Abdul, with a face like a thunder cloud, accompanied him to where Blue and Matthew were working and stood close by to hear what was said.

"So, you are the two young men who helped rescue my future bride, Miss Rachel Coleville-Grey. I am Sir Chester Peggleton. You have earned yourselves a just reward for your honesty and trustworthiness," he said, holding out several gold coins in the palm of his hand.

Abdul's face brightened, and a smile beamed across it as he heard Blue thank Sir Chester, take the coins and ask after the coach-driver's health.

Matthew stood by, bewildered and horrified, staring at the portly figure of an old man. Matthew, his voice full of disbelief, disgust even, said to Blue after Abdul and Sir Chester had walked away, "How could that lovely young girl want to marry an old person like him?"

"There are various reasons, money is one."

"No! She wouldn't marry for money!" Matthew cried out. A vivid picture of the beautiful young girl whom he had held in his arms the other day, came before his eyes. The softness of her velvet cloak and her delicate perfume. The first time he had held a young woman in his arms. He had wanted to hold and protect her forever. The very thought of that old man with that lovely young maiden made him feel sick.

"Oh! No! She couldn't!" he uttered aloud, walking away, wanting to be alone. Blue didn't see Matthew again for the rest of that day. When he did return it was late evening, almost dark. Blue made no comment, he could see he was still upset.

Working with Abdul was a pleasure for Blue, but, over this past week or so, taking note of Matthew's attitude and woebegone face, he thought they had better move on, and get away from this area.

Abdul was sad they were leaving so soon and said, as Blue thanked him for his hospitality, "If ever you get into a muddle, get in touch with me. I'll be in the East of England in the spring."

With little to say when Blue told him they would be leaving Abdul earlier than anticipated, Matthew started to pack his things in a most lethargic manner. A few days later, in bright sunshine, they began their journey towards the East Coast.

Chapter 16

On the course of their travels, approaching any large town, the two lads would dress themselves in clown attire, paint their faces, then prance and juggle their way along the streets, with Prince following at heel and Matthew playing his cheerful music.

People stopped to look, some joining them, shopping baskets on arms, dancing over cobble stones, their children following behind hopping and skipping, almost like the Pied Piper, Blue thought.

Some children were barefoot, others wore shabby, well-worn boots, some children looking very impoverished, but after seeing the clowns and the little dog, nearly all had smiling faces.

On one such occasion, Blue walked on stilts, his long, billowing trousers flapping in the warm breeze. Upon reaching the town market place, Matthew halted the wagon.

"We may not be welcome, Blue," he shouted, seeing a group of white clad Morris Men dancing in the square.

With a flourish, the music of both fiddler and concertina players ceased. One of them shouted, "'tis warm work dancing, come and join us. We're having a break."

The dancers passed around an earthenware jug, filled their tankards with a golden liquid and began drinking.

Blue, tall on his stilts, was able to reach over the heads of people to pick a plum, orange, apple and lemon from the fruiterer's well-displayed stall and with them began to juggle, at the same time laughing and making funny facial expressions.

"How dare you?" shouted the alarmed fruiterer. "Come on, give them back or pay me!" he continued, raising his fist, his weather-beaten face turning pink to purple.

Blue tossed a coin towards the angry stallholder, telling him to keep the change, and strode away as the man delved into a box of plums in order to find the coin.

Dropping the fruit at the feet of a child, Blue took the Morris Dancers' wooden sticks, throwing and catching until six sticks were circling through the air. He dropped one, Prince retrieved it, took it to Matthew, who tossed it to Blue. He did this a couple more times and Prince carried out the same procedure.

Giving back the sticks, he asked the men for their hats. Willingly they threw them to him, enjoying the entertainment as much as the crowd. The many silver bells on the hats jingled as they were tossed high and caught. Music from Matthew's accordion encouraged the Morris Men to dance again. A large crowd had gathered in the tiny square, overflowing onto the road, stopping all the horse-drawn vehicles, with some drivers shouting and grumbling, while others were enjoying it, with a grandstand view. Completing the show as usual, Prince pulled the cord of Blue's pants, to hoots and shouts of laughter.

Jumping from his stilts, Blue shook hands with the fruiterer and dancers.

Sitting with Matthew that evening, Blue confided, "I adore giving impromptu performances in these towns and villages, watching dull faces brighten with smiles. I am doing exactly as I dreamed. My ambitions are being fulfilled."

Matthew made no comment. His heart was heavy. The joy of wandering into a village church, in search of an organ to play, had gone. Whenever he played Madame Clare's lullaby, the words and Rachel Coleville-Grey's beautiful face haunted him. He said nothing of this to Blue and his friend was also unaware, that, on the day Sir Chester Peggleton came to the fairground, the urge for him to see Rachel was so great that he had gone to the large villa in Memorial Square, where Rachel resided.

Darkness was falling as a carriage arrived at the front door of the villa. Light shone as the door of the villa opened and a black-suited servant emerged to open the carriage door.

Hurrying over the cobbled street he was quite close to Rachel as she was about to place her foot on the carriage step.

Wearing a short, white fur cape over her long pink, sequin-spangled gown, she looked entrancing. He had spoken to her and as she turned her head to look at him, two large diamond clips sparkled in her blonde curls. She recognised him immediately, and giving a sharp exclamation had hurried into the carriage.

He well remembered the servant shouting at him as he reached up to the coachman, asking if would give this letter to his passenger, and throwing a coin on his seat for his trouble.

Failing to get another glimpse of Rachel, he had returned, in despair, to their wagon.

Late summer saw the two travellers in East Anglia. Both had acquired a weathered look and a penchant for silk, floral waistcoats, brightly coloured neckerchiefs and bowler hats.

Their first ever encounter with opposition for overnight resting came on the outskirts of a small village. When parking the wagon on a piece of roadside grassland adjoining a wood, a burly man carrying a gun shouted at them.

"No place here for Gypsies. You'd best be gone 'afore morning and mind that dog. If I catch either of you in the wood, you'll be 'afore the beak' in no time."

Prince growled with ferocity, the first time he'd ever taken sides.

"If you let that animal come after me, I'll shoot it!" he said as he turned and hurried away. Neither had said a word. Both were speechless, having met no one like him on all their travels. They wondered who he was, as he disappeared into the wood.

In fact, they hadn't understood the dialect of this man. Hoping all the village people were not the same, they set off to find out.

A Smithy and Butcher's shop were first to be seen, then a large farmhouse and milk parlour. In the centre of the village were pink washed, wattle and daub houses. The tiny windows were bedecked with net curtains. The rooftops held thick, reed thatch.

On the whole, it gave one the appearance of a sleepy place.

Tall stems with seed pods and the last bright flowers of summer adorning their tips, leaned at all angles against the cottages and walls.

A rough road between an ivy-clad flint wall and a plantation of hardwood trees led to a village shop, part of which was a dwelling. An overhead bell rang loudly, by the opening of the shop door. The shopkeeper, drying her hands on a cloth, came quickly from another room.

Blue asked for bread. She replied in a very friendly and pleasant manner that they would find bread in the next village at the bakehouse.

Because of her friendliness, they enquired the name of the man who carried a shotgun and why did he carry it?

She answered, "I expect it was the gamekeeper for the Big House. He doesn't like folk trespassing. If you are parked on the stretch of green beside the road, it is Common Land and you are allowed to rest a night or two."

Making a few purchases they thanked the lady, set the door-bell ringing again and made their way through the graveyard nearby and stepped inside an old thatched Church. A man was busy shovelling fuel into a large furnace. Nearby, a stout wooden ladder rested beside an inner tower wall, leading to a trapdoor high in the ceiling of the tower.

The man stopped his work, wiped the perspiration from his brow and, ignoring the visitors, walked up the aisle and placed a hand over a floor grating. Seemingly satisfied, he returned to the furnace, checked a flue on the metal chimney and turned away, not having uttered a word to his onlookers.

This day being a Saturday, Matthew asked him if a service was taking place the next day. The man nodded.

"What time?" asked Matthew, not to be put off by the lack

of response.

"Eight, half-past ten and three o'clock. Bells'll ring," the Stoker informed them, eyeing the two up and down, but passing no comment.

Thanking him, Matthew walked towards the enormous organ, its gold and blue pipes almost reaching the rafters. Situated in front of an intricate screen and opposite the three-tiered pulpit, stood a large square box-pew. Inside this pew were carved wooden seats and red felt hassocks.

Slabs of engraved marble, attached to the walls, gave names of deceased dignitaries. Blue, wandering around reading these, came across one dedicated to a Rev Coleville-Grey, one time Rector of a nearby village. The name set Blue thinking ... it couldn't possibly be a relative of Rachel, surely fate hadn't led them ... He looked at Matthew still admiring the organ, and with a shrug decided not to mention this to his friend. Remembering Prince tied to the rail outside, he suggested they both left.

Sunday morning, walking along the gravel path to the church, hearing a bell tolling for the mid-morning service, Blue could see in the distance a stretch of glistening water and cattle grazing. Another church stood out against the clear blue sky, all looking pleasantly inviting to explore.

Once inside the Church they found many people, old and young, possibly dressed in their Sunday Best, as they did back home.

Heads turned as the colourfully dressed travellers found seats for themselves at the back of the Church.

A young man carefully pumped the organ bellows and the organist, a woman, began to play. The furnace-man, now neatly dressed in a well-worn black suit, walked to the door to greet a number of people entering. Accompanying them, he opened the door of the box-pew to allow them to enter.

Blue thought for one moment, by Matt's white face, that

his friend was about to faint, for who should be making herself comfortable in that high-box pew but Rachel Coleville-Grey.

Blue just remembered to stand as the Clergyman came into view, but little else, save nudging Matthew every so often, to stand or sit, and drop a coin into the collection box. Matthew's attention centred solely on Rachel Coleville-Grey.

The service over, everyone standing, the honoured party from the box-pew, preceded by the Vicar, walked down the aisle. Blue placed a restraining hand on Matthew's arm, much to his annoyance, but he waited until the local people had left.

At the Church door, shaking hands, the Rector said to them, "I'm pleased to see you. Both new here, I understand. Visitors to our lovely village. Caravan dwellers, I am told." He noted their clean and tidy, although gaudy, appearance.

Matthew, still looking vacant, said very little, with Blue making most of the conversation and answering the Rector's questions.

"Before we move on, my friend, here, may he come and play the Church organ?"

"Why, yes, by all means," the Rector replied, astonishment flitting across his face. "The Church is always open. You are most welcome. Harvest Festival is approaching. We decorate for the festival, sing thanksgiving hymns, but there, I don't suppose you know …"

The Rector's voice ceased for a moment.

Matthew, who by now had pulled himself together, smiled and said, "I'm sure I could learn."

"Hmm!" The Rector cleared his throat, looking doubtful, "Yes … Well …"

People waiting to leave the Church began to mutter, getting impatient, especially the stoker, so the two travellers moved quickly away, passing little groups of folk, to whom Blue raised his hat, wishing them a 'good-day' but received no acknowledgement.

He thought of the Church meeting in Adelaide and the Green family and felt a little homesick as they made their way back to their wagon.

"No doubt our friend is waiting for us, Matt," he said as they approached the greensward. Blue's sharp eyes had seen a movement and glint of steel in the copse.

Ignoring him, they tethered Silver, and began cooking. The delicious aroma of fresh, sizzling pork and onions over the fire was too much for the Gamekeeper.

Prince gave a growl. The Gamekeeper came towards them, empty handed. Prince, who was tied to the wagon, growled even louder. Dressed exactly as the day previous, almost like a uniform of tweed jacket and plus-fours, long woollen socks and boots, the Gamekeeper stopped by the fire and looked into the pan.

Blue, commanding Prince to stop his noise, asked the man if he would care to join them.

"Don't mind if I do, smells jolly good."

Accepting the invitation, he removed his soft cap, tossed it to the ground and sat on it, accepting a large chunk of bread, topped with pork and onions.

"Tea?" inquired Matthew, watching the man closely, comparing his facial features to those of a ferret.

"Aye," said the Gamekeeper. "I said to myself yesterday, those two aren't like the rest, didn't swear at me or want to fight like others who stop here."

Spoken in the same dialect. Most difficult for the travellers to understand.

Taking from his pocket a large shut-knife, he opened it and wiped the blade on his coat sleeve, sliced his food and commenced eating. Grease from the pork ran down his chin. This he wiped with the back of his hand, enjoying every mouthful. Eagerly, he accepted another large wedge, yet always scanning the horizon for any sign of movement.

"Tell us a little about the village, if you will. The Church is very old. Is there a Manor House?" asked Matthew calmly, although his heartbeat was erratic.

They had to wait for some minutes, as another large portion of food was pushed into the fellow's mouth, followed by gulps of tea.

Again in a broad dialect, he spoke.

"Yes … Manor House is in the Park, up past the rookery. You get to it through the big iron gates, off the road to the Church."

He stood up quickly, eager to be gone, speaking with great haste.

"I'll not worry you two gentlemen for a few days, but don't hang about too long, else I'll get a ticking off from the Governor, or the sack. Nasty one him. Don't do to cross him. Look like his carriage coming."

Pulling his cap into shape, with no word of thanks, he hurried back into the wood, out of sight. A minute or so later, with great speed, a coach and four containing one occupant rattled by on the rutted, stony road.

Seeing his friend propped against a wheel of the wagon, completely relaxed, enjoying the late afternoon sunshine, Matthew pushed a long piece of wood further into the fire.

Brushing his clothes, he said to his mate, "Think I'll take a walk before sundown."

Blue gave a half-hearted grunt, but saw, from the corner of his eye, Matthew limp away in the direction of the village.

Matthew, following a cart-track, avoided the centre of the village, taking what he thought to be a shortcut to the park. It was. Cattle grazed contentedly around clumps of giant oak and beech trees, and, in the distance he saw a large lake.

Half-hidden from view, on the far side of the mere, stood a church and farmhouse. Sauntering along, he came upon a stone-built bridge with white side-railings. This looked strong and wide enough for a vehicle to pass over.

Leaning on the railings he watched mallard and small black water hens scurry towards the tall green and brown bullrushes. Small fish, in shoals, flipped about, churning the silt below, while dragonfly darted hither and thither near the surface of the water. Continuing his journey he found a well-maintained shingle road leading to a large house. Across the road, at the entrance to the house, were two very large, black wrought-iron gates.

A circular flowerbed in front of the house looked colourful; this was surrounded by gravel and had space enough for a horse and carriage to manoeuvre.

Two stone columns, one on either side of the heavy oak door, supported a semi-circular porch. Large windows, evenly spaced between grey stonework on ground and upper floors, were topped by a grey slate roof.

More buildings stretched on either side and beyond.

This place is very old. Nothing like it back home, he thought.

He then concealed himself on a low branch in a clump of trees by the roadside, where he had a perfect view of the front of the house.

Sitting there until dusk, and seeing no movement, he was on the point of leaving, when he heard the rattle of carriage wheels and angry shouts from someone urging horses forward.

The carriage passed close to him, as two black-suited servants ran to open the gates. As it passed he saw two men on the driving seat. The one with the reins, driving like a madman, was the gentleman who had accompanied Rachel Coleville-Grey to church; the other, hanging on to the seat for dear life, was Jacob!

Did Sir Chester Peggleton own this large establishment, he wondered. Rachel living in his house! Oh! No! He couldn't bear the thought of it.

With a heavy heart, he began his return journey. Pausing on the bridge, he asked himself, what beautiful young woman would look at a person who had only one leg? Not one accustomed to handsome escorts and society gatherings!

Leaning against the railings, his flute pressed against his ribs. Taking it from his pocket, he began to play Madame Clare's lullaby. Music echoed across the water, firstly as a sad lament, remembering Rachel's beautiful face as he held her in his arms. What if he had to return home leaving the love of his life in England! He felt sure he would die! His heart broken!

Then his thoughts turned to Hans and Mitzy, together, sharing their love and happiness on the other side of the world.

Vowing not to give up hope, gradually his poignant lament changed tempo to the lilt of the lullaby. Somehow, he would meet Rachel Coleville-Grey.

The great yellow ball of a full moon rose over the trees, silhouetting the distant church tower and glistened on the water. He ceased playing and offered up a prayer.

Blue asked no questions when he returned, just handed him a mug of steaming tea saying, "Earlier this evening a maniac carriage driver drove by, no respect for his animals. A man sitting beside him looked like Jacob!"

Matthew, sipping his hot tea, had his mind on other things. Casually he asked, "Do you think the gamekeeper will make us move?"

Blue, giving Prince a piece of cold meat and hard biscuit for his supper, replied, "Doesn't matter if he does. Over the other side of the village, there's a patch equally as good. I've had a nosy around."

Early next morning, Blue awakened to the sound of men's voices and the rumbling of farm wagons. Sliding from his bed, he quickly dressed, opened the door and was greeted by a clear, blue sky and hedgerows wrapped in a veil of mist. Cobwebs glistened like jewels in the early morning sunlight, and more men walked past, each carrying a scythe.

Blue held his hand up in greeting. Collecting Prince, he decided to follow and watch them working, everything a new experience.

"Mind if I watch?" Blue asked, standing near the group of men.

A grunt from one, and a grin or two from the others seemed promising.

In a field of growing corn, one man began to scythe a width, followed by another and so on, stopping at regular intervals to sharpen the scythe blade. The first man setting a steady pace, perfect rhythm in every movement. On and on, up the field, each man leaving a neat row, later, to be gathered, tied and stoked, possibly by women from the village, so Blue was told by a more amicable man in the group.

Blue sat on the bank watching, waiting for their return.

Beside him were well-worn coats and beneath them, to keep cool, bottles of cold tea, a corked, earthenware bottle, similar to that which the Morris Men were using. Perhaps this one contained home-brewed beer. Also a number of white linen bags of food. After scything three times around the small field, the sweating workmen stopped for food, vitals, they told him, and eagerly seeking the liquid, drinking it direct from the bottles. Large chunks of bread, spread with dripping or lard, were taken from the bags and cut using various sized shut-knives. After some brown skinned onions were passed around, they began talking in the same dialect as the gamekeeper, discussing a forthcoming harvest supper or hawkey as if it was a most special event, practically ignoring their bystander.

One man suddenly surprised Blue by asking him, "What do you do for a living? – nothing?"

"I make a fool of myself – I'm a clown," Blue answered.

"You're no fool if you do nothing," another man said. The others laughed.

"That's right, I make folks laugh," Blue countered, grinning.

"I 'spect that dog pick up a dinner or two?" the first man stated as a matter of fact, looking at Prince.

"Oh, no. He's also a clown."

"Pull t'other one, it's got bells on," scoffed another member of the group, busy eating his food.

Blue noticed this man's trousers were held at the waist with a piece of twine. Given the command, the dog trotted to the man, jumped up and pulled at the hanging twine. Of course, the knot was too tight to release the cord and trousers.

"Call it off! Call it off!" the man shouted, taking off his bowler hat with one hand, holding his trousers and food with the other, thwacking Prince with the hat to let go the twine. Seizing the hat, the dog made off, knowing his routine to perfection.

Blue gave chase for a moment or so, then returned to sit on the bank.

The men doubled up with laughter, then looked with amazement as the dog trotted back and laid the hat at Blue's feet and sat down, as if nothing untoward had happened. Making sure the hat wasn't damaged, Blue gave it back to the owner as a man called out, "Find out what else he can do, Olly," setting the men off in a peel of laughter again.

Bidding them a cheery "Good-day," Blue left them, realising he was hungry, so returned to the wagon.

That same afternoon, opening the studded, oak porch door, leading into the village church, the sound of female voices made Blue and Matthew hesitant about entering.

"Do you think folks have started to decorate?" whispered Matthew.

Peering round the inner door, Blue said quietly "No. Two women are sitting together, one is weeping. Shall we return later?"

Before he could close the door, Prince gave a loud bark, perturbed at being left alone.

Hearing the sound, one woman quickly arose from her seat and looked around, the other hastily dabbing her face.

Walking up the aisle towards the women, they assured them they had only called to play the church organ.

Matthew's face paled. Blue, looking closely at them, said, "Haven't we met somewhere before?"

Appearing incredibly surprised, Blue held out his hand.

"You are the two ladies we rescued from the carriage. Are you in some kind of trouble?" he asked, very concerned, looking from one to the other.

"Not really in trouble," Kate said, taking hold of Blue's hand. "Yes, we are those same ladies, I do remember you. I'm Kate."

Rachel had regained her composure and had gathered together her scarf and gloves, saying to her companion, "We must be going before we are missed."

Matthew, who could contain himself no longer, asked, "Miss, you haven't married Sir Chester Peggleton, have you?"

At the mention of that man's name, a look of horror crossed her face as she shook her head. What could this man know of Sir Chester Peggleton? The very thought of that fat, pompous man nauseated her.

Relief flooded Matthew's face.

"If you are in trouble, please may we help?" he pleaded. "We are genuine and honest. True as we stand in God's house."

She looked at him, aghast. In no way would she contemplate divulging her personal life to a total stranger.

"Stay and hear Matthew play the organ. Be our guests, just for a while, his music will perhaps cheer you," Blue suggested, feeling slightly embarrassed by Matthew's questions.

Matthew reluctantly moved away from Rachel's side. Seating himself at the organ, while Blue pumped the bellows, he began to play.

Naturally, his first choice was the lullaby. Rachel sat, puzzled. Where had she heard this beautiful melody before?

Memory quickly flooded back to the other evening, and her cheeks paled, as she remembered the scene with her cousin, Neville.

He had arrived home in a diabolical mood and confronted

her with the fact she was penniless and commanded her to accept Sir Chester Peggleton's offer of marriage or the estate would have to be sold in order to pay debts.

When asked, "Whose debts?" he had replied, "Your late father's, of course!"

Near to tears, she shook with apprehension, as this was the first time she had summoned enough courage to accuse him the debts were his and his alone, and most certainly not her dear father's. And, debts or no debts, she would not marry Sir Chester. Thinking her cousin about to strike her, she quickly moved away from him. Then something made him change his mind. The vicious hate left his face, only to be replaced by an evil grin while issuing an ultimatum: "You marry him or else! Darling cousin."

Grabbing her, he gripped her arms, causing her to cry out in pain. Thankfully, Kate came into the room. Quickly releasing her, muttering at Kate, he left. Rubbing her bruised arms, Kate soothed and calmed her, then helped her upstairs to her sitting room overlooking the parkland and long-water.

The lullaby the young man was now playing was the same as that which had drifted through her open window, as she had sat wishing her dear Mama and Papa were still alive.

No one had heard the Chancel door of the Church open, or the Rector make his entrance, until he applauded as Matthew finished playing.

"Beautiful, most beautiful. How good it is you young people know each other. Miss Rachel, tell me the name of your talented friend."

She hesitated, then said, "Matthew, I think, Reverend Peake."

"Well then Matthew, these are the hymns I have chosen for our Harvest Service. Will you play them for me now?" asked the Rector, handing Matthew the large hymnal. Giving him no chance to refuse, he sat himself beside the two ladies on the hard pew seat.

Listening, eyes closed, mouth occasionally moving, the Rector seemed oblivious of his surroundings.

"Something the matter, my dear Rachel?" he asked, during a lull in the playing.

"Kate and I must go home," she merely answered.

"Oh, my dear, must you? I thought, perhaps, you and your friends might give us the honour of your company over tea. I am sure my wife would be delighted. We have so little young company since our family left. Spare us a little of your precious time, my dear," he said, persuasive enough for Rachel to agree.

After Matthew had finished, Reverend Francis Peake shook his hand, delighted by his rendition of the hymns, and, after asking their names, invited them to join him and the ladies to take tea at the rectory.

Warmth greeted them outside the church. They accompanied the Rector and the ladies through a small iron gate into a rambling garden, following a well-worn path across the lawn towards the house. The lawn hadn't been cut for some time, letting the late summer wild flowers bloom at will.

A creeper, beginning to show autumnal tints, practically covered the front of the white brick, three-storeyed rectory, its younger shoots trespassing on to some of the many large sash windows and towards the grey, slate roof.

Ascending the three well-worn stone steps and into the house, the Reverend called his wife to meet his guests.

Bustling into the large hall, she greeted Rachel and Kate warmly, happy to see them. Smiling at the two brightly clad young gentlemen and not quite knowing what to say, she was helped by Blue, who introduced Matthew and himself.

Matthew, looking at the wife of the Rector, immediately thought of his mother, face red from cooking, cleanest of clean white apron flowing to the floor, wisps of hair that could not be persuaded to stay in the small knot at the back of her head, straying to each side of her face.

"I have been jam-making," she told them. "So many black-berries and lots of apples."

Looking pleased, she added, "I've had a lovely time!"

To her husband she said, "Take them to the drawing room, Francis, dear, while I get Peggy to make some tea."

The drawing room was large. A long casement window overlooked a sunken front lawn and rose garden. The room held an assortment of furniture from various periods of time, well-worn, but comfortable. Rugs, made from oddments of cloth, were scattered over the well-polished wooden floor and, judging by the burn marks, each rug in turn had been placed in front of the big, open fireplace.

Showing the ladies to the sofa, the Rector bade the others find a seat, seating himself in a leather chair, which had definitely seen better days.

"Tell me, young man," the Rector, always straight and to the point, said, "How did you lose your leg?"

Briefly Matthew told him of the calamity with the wagon, but not where it happened.

"I must say, you get about very well. Now Rachel, my dear, you have not exercised my horse Blossom of late. She is getting fat and lazy."

The Rector, looking towards Blue, asked, "I don't suppose you ride?"

"Yes, Sir, we both can. Matthew rides much better than I. He was literally born in the saddle," Blue replied.

"You amaze me!"

Assuming the young people knew each other, the Rector said, "No wonder you have Rachel for a friend, eh, my dear? You also live in the saddle, as the saying goes."

A knock at the door interrupted his conversation. Peggy, the maid, entered, bearing a tray of tea and cakes, with Mrs Peake following and helping the maid arrange the tea things on the table.

Kate noticed both young fellows stand and offer their seat to the now very tidy Rector's wife, but she proceeded to pour the tea into elegant china cups and enlisted Matthew's help to pass around the tea.

Delighted at having young people in her home again, she asked their names, muddling them from time to time, but had everyone laughing and talking and making plans for the Harvest Supper.

Still with the Supper in mind, Mrs Peake appealed to Rachel to attend, assuring her the village people would be very pleased to see her. Then she asked of Blue, "Have you ever been to a Harvest Supper?"

"Very similar, Ma'am. Sheep shearing over, we celebrated, Matthew especially, he's the musician. Sure does add life to any party."

"Will you both be around for the Supper?" she asked.

"No, Ma'am. I think not. We have to find another place to stay. A gamekeeper has told us to move on."

Before Blue could say more, Francis Peake said excitedly, "We've plenty of room in the orchard for your caravan, move in here! Please come."

For a moment after making his request, the Rector was silent. He had prayed for guidance, knowing Rachel's problems with Neville. Was the arrival of these two young men Heaven-sent?

"Well ... if no one objects ..." Blue half-questioned. "Would be wonderful for a time, eh, Matthew?"

Judging from the look on his face, there was no need for him to answer.

Gradually, daylight began to fade.

"I'm sorry to break up your tea party, Mrs Peake, but we must get home before dark. Thank you for the tea. I will come to ride Blossom soon, I promise," Rachel said, rising to leave.

"May we give you both a lift home? Our horse and wagon are in the plantation. You are most welcome."

Rachel hesitated at Blue's invitation.

Kate, taking the matter into her own hands, accepted for them both, mentioning the fact she did not like walking along the park road at dusk.

"Very sensible Kate, then you can pull in here this evening," the Rector concluded, looking very happy, shaking each one by the hand.

Untying Prince from the iron boot-scraper beside the rectory steps, Blue said aloud, "Meet the Prince of Dogs," whereupon Prince sat, and lifted his paw for someone to shake.

Rachel could not resist the dog's offer. She stooped, took the paw and acknowledged his greeting. Prince licked her hand. She laughed. Looking at Matthew, she said, "He likes me!"

Walking the short distance to the wagon, Matthew asked after Rachel's parents and was told they were both dead: her father dying tragically, shooting game.

"I was eight years old when my Mama died. Kate has taken care of me, since my birth, haven't you, my dear Kate? I have a cousin, Neville, who helps run the estate."

Even the mention of his name made her wince. She said no more.

"Do you remember this wagon, Ma'am?" Blue asked, helping them aboard.

"Kate told me after Jacob was settled in hospital, a Kangaroo Clown had rescued us!" Rachel told them, accepting a rug from Matthew to place over their knees.

The park gatekeeper was opening the heavy iron gates as the wagon approached, wondering, no doubt, what the Mistress of the Hall was doing aboard such a vehicle. Jacob, looking very perplexed, was waiting for them on the bridge, unable to believe his eyes as Miss Rachel and Kate sat side-by-side on the wagon seat.

Invited aboard, Kate began telling him the afternoon's happenings.

Reaching the gates of the Hall, Jacob suggested they did not take the wagon any further, giving the explanation: "Master Neville is behaving like a mad bull. Sir Chester Peggleton called this afternoon."

They heard Rachel gasp as Jacob continued, "Kate, my dear, you had best stay upstairs with Miss Rachel and I will get Cook to send you supper."

Helping Rachel alight, Matthew managed to say to her, "Remember where we are should you need help. God bless," he added, retaining her hand for as long as possible.

Their site was ideal in the rectory orchard. Silver shared the paddock with Blossom, enjoying his freedom as the two horses galloped together.

Showing a great interest in the wagon, they invited Francis Peake inside. The Rector was amazed and complimented them on its cleanliness, accepting the cup of tea Blue offered. An hour passed on this bright, autumnal morning, as Mrs Peake, seeking the whereabouts of her husband, found all three sitting, enjoying the warmth of the open fire.

"My dear wife, I had forgotten how peaceful it is in our garden."

Taking note of his face, she could tell he was very happy.

"I have a large blackberry and apple jam pudding simmering on the stove. Should you both care to join us, lunch will be served at one o'clock," she informed them as she was preparing to leave.

Accepting her generous offer, they promised to be on time.

The enormous steaming pudding was brought to the dining room on a large oval dish and placed on a side-table, by Peggy, who then began to serve.

Blue or Matthew had not seen such a large pudding since they were at the Homestead. Standing on the polished table were two large jugs, one containing cornflour sauce, the other cream. The pudding was set before them. They waited. The

Rector, after clearing his throat, said Grace.

During the meal, the Peakes spoke of their own family; two sons, both Missionaries, one in New Zealand the other, South Africa, and how much they were missed.

The pudding and sauce were delicious. Peggy returned, bringing cheese and salad, telling the Rector someone wished to speak with him.

Francis left. Conversation at the dinner table continued, with talk of the Church and village affairs. Mrs Peake answered the boys' numerous questions.

Matthew had seen another set of iron gates inside the park and asked what lay behind.

Happily, Marjorie Peake enlightened him by saying, "The Gardener's Cottage, a well-established, walled garden, with peach houses, cherry and plum trees, all forming a part of Rachel's estate."

Mrs Peake, a most knowledgeable person on village affairs, past and present, could have entertained her avid listeners for much longer, but suddenly realised the time, telling them it was time for her to leave to make visits to sick parishioners.

The two, not wishing to delay their hostess, thanked her for the most delicious meal and returned to their new location.

Talking together on the news gleaned from the Rector's wife, they realised many people in the village were very poor, and some of their dwellings were very damp. Many folk didn't seem very happy with the way the estate was run.

Chapter 17

Very early the next morning, a loud rat-a-tat on the side of the wagon, and a bark from Prince, brought Blue quickly from his bed. Pulling on his silk dressing-gown, he opened the door and exclaimed loudly enough for Matthew to hear, "Well, 'pon my soul, Miss Rachel on her horse! Good-day!"

"Who's coming riding with me? I want to find out if you really can ride!" she said, her horse moving around eagerly, raring to go.

Dressed immaculately in riding habit and black silk top hat, she looked a perfect picture. Blue yawned.

"Excuse me!" he apologised. "If you can wait a moment, it will have to be Matthew who joins you. I don't get about too early," he said, telling a slight untruth. Walking towards the grey ashes of the fire, he gave it a poke and asked her, "Would you like some tea?"

Accepting her refusal, he said, "Tell me where the Reverend keeps Blossom's tack, I'll fetch it for Matthew."

Neatly she dismounted, looped the reins around a post and accompanied Blue to the saddle room.

Blossom trotted over to the gate and nuzzled against Rachel, while Blue placed the saddle on the mare's back, with the pretext of fixing the straps incorrectly.

"Oh, let me do it," she intervened, expertly tightening the girth.

Matthew, by now tidily dressed and smiling, touched his forelock, wished her a "Good morning," and clipped his piece of metal to the stirrup.

"A drink before you leave, Matt?"

Seeing his shake of head, Blue said, "I'll have breakfast for the two of you on your return, in say ... an hour?"

This was said with a smile as Matthew helped Rachel on to her horse, then expertly seated himself on Blossom.

Rachel noted the way he clipped his aid into the stirrup, thinking how handsome he looked under his broad-brimmed hat. Also, how well he sat and spoke kindly to the mare as they moved away, out into the village. No doubt tongues would wag, but she did not care.

Riding beside Rachel along a broad bridleway, with men busy in the fields and birds trilling high in the clear, blue sky, not in his wildest dreams had Matthew envisaged such ecstasy.

Following the bridleway past fields of root crops, high hedges, small spinneys and wild flowers, they eventually came upon an Abbey and a group of tiny, windowed cottages. The cottages were coated with lathe and plaster, pink washed and with a deep, thatched roof.

Little conversation passed between them, save for Matt occasionally asking what the workmen were doing in the fields, as everything was so different from his home country.

A mouth-watering aroma of newly baked bread greeted them from a bakehouse. Seeing a young man at the shop-door, Matthew turned to her.

"Freshly baked bread for breakfast. Blue would be delighted. You order, Miss Rachel, I will pay."

She ordered a cottage loaf, baps and Suffolk rusks. The young man packed the items into the Reverend's saddle-bags attached to Blossom's saddle. Matthew paid, giving the helper a token for his trouble. "Good we have these saddlebags. I guess the Rector needs them."

Rachel then spoke of Francis Peake. She told him some people relied on him for many things. His home-made cough linctus was excellent, as were his other remedial medicines.

A small river and the sound of rushing water gave Matthew the cause to stop and look. Hissing water roared through large archways beneath a grey wooden-structured mill.

Matthew was fascinated, and listened to her explanation as to how the mill worked. Looking at her small fob watch, she said, "Time to go."

Nudging her horse she cantered towards a vast apple orchard, over a ditch and, at a gallop, out into the fields. Matthew followed, giving the mare her head, pleased the horse was sure-footed, until they were back on the bridleway once again.

"Satisfied?" he asked with a smile. Seeing her flushed cheeks, he felt his heart turn a somersault. Gee, she was beautiful!

"Yes, quite satisfied. I'm hungry!" she told him.

Matthew laughed aloud and thought, how often have I heard that saying!

Blue saw them return and ride over to the paddock. What a handsome couple they made. He sincerely hoped Matthew's heart would not be broken.

The savoury pancakes were ready and waiting.

"Did you have a good ride, Rachel?" Blue asked while serving the food. Delighted by their purchases, he placed the baps within her reach.

"Yes. Wonderful! Matthew rides well. Somehow one doesn't notice he is … um … has …" she hesitated, lost for words.

"That is sure right! There is nothing Matt cannot do!" Blue warned her.

Laughing, Matthew teased her, telling her they would have to wash the dishes after breakfast, as Blue had done the cooking.

She grimaced, but continued eating and enjoying her food. Eventually, Rachel said she had to leave or Kate would worry.

Although it was on both of their minds, they did not ask what happened to her cousin the previous night.

No doubt, Blue thought, she would tell in due course, if she came again.

When Rachel arrived back at the Hall, she found Kate very agitated.

"You've been out riding much longer than usual. I began to get worried."

"I've been riding with Matthew. Had breakfast with them, in fact, and I am feeling much better."

Kate looked at her, horrified.

"What will folks say? They will think you a wanton hussy!"

"Matthew is very nice and handsome. I will go again tomorrow," Rachel tormented.

"Whatever has come over you, Miss Rachel? Pray Master Neville doesn't hear of this, or the fat will be in the fire."

Kate sat down, her mind in a turmoil. No matter what she said, Rachel would have her way.

Riding with Matthew became a regular habit. No more knocking on the wagon, Matthew waited for her on the edge of Broom Wood. On one such meeting, Rachel reminded him, "I'm helping Mrs Peake at the Harvest Supper. You are going? You will be there?" she asked, seeking assurance as if her life depended upon it.

"Of course! I shall be taking my accordion," he replied, pretending that was his only reason for attending.

Sliding from her horse, she stood in front of him. Temptation was too great. Gathering her into his arms, he kissed her tenderly, murmuring, "My darling Rachel!"

Releasing her, he apologised. "This is madness. I'm only ..." Hesitating, he said, "Part of me is missing." Not daring to look at her, he anticipated this was the end. She knew so little about him.

Rachel, placing her hand in his, said, "Perhaps this is madness, Matthew, but I love you as you are!"

Unable to believe he had heard correctly, looking into her lovely eyes, he slid his arms around her waist, pulling her to him, and kissed her passionately.

"I have loved you from the moment you fell into my arms, my dearest, after your road accident. I have thought of you and longed for you and fate has brought us together, my most beautiful darling."

Later, sitting on the trunk of a fallen tree, Rachel laughed and said, "Matthew dearest, I don't even know your surname!"

Happily, with his arm around her waist, he answered, "It is Dere. Matthew Dere."

Sighing contentedly, she thought, "Matthew Dear," thinking in the terms of an endearment. "My Matthew Dear."

"The spelling, my love, is 'Dere'." Planting another kiss on her cheek.

"We have a great deal to learn together. I am so happy. The Harvest Supper?"

So very reluctantly they parted.

Dressed ready for the Harvest Supper, Rachel and Kate were waiting for Jacob to bring the carriage to the door.

Neville, walking from the library, asked, "You both going out? Where may I ask?"

"No business of yours, dear cousin," Rachel answered sarcastically, "but if you must know, we are helping at the Harvest Supper in the village."

"Oh, a serving wench now, are you?" he retorted.

A servant called, the carriage was waiting, thus avoiding another scene.

Left alone in the large hall, Neville paced the floor. For him, time was fast running out. If only he held the reins of this estate, not that old, penny-pinching Solicitor, Clinton Howard, things would be different.

Within a few months Rachel would be twenty-one, with jurisdiction over her money. Unpaid accounts were accumulating and people were clamouring for payment. Neither Clinton Howard nor Rachel knew of this.

To devise a scheme whereby Rachel married Sir Chester Peggleton was a must, and soon! His own future would then be assured.

Sir Chester, from whom he had borrowed money heavily, promised to relinquish all debts, a condition of this marriage, and into the bargain let him live here. Otherwise, legally, when his cousin married, he would have to leave this house.

Neville pulled the bell rope and waited. A young maid appeared. He demanded the housekeeper came to him immediately in the drawing room.

Noticing he was in one of his ghastly moods, she scurried away.

The housekeeper took quite a time to make an appearance, thus making him even angrier.

Mrs Myra Crispe walked into the drawing room. Wearing a shabby dressing-gown, her long hair pulled untidily into a ribbon, she saw him grimace at her unkempt state.

"It's my evening off, Sir, if you don't mind!" she told him, pulling her gown belt tight.

"Been at the wine again?" he asked. "I have noticed my table wine is being tampered with. Strange how the wine merchant still delivers and the grocer does not. How come?"

This was sarcastically spoken and with a repugnant leer on his face.

Suddenly he remembered he had to be cautious, as this woman knew far too much.

"If that's all you've called me here for ..." her speech was slightly slurred, "I'm going."

"Not yet, Crispy, my dear friend. I have a lady-friend visiting me at the weekend. I want the best bedroom prepared. I have given you ample notice this time. She is to have all the luxuries to which she is accustomed. Inform Cook. You all know Lady Eleanor's wishes well – very well."

He walked towards her menacingly, tossing a coin but not giving it to her, knowing no one had received any wages for almost a month.

Leaving behind a stale odour of alcohol, Myra Crispe

hastily made for the door, muttering to herself, "Heaven forbid! Eleanor Paget indeed, and her husband not dead and gone yet!"

If anyone thought the Harvest Supper would be a mundane event, they were wrong. The old tithe barn had been swept clean and prettied with sweet-smelling herbs and fresh pine sawdust scattered on the floor. Benches and tables were set about the room, two tables covered with clean, white cloths ready to hold the food.

A group of women from the village were in the barn when Rachel and Kate arrived with their food. No one spoke to them.

The Rector's wife came, telling everyone to help place the food from the various baskets and boxes, which had been provided by all and sundry, on to the tables.

The variety of food looked really appetising; cold cooked pickled pork in neat slices, brawn, meat and potato roll, three huge rabbit pies, jellied eels, apple tarts, summer puddings and small loaves of bread.

On another table, cheese, a bowl of hard-boiled eggs, a variety of homemade pickles and raw sliced onions.

Finding the mistress of the Hall quite a friendly person, some of the helpers began to chat to her.

Lanterns glowed, their light reflecting on the bottles of homemade wine, ginger beer and cordial, and, standing to one side, two large casks of ale, partly provided by the local brewery. Everything was ready.

The villagers began to arrive, dressed in their Sunday Best clothes, shoes and boots clean and shining, the ladies carrying plates and cutlery for themselves and their menfolk.

Some of the men wore well starched, white collars to their shirts or a kerchief around their neck, pretty waistcoats and worsted trousers. The majority of men, with their shirt sleeves rolled to the elbow, seated themselves near the casks of beer, while the women arranged themselves in groups around the room. Kate had found a friend and sat chatting to her.

Reverend Peake began by giving a speech, or one could call it a short sermon and ended by saying 'Grace'.

After many loud 'Amens' the Supper, or Hawkey, began.

Rachel looked for Matthew and found him tucked away, leaning against a wall. Just as the other women were doing for their menfolk, she helped him to a plateful of food. Blue, dressed in his clown attire, his face painted, made a dramatic entrance, walking on his stilts. Tall enough to reach over heads, he helped himself to food, avoiding the greenery suspended from the rafters, in such a fashion, causing much laughter. Later in the evening he began his juggling act.

Blue, using five balls and picking up a hard-boiled egg from the table, tossed and caught it with the others, finishing by popping the whole egg into his mouth. Pulling numerous funny faces and performing the subsequent antics involved in trying to chew and swallow the egg, caused great hilarity.

Finally, to much amazement and great applause, he removed the egg from his mouth, bounced it on the floor for all to see, but, it was not the egg, it was a white celluloid ball, which bounced.

"Where's the dog? You want to see him again, don't you, Olly?"

Prince was brought in. Twisting between the stilts, bowing, walking on two legs, retrieving and of course the inevitable pant-showing.

"Bet your pants aren't such a pretty sight, Olly," shouted one of his mates.

John the fiddler began playing, setting feet tapping. Others with spoons, bones and a comb and paper, joined the happy group.

As the evening wore on, Matthew, fancily dressed, played a medley of Music Hall songs on his accordion. Blue, having learned words to some of the choruses of these, did his best to encourage the happy villagers to sing along.

Due to body warmth and ale, the people were getting more relaxed. A portly gent, wearing hobnailed boots, did a tap dance, keeping in time with the beat and rhythm of Matthew's and the fiddler's music.

A lady in a dress with a tight bodice joined him in the centre of the floor, hoisting her long skirt, and she too began to dance.

To calls from the onlookers of "Faster! Faster!" having been instrumental to this type of performance before, no doubt, the fiddler increased his tempo.

On and on the two danced, reeling, hopping and stamping. Shouts and whistles egged them on, until, gasping for breath, both collapsed on a bench seat.

After the clapping and shouts of "Bravo!" died down, the fiddler began playing a waltz. A youth crossed the floor and asked a young lass to dance. Others did the same. Matthew, discarding his accordion, escorted Rachel on to the dance floor and danced with her in a most correct manner, both knowing eyes were following their every step.

"Did you like the food I brought?"

To his answer, "Yes. Delightful," she said, "I learn something new about you every day, Matthew Dere."

He smiled, a loving look in his eyes, and asked, "Will you marry me one day?"

The sudden question caught her by surprise.

"Think well before you answer ..." he said. "We can't talk here, my love," and led her from the crowded floor, into the dark night.

"As I said," he continued, not daring to touch her by taking her into his arms, "Think well before you answer. Part of the year, Blue and I must travel. You know so little about me. Will you trust me? Could you leave your wealth and servants behind? Travel with me, take the rough and tumble of circus life? You have only known me for a few weeks, but I have loved you with all my heart, for many months, since I first saw you and I will love you until I die."

Without hesitation she pressed herself to him, wondering

155

why he didn't bestow a kiss upon her lips. Putting her face to his, she whispered, "I love you," realising afterwards, with dismay, "Oh! My face is covered with grease-paint! What a clown I am!" She rubbed hard at her cheek, laughing.

His arms enfolded her. Never having experienced the feeling now running through his body, he was reluctant to release her and rejoin the party.

Humorous yarns, recitations and jolly songs added to the entertainment. It was well after midnight when people began to drift away.

Work began for the horsekeepers at four in the morning. Pratty, the carrier, stood-by with his carrier cart, anticipating a few of his friends might be incapable of walking home. Laughter and merry voices echoed along the lanes and roadway in the dark village, each one in agreement, this hawkey had been one of the best for many a year. Rachel, bubbling with excitement, could not keep her news to herself any longer. Seated in the carriage next to Kate, she said, "Oh, Kate. I've had the most wonderful evening and Matthew and I are to be married!"

Rachel couldn't see the look of horror on Kate's face as she cried out, "Rachel! You cannot mean it? You've only know him for a few days! You know absolutely nothing about the young man, why, he could be an out-and-out scoundrel, a rotter!"

"I know all I want to know. I love him, Kate. He is the most important person, except you, in my life," Rachel replied candidly. "I feel like a song bird released from a cage."

"You have had too much parsnip wine to drink!" suggested Kate.

"Not intoxicated with alcohol, just love, Kate. I am determined to marry Matthew."

Then she said very seriously, "Neville will not be told until the very last moment. It will be a secret."

Blue, hearing Matthew's news, said, "You realise the problems you'll both have? Sure do wish you good luck, my friend.

You haven't let the grass grow under your feet."

Blue wished afterwards he had not said anything to remind him of his disability, but Matthew only laughed, overjoyed and on top of the world.

"A secret, Blue, until we get that Neville fella sorted. OK?" Then he said, quite seriously, "There are problems at the Hall. Rachel and I have had long discussions."

"Count on me, my friend," said Blue, slapping him on the shoulder.

Morning saw Matthew again make ready for his meeting with Rachel.

"Breakfast as usual?" Blue asked from under the covers of his bed.

"Sure. We will be hungry," Matthew answered, his face wreathed in smiles.

To Blue's surprise, the couple returned earlier than usual. Blue greeted a radiant Rachel, kissing her on both cheeks.

"You have made a wonderful choice. May you both enjoy untold happiness."

"That is quite some speech, Blue. You been rehearsing all night? Hurry with those eggs, I'm ..."

Matthew was silenced as Blue tossed the teapot for him to make tea.

"We have planned a Christmas Wedding, Blue," Rachel told him happily. "If Francis agrees. We'll pop in to see him after breakfast, if he is at home."

Looking at the happy pair, Blue remarked, "You will have quite a lot of sorting out to do, Matt ... with Reverend Peake, I mean," he added, seeing a look of alarm on Rachel's face. The Rector, when consulted, accepted the suddenness as a matter of course. He told Rachel he quite liked the idea of a Boxing Day wedding and congratulated them both. Naturally, their secret would be safe with him, but they must understand, legal arrangements had to be made.

Speaking seriously to Matthew, he said, "We will talk together later, if you agree?"

"Definitely. Sure, Sir." Matthew shook the Rector's hand, with the feeling this kind soul could be trusted.

Rachel decided it was time Matthew escorted her home, asking Blue to join them when he was ready. They would have lunch there.

Arriving at the Hall stables, two young stable-lads came forward to take their horses. Jacob appeared. "Is my cousin at home, Jacob?"

"No, Miss. Out riding."

"Good!" she replied. "Matthew, I will be able to show you my home without interruption."

Walking along, Rachel explained that the servants' quarters were built practically underground. The big stone-built Hall, set in neat trimmed lawns and gardens, overlooked a lake. They made their entry through a semi-circular sun lounge, filled to capacity with large green and flowering plants in ornate containers. Crossing the mosaic floor, they entered a spacious drawing room. The room held well-polished elegant furniture, and matching gilt and pink upholstered chairs and chaise-longue. Portraits in oils of handsome men in naval uniform and beside them, beautiful ladies in magnificent gowns, adorned the walls. A crystal chandelier hung from the ceiling. In awe, Matthew looked about him, taking in the enormity of change for Rachel when she became his wife. Would their love be strong enough?

Rachel selected a bell rope and gave it a pull. At that precise moment a doorbell rang.

"Blue, I expect."

Putting a restraining hand on Matthew's arm, she said, "A servant will go."

"A Mr Blue, to see you, Miss Rachel," a manservant announced in a sombre voice.

"Show him in, please, Burroughs."

As Blue stepped forward, looking about him with surprise, Rachel greeted him with a hug. "Welcome to my home."

Kate appeared suddenly, looking flushed and upset and near to tears.

"Please don't be upset, Kate dear. I know this is all very sudden. I love Matthew and he loves me and we plan to marry on Boxing Day," Rachel said, thinking Kate was still upset by her plan to marry after such a brief courtship.

So preoccupied was Kate, Rachel's words went unnoticed.

"Miss Rachel, Mrs Crispe has been ordered by your cousin, Neville, to make ready the best bedroom for Lady Eleanor Paget. She is coming to stay!"

Kate continued, "He even told Cook to prepare Her Ladyship's favourite dishes. I've had quite an argument with the housekeeper."

"I'll take care of it, Kate, dear. You talk with Matthew and Blue."

Leaving them, Rachel went in search of the housekeeper.

Through the large windows, Blue saw woodlands, with their leaves now turning yellow to bronze, stretching to the long water. An ornamental wooden bridge spanned the blue lake. Deer grazed the parkland, undisturbed. Blue wished he was an artist, the view was magnificent. Built on a small rise, Kiddsmere Hall was so positioned to receive any available sunlight from morning until night. Blue walked into the sun lounge amid the potted ferns and palms. Outside, a gardener was busy tending the roses, while other men cleared leaves and trimmed the already very short grass. Rachel must be very rich to have such a bevy of servants.

Hearing Rachel's voice, Blue returned to the drawing room and to a much calmer Kate.

"I will have a great deal to say to my cousin, Neville, when he returns. I have the key to the guest bedroom, Kate. We will finish our tour of the house, then find out what Cook has for lunch."

Rachel very rarely visited the kitchens or servants' quarters, but after that little set-to, aimed to find out for herself what else had been happening. Therefore, the first place to show her husband-to-be would be the kitchens.

Cook, with the help of five young maids, had been very busy. Two succulent fowls and a large ham were arranged on silver serving dishes, accompanied by two freshly cooked ribs of beef. Vol-au-vent cases, placed on a cooling tray beside choux pastries, awaited fillings.

"Are we having a party, Cook?" Rachel asked.

Cook looked at her and realising Miss Rachel was unaware of this weekend's party, said: "Some guests are staying, more coming for supper."

"Strange, I knew nothing of this. Master Neville's arrangements?"

"Yes, Miss," The hot and flustered Cook replied.

"Never mind. I will sort it out. Send lunch for four to the dining room, Kate will join us. One of those birds will do nicely, with all the trimmings, in say, one hour, please Cook."

The Cook asked fearfully, "What will Master Neville say?"

"Don't worry, I will inform him in no uncertain terms."

Leaving her, they accompanied Rachel down more steps, passing damp, dark and dingy places, smelling of stale food. Sculleries, with servants working at numerous jobs. A laundry room, full of steaming coppers and wet clothes. No one looked very happy at their work, Blue noticed. He would hate to work in this place, no disrespect to Rachel or her family. Give him the open country and happy travellers, were his thoughts, as they retraced their steps.

A pristine white cloth and napkins, gleaming cutlery, crystal glasses and a bowl of roses on the large dining table made a very attractive setting. The dining room, also very large, contained heavy cabinets and side tables. On one of these was an array of crystal decanters.

"A vast difference from our meal table, eh, Matt?" said Blue, moving two dining chairs in readiness for the two ladies to seat themselves.

"I thoroughly enjoy my breakfast with you both," chipped in Rachel. Then, looking around asked, "Where is my boy, Prince?"

"Outside in the wagon. I wouldn't bring him in," Blue explained.

"He must come in. This is part of his home now."

Then she asked, "May I fetch him?"

"Of course." Blue handed her the key to the wagon door.

She soon returned with Prince and commanded him to sit beside her chair, and was delighted he obeyed her command.

About to start their pudding, they heard the peel of the doorbell, followed by a commotion of loud voices.

Burroughs entered the dining room, apologising to Rachel for the intrusion and, trying to close the door behind him, very quickly said: "Lady Paget has arrived, Miss ..."

Before finishing his sentence, Lady Paget pushed open the door saying, "Darling Neville, sorry to disturb your lunch, I've arrived early ..."

The expensively dressed, attractive woman in her late thirties, paused in mid-sentence and surveyed Rachel's colourfully attired guests and the dog. In a haughty manner she asked, "Where is Neville?"

Rachel, ignoring the woman, said, "Burroughs, take Lady Eleanor's luggage, and show her to Master Neville's rooms in the East Wing. Mrs Crispe has been informed."

Bereft of words, Lady Paget followed him.

"Whatever has happened to you, Miss Rachel? Your behaviour is most unusual! I fear Master Neville's temper will be aroused out of all proportion," Kate said woefully.

"Kate, I noticed things today which did not please me. Matthew and Blue have made me open my eyes. With their and your help, I mean to set things to rights. Neville has had his own way for too long!" Rachel stated with defiance, toying with the remainder of her lunch.

Matthew was about to ask more questions about the estate, when the dining room door suddenly opened. This time a very dishevelled-looking man came into the room.

Seeing Rachel and her guests, he exclaimed, "Oh! Lady Eleanor not here?"

"No, cousin, she is your guest. If you want to entertain, do so in your own apartment," Rachel told him angrily.

Crimson-faced and speechless, he hurried away, slamming the door behind him.

"Matthew, dear, that was my Cousin Neville. I believe Grandfather thought, one day, Neville and I would marry. I shudder at the thought."

Seeking Matthew's hand and looking into his eyes, she said, "Oh, Matthew dear, I wish we were to be married tomorrow."

Kate, giving a horrified look, reprimanded her. "Miss Rachel, you should not talk like that. What has come over you?"

Rachel, interrupting her, said, "I don't think you heard what I told you this morning, my dear Kate. Matthew and I plan to marry on Boxing Day, the 26th of December. We are keeping it a secret, especially from Neville."

By the sudden paleness of Kate's face, as she looked from one to the other, Blue thought her about to faint, so handed her a glass of water.

Chapter 18

Reverend Peake quite liked Blue popping into the rectory for a chat and a laugh. Today he was mixing a cough syrup and Blue was making notes of the ingredients and the preparation. As well as being Rector of this parish, Francis was noted for his generosity. As they were talking, Mrs Peake's voice could be heard, calling for her husband to come quickly.

The moment the Rector arrived by her side, a young boy at the rectory door, almost breathless from running, asked, "Can you come quick, Sir, Olly's fallen from the corn-cart. Hurt something bad. Nurse isn't at home." Then he explained where Olly could be found.

"It would be quicker to take my wagon than you saddle up Blossom. I've bandages and things you might need," suggested Blue.

Francis agreed. They found Olly lying in the field, his head pillowed on someone's folded jacket, his leg twisted at a peculiar angle.

"Parson, I've had my lot!" Olly gasped between stabs of pain.

The Rector held Olly's hand while Blue gently probed the damaged leg.

"You have broken your leg, my friend," said Blue, carefully beginning to unbuckle Olly's buskin and remove his boot.

"'Tis my hip that hurts most," Olly told them, his face wreathed in pain. Blue snipped the trouser seam, fetched splints and bandages from the wagon, and said, "Clean break, I think, Sir," as the Rector placed a hip flask to Olly's lips.

Deftly, Blue manipulated the leg into splints and bandages then proceeded to examine the hip. The workmen stood around, silent, watching.

Olly, by now becoming dozy, grimaced at Blue's gentle exploration of his hip then letting out an almighty yell and swearing as Blue gave him an terrific jerk.

"Good God!" said Francis, as Olly's face began to show a less painful expression, and moved his body slightly, with great caution.

The young errand boy arrived with more helpers and a hurdle. Gently, they lifted the patient onto the hurdle and into the awaiting corn-cart.

"Thought it would be my box you would be bringing," was Olly's greeting to his mates.

One answered, "Old Davil don't want yew yit!"

Taking Blue by the hand, Olly quietly spoke to him, "Thanks. You're a magician as well as a fool!"

Blue smiled. Olly's work-mates carefully trundled him back to his home in the village to await the attention of a Doctor.

After this incident, Blue made a habit of visiting Olly, his wife, Mary, and their five children in their small, farm cottage. Often he took gifts of flour and other items of food and candles, which the couple were loath to accept, especially given by a gypsy. Soon Blue's easy, friendly manner overcame any prejudice. From this friendship, be learned a great deal about life in the village and the 'goings-on' at the Hall.

"Neville-the-Devil' was the local nickname for Rachel's cousin. He had no respect for his workers or animals. No one liked or had a good word to say for him.

Just to show his authority, the inside walls of the estate cottages were colour-washed with red ochre, making the small windowed rooms even darker.

Neville regularly called on the elderly widows, asking if they were happy and comfortable in their cottage.

Answering him in the affirmative, he made them move into another dwelling when it became vacant, for sheer spite. One old lady of whom Olly spoke, was very wise and complained bitterly of the damp and rot every time Neville called. She remained in her cottage, quite happily.

Olly could have told endless tales of Neville's devious methods. He only wished, like many other people, that Miss Rachel would find herself a good, decent husband, to help run the estate.

Matthew and Rachel were also soon to learn for themselves her cousin's treachery and trickery, when visiting a tenant farmer. The farmer confronted them at his farm gate, a very angry man, not letting them enter.

"But why?" asked Rachel in all innocence. "Tell me why you are so angry?"

"If you don't know, then ask that sly cousin of yours," he replied angrily, banging his fist on the gate.

Hearing the commotion, his wife appeared, asking in a none-too-friendly manner, "What has she come for? Tell her there will be no more ham or poultry until she pays for what she has had already! How does she think we can live?"

Rachel's cheeks had turned pale. Speaking quietly, she asked, "Tell me more of this if you will. May we come in?"

Rather unwillingly, he opened the gate, letting the pair through. Sitting at the kitchen table in the farmhouse, they listened to the farmer's many grievances, assuring Rachel it was the same situation all over the estate and beyond. Debts!

"Why, your staff at the Hall are often left without payment!"

Noticing her horrified look, he asked, "Where does Clinton Howard live, he was always fair. He has not visited us for a couple of years. When your grandfather was alive, it was a pleasure to live here."

Thanking them for the information, but promising nothing, they left to visit the next farm. There they heard a similar story. This time Rachel gave assurance the matter would be looked into.

Telling nothing of this to Neville, she and Matthew would consult Mr Howard at his London address. But for the moment, the pair had important arrangements to attend to before making a trip to London.

The promised, confidential, discussion between Reverend Peake and Matthew had taken place, with Matthew supplying details of himself and his home in Australia. When Matthew gave the Rector his passport and also broke the seal on the envelope given to him by his father, Francis Peake accepted Matthew's story.

Ben Dere had been very thorough, listing names and places of contact. The Rector was overjoyed, as a great burden had been lifted from his shoulders.

Naturally, everything he had been told would be treated as confidential. He and his wife thought a great deal of Rachel, and felt she was in need of love and protection. She had endured a very unhappy life.

Matthew had explained to him how, and when, he had first met Rachel and his instant love for her. His wish for her to see another side of life, away from her home. She knew nothing of his wealth; because of his disability, he had to be sure her love was for him and not his wealth. He was absolutely sure this was so. They were both deeply in love and he would die for her!

With so many problems on the estate, especially concerning her cousin Neville, who, they felt, would do everything in his power to stop the marriage, was their reason for secrecy.

Trusting the relevant legal documents could be obtained, Francis Peake promised he would conduct their wedding ceremony on 26th December, as they wished.

Needing a caravan for himself and Rachel, now was the time to visit the estate carpenter. Matthew found the man busy in his workshop.

The carpenter didn't look or speak until Matthew introduced himself. When asked if he was skilled enough to make a traveller's wagon or gypsy caravan, half-heartedly he told him he could, given time and better wood than he was, at the moment, using. Matthew laid some plans on the rough bench. The carpenter looked. After great discussion, Matthew gave him to understand he wanted the caravan made as quickly as possible and suggested he found another skilled man to help him. This pleased the carpenter. Good wood and extra money, nothing would stop him, and promised it would be ready at the beginning of the new year.

Matthew then went in search of Jacob at the stables.

Finding him in the harness room, he said, "Jacob, I want you to get me a horse."

Jacob looked towards the various stables, then asked, "You want a filly?"

"No, something to pull a caravan, Jacob. Say nothing to Kate, there's a good fellow, or to Rachel."

Jacob couldn't believe he had heard correctly, but at that precise moment a shemozzle became apparent in one of the stables.

"Have to leave you for a moment to quieten those lads. They get mighty upset at times," Jacob said, quickly making for the stables.

Upon Jacob's return, Matthew asked the reason for the disturbance.

"Poor food and very little pay, that is to say, when Master Neville feels like paying."

"Is Neville at home?"

"No. He left with Lady Eleanor same night as you lunched with Miss Rachel. Her Ladyship was carrying on something alarming." Jacob stopped talking, thinking it best to say no more.

Matthew went into the house in search of Rachel. He found her in tears, in the sitting room with Kate beside her.

Taking her in his arms, he kissed her and asked why she was so distressed.

"Oh! Matthew dearest, it has been such a terrible week. Now look at this!"

Pulling a letter from her pocket, Matthew read, "Marry Sir Chester or else!"

Still holding her in his arms, he asked, "You think your cousin wrote this?"

"Yes." Between sobs, she told him the accusations Neville had made, that the estate debts were of her father's making.

"The sooner we see your Mr Howard in London, the better, my love. How soon can you and Kate be ready to travel to London? By morning?"

As an afterthought, he said, "It is possible Blue will want to accompany us."

With knowledge that her house in London was always at the ready, they agreed to consult Jacob and travel in the morning.

Blue was delighted at the prospect of seeing London. At dawn they began their journey. With him sitting comfortably beside Jacob on the coachman's seat, the Coleville-Grey carriage rolled along the turnpike. Jacob, who knew the route well, elected to call a halt at an Inn, used by Neville, to spend the night. Midday on the morrow should see them comfortably settled in Coleville House, Cavendish Row. Rachel, who had not visited her London home for several months, was looking forward to her stay.

Arriving at the Town House, they were met at the door by Mr and Mrs Maslin, the housekeeper and her husband, both middle-aged Londoners.

"Sorry we've taken you by surprise," declared Rachel, "but you always keep the place immaculate and in readiness for Mr Neville. We have brought food with us."

Very surprised, the caretakers viewed Rachel's choice of companions with amazement, especially the dog, but made no comment.

Before entering, Blue had surveyed the tall building. Five-storeyed, he guessed. Nicely set between other brick-built, imposing houses, in a very select area.

Quickly unloading the luggage, Jacob took his carriage and horses to the stables, returning with the phaeton and fresh horses in readiness to take Miss Rachel and Matthew to Clinton Howard's Thames-side offices.

Upon reaching these offices and the assistant telling Mr Howard of Rachel's arrival, he welcomed her into his office immediately, delighted to see the young woman.

Dressed in pinstriped trousers and black coat, Mr Howard looked an old man, his hair and beard grey, not at all as Rachel remembered him, when he last visited Kiddsmere Hall.

Rachel introduced Matthew as her 'kind friend and confidant'.

Unaccustomed to such colourful garments worn by gentlemen, Mr Howard looked quizzically at Rachel. "Are you sure you want this person to know your personal business?"

As a show of approval, she placed her hand into Matthew's strong clasp and smiled. But, her smile quickly vanished as she listened to the solicitor quietly reprimanding her, before she had explained the reason for her visit.

"Your personal expense accounts, my dear, which Neville always pass on to me, are very high."

"Neville tells me you vet everything and I see by your signature on the dress-maker's statement, your extravagance for clothes."

Bereft of words, Rachel listened as he continued. "Also an account from a jeweller for a diamond ring." Opening another folder, he leafed through more papers.

Timidly, Rachel asked to see those accounts, knowing she had not purchased new garments for a very long time and most certainly not a diamond ring, because her cousin had told her they had very little money.

Clinton Howard passed the accounts to her.

Looking them over, she immediately declared, "I have never purchased these items, Mr Howard, and most certainly, these are not my signatures." She handed back the papers.

Taking little notice of her, the solicitor continued, "You increased the rents from your tenant farmers, having disregard for my or Master Neville's wishes. The letter which I sent, you completely ignored!"

Rachel felt nauseated. Never before had she been accused of such falsehood. No wonder her tenants felt bitter towards her.

"Please listen, Mr Howard. I can assure you I know nothing of a letter or how much my tenants pay. Please, believe me. Neville did tell me you had increased the rents, which he himself collects. He also said we must cut down on food, as too much was being spent in the servants' quarters. Oh! Mr Howard, something is seriously wrong! Of late, I and Matthew have heard so much from disgruntled tenants. I have promised to do something about it. That is the reason why we are here today! I do not think my dear father deliberately ran up debts. Mama told me nothing, only to take care of our family heir-looms ..." Her voice was beginning to falter.

"Your father's debts?" Mr Howard repeated aghast, at last taking notice of what she was saying. "Your father left no debts!"

"But Neville said ..." Rachel became silent, looking wide-eyed at Mr Howard, and he at her, as both of them realised the truth. Neville had been making false statements.

Matthew took the threatening letter, which Rachel had received, from his pocket and handed it to Mr Howard to read.

"Well! Well! Who could have written this?" he asked.

"I think it was Neville. I will not marry Sir Chester Peggleton, I am marrying this young man on this coming Boxing Day," she quietly stated.

"Neville knows nothing of this. We do not want him to know. He is not to know!" she said most emphatically.

Taken by surprise, Clinton Howard looked from one to the other as she continued, "My Matthew is a travelling musician with his ... our friend Blue," she corrected. "I aim to rove the country with them, after we marry, so you will be left entirely on your own to run the estate. I know the terms of my grandfather's will. Neville has to leave the house. Find another place to live. But tell me, please, what are we to do for the present? Have we enough money to pay our debts?"

"Oh! Yes! Yes! You have money. Your investments are very sound. We will get a good agent. We have enough time to find someone," he stated without hesitation.

Talk passed between them, concerning the agent and the accounts and the immediate running of the estate. He found Matthew a very sensible person. After partaking tea with the solicitor, it was quite late when the couple left.

Mid-morning the following day, Matthew insisted upon taking Rachel shopping. Calling a cab, he instructed the cabby to take them to a reputable jeweller and wait.

Inside the Jeweller's shop, a young assistant came forward and politely asked their needs. Matthew asked to be shown a tray of betrothal rings.

Taking note of his customer's colourful attire, the assistant produced a tray of cheap dress rings.

"Not trash!" said Matthew, pushing the cheap baubles away.

"What price, Sir?"

A well-dressed, elderly man came forward from the depths of the shop, placed a chair beside the counter for Rachel's use, sending the assistant to fetch another, more expensive selection.

Looking at the tray of rings before her, Rachel chose a large amethyst and diamond cluster and tried it on her finger.

"Matthew, darling, this fits perfectly. I would love this," she said, twisting and turning her hand, admiring the ring.

Matthew then asked to view some wedding rings. After both selections were made he discreetly made the payment, taking their purchases.

The delighted jeweller then ushered them to their conveyance, wishing them joy and great happiness.

In the privacy of the cab, Matthew knelt before her, declaring his eternal love, asking again if she was certain she wanted to marry him. Without hesitation, she gave her reply, placing his hand against her cheek lovingly, and said very seriously, "My life would be nothing without you Matthew, dearest. I'm willing to travel the whole world with you."

"My darling Rachel," he whispered. "My beloved, I adore you."

After placing the ring on her finger, he swept her into his arms, murmuring endearments, tenderly kissing her lips, hardly daring to believe her declaration.

"Where to, Guv?"

The voice of the now impatient cab driver brought Matthew to his senses.

The moment after returning with Matthew to Cavendish Row was for Rachel to find and show Kate her engagement ring.

"I hope you do not live to regret your hasty decision. As I have said before …"

Rachel interrupted her.

"Dear Kate. Don't worry! I'm so happy! I'm walking on air! I'm in love!"

Blue decided a celebration was called for and booked five seats for a Variety Performance in a London Music Hall.

Asked would she like to go to the show, Rachel, at first, hesitated. Someone once informed her such places were unclean. But she was about to become the wife of an entertainer, so gracefully she accepted for Kate and herself.

Jacob did not hesitate for one moment, he loved the Music Hall.

In the meantime, from Jacob's directions, Blue found the London Solicitor, Jeremiah Blizzard, brother to Ben Dere's Australian Solicitor. Jeremiah was very pleased that at long last Blue had made contact with him, because of news received from his brother of a gold find on Everest land. Jeremiah was still awaiting more details. His brother had written from Adelaide, telling him to pass the message to Blue as soon as possible.

"Of course, I had no idea where to find you and neither had he. Now you must keep in touch."

Blue thanked him, giving Mr Clinton Howard's name and address, saying, through him you can contact both Matthew and I.

Excitedly, Blue hurriedly returned to Cavendish Row to give Matthew his news, not really knowing if his family was very rich. Whatever the outcome, it would remain their secret.

After a day spent shopping and sightseeing, the evening to visit the Music Hall had arrived. Now ready and waiting, Rachel surveyed her party and felt proud. She, herself, was wearing a pleated and tucked gown of pink taffeta, and Kate's black taffeta and lace trimmed gown, suited her perfectly. Both wore flower trimmed bonnets.

Matthew looked magnificent in his blue silk shirt and tight black trousers with knee buckles. Smiling, she walked towards him, placing her hand on his arm and gave him a kiss upon his cheek.

Kate made sure Jacob was suitably attired, certain his white shirt was clean and creaseless. A gold, frilled-fronted shirt, black cummerbund and green silk trousers, enhanced Blue's mass of blonde, curly hair, giving him the appearance of a young Norseman.

Maslin announced the arrival of the carriage. It had been decided that Jacob should have the evening free of encumbrance.

In a short time, travelling through the dimly lit streets, the Coleville House party alighted in front of the large theatre, to mingle with an assortment of well-dressed ladies in plumed hats and colourful gowns. Some of those ladies' escorts were dapper and dandy menfolk, dressed in evening attire, while others sported checked suits. A happy and smiling crowd, looking forward to an enjoyable evening of entertainment. Blue directed his party through the jostling crowd to their reserved seats. Around them, gold and red decorated walls supported painted angels in the dome-ceiling, and gas wall lights gave a soft, mellow glow through tinted-glass globes. A large white curtain, hiding the area of the stage, had a number of tradespeople's names emblazoned across it, and heavy dark curtains hung to the sides.

An aroma of exotic perfumes and cigar smoke filled the auditorium. Several musicians took up their instruments in the orchestra pit at the front of the stage and struck up with a rip-roaring opening tune.

The lights dimmed. The audience quietened and the giant curtain arose, revealing delicate, painted scenery and a troupe of prettily dressed girls dancing, occasionally daring to show a black stocking-covered leg, causing riotous shouts and whistles. The compere announced artists who then sang Cockney songs and operatic duets. From time to time the audience was encouraged to participate.

To obtain attention and sometimes to restore order, the handsomely dressed compere banged his gavel onto the wooden rostrum on which he was standing.

"Our next performer," he subsequently announced, "is a sharp trickster, tormenting us with tantalising trickery. Remember, the quickness of the hand deceives the eye; none other than your old friend from Wethergate, the one and only, Leonardo Crutch!"

Bringing the gavel down to a roll of drums, a flash, loud bang and a cloud of smoke, through which a choking Leonardo appeared in the centre of the stage.

The man, his face painted white, dressed completely in black, a long cloak hanging from his shoulders, took a well-worn top hat from his head and bowed to the audience. Smoke curled from within the hat as he deftly removed not one, but four or five cigars from the lining of the hat. Giving each one a puff, he popped them into his mouth and chewed. More burning cigars were taken from his pockets and from behind his ears, and deftly stacked away, hidden from sight.

Playing cards were fanned out in his hands or being produced from unusual places, all happening so quickly, holding the audience captivated.

Carrying a small table, a scantily-clad female assistant joined him. More shouts and whistles. Leonardo emptied his pockets, placing various items on the table and, during this, a loud bang, and from the canister shot forth endless yards of coloured silks. More tricks from his sleeves at a fast pace enthralled the audience, until he had completed his act. The applause was tremendous.

Blue hardly remembered the latter part of the show, so engrossed was he with Leonardo. Here was the man Barney said would help them when they arrived in England. What luck!

"Have you ladies enjoyed this evening's entertainment?" Blue asked. "I know Jacob has, I heard his laughter. Leonardo is very popular, Matt. Do you remember his cousin, Barney? We must meet Leonardo. Shall we go to the stage door?"

Each agreeing that it had been a wonderful evening they returned to the foyer. Blue made enquiries of the whereabouts of Leonardo.

A door-keeper gave him directions. Through dark passage-ways smelling of stale odours, they finally reached Leonardo's dressing room.

Leonardo came to the door, answering their knock, a much slimmer man than anticipated when seen on stage, now devoid of make-up and bulky clothes. Although his brown suit looked well-worn, he appeared clean and neatly dressed.

With a smile, he asked their business.

"Nothing in particular," Blue replied, "just that we met your cousin, Barney Crutch, on our travels. He asked us to make ourselves known to you, should our paths cross."

"Well, I'm damned! Barney! Last I heard, he was in Australia. How was he? Doing well?" Leonardo said, shaking Blue by the hand. "I bet he was," laughed the magician, answering his own questions. "Still in this business? It's nice of you to call."

Blue wanted to ask so much, but with Leonardo doing all the asking, he promptly invited him if he would take lunch with him tomorrow.

"Good idea! Where shall we meet?"

Rachel answered for them.

"Come to my house in Cavendish Row, at noon, if that suits you?"

Searching in her evening bag, she gave him her card.

"Delighted, Miss. I can hardly wait."

Finally releasing Blue's hand after giving it another vigorous shake, they took their leave of him.

Once outside the building, they scrambled happily into a waiting carriage. Matthew hummed a bar of music, a tune to one of this evening's songs and with gusto and merriment they sang some of the words, ending in a muddle and out of tune but into a crescendo of laughter. Rachel snuggled even more closely to her beloved.

"I have never enjoyed myself so much as I have this evening! Thank you, Blue."

Jacob spoke, "Your friend, the cigar smoker, now, he was good. But Kate liked the opera singer best, didn't you Kate?"

Kate, giving an audible sigh, said, "Yes. Thank you, Master Blue. I've never been to such a place before. We were always told most horrid tales about such places, but the performers were beautiful! Just think, Mr Leonardo, coming to lunch tomorrow!" This was said with such awe that Matthew said to Jacob, "Jacob, you must hurry and get a ring on Kate's finger, before she gets carried away!"

"Aye. Maybe I ought," said Jacob in all seriousness.

"I think that's a proposal of marriage, Kate, dear," laughed Rachel. "I'll soon be off your hands and you'll need someone to look after."

"Stop your tormenting!" came from a flustered Kate, thankful they were nearly home.

Chapter 19

Eager to hear more news of his cousin Barney, Leonardo arrived at Cavendish Row punctually at noon. Taking note of the select buildings, he commented to himself that this area was certainly different to his one-room accommodation in the grime of a London back street. He pulled the bell-pull and waited. A uniformed manservant opened the door and ushered him into an elaborately furnished sitting room, where he was first greeted by the tall, blonde-haired young man to whom he had spoken last evening, who had by his side quite an unusual sight; a dog.

Learning this young man's name to be Blue, who then in turn introduced him to the beautiful young lady, he thought these two could be brother and sister, but found they were not. Finally, he was introduced to the handsome, disabled young man.

Memorising their names, Leonardo accepted a glass of wine, and, with total amazement, learned these two young men were indeed clowns.

Rachel left the menfolk in order to make ready for lunch.

"Tell me more of Barney," Leonardo requested.

Happily they did so, but did not mention to him that Australia was their home.

Easy, happy conversation flowed over lunch, with intermittent laughter, something to which Rachel was not accustomed. Talk turned to Leonardo's family. When treading the boards, as he described his work, he only managed to see his wife and family and return home to Wethergate, once a month. They had two healthy lads, but sadly their young daughter had fallen and injured her back, suffering endless pain. She was quite helpless, relying upon his wife for almost everything.

His wife tried hard to make ends meet, explaining he received very little pay for his efforts at the moment. "But at last I am becoming well known and popular."

Now in the sitting room, Rachel smiled at Leonardo and asked to show them one of his cigar tricks.

Taking three cigars from his case, he popped them between his lips and endeavoured to light each at the same time with a single match, this done in a most comical manner. Kate had joined them. They watched, transfixed, as his nimble fingers switched the lighted cigars from one hand to the other with great dexterity, disposing of them without a trace, giving a laugh at their astonishment, only to produce each glowing cigar from his different pockets.

Soon it became time to bid them a fond adieu, in order to make ready for his evening performance. He assured them they would meet again; most certainly at Wethergate Fair.

After Leonardo had left, Kate remarked, "Didn't even bother if he caught fire, anywhere!"

The following morning, a messenger arrived at the Coleville residence, delivering a large bouquet of carnations. Rachel, opening the accompanying envelope, read, "To a wonderful hostess and beautiful chaperone. Rachel Coleville-Grey and Miss Kate. Five seats reserved for Saturday's evening performance."

Signed: Leonardo.

Taking the flowers, Rachel quickly went to Kate's room. Hardly waiting for Kate's "Come in", she opened the door, saying, "Look, Kate. From our new friend," handing her the bouquet and card.

Kate looked flushed and fumbled with the envelope. "Are you well, Kate dear?" Rachel asked, very concerned.

"Yes. Oh, yes! Very well, thank you," she continued, feeling very embarrassed. "Last evening, Jacob asked me to marry him." Almost in tears, she said, "I accepted!"

Rachel hugged her. "Wonderful! Wonderful! Why do you cry? You should be so happy. Just as Matthew and I. When will you marry? Jacob's room is not suitable for you both. We will make an apartment in the house, and you will both be able to look after our home while Matthew and I are away."

Rachel was speaking with great excitement and gusto, until Kate quickly interrupted her.

"Miss Rachel, you are moving too fast! Nothing is decided yet."

"Hurry Kate, read the card, then let us find Matthew and tell him your news. What shall we wear for our evening out? May I buy you a new gown, Kate? This is a special occasion. Come shopping with me this afternoon!"

Kate was overwhelmed. "Oh, Miss Rachel, I can hardly think straight!"

They found Matthew leafing through sheets of music in the music room. Taking little notice of their entrance, he asked Rachel if she had relatives who were musical.

"Yes. My grandmama played this spinet. Matthew, listen darling, Kate and Jacob are engaged to be married! And Leonardo has sent these. We must celebrate!"

"Wow-oh! Kate!" Matthew shouted.

Rachel, about to ring for Maslin, saw Blue returning from walking Prince, and told him Kate's news.

Blue, gathering her into his arms, twirled her around, ignoring her cries of alarm and, before releasing her, planted a kiss on her cheek. Leaving her scolding him and smoothing her dress and hair, he went in search of Jacob.

When a smiling Jacob entered the room and stood beside her, Kate felt quite embarrassed and emotional. Never had she known such attention.

Blue found a full decanter and some wine glasses.

"We really should have champagne. Blue, this is Port!" Rachel told him, accepting the glass of wine.

Matthew arose from the music stool, smiling, and shook Jacob by the hand.

"Congratulations! May you both have a wonderful life together in our home. Thank you, Kate, for your devotion to my lovely fiancée. God bless you both," he said, calmly bestowing a kiss on Kate's cheek.

Returning to his seat at the spinet, he began playing a beautiful song.

"Just for you, Kate."

For the next half hour, Matthew entertained the happy group, playing a selection of melodies found among the sheets of music. They all listened, enthralled, knowing by the look on his face that he was enjoying every moment, and would have continued but for the fact Maslin announced, "Lunch is served."

"Your grandmama had an excellent taste. A wonderful choice of music, my love."

The ladies' afternoon shopping spree proved very successful. Rachel chose to visit her favourite salon. Leaving Kate to try several gowns, and unknown to Kate, Rachel asked to view some wedding gowns. Delightedly, they brought her several from which to choose. Immediately one in particular caught her eye, and, after a few minor alterations, suited her perfectly. Satin slippers and an imitation fur cape completed her ensemble. All her purchases she would arrange for Jacob to collect in due course. Looking at Kate's final choice, Rachel declared, "Kate, you look lovely in velvet. Dark blue suits you perfectly. See for yourself in the long mirror."

Kate glanced in the mirror, saying, "Fine feathers don't make fine birds, Miss Rachel. True, it feels very warm and comfortable. It's often a bit draughty at home. Colour is nice as well. Real velvet!"

With great reverence and pleasure, she ran her hands over the soft folds.

"Thank you, Rachel dear."

The week had been a busy one for them all. Now, this Saturday evening, with trunks and boxes packed and ready for their homeward journey to Kiddsmere on the 'morrow, they were again waiting for a carriage to take them to the Music Hall, and could talk of nothing but the forthcoming evening's entertainment, wondering what new tricks Leonardo, literally, had up his sleeve.

To a packed house, the Variety Hall dancers surprised them with a new routine, pretty silk gowns, feather boas and a variety of parasols. The singers sang a selection of new songs and the monologues and bawdy jokes, as with Leonardo's tricks, were all different, and cleverly introduced by the dashing compere, and to great acclaim.

"It's a shame the show has to end," Rachel declared, having enjoyed the evening thoroughly. They all shared her sentiments, as the final curtain came down.

In order to thank him, they found their friend in his dressing room, packing a canvas bag. Yes. He was returning home in the morning, to Wethergate.

Rachel asked in which direction was Wethergate, as they planned to leave for home early the next morning.

Jacob enlightened everyone, by saying, "If you took the Forest road, you would pass close to Wethergate. Master Neville often goes that way."

Asking Leonardo if he would accept a lift, after much discussion, Rachel invited him to spend the night at Cavendish Row in order to be ready for an early start.

The cigar-smoking magician accepted the offer with great delight and courtesy.

"I feel Lady Luck is at last smiling upon me. I am most grateful and so pleased to have met you," said a happy Leonardo Crutch, as they were approaching Wethergate. For him, it had been a most pleasant stay at the house and a delightful journey home.

Passing through a large, ornamental gateway, the road zigzagged amidst gorse, bracken and heather-covered heathland.

"This is the place where the traditional Goose Fair is held each year. Bargaining and merry-making continue for a whole week. Where I first started my tricks, many years ago," Leonardo told them. "It is always great fun at the Goose Fair." He then gave Jacob directions to his home, in the main street in Wethergate.

Helen Crutch, his wife, was not the only person to wonder why an elegant carriage had stopped in front of her house. Several neighbours were also inquisitive. Helen stood at the doorway of the cottage as her two boys raced to the gate after hearing their father's call. He also beckoned his wife to come and meet his friends.

A tall, painfully thin, young woman joined them. Quite pretty, about thirty years of age. Leonardo introduced her, asking if she could manage to provide a warm drink. Placing his arm around her shoulders in a loving manner, "A pot of tea, perhaps?" he suggested, kissing her cheek.

"I think I can manage that," she answered willingly, returning his kiss and smiling.

Noticing Rachel's expensive fur-trimmed clothes she thought of her own over-washed and darned garments. Her house was clean, but with two hungry boys to feed, a large pudding, steaming away in a boiler on the black stove, was not suitable food for such genteel folk as these. She wondered to herself how her husband had become involved with this 'upper-class' set.

Rachel, noticing Helen's hesitation, quickly asked, "May we share our hamper with you and your family, Mrs Crutch? I'm sure it's much cosier in your house than on the roadside."

Very pleased to be home, Leonardo hurried into the house to see his daughter, leaving Helen to escort his friends.

"Our daughter, Annabel, is not quite so well today," Helen

told them. "The weather has been so damp. We always blame the weather," she said with a laugh, inviting them inside the cottage.

A long, low Ottoman, pulled close beside the hearth for warmth, held a delicate, pale-faced girl, holding on to her father's hand as he sat beside her.

A bright red ribbon, matching her red dress, held her limp, dark hair. A colourful patchwork quilt covered her legs. Propped against the pillows was a ragdoll, which had a long woollen pigtail, whose name turned out to be 'Matilda-Jane'.

"And how is Matilda-Jane today?" her father was heard to ask his daughter.

"Pleased you are home, Daddy!" she replied in a tired voice.

Her father held the ragdoll and, using it as a puppet, introduced his daughter to Rachel and Kate. The child laughed a little, so he continued with his game, introducing Matthew and Jacob. When he came to Blue, he said to his daughter, "Now you guess his name, I will give you a clue," and began to recite a well-known nursery rhyme.

"Oh! Not Boy Blue?" she giggled, looking at Blue.

"Right first time. Well done." They sang her praises.

Kate began unpacking the hamper with the help of the two boys, David and Richard, who chatted to her amicably. Very soon Helen's table was laden with cooked meats and pies, a variety of cheese and paté, bread rolls and dairy butter, rich cookies, crystallised fruits, fresh pears and apples.

Helen surveyed the room and the people. Quite unbelievable; Leonardo's rich friends happily sipping tea, eating and talking as if they had known each other a lifetime.

The pudding was forgotten on the stove, until Matthew, with a twinkle in his eye, asked Helen what kind of pudding she had made.

"Spotted Dick. The boys love it."

"Shall you be sparing a morsel?" he asked, licking his lips.

"By all means," came her rejoinder, going to the stove,

lifting the bag of pudding onto a warm plate.

Matthew watched, recollecting the same technique at the Dere Homestead, on the other side of the world.

"Matthew … Matthew!"

Rachel, giving his arm a tug, said, "Helen asked is that piece large enough? You were miles away, my darling!"

"Sorry … Oh yes, splendid," he said, accepting the plate and large piece of pudding.

"It looks delicious," he added, spooning a large piece of the pudding into his mouth, following with shouts of, "Oh! Ah! It is very hot!"

"What can you expect?" Annabel asked, giving a little giggle.

She had eaten very little, enjoying a few small pieces of cold meat and some fruit with fresh cream, fed to her by her father.

Poor child, thought Blue, taking notice of her pain-filled face. Confined to that bed, by what? A fall, Leonardo had said. He felt compelled to ask her mother what was wrong and the treatment, if any, she had received.

"Our village doctor does what he can to relieve the pain with a medicine. His friend from a college came to see her, said something about using needles in her back, but that upset Annabel so much, she had nightmares, and to placate her we promised not to try that remedy."

Helen told Blue all this quietly in order that her daughter should not hear.

"When did this happen?" Blue asked, walking over to Annabel.

Looking very frightened, Annabel pulled the covers close around her.

"Six months ago. It is her back," Helen told him.

Blue smiled at her and began telling her a story of a young boy who had had an accident, and was lying in his bed, just as she was, in great pain. A kind doctor, his wife and son came along, just by chance.

"Days later, when the doctor's young son visited the sick

185

boy to cheer him a little, what do you think he took with him as a present?"

Annabel, now very interested, asked, "What?"

Matthew, like everyone, had been listening and, quickly taking his flute from a pocket, began to play a merry tune.

"Mrs Crutch, may I run my fingers down your daughter's spine? I promise not to hurt her."

Helen looked towards her husband for assurance. They both agreed.

"Annabel, your daddy will turn you onto your tummy, but remember, you must listen to the magic flute."

This little girl could only be about seven years old, but so very thin, Blue thought, as his fingers carefully, methodically traced her spinal column. Many times had he watched his father find an offending vertebra and been told to do just as his father had done and had been amazed at the quick recovery of the one-time cripple, after the repositioning of the offending disc. His father had also told him of the implications of this method. He hoped this child's problem was a disc.

"You still listening to the magic flute?" Blue asked, coming to the end of his probing and manipulation. She could only give a grunt in answer as Blue gave her back two sharp taps on an offending disc.

Was it any wonder this child had suffered?

"Fine, Annabel, you have been very good. Now turn over."

Matthew, still playing the flute, had seen and marvelled at Blue's skill before, helping their traveller friends and fellow artistes, and wondered if his friend had healing powers in his hands.

Her parents watched with bated breath, as their daughter moved very cautiously, afraid the pain would strike. They waited for their daughter to scream. No sound came, as she did as she was asked.

Blue encouraged her to put her feet to the floor and held her as she took a couple of steps. The child looked from Blue to Matthew in wonder and then to her family.

"The magic flute made the little boy better?" whispered Annabel.

Blue grinned and nodded.

"Of course! He had to stay in bed for a while because he was so very weak. I think Matthew should come back and see you again, bringing the magic flute, don't you?"

Blue gently returned her to her bed.

Very quietly she said, "Yes, come again with Boy Blue and bring your lovely princess," giving Rachel a warm smile. Cautiously pulling the bedcovers over herself, she went to sleep.

Leonardo and Helen were speechless. Tears of joy ran down Helen's cheeks unchecked. Clasping Blue by the hand, she gazed into his face and whispered, "It is a miracle. How can we ever repay you?"

Blue shook his head and passed a nonsensical remark, thus bringing a very watery smile to Helen's face. Leonardo was bereft of words, totally uncharacteristic for him; he just gripped Blue's hand.

Chapter 20

After their return from London, Rachel kept her promise, and newly decorated and furnished rooms in the Hall were ready for Kate and Jacob, whose banns had been called. Kate Ellis and George Jacob were to be married at Kiddsmere Parva Church. Kate in her late fifties, had blossomed, partly due to Jacob's attention, but the other reason being that Rachel now had Matthew to help her. The more Kate saw of the young man, the more she liked and trusted him.

All outstanding debts had been met. People accepted Matthew as a friend of Miss Rachel. Kate or Matthew barely left Rachel's side, afraid for her safety.

Since Lady Eleanor Paget left the Hall 'in a great huff', nothing had been seen of Neville. An invitation from Sir Chester Peggleton for Rachel to pay him a visit had been politely refused, but an air of apprehension hung over the house.

Jacob and Kate's wedding day dawned, and still there was no sign of Neville.

With Rachel, Matthew and Blue as witnesses, and a few faithful servants present at the small Church, Reverend Clifford Dent, the Rector of Kiddsmere Parva officiating, Jacob and his beloved Kate made their marriage vows.

A special roast turkey celebration lunch had been prepared for everyone at the Hall, to which Reverend and Mrs Peake, as well as Reverend Dent and his wife had been invited.

Jacob insisted it was his duty to provide the beer, telling Matthew, "otherwise it would be said that Old Jacob was too mean to wet one's whistle, the day he got spliced!" Served in the Hall ballroom, every servant, with the exception of those preparing and serving the food, sat down to lunch.

Kate, wearing her blue velvet dress, with added contrasting cream lace trimmings, looked wonderfully happy. Cream gloves, navy straw boater hat, its cream ribbons neatly hanging over her tightly pinned hair, and to complete her ensemble a pair of serviceable black boots.

Beside her, on the table, lay a posy of cream and pink carnations, her wedding bouquet.

After the cake-cutting ceremony, Matthew, with glass in hand, stood beside them.

"Let everyone stand and raise their glass. On behalf of Miss Rachel and myself, I wish to propose a toast. Good health and longevity to Jacob and his charming wife, Kate."

Raising their glasses, all echoed Matthew's words. "Jacob and Kate."

By courtesy of Blue, the glasses had been filled with champagne.

Sporting a cream carnation in the buttonhole of his neat black suit, Jacob gave a short speech, thanking Miss Rachel and both Reverend Dent and Reverend Peake and special thanks to the two young men who had changed their lives completely and brought them such great happiness. Looking at his wife, and seeing she was shedding a tear or two, he promptly, to the amazement of everyone, produced a clean white handkerchief, and wiped and kissed her cheek.

His friends whistled and called for more as another shouted, "Hope he don't keep you awake at night, he what ya call snore!" This brought much laughter.

The newlyweds would spend a short honeymoon with Jacob's family in Norfolk. To please Matthew, Rachel agreed to stay at the rectory until their return. A truly amicable arrangement, as Marjorie Peake looked upon Rachel as a daughter.

Since their first meeting with Helen Crutch, they had visited Wethergate twice. In a day or so, they were setting off again to see Helen, this time with Francis Peake accompanying them.

He had become very interested, wishing to see the result of Blue's manipulation of Annabel's back.

Arriving at Wethergate, Helen, most pleased to see them, made them welcome. Blue noticed a great improvement as his fingers probed and massaged her child's back, trying to get unused muscles to work more freely. Francis watched, telling Blue he had a friend in college very interested in therapy.

"You two should meet sometime. He knows the method does not always get approval."

Blue nodded, saying to the child, "Your mother has been working wonders on your back, you'll be running again before Christmas!"

Helen looked much happier, even younger. Every day she gave thanks for her daughter's recovery, carrying out Blue's instructions diligently.

"Helen, would you like to come and have a holiday with us?" Rachel asked. "Jacob will fetch you and the family. We have a large garden. Perhaps it will snow soon. David and Richard would love it. Blue could carry on with Annabel's treatment."

"Are you sure? You hardly know us, Rachel." Helen looked doubtful.

Rachel held Helen's hand. "It would give me great pleasure, and I'm sure Reverend Peake will vouch for us. Come next week," she suggested, hoping Helen would agree that a short holiday would do them good. "Come to Kiddsmere, be waited upon and spoiled a little."

Finally Helen agreed, but she would wait until Leonardo came home, then Jacob could fetch them, in all about ten days, perhaps.

Back at Kiddsmere Hall, Neville tugged impatiently at a bell rope, having searched unsuccessfully for his cousin Rachel.

Myra Crispe hurried to answer the call. Of late, the running of the house had been taken from her.

"Where do I find Miss Rachel?" he snapped.

"With the Peakes."

"Have you considered my request?"

He saw her look of fear.

"No! No! I couldn't hurt that young woman!" Myra put her hands to her face. "You had best think again."

Walking towards her menacingly, he put his hands around her throat.

She struggled to free herself. Releasing her, he pulled a large bottle of liquor from his luggage, uncorked the bottle and passed it under her nose, in a tantalising gesture.

Myra Crispe grabbed at the bottle. He was too quick for her, and giving a wicked laugh, placed the bottle on a table out of her reach.

"So you must get on with it, my friend, and quickly. I'm losing my patience."

As she turned to leave, he said, "Here, take this," holding out the bottle.

Snatching the bottle from his hand, she left quickly, before his temper erupted further, making for the sanctuary of her room, his wicked laugh echoing in her ears.

Immediately after this episode with Myra Crispe, Neville went to the carpenter's shop. Seeing a caravan in near completion, he shouted at the carpenter, "What the devil are you doing? Who gave you orders to make this?"

"Mr Matthew, Sir," the carpenter answered, picking up a large hammer in readiness.

"Mr Matthew!" Neville repeated, nearly choking, his face fusing to bright red. "That travelling scoundrel!" he shouted. "I suppose Miss Rachel ordered the wood." Neville demanded, "Who's paying?"

"It is all paid for. Came special delivery. Don't know who's paid," the carpenter told him, returning to his work.

In a blinding rage, Neville made his way to the stables. He

yelled for Jacob. A young stable-lad came running towards him.

"Where is Jacob? Why isn't he here when I want him?" Neville demanded of the lad.

"He's taken Miss Kate … er … I mean his wife, Mrs Jacob, to see his family. They are due back soon, Sir. I'll get your horse ready, Sir."

Seeing Neville's face contort with anger, the lad wanted to get away from him as quickly as possible. He'd experienced the likes before. Thank goodness Neville had no whip in his hand, otherwise he would have lashed out before now.

"I don't want my horse. Look at the state of this yard, get it cleaned!" he yelled.

The lad knew the yard was immaculate. All the stable boys liked Jacob and had promised to keep everything in order while he was away. Only a bucket of water stood by the horse trough.

"Lazy lout! Do as I ask!" Still shouting, he picked up the bucket and threw it at the young boy. As luck would have it, the boy ducked and the pail missed, but the lad was drenched by the water.

Neville turned and made for the scullery. The lad, having a good idea what Neville was about to do, quickly fetched a pitchfork, shouted to his stable mates for assistance and ran towards the servants' quarters.

Hearing the shrieking from one of the maids, he knew exactly where to find the Master, and, holding the fork, advanced menacingly, demanding the girl be left alone.

Neville leered and jeered at the lad, then, seeing the other boys assembling behind him in the passageway, pushed the young, dishevelled maid away. Realising his predicament, he grabbed the girl again, using her as a shield in order to pass the angry lads. Making his escape, Neville shouted at them, "I'll sack the lot of you! No food for you today!"

He pushed the young girl into the midst of the protesting boys.

192

Continuing through the house, Neville encountered Burroughs carrying a laden tray and enquired of him where he was taking it.

The Butler told him he was going to Mrs Kate's rooms, as they were returning this evening.

"They?" asked Neville, uncouthly, still upset by his previous ordeal.

"Yes, Mr Jacob and his wife Kate. A fine couple, if I may say so, Sir."

With Neville following, the butler continued his journey. Reaching the apartment, the suite of rooms were warm and comfortable. An open fire blazed in the hearth. A posy of sweet smelling herbs awaited Kate and her husband.

Neville couldn't believe his eyes. Noisily, he opened and closed doors.

"Has my cousin Rachel gone mad? What with gypsies and servants taking over the house ..."

After depositing his tray, Burroughs said, "If you don't mind, Sir, I wish to lock this door."

"Your polite way of getting me out, eh, Burroughs? I can see I've been away too long." With this threat he left the butler to his duties.

"Not long enough!" remarked Burroughs, when Neville was out of earshot, making quite certain the door was securely locked.

When Jacob presented himself at the rectory in order to collect Rachel, he told of Neville's return, but said nothing of her cousin's set-to with the stable lads. Hearing this news, Rachel paled, saying, "Matthew must know!"

Without hesitation, Matthew said he would accompany her and Jacob home.

"My love," he comforted her as they sat together in the carriage, "Neville would not dare do anything to harm you!"

"Matthew, darling, he's a beast! You do not know him as I," she shivered.

"Be brave, my love, it will not be long before we will be together – always," he said, taking her in his arms, kissing her tenderly.

Standing, looking from his apartment window, Neville saw Rachel return with Matthew by her side. Neville cursed loudly. Then, with a shrug, he realised he could bide his time; Myra Crispe would surely act soon.

Thoughtfully, he placed another bottle of spirit on the table. Soon he would pay the housekeeper another visit.

Taking leave of Rachel, very discreetly, just before her time to retire for bed, Matthew returned to the rectory.

Kate went to Rachel's apartment as normal that same evening, collecting the tray with Rachel's nightly cup of hot milk, placing the cup beside her bed. She stayed talking happily to her for a while. After Kate left, Rachel locked her door, removing the key from the lock, having made sure Kate had her duplicate key.

Early the next morning, Kate came to Rachel's room and drew back the curtains.

"Morning, Rachel dear. You did not drink your milk!" Kate scolded, seeing the full cup of milk standing at her bedside.

"No, I quickly fell asleep, thinking of Annabel, Helen and her family, soon coming to stay with us," Rachel said with a smile. "Cook's cat can have the milk. I'll have my breeches and riding jacket, please Kate. I'm meeting Matthew this morning."

"Oh, Miss Rachel, you should wear your riding habit!" Kate retorted with admonishment. "Think of the talk in the village, those gossiping tongues!"

"You must admit, Kate, I look divine in breeches!" she tormented, jumping from her bed, eager to be away.

An hour or so later, Neville was waiting patiently in the stable yard while Jacob saddled his horse.

"Sly old chap you are, Jacob, married Kate, and didn't say a word to me," he said, giving Jacob a dig in the ribs.

"That's right, Sir, on the spur of the moment, like. Should have tied the knot before," was Jacob's amicable reply.

"I haven't seen Miss Rachel, she's well, Jacob?" Neville casually asked.

"Yes, Sir, gone riding long since. Picture of health! Ready for you now," he said, giving Neville a lift into the saddle.

Neville rode away like a madman, anger festering within his whole body. So, the old besom, crafty old devil, expected another bottle of whisky – blackmail! That's what it was, sheer blackmail! Wait until I return. Just you wait, Myra Crispe, he thought, whipping his horse furiously as he rode along.

It was mid-afternoon. Myra, in her room, stood behind the closed door. Hearing the chink of glass, she opened her door tentatively, and reached for the bottle. A hand grabbed hers. Tipping her off balance, Neville pushed his way into her room, quickly closing the door.

"So, you scum, time is short! When?" he hissed, gripping her by her hair, his other hand over her mouth to stifle her scream. "You have done nothing!"

"I have tried!" Myra gasped, tears beginning to fall.

"Don't lie to me," he said, giving her head a mighty jerk. Seizing a pair of scissors, he began cutting off large chunks of her hair close to her scalp.

"No! Oh! No!" Myra cried out, seeing locks of her long hair falling to the floor.

Releasing her, she collapsed on to the floor, sobbing, grovelling, gathering the long strands of hair together.

"Mark my words, it had better be tonight, or next time you will be shorn!" Uttering more threats and abuse, Neville left her.

It was after midnight. Kate heard Rachel's call.

"Kate! Kate!" she shouted at the top of her voice, pulling the bedside bell rope. Groaning and calling again, doubling herself in her bed as pain racked her body. Kate rushed into the bedroom, and heard Rachel say, "Kate, I feel so ill. I think

I am about to die."

Jacob, who had followed his wife, took one look at Rachel and said to Kate, "I'll go and fetch the doctor. Perhaps it is something she's eaten. Try and make her vomit."

In the darkness of the night, Jacob thought he'd never reach the rectory or the doctor in time. Shouting for one of the stable lads, they bridled two horses, one of which he would ride, the other he would leave for Matthew.

Hammering on the wagon, he shouted to them, "Rachel is very ill and I am going for the doctor."

Blue threw on his clothes, then helped Matthew to dress. Both seated on the one horse, they galloped to the Hall.

An anxious Kate met them, saying: "She only wants to sleep! Violent cramps in her stomach, Master Matthew. I've tried to make her vomit like Jacob said."

Kate hurried with them to Rachel's room.

Rachel moaned, drawing her knees to her stomach as the pain struck again.

Blue looked at the writhing girl and knew instinctively what he had to do. Racing to the kitchen, he turned up the wick of an oil lamp in order to find the large jar of mustard powder that he had seen on the shelf of the dresser.

Mixing a large quantity of mustard powder with water, he chased back to Rachel's bedside.

Slapping her cheek, almost brutally, he ordered her to drink the mixture. Blue placed his arm behind her shoulders, lifted her and poured some liquid into her mouth, pleading desperately, "Swallow! Rachel, swallow!"

She obeyed. Spluttering and gasping for breath, Blue gave her more of the liquid.

"Be ready with your basin, Kate!"

Within seconds, Rachel vomited. Blue continued the purge until he was satisfied enough had been accomplished. Rachel was on the point of collapse.

He then sent Kate to the kitchen to mix a weak solution of flour and water.

Gently, Matthew sponged Rachel's forehead, cradling her in his arms, quietly whispering words of endearment and encouragement until Kate returned.

It was his turn then to persuade Rachel to drink.

By the time the doctor arrived, the remedy that had been administered appeared to be having results.

Leaving her with the doctor and Kate, the two young men adjourned to Rachel's private sitting room.

The doctor examined Rachel while listening to Kate's account of her malaise, saying very little. Taking a small box of pills from a big bag, he gave Kate instructions of administration.

"Keep her quiet. Some very light broth later, but for now sips of water. I will call back to see you about noon," the doctor said, speaking to both Rachel and Kate. Looking at the pale, lethargic young woman, he said, "A day or so should see her about again. I need to have a word with the two young men."

In the sitting room, the doctor told them, "Just in time with your treatment, I should say, young man," looking towards Blue. "What do you think caused this? Any ideas? A real stomach upset; a touch of food poisoning, without a doubt."

"As Kate will have told you, she had eaten nothing other than that which has been prepared in the kitchen. The only thing we can think of is this milk," said Matthew, drawing his attention to the half-empty cup.

"If you are correct, this is terrible and the symptoms certainly point to a form of poisoning," the doctor stated, very concerned. "I will get this analysed."

Taking a container from his bag, he poured the milk into it, then carefully placed both cup and saucer into a paper bag.

After the doctor had left, Kate tried to remember who it was who had brought the milk. Cook would know. She would be asked first thing.

Blue wandered back to the kitchen with Jacob to make some tea.

"Jacob," Blue asked, "How did you know Kate had to make Rachel vomit?"

He replied very emphatically, "I have seen animals much the same and they purge themselves. Just came to me."

"No milk in the tea, Jacob, my friend!" said Blue, slicing a lemon.

Taking the tea back to Rachel's sitting room, Kate said to them, "I have been thinking, Blue, I went to the kitchen yesterday morning and I didn't see any sign of Cook."

"Don't worry now Kate, wait until morning." Looking towards Rachel's bedroom, Blue said, "Warm water only for Rachel to sip. Would you care to take a rest?"

Blue knew quite well it would be horses' work to drag Kate from Rachel's side.

"Thank you, but no. Rachel may want me for something, Blue dear," she said, returning to her charge.

What would folks say if they knew Miss Rachel was left unchaperoned, with two young men in her bedroom! Unheard of! But I would not be without them now! she admitted to herself. So distraught was Matthew, Kate agreed he should stay with her. The night seemed endless as they sat by the bedside. Once or twice Rachel called out in her sleep and Matthew moistened her lips, and murmured reassurance. At long last dawn began to break.

Jacob looked in, saying it was time to tend his horses and they would find fresh tea in the teapot. Blue, going with Jacob, told him he was going to the kitchen.

There he found four maids busy preparing breakfast, as well as a young man tending the giant cooking range.

"Cook not about yet?" he asked amicably.

One of the girls answered. "We haven't seen her this morning. She was unwell yesterday."

"Oh! Did she say what was wrong with her?"

"Cook thought she had caught something from her cat. He was really ill!"

"Dead, poor thing! Upset her something alarming," another young maid said, giving the explanation for Cook's absence.

This news set alarm bells ringing in Blue's mind.

"Oh, by the way, we have no fresh milk, send someone to the farm for some, please," Blue requested.

Leaving them to their work, with haste he made his way back to Kate.

"Kate, will you come with me to Cook's room. She wasn't well yesterday."

Hurrying through semi-dark passage ways, they reached her room.

Knocking on her door, Kate called, "Cook, it is Kate. Are you unwell?"

Hearing a voice from within, she tried the door. It was locked.

They waited. Then heard the turn of the key and saw a poorly looking Cook open the door.

Kate stepped inside, very concerned. "My dear, can I get you something?"

"No thanks, Kate. My stomach pains have gone. But I still feel very shaky. My poor old cat, Thomas."

Mentioning his name, she began to weep.

"I bet that keeper put some poison down. Then, I say to myself, why should I get it if it is poison? So it must be something catching, going about! I will be in the kitchen later. 'Tisn't often I am ill. Those young girls are very good."

Kate told her not to hurry back to the kitchen. She would send one of the girls with some broth and a drink.

Blue, overhearing all the conversation, said thoughtfully to Kate, "Does seem strange, doesn't it? How could she get poison from her cat, if it was poisoned?"

Like Blue, Kate had no answer.

Kate left him and made her way to the kitchen to give her orders and make a few inquiries.

"One of you," she said, speaking to the kitchen staff, "please take some broth and some tea to Cook's room. Been quite poorly, she has, poor soul. By the way, who took the milk to Miss Rachel last night?" Kate asked, in an apparently unconcerned manner, although her heartbeat had quickened considerably.

"Elsie said she was taking it," one of the girls answered.

"Where is Elsie now?" Kate asked, looking around for the girl.

"Crispey, er … Mrs Crispe wanted to see her. We haven't set eyes on her since. We don't know why she was wanted."

Seeing they were busy, Kate reminded them about Cook's broth, then thoughtfully walked upstairs to her own rooms.

When she eventually reached Rachel's room, she found the doctor had returned and was quietly talking to Blue.

As soon as he saw her, the doctor asked, "I would like to see your cook, please Kate. Will you accompany me?"

This time, the cook's door was not locked.

Kate knocked, saying, "I have brought the doctor to see you!"

Cook, who hadn't heard what Kate said, replied, "Come in my dear. Isn't she kind, Myra has just brought me some broth. 'Drink your tea while it is hot,' she said, 'It will do you good'. I was just about to have a sip."

Seeing Cook lift the cup and saucer, at that precise moment, something jogged Kate's memory. Myra! Myra Crispe brought the milk for Rachel last night.

"Don't drink it!" Kate shouted, rushing to her side. "Don't drink it!"

Alarmed, she put the cup back on the saucer, looking at Kate, wondering whatever was the matter.

"I have just remembered. It was Myra who brought the milk last night." Beginning to tremble, Kate sat herself on a chair.

Taking the cup of tea and smelling it, the doctor said, "Could be all right! But I will have it analysed."

Looking at the trembling Kate, then at the doctor, the cook asked, "Whatever is going on? What is this all about? Why are you here, Doctor?"

"We think someone tampered with Miss Rachel's bedtime milk," he explained.

In a disgruntled voice, the cook said: "I don't expect she drank it. She didn't the night before. I tasted some of it to find out if Kate had put a drop of brandy in, as I know you sometimes do if the poor girl cannot sleep," she said, looking towards Kate. "You hadn't, so I gave it to Thomas – my cat. I didn't want to make my poor old puss tipsy!"

Talking again of her cat, she stopped and began to weep.

"Thank you, Cook, I think you have given us answers to a lot of questions. Are you feeling better today?" the Doctor asked, taking her pulse.

"My stomach is much better," she said, wiping away her tears. "The pain has gone. I was very sick. Thank you, Doctor." Watching the doctor carefully remove her cup of tea, she said, "I will go to the kitchen and make myself some tea later."

With a promise to see her again, the doctor and Kate left.

In the meantime, Blue wanted to find the young maid, Elsie, wondering why she was missing. No one had seen her this morning.

He sought out Jacob at the stables, telling him the doctor had informed the Police about his suspicions. Now, a maid named Elsie was missing. Had he any idea where she could be found. Was she a lass from the village? Could she have gone home?

"Maybe one of the lads can help us," Jacob suggested, looking towards the stables.

He knew one of the lads and Elsie were courting. Calling him over, he said, "Johnson, when did you last see your Elsie?"

The young lad looked very sheepish.

Jacob assured him, "Come lad, she's done no harm. I'd

stake my life on it!"

Johnson looked at Blue.

"Old Crispey give my Elsie a minute's notice, said she's stole some soap. My Elsie'd never steal a thing!" he said, stating this fact with great conviction.

"Where is she now?" Jacob asked again.

Very reluctantly, he answered, "In the hay-loft. She'd nowhere to go."

"Good lad," Blue said, patting him on the shoulder. "Go and fetch her."

Elsie, frightened and very cold, accompanied Blue and Jacob into the warm kitchen.

Placing a chair near the stove they told her to take a seat and she was given a warm drink.

"Elsie," Blue began, "Tell us what happened last night. Don't be afraid. Just tell the truth. Did you take the milk to Miss Rachel's room?"

She looked around and began to tremble.

"No ..." she said, "Well ... I did part of the way, then Mrs Crispe took the tray from me. She was right upset. Said I wasn't to go into Miss Rachel's room because Miss Rachel had seen me steal some soap. I was to leave that very moment, without references!"

Elsie began to cry.

"I've never stolen anything! Miss Rachel's always been so good to me. That's the truth, I swear, that's the truth," she sobbed.

Jacob, putting his arm around her, tried to comfort the girl. She sobbed and sobbed, uncontrollably into his jacket. Giving her his clean handkerchief, he said, "I believe you lass, stop your crying and dry your eyes."

At that moment, Cook, neatly dressed and ready for work, walked into the kitchen and sat herself in her usual chair. Seeing a very distressed Elsie, she asked, "Whatever is the matter dear, you got stomach pains?"

Elsie shook her head, wiping her eyes.

A loud knock on the door made everyone look around.

A youngish man, dressed in a dark serge suit, stepped inside. "May I come in?"

"You're in!" snapped the Cook.

"Oh … yes … quite so. Which of you is Mr Blue?" the man asked.

As Blue moved forward, he said, "I'm Inspector Rush."

Elsie gasped, "I didn't take the soap!" then fainted.

Later, sitting quietly, sipping some water, assured by the Inspector he had not come to arrest her, Elsie was persuaded to repeat her story, which the Inspector wrote down word for word, occasionally asking questions.

He then asked to hear the Cook's story, about her cat and her own illness.

Elsie listened, unable to understand it all, especially when he advised both herself and the Cook to stay alert and prepare their own food and drink.

Afterwards, as the Inspector walked with Blue from the kitchen, he said, "Awful business this, Mr Blue. I will need the cat for a post mortem. The gardener will remember where he buried it, no doubt. Now to find Mrs Crispe and talk with her."

When asked, Burroughs, on duty by the main door, said he hadn't seen the housekeeper since breakfast. Their continued search failed to find her. Mrs Crispe was not in either of her rooms and no one had seen her for some time.

Blue looked in on Rachel. Colour had begun to return to her cheeks. She slept, with Matthew still holding her hand, dozing at her bedside. Kate, sitting in the room, quietly asked, "Is Master Neville about? Have you seen him? I've been wondering if he has had a hand in this? My Jacob heard tell, Master Neville has been in a filthy temper of late."

"Difficult to say," Blue answered in a whisper. "I'm away

to fetch Prince. Remember, the Inspector will be around for some time."

Blue followed the footpath across the grassland and over the bridge. A brisk walk would do him good. Calling at the rectory, after collecting Prince, Blue gave Mrs Peake the sordid details. The Reverend was not at home.

"Well, for anyone to do such a thing!"

She sat down, trying to digest the information. Her legs had gone weak.

"I can't believe it! Who would do such a dreadful thing?!"

"At the moment," Blue replied, "No one knows!"

Chapter 21

Inspector Rush, hidden by bushes on the edge of the shrubbery, saw a man casually walk from the cover of a clump of beech trees and make his way towards the Hall. The man had a shotgun resting on his arm and carried a brace of pheasants.

Assuming this man to be Mr Neville Coleville-Grey, the Inspector unobtrusively followed. At the game-larder beside the kitchen, he heard him shout orders to one of the backhouse boys to hang the birds, and saw him open the passageway door leading into the kitchen.

Cook, still feeling unwell, sat at the kitchen table holding a cup.

The man looked at her and said sarcastically, "Drinking our best Port?"

Giving her no chance to reply, he said to the maids preparing vegetables for lunch, "My lunch will be served in my dining room. I refuse to eat with dogs!" Neville spat out the words.

Unnoticed, the Inspector had followed him into the kitchen, so Neville was quite startled when the Inspector asked, "I believe you to be Mr Neville Coleville-Grey, am I correct?"

Neville spun round, saw the man and asked uncouthly, "Who are you? What do you want?"

"A talk with you, Sir, somewhere in private. Is your gun loaded? I am Inspector Rush." Neville broke open the gun. It was empty.

"Satisfied?" he asked, and turned to make his way to his own apartments in the east wing, followed by the Inspector.

Unlocking the door, Neville invited him inside, at the same time excusing himself for a few moments. He requested the man to take a seat then left the room.

Several minutes elapsed before Neville, in a nonchalant manner, returned to the room, bringing with him an aroma that the Inspector defined as 'alcohol'.

"Why are you here, Inspector? Something wrong? I know the servants are often up to no good, or are you looking for a plague of gypsies?!"

"Not the servants, Mr Grey, just looking for the housekeeper. She has her rooms in this wing, I believe. Gone missing, she has. Have you seen her of late?" the Inspector asked, his notebook at the ready.

Carefully, Neville thought. "Not since yesterday," he answered.

"What time would that have been?" he quizzed.

"I really cannot remember," Neville cautiously replied.

"Wouldn't have been in the evening, would it, Mr Grey?"

Quick to answer, he said, "No. Oh no, I happened to be with a friend last evening."

"Thank you, sir. That is all I want to know for the time being. You won't mind your apartments being searched? Don't leave the house, Mr Grey, I would like you to be present when the search is made. Mrs Crispe must be found."

The Inspector pocketed his book, shook Neville by the hand and quietly left.

Neville closed and locked the door behind him, wondering what had happened, if anything, to his cousin Rachel. Was she dead? Rubbing his hands together in anticipation, he began pacing the floor.

No matter what that stupid Inspector said, he thought, I must get to London and be quick about it. Plans began to form within his brain. Firstly, to know the condition of his cousin. Darkness comes early … his carriage ready … No, he must calm himself! Wait until lunch was over.

In the darkness, Neville walked from his room. Arriving in the main hallway, he was about to climb the wide staircase leading to his cousin's apartments, when, "Can I help you, Master Neville?" asked Burroughs politely, stepping from the shadows into the dimly lit hallway.

"Oh! Yes ... er ..." Neville stammered. "Is my Cousin Rachel unwell? I haven't seen her."

"Very sad. Very sad indeed, she ..." Burroughs stopped in mid-sentence, and taking his handkerchief, gave his nose a resounding blow.

Matthew, hearing voices, walked down the stairs.

"So we meet at last, Neville Grey. Cheat! Thief! Blackmailer! Possibly a murderer! I should run you through."

Matthew's voice was ice-cold, his temper blazing.

"May the Devil take you, Neville Grey!"

At first Neville was taken aback. Then he shouted at Matthew, "Oh! It is you, organ-grinder! So, I am a cheat and thief."

Neville gave a wicked laugh.

"You have room to talk. Behind my cousin's back, you are feathering your nest. A caravan in the making! Loan of horses! What else, may I ask, skunk?" Neville spat out, sneering.

"I am not afraid of you or your accusations. Go back to where you belong, with the robbers and vagabonds, before I throw you out!" Neville stepped forward.

Burroughs hastily put a restraining hand on Neville's arm. Shrugging it off, he ascended the stairs.

Matthew, too quick for Neville, kicked out with his artificial leg into Neville's stomach, sending him reeling down the steps onto the floor, gasping for breath.

"Leave him Burroughs, and fetch me a glass of water, please," said Matthew, his eyes not leaving the groaning Neville for a moment.

Taking the glass, he threw the water into Neville's face, telling him, "Get back to your own apartment, Mr Grey, and stay there."

Gingerly, Neville rose to his feet, holding his stomach. As he staggered away he swore, "I'll get you for this, impostor!"

Midnight was almost upon them. Matthew and Blue had taken turns to keep watch, but had seen no sign of movement from Neville's apartment during the evening.

Maybe they had made a mistake. Mrs Crispe was still missing. Suddenly, Blue heard a noise. Carriage wheels on the driveway, going to the east wing.

Quickly he aroused Matthew asleep beside him.

"Something is afoot."

A few moments later they heard the carriage being driven away at great speed.

Blue raced with the lighted lantern and placed it on the high wall, giving the signal, while Matthew went to awaken Jacob and Burroughs.

It was not long before the clatter of hooves and the carriage wheels warned them of the approaching posse.

Meeting Inspector Rush at the front door of the Hall, they saw Neville handcuffed to a Policeman.

Neville, making loud accusations against being detained, repeatedly swearing his innocence, while another Policeman, holding a lantern, opened the carriage door. To his surprise he found a large bundle on the floor of the carriage.

With the help of Burroughs, they carried the bundle and deposited it on the floor in the hallway.

"What on earth is it?" Blue questioned. "It looks like a body!"

A policeman unwound a long rope and turned back the large thick blanket.

"It is Mrs Crispe!" announced an amazed Jacob. "Is she dead?"

She gave a moan.

"We'll get no information from her tonight!" Inspector Rush declared with little sympathy. She has been drugged or is drunk!"

He turned to Neville, pointing a finger at him.

"You, Neville Coleville-Grey, are under arrest for attempted murder, also with the abduction of this woman, possibly against her will."

"You've no proof!" Neville jeered.

The Inspector, taking no notice of him, ordered, "Take them away to the town gaol. You will have to watch him, 'tis said he has a vicious temper!"

Mrs Crispe, moaning and groaning, was lifted into the Black Maria.

"She will be taken care of tonight. We will get a statement from her after she has sobered up, if that is the case."

Bidding them 'adieu', the Inspector and his troupe set off for the town.

"Stone-the-Crows!" said Matthew. "What we all need is a stiff drink. Burroughs!"

Chapter 22

News soon spread of the dreadful happenings at the Hall and the village was alive with gossip for days. Many villagers said Master Neville had received his just desserts, but wondered what would happen to the estate.

Thankfully, Rachel was making a good recovery, albeit slowly, but, with Matthew by her side and her strong will, she should soon be up and about again.

Inspector Rush had given them the assurance that Neville and his accomplice, Mrs Crispe, were the culprits. Mrs Crispe had confessed.

With Helen and her family due to arrive in a few days, having decided Rachel was well enough to have guests, the servants prepared Rachel's old playroom and rooms in readiness.

Rachel was looking forward to their visit, it would help to take her mind off 'her brush with death' as she referred to the horror she had endured.

Upon their arrival, Helen and her children found Rachel's home awe-inspiring, but the children soon lost their shyness, investigating nooks and crannies, talking to everyone they met.

The big house soon became full of laughter and happiness, helping Rachel to put her traumatic experience to the back of her mind, assured that Neville would stay locked away.

Excitedly, she began counting the days to her wedding day.

A quiet wedding ceremony at Kiddsmere Church, followed by a grand feast in her large ballroom, for her staff, tenant farmers and the village folk, was all she asked, and Matthew was in agreement.

Reverend and Mrs Peake, as well as the Dents, Mr Clinton and one or two other local dignitaries who had been friends in the past, would partake of a private lunch in the dining room immediately after the wedding ceremony.

Leonardo, Helen and their children would return to the Hall on Christmas Eve and stay for a few days, as Annabel had agreed to be Rachel's bridesmaid.

Annabel's improvement in health was remarkable. Blue was her 'Knight in shining armour', with her following him around, even learning to juggle.

The day came for Helen's return to Wethergate.

"Time has passed so quickly. It is hardly worth your while going home, Helen, you'll return again soon," Rachel said, watching her pack their few belongings.

"And I shall miss you! You and the children have been a great help to me after my ordeal."

"Dear Rachel, thank you, it has been wonderful, but I promised to be there when my Leonardo returns home!" Helen told her shyly.

A quietness descended over the Hall again after the departure of Helen and her children. Feeling much better, Rachel made her usual tryst for their ride and breakfast with her beloved and Blue. The Peakes were delighted to see her.

Days passed quickly, with everyone busy making preparations for a large party. Kate had informed the staff to prepare for a 'large celebration party', with no mention of a wedding, leaving everyone to think the dismissal of Neville was the cause to celebrate. Walking in the garden, talking of their forthcoming wedding, Rachel said, sympathetically, "I feel so sad for you, Matthew, dearest, no family, no one but Blue to give you support on our important day."

"Trust me my love, when you meet my family, we'll have a most wonderful celebration!" Matthew told her.

Although Rachel was well wrapped in a fur coat, protectively he guided her towards an arbour, away from the chill wind. Pale sunshine filtered through the bare branches of a climbing rose, and winter jasmine flowered in the shelter of the arbour woodwork.

"You tell me so little about your family or home, Matthew, will they like me, do you think?" she asked nestling close to him.

"They will love you, my darling!" he said, placing a finger under her chin, "but not as much as I love you, and to think I almost lost you!"

Turning her beautiful face towards his, he covered her lips with his in a long and passionate kiss.

At lunchtime on Christmas Eve, Leonardo, Helen and their family arrived by carriage from Wethergate. Jacob and a stable lad had driven to fetch them.

Giant logs of burning wood filled the large fireplace in the entrance hall, sending out a most welcome warmth.

The frost outside had set in with a vengeance. Red-berried holly and sprigs of mistletoe hung from the ceiling and red candles stood in lanterns, waiting to be lit.

The excited children didn't hesitate, but darted off in the direction of the kitchen to see Cook, with whom they had made a great friend on their previous visit.

They found her busy with her helpers, making pies and spiced buns, a thick soup and savouries, in readiness, she told them, for the carol singers, who regularly called on Christmas Eve.

After lunch, Helen's two boys eagerly explored Rachel's extensive garden, climbing among the branches of the gigantic oak and cedar trees, swinging on low, curved branches, until darkness forced them indoors.

After an early supper, Rachel and her guests were joined by twenty or so carol singers.

The singers from the two parishes had amalgamated to enjoy the fun and food provided. Listening and singing, at the end, Rachel helped to distribute the hot soup, mince pies and all the goodies made by the Cook.

Francis and his wife, as well as Reverend and Mrs Dent, were delighted Rachel had asked the carol singers into the large hall to sing their carols. Master Neville always made them stand outside, whatever the weather.

A real English Christmas was a new experience for both Blue and Matthew. Back home the weather was warm, hot even. Last Christmas-tide they spent on the edge of a very large forest. Now, here they were in this beautiful old mansion, enjoying every moment. Fate had sure dealt them a good hand!

Drawing Matthew to her side and holding him by the hand, Rachel announced proudly to the gathering of singers, "This young man, Matthew Dere, will become my husband soon. We plan to marry, by Special Licence, at Kiddsmere Parish Church on Boxing Day."

No one dared to speak, it had come as a great shock, until an elderly gentleman stepped forward, wishing them, "Good Luck! Good Health! May all your troubles be little ones!" said with a twinkle in his eye.

A chorus of best wishes followed, taking great note of Matthew's colourful attire and his handicap, no doubt, to be discussed in great detail with friends and associates at the earliest possible moment.

The Church service on Christmas morning, always well attended, saw the Hall pew full of unknown folk; at least, to the locals, they were unknown.

Reverend Peake ended his sermon with the usual blessing and then to the amazement of the congregation issued an invitation.

"On behalf of Mr Matthew Dere and Miss Rachel Coleville-Grey, for those in the two villages to come and enjoy 'Afternoon Tea' at four pm, at the Hall, tomorrow, the 26th December, in celebration of their marriage that very same day."

Reverend Peake smiled at Rachel and her guests. A complete hush followed, until the organist began to play.

Together, Rachel, Matthew and Reverend Peake walked

with their friends down the aisle.

After their light lunch, Leonardo offered his arm to his wife, suggesting a quick stroll in the garden, "If Rachel and her friends will excuse us?" he asked politely.

Helen looked very trim and neat, dressed in her grey taffeta gown, her husband's Christmas gift. A wide, grey belt with silver clasps, encircled her slim waist.

Rachel watched as Helen draped a large, thick, black woollen shawl over her head and shoulders.

Tomorrow, Helen's wish would come true, for underneath the green tree in the hall, in a pretty wrapper, along with other parcels, for each and every one, was a black, astrakhan cloak, a gift to her from Blue, Matthew and herself, after Helen once confided to Rachel her dream of owning such a cloak.

Tomorrow! Her own wedding day. Rachel's heart gave a leap, and excitement bubbled as she looked across the room in Matthew's direction. Their eyes met and he smiled. The evening meal. Roast turkey and all the trimmings, plum pudding and rich sauce, mince pies and a variety of cheeses, turned out to be one of the happiest and most enjoyable Rachel and Kate could remember. Especially for Kate, with Jacob by her side.

Referring to his surprise announcement that morning in Church, "As one would expect, one could have heard a pin drop in the Church, such was the silence," Francis said after he and his wife had joined Rachel and her friends at the Hall for Christmas dinner, that evening.

"You will have a great number attend, my dear, I hope you are well prepared!"

Rachel assured him they were. Chairs and benches had been acquired and the amount of food tremendous!

Since Mrs Crispe's arrest, Kate had taken over the running of the house, much to the delight of everyone, pleasing Cook enormously, practically giving her a free hand when ordering supplies.

Sitting around the dining table, Leonardo began relating some laughable happenings from his experiences in the Music Halls.

He told of the time when he had not completely extinguished one of his cigars which he had placed in his back pocket. Warmth began penetrating his flesh, so he sat and rocked back and forth, much to the amusement of the audience.

Having seen his act, Kate and Jacob laughed until tears rolled down their cheeks.

"No laughing matter, at the time," Leonardo told everyone. More of his tales and the manner in which he told them, had everyone in fits of laughter, including the Rector and his wife.

His children begged for more stories, but with a smile, he told them he had talked far too much and it was Matthew's turn to entertain. Matthew suggested they retire to the drawing room for more comfort, offering his arm to escort Rachel.

Blue noticed the wince of pain Matthew gave as he vacated his chair. He had seen and dressed the abrasion on Matthew's leg, but the leg iron appeared twisted somewhat, from his encounter with Neville on the stairway, no doubt.

Francis Peake had been told of this and was also concerned.

Blue asked Francis if he had heard if the young doctor friend of his from Addenbridge studying limb replacement, had obtained the position he so desired at Cambsworth hospital.

"Yes, I should have told you, but I have been so busy delivering the Christmas sausages to the widows and widowers on the Charity list, I forgot. I received news from him yesterday. He is ecstatic and has invited us to visit him in the New Year. I believe I mentioned I knew his father very well. A clever man. This son takes after him!"

Blue and Francis, when entering the drawing room, saw Matthew preparing to play music on his accordion for pass the parcel with Annabel and the two boys. One would think he had no care in the world. Prince lay stretched out in front of the glowing fire. Blue fondled his ears.

Music and laughter filled the room as the large parcel revealed forfeits and small presents. The children, not having experienced the like before, enjoyed the forfeits, especially those to be performed by the adults. Pulling funny faces at people was no problem for Blue, he caused much hilarity. Sing a song. Say a nursery rhyme. Hop on one leg. So many, Mrs Peake was reminded of her two boys and the pleasure they had had with this simple game. Sadly it became time for departure, Blue and Matthew escorting the Peakes to the rectory.

"'Till tomorrow, my love," Matthew said, bestowing a kiss on Rachel's cheek. "Take care of her, Kate."

The morning of Boxing Day dawned clear but very cold. Clinton Howard arrived at the Hall early, after spending Christmas Day with friends in the nearby town.

Readily attired in his morning suit, a grey top hat and sporting a gold pocket watch across his gold silk waistcoat, with a white, winged-collared shirt, decorated at the neck by a pale green silk cravat, he was almost unrecognisable. He had agreed to act as a father figure in the wedding ceremony, by giving Rachel away.

Reverend Peake would have liked that honour, but considered it his duty, and a great pleasure, to perform the wedding service.

At precisely 12 noon, in brilliant sunshine, Clinton Howard, Rachel and her bridesmaid, Annabel, stepped from their carriage at the main church gate to make their way to the church.

A few of her close friends and associates awaited her arrival. The bridegroom and his best man had arrived very early. Matthew, full of nervous energy, had arisen at an unearthly hour, attended to the horse and set the fire going. To the crescendo of organ music, wearing a white fur cape over her diamanté studded, long cream silk dress, a short veil held in place by her late mother's tiara, on the arm of Clinton, Rachel

216

walked towards her husband to be, looking a picture of beauty and happiness. In this magnificent church, they solemnly made their wedding vows. An east wind carried the sound of the merry peal of bells over the frozen lake towards the Hall, declaring the wedding ceremony over, and the village now had a new Lord of the Manor.

The leader of those bells was a delighted Olly, now recovered and hopeful of a better standard of living, having had many happy encounters with Blue and Matthew.

Chapter 23

The procession of carriages had left the main gate, duly making their way to the Hall. A group of onlookers of various shapes and sizes, some elderly and gaunt, others plump and in their prime, each wearing what one would term their 'Best' clothes, were all in deep discussion and giving their personal opinion of the event. Gossip, in abundance, had been circulating the tiny village for some time, no one believing Miss Rachel would consider marrying a travelling minstrel.

Now before their very eyes, with a special licence, she had married her 'Matthew Dear', as she always referred to him.

"A white fur cape and her long cream silk dress trimmed with fur, jewels and lace! My! Didn't she look a picture!"

"Her bouquet of carnations came from their hot house. That old, bearded man beside her was Mr Howard. He looked smart. He came all the way from London."

"That little kid, her bridesmaid, didn't look a strong one. Warm and pretty in velvet. Like a forget-me-not, with her pink carnations, blue cloak, dress and bonnet."

Two women standing by the church gate continued their discussion.

"Whatever did you think to the way her fellow got himself up?"

"Long blue jacket, trousers all tight around his legs, gold braid tied on here and there and a blue silk shirt. Fancy! Even the dog had a collar of frills, and a hat!"

"A hat!" one of the women repeated, astounded. "What her old grandfather would have said, I just don't know! Still, time will tell. Not all that good, you know, her marrying a cripple. But I did hear say, she plans to go about with him in his caravan, just like the gypsy he is. He's feathered his nest all right! Mustn't stay talking any longer. Should be a good do this afternoon up there. Better be early to get a seat!"

The plumper of the two ladies stepped back a pace, treading on the toes of a young fellow who had been busy with pencil and notepad, unobtrusively eavesdropping.

"You should look where you're going!" she accused him angrily. "Could have had me over!"

The young man, with a pained expression on his face, hopping on one foot, doffed his cap in apology.

Leaving him, the two women departed, joining another group of people further along the road, undoubtedly to exchange more items of gossip.

In the first of the procession of carriages were Matthew and Rachel.

"My most beautiful, adorable bride, my darling wife!" Matthew tenderly gathered her into his arms, his lips seeking hers and her returning his kiss. "I will love you forever."

Blue, his wagon decorated with ribbons and accompanied by the Crutch family, who had insisted upon travelling in his vehicle, arrived at the Hall in time to see Matthew gather his wife into his arms and carry her over the threshold.

Servants, neatly dressed in their best uniforms, were on hand to administer to the few chosen guests, with Burroughs as Chief in Charge. Gradually the guests arrived. Kate, because Jacob was driving the happy newlyweds, had arrived with the Peakes. Champagne and caviar was offered and soon the Hall was filled with happy people. Rachel had sent invitations to her tenant farmers and their families.

To Captain and Mrs Long, Admiral Bourton and his wife Lady Amelia, great friends of Clinton Howard. Of course the Reverend and Mrs Peake, and also Reverend and Mrs Dent, very good friends of Kate.

All the guests, now gathered in the warm drawing room,

were very pleased to see Rachel and her husband so happy.

The children had been delegated to the large nursery, where a luncheon table had been prepared especially for them, supervised by Annabel's favourite servant and friend, Elsie.

Burroughs announced lunch. Matthew led his wife and guests into the dining room. The room had been beautifully decorated with flowers. On a side table stood a large, iced wedding cake, its pink and silver trimmings blending with arrangements of fresh pink carnations and trailing fern, which cascaded down each corner of the white lace table covering. More pink carnations and fern, grown in the Hall's own carnation house, graced an impeccably laid dining table, matching the neatly arranged pink table napkins.

Before Matthew could take his place at the table, Burroughs approached him, bearing a tray on which lay a printed card.

Matthew read the card, dropping it back on the tray, saying, "Send him away. No newspaper correspondent! Thank you Burroughs."

No one at the table felt ill at ease for long, as Leonardo, with great wit, proposed a toast to the happy couple, as well as to Kate, setting general conversation in motion after Matthew laughingly told him that the toast came at the end of the meal.

"Ah! But I like toast with my soup, don't I, Helen?" Leonardo answered, laughing. The banquet continued happily, as each course was served. Soup, salmon, beef, game and turkey, accompanied by numerous vegetables and sauces, this followed by a selection of delicious puddings, jellies, creams and meringues.

Cook and her staff had excelled themselves.

Lady Amelia Bourton, with a very astute mind and train of thought, watched the two young gentlemen who had taken the village as if by storm; one capturing the heart of the owner of the estate. Both had impeccable manners, she noticed and were quite appreciative of her husband's and her gift of caviar, a luxury of which both had knowledge, mentioning a friend known to them as Freddie and his acquisition of luxurious delicacies.

Foolish clowns they may be, but hidden depths beneath their glamorous attire made one wonder and sincerely hope dear Rachel had not been duped. She guessed Francis knew more about those two young gents than he cared to admit, being very cautious when questioned, with no enlightenment as to their nationality or circumstances. Discretion was second nature in his position as a confidant, no doubt.

One might expect Kate to be included at the table, but not Jacob. Poor Kate had tried very hard to chaperone a strong-willed Rachel. To slip away for a clandestine meeting in the garden, or a pretext visit to one's hostess' room was one thing, but to let her ride hither and thither with her beau!! Whatever was the world coming to?

Anyway, both tenant farmers, Gerald, George and their wives, declared their lives had become worth living again, since Neville's departure.

I will score a first, I'm sure, when visiting friends, to tell them, 'Taken along to the Wedding Ceremony and celebration luncheon and a place in front of the dining room fire – a dog! Yes! A dog!'

The only person who appears to be out of her depth is the lady named Helen. But she is rather sweet.

So lost was she in her melee of thought, Captain Long, sitting next to her, gave her a prod and asked her again, "When will the Admiral join his ship?"

"Oh! In a few weeks," she replied.

Later in the large ballroom, the villagers began to assemble. Some had walked, others conveyed on farm wagons or carrier cart. It would be dark when they returned home, so they had arranged their transport accordingly.

Long trestle tables, covered in white damask cloths, were piled high with ham- and turkey-filled sandwiches, small beef pasties and pork pies, slices of cheese and twists of bread. Chocolate and pink iced fancies, jam and lemon tarts, mince pies and currant buns. A large tea urn, surrounded by cups and saucers, stood ready and waiting.

A smiling Francis Peake greeted them on behalf of their host and hostess and told them that they would join them after tea. With no more ado, he said a prayer, letting the feast begin. Looking around, he would hazard a guess to be well over a hundred folk present. Cups of tea washed down the numerous savouries and sandwiches, followed by the cakes and slices of rich, plum cake. Finally came dishes of red and yellow jelly, topped with delicious cream.

Happy faces turned towards the door as Matthew and his bride entered. Many stood to welcome them, while others sat clapping. After a short speech of greeting by Matthew, he then suggested they made a space for dancing. In no time at all the tables were moved to one side and a large screen was removed from a corner, revealing two pins of ale.

Matthew, never without his flute, and remembering the happy 'hawkey', began to play. First the clog-dancer with his ladyfriend took centre stage, then an elderly man asked Rachel to join him. Gathering the long skirt of her wedding gown, she smiled and hopped from one foot to the other in tune, while her partner shook and tapped his feet in rhythm, noisily snapping the hobnails in the soles of his boots on the wooden floor.

Glasses were re-filled, amidst much laughter and merry-making as Matthew played his accordion. Folk danced while others sang and the afternoon soon became evening.

Children raced happily, mingling with the dancers.

Discreetly, Burroughs informed Matthew that some of their personal guests were ready to leave and that Reverend Peake wished to speak.

With a nod of agreement to the butler, Matthew said, raising his glass, "To absent friends and loved ones." Then he played his favourite piece – Madame Clare's lullaby – now happily assured his loved one was by his side.

With his arm encircling his wife's waist, Matthew and Rachel listened as Francis thanked them, on behalf of all those present, for this wonderful celebration of their wedding.

The clog-dancer jumped onto one of the tables, and, before the Rector could finish his speech, at the top of his voice shouted, "Long may they live!"

Raising his tankard, he said, "The best we've known in this here Hall. Good luck, young fella! Take good care of her!"

Encouraged by a chorus of good wishes and whistles, Matthew acknowledged their sentiments by giving Rachel a resounding kiss, bringing blushes to her cheeks.

With great regret, the happy couple left the merry-making, which would continue for another hour or two.

Mr Howard, now returning to his friends in town for a few days, said to Rachel, "Before I return to London, we must talk about a new agent, now that rogue cousin of yours is in custody. I understand from your … husband," Clinton Howard cleared his throat, "You are both staying here until this inclement weather departs."

He peered over his glasses at this beautiful young woman, wondering if she had the stamina for 'living under the stars', so to speak.

Taking a letter from his pocket, he handed it to Rachel, saying, "From your friend, Lady Pearl Drinkstone. Rather worried. Got in touch with me. Has not seen you all season."

"I did not have to go to the ball, Clinton, I found my darling Prince Charming here on my doorstep," Rachel told him happily, hugging Matthew's arm as he stood close at her side.

"I wish you a fond adieu and will see you again in a few days' time. Burroughs has signalled my carriage awaits."

Most of their guests had gone. Leonardo and Helen had also taken their leave, going with their children to their suite of rooms. Only the Reverend and Mrs Peake and Blue remained. Blue looked lost and forlorn. Only then did he realise his life would never be the same again.

Francis had seen that look of dismay on Blue's face, so after saying farewell to his host and hostess, calmly said to Blue, "Care to come to the rectory? I have something to discuss with you, Blue. About the future."

"Your eyes miss nothing, Sir. Feeling sorry for myself, Francis. Mind you, I'm sure pleased for Matthew," Blue said, snapping the lead clasp on to Prince's collar. Turning to Matthew and Rachel, he said, "I guess I'll have no takers for tucker at sun-up!" giving his friend a slap on the back and Rachel a kiss.

Strange thing, emotion, thought Francis, as this was the first time he had noticed Blue's Australian accent.

Chapter 24

Days lengthen and the cold strengthens. An age-old adage proved true. Blizzards raged and frost seemed to penetrate to the marrow.

Much of Blue's time was spent with Francis at the rectory, helping to administer to the sick, who invariably found the vicar's remedy for ailments less costly than from the doctor.

A young mother, holding her small son on her lap, had come to Francis for advice.

"Rickets," diagnosed the vicar, shaking his head. Blue, also in the room, saw for himself the condition of the child's wizened, misshapen legs and listened as the rector told her to go to the Hall and buy two pen'eth of dripping to mix with her son's vegetables. The rector, seeing a look of consternation on her face, delved into his own pocket and gave the woman two pennies.

With thanks, she bade them a 'good-day' and set off towards the Big House. Francis sighed heavily; that child had a mother to care for it and was in some ways blessed. Turning to the many afflictions suffered by the children resident in the gaunt orphanage attached to the Cambsworth Hospital, his heart bled for them in their situation. Their need for food and clothing. Having received a plea for help, the rector decided to pass the letter to Blue.

"You know, Francis," he said after reading the letter, "My wish has always been to travel and make those I meet laugh, using my foolery and other gifts given to me. I would dearly love to help the children. For the past weeks I have been lost, whiling away my time until we move on."

Blue smiled. "You have suddenly lifted a weight from my shoulders. Your faith, Francis, moves mountains! How far is it? When shall we go? Next week?" he asked, picking two paper-weights from the desk and beginning to juggle.

When told of the impending visit to Cambsworth, Rachel immediately offered the use of their carriage and Jacob as driver. A distance of some thirty miles or so, after an early start, they could reach their destination before nightfall. But an overnight rest might be inevitable. Much depended on the weather.

Francis, eagerly looking forward to a short break, began asking those he thought might have a little something to spare, like soap, clothes and food, which he thought would be useful in the children's home.

By the time he and Blue were ready to leave, and with the generosity of many people, an enormous pile of garments and a few luxuries had been forthcoming.

The Reverend and Blue, well pleased, loaded the carriage.

Prince, who had taken kindly to the luxury of a warm rug by the rectory fireside, sensed something different this morning and moved close to his master's feet. Blue absentmindedly stroked the dog's head as they sat in the breakfast room, waiting for the arrival of Jacob and the carriage, and for Francis to finish his cup of tea.

This morning they were setting off to Cambsworth.

The morning was cold and dark. Later, Blue noticed the hoar frost upon the hedgerows. Lacy cobwebs clung to the seared and bent stems of bracken and cow parsley. Oak and elm trees stood bare and sinister, as patches of freezing fog drifted and swirled, breaking occasionally, letting through a patch of blue sky, as their carriage rolled along the turnpike. Not a very good journey at all.

Over half the journey completed, Jacob called his horses to a halt outside a tavern. A burly man, wearing an apron over his clothes, came out of the tavern doorway, calling to another person to come and assist the travellers, after recognising Jacob as one of his regular customers.

"Hare and Hounds. Finest Ales," Francis read aloud as his carriage door was opened by the man wearing the apron.

"Pleased to meet you Reverend, Sir," he said, noticing Francis' ecclesiastical attire. "I keep a good, clean, honest house, if I may say so, Sir … er … Reverend," said the Innkeeper, doffing his bowler hat.

"I am sure you do! Otherwise our good man would not have called here!"

Francis stepped down and followed the man, Blue and Prince beside him, leaving Jacob in charge of the laden carriage and horses.

Within the tavern, in an enormous inglenook fireplace, a fire burned brightly. The room was comfortably warm. A large ham hung from a long chain and hook in the chimney-piece and attached to the bress 'ummer, a copper hunting horn, in need of cleaning. Pictures of red coated huntsmen in precarious positions on and off their sturdy steeds, surrounded by packs of opened mouthed hounds, gave colour and life to the walls of the large, dark, oak-beamed room. A stuffed fox in a glass case, its mouth open wide displaying a set of strong, white teeth, had pride of place on a window ledge.

A noisy group of men, seated around a wooden table enjoying ale and thumb-pieces of bread and cheese, suddenly stopped their noise to observe the odd couple who had just entered, one giving the appearance of a gypsy, the other, a vicar in clerical attire. The latter quickly making for the fire to warm his posterior.

Eventually, after passing a few crude remarks, the men continued eating and making noisy conversation.

Blue ordered a warming meal for three, and, to the surprise of Francis, a jug of mead.

Prince, sitting quietly on the clean sawdust-covered floor, watched a man from the group walk over to the bright fire, kick a piece of wood with his booted foot, sending a meridian of sparks up the chimney, then take an iron poker and thrust it in the red-hot ashes. A moment or two passed, after which he removed the poker from the fire and plunged it into his tankard of ale.

The hissing sound brought Prince quickly to his feet. Walking on hind legs, he peered inquisitively into a basket of firewood. Curiosity satisfied, lowered himself, using his two front feet only, he walked back to Blue, back legs held high in the air.

"What's up, Jabez?" asked his companion, seeing him with his mouth wide open and speechless, his ale cooling.

"What made him do that?" the man named Jabez asked of Blue.

"Once he worked with a snake charmer. My dog, Prince, never forgets a trick."

Another asked, "Oh! Does he know any more tricks?"

"Yes," replied Blue.

One portly gentleman, getting to his feet rather unsteadily, said, "Bet he can't stand on his head and waggle his tail!" He turned, sniggering, to his mates.

"What's your wager?" Blue asked in all innocence. Jacob, who had by now joined them and Francis, sat silent.

"A golden guinea," the man said with bravado. Pulling a long-john from his pocket, he placed a coin on the table in front of him. "Bet you haven't got a coin to match it, by the looks of you!"

Laughing, Blue replied, not even attempting to put his hand in his own pocket, "What! Another wager, good sir."

"Yeah!" the befuddled man answered. "Yeah!" placing another gold coin beside the first. "Now, show us the colour of your money – what's your name?"

At that moment, the Landlord entered, carrying a large tray full of steaming hot meat and vegetables.

"Ah! Landlord! Will you hold the golden purse for us?" Blue asked, relieving him of the laden tray and putting it on the table in front of Francis and Jacob.

"Of course I will," he said, then asked, "What's old Roger up to now? His usual tricks?"

"No! 'tis that dog yonder who's to do the tricks!" They all laughed.

"If it can!" said another, pointing to Prince.

Quickly, Blue picked up the two coins from the table, showed the gambler his own gold coin, saying, "That one is mine!" and gave only two coins to the Innkeeper to hold and called Prince to come forward.

Blue, taking a small ball of wool from his pocket, commanded the dog to stand head down and hind legs uppermost. He placed the wool on the dog's tail, and quick as lightning, Prince flicked his tail and caught the ball between his teeth, laying it at his master's feet.

"Good boy! Good boy! I keep the gold, my friend? Satisfied? We are truly thankful for your generosity, are we not, Vicar?"

Blue handed Prince his usual sweet meat.

Blue, giving Francis no chance to say anything, said, "We must not linger, our food will cool and daylight will soon be fading. We have a journey to complete."

Picking a large slice of meat and bone from his plate, he gave it to Prince.

The gambling man made his way towards the outer door, asking as he went, "Want to sell him for a guinea or two?" pointing to the dog.

"Not so likely, my good man. Earn us many a dinner, does he not, Reverend?" Blue said, looking towards his friend for approval.

But Francis sat with eyes tightly closed, hands clasped together in a moment of prayer. Well refreshed, the remainder of the journey proved uneventful, arriving at the grey stone orphanage just before dark.

An odd gas street lamp or two gave enough light to see the wrought iron gates of the Home, where the gatekeeper, an elderly man, enquired of their names.

Francis answered.

Recognising his voice and name, the gatekeeper immediately unlocked the gates, letting the carriage and horses into the courtyard.

Chapter 25

Inside the Orphanage, Blue again became aware of the aroma of stale food, reminding him of the airless, underground kitchens at Kiddsmere. It was nauseating.

A few lighted candles flickered in iron holders attached to the walls, giving the minimum of light, showing them a long, cold passage to a dowdy sitting room.

There they found Mrs Lily Cook, whom Francis introduced as the Matron in charge of the orphanage.

Lily Cook was a thin middle-aged woman, dressed in a long black afternoon dress of taffeta, causing her very pale face to look ghost-like. Her dark, brown hair, with a centre parting, was worn cartwheel fashion and pinned over each ear, making her appear a severe, formidable person. On a chain around her waist, numerous keys jangled as she moved forward to greet them, expressing pleasure on his arrival, saying, "Francis Peake! So good and kind of you to visit us!"

Turning to Blue, she said, "You must be Blue, the young person of whom Francis wrote. Come along in and join me for some tea."

Her looks belie her warmth, thought Blue.

Listening, as Francis outlined his plans to Mrs Cook, Blue heard him tell they were lodging for the next day or so, with his doctor friend in the adjoining hospital. He was expecting them. The Rector then asked if the young orphan lad, of whom he had met and spoken to on his earlier visit, would be ready to accompany them to the Blacksmith at Kiddsmere.

Blue learned that Sam the village Smith had offered to take a young lad and train him in his trade. The lad would sleep over the traverse in the Smithy and light the fire early morning, in readiness for the Blacksmith to commence work.

The boy would be well cared for by the Smith's wife, and given the opportunity to start a new life. From what Blue could make out, Francis often found workplaces for the stronger boys from the orphanage. Some were very happy in their newly-found lodgings, enjoying a certain amount of freedom, whilst others, unable to settle, returned to the orphanage until a suitable place was found. It depended greatly on the family to whom they were billeted and their kindness.

Leaving the Matron to her duties and with thanks for the tea and scones, Francis and Blue walked through more dim, musty, passageways leading to the hospital.

Looking through an open doorway, Blue noticed rows of iron bedsteads. He hesitated. Francis took hold of his arm and said, "Tomorrow."

Cold, refreshing night air greeted them when they opened the outer door and crossed to where the doctor's quarters were situated.

Jacob, with Prince beside him, let them in, saying, "The carriage has been unloaded. The young doctor will not be away long, says I'm to show you to your room."

Blue noticed a table had been set for supper and a fire burned brightly in the grate. Following Jacob and Francis up the narrow, stone stairway, he wondered for what purpose these buildings had been built. A monastery, perhaps, taking note of the small solid iron-studded doors, set in thick walls of stone blocks. All very old.

The door that Jacob opened from the landing led into a surprisingly large room. An oil lamp burned quite brightly, showing two iron bedsteads and neatly made beds. Three wooden chairs, a laboriously carved, marble washstand, complete with a large white china basin and copper water jug.

Jacob had brought their few belongings to the room earlier, and these he had arranged on a wooden table. Jacob's lodgings were elsewhere.

Blue sat himself on the edge of one of the beds and watched Francis remove his leather boots, and, with immense pleasure, push his feet into his well-worn slippers. Hardly had they cleaned themselves when Jacob knocked on the door, telling them the Doctor had returned.

Doctor Joshua Stone, a young man, greeted Francis with great affection.

They knew each other well. Joshua sported a very curly black beard and had thick black hair. Painfully thin and very tall, Blue thought as he shook hands with him, a good meal would do him good. His dark suit, almost threadbare, matched a frayed shirt and well-worn shoes, but he was jolly, with an impish grin and twinkling eyes.

A steaming jug of cocoa stood on the supper table, and next to it a vegetable tureen and a plate with three thinly sliced pieces of cold meat.

Joshua poured the cocoa into three beakers, telling his guests to be seated and help themselves.

Lifting the lid off the tureen, they found a mound of small potatoes, boiled in their skins, as well as sliced carrots. The vegetables were lukewarm, but edible.

Hospital talk dominated the conversation, and, as Blue listened, he realised Francis relied on young doctors to keep him up to date with new medicines.

Deliberately, Francis turned the discussion to the subject of bones and muscles, drawing Blue into the conversation, who could then tell how his father taught him various techniques of joint manipulation.

"But," Blue advised them, "I am a clown, not a doctor!"

So, the evening turned into early morning, which no one noticed, until Prince, sitting by the now empty fire-grate, whimpered. Blue gave him a large, hard square biscuit, promising a walk shortly.

After a comfortable night and a large plate of porridge for breakfast, Blue walked to where, the previous evening, he had seen the long room and rows of beds.

He took the liberty of entering. The walls were white-washed. Small Gothic-type windows were set high up in the walls, thus one could not see out or in. Beds, with meagre coverings, but spotlessly clean, held children of all ages.

On their knees, women of varying ages and sizes, were scrubbing the stone floor, carefully mopping up the excess water, while a few nurses scurried to and fro, in an attempt to quieten some of the crying children.

Blue watched the busy scene as Joshua and a companion moved from bed to bed.

"Wish we had more money for medicine and equipment, even bandages." Joshua's words of the previous night came to his mind. Here he saw the reason why.

For some of the children any remedy would be too late, but it would help to relieve their suffering. Disease-riddled bodies, misshapen limbs, Blue's gaze rested on the children woefully. Unable to endure the scene any longer, turning on his heel, he left. A walk was called for, so, collecting Prince, they made for Cambsworth Town Centre. This morning the fog had lifted somewhat, and had been replaced by a very chill wind. They wandered along the pavement towards the market place, occasionally stopping to glance in a shop window or doorway.

Noticing a heap of newspapers inside the Telegraph Office, he decided to step inside. More papers covered a table and a wooden bench, encouraging people to sit and read or buy. A man behind a wire grill at the counter took little notice when Blue selected a paper and began reading.

"Vagabond feathers his nest while cousin is in prison," he read. "The cousin, manager of a large estate at Kiddsmere, Suffolk, is imprisoned under suspicious circumstances, along with the Housekeeper of the Hall.

"The housekeeper has admitted that she was forced to obey him to commit murder. Fortunately for the housekeeper, the Owner of the Hall, Miss Rachel Coleville-Grey, survived the ordeal."

Blue looked at the date on the paper, took it across to the shopkeeper and asked if he could purchase it.

"Yes. Fine. It is an old one! Cost you a half penny."

Blue paid the man then hurried back to find Francis. He was in Joshua's living room. Francis read the report, which also included details of the marriage of Rachel and Matthew, last December.

"As you know, Matthew is not a vagabond out to feather his nest," Blue protested, when Francis had finished reading. "How on earth did that paper get hold of those details?" Blue wanted to know.

Francis sat and thought for a moment.

"Maybe Sir Chester Peggleton had a hand in it. He desperately wanted Rachel for his wife. I believe he offered surety for Neville. Could be jealousy or spite. One never knows!" Francis concluded.

Blue turned away and gazed out of the window, thinking of his two very dear friends, Matthew and Rachel, of the love they shared and those happy breakfasts. Matthew was no money grabber!

Francis' reading aloud and the rustling of the newspaper interrupted Blue's train of thought.

"'Australian finds gold.' You know, Blue, we could do with some gold here to help Joshua and his friends in the laboratory and on the ward!"

"Where was it found?" Blue was now very interested and, looking over Francis' shoulder, read for himself: 'Brent Gordon, railroad surveyor-excavator, uncovers gold seam. Government inquiry as to who holds the mining rights!'

"Wowee! Good on you, Brent! I wonder where?"

Francis looked at him inquisitively. "You know this Brent Gordon?"

"Sure! We thought at one time he wanted to marry Matthew's sister, Rebekah ..."

His voice faded as new thoughts entered his head.

"My father! I must get in touch with my father in Justville. Come with me to the Telegraph office, please, Francis," he begged of him.

Francis agreed.

A considerable amount of time and money was spent with the telegraph clerk, in an endeavour to get a message to Blue's father, requesting information regarding the Gold find. In frustration, the two of them left the office, wondering if the message would ever be received in that small Australian town.

Blue could think of nothing but the implications of the gold find. What reason had he that it could affect his father? That it could bring prosperity to his hospital and the orphanage? He had a strange, uncanny feeling it could, even though Francis tried to make him see otherwise.

Francis prayed Blue would not be disappointed.

Their return home to Suffolk was imminent, and no news via the Cambsworth Telegraph Office caused Blue great anguish. To contact Mr Blizzard in London for information had not occurred to Blue, until experiencing a vivid dream in the middle of the night. His shouts awoke Francis.

"I am so sorry, Francis, I've been dreaming! I have to go to London in the morning. Why I did not think of Mr Blizzard before, I just cannot imagine!"

Francis, feeling it was useless to argue with him, still partially asleep, murmured in agreement.

Thinking he would be unable to sleep again, he began mentally preparing his sermon for Sunday next with these sick children in mind, and of Blue's desire to help. In the darkness of the room, Francis began to quietly recite the words of his favourite prayer. When the Rector next opened his eyes, it was daylight. He could not believe it!

Blue's bed was empty and neatly made.

Francis found him sitting at the breakfast table, having already eaten breakfast, spoken to Joshua about a coach leaving for London, and had taken Prince for a walk.

"I am sorry I disturbed your sleep, last night, Francis, so I let you sleep on," Blue said apologetically.

"No need to apologise. Do you have to go to London?" he said, accepting a cup of tea. Blue assured him he felt so sure it was necessary. He would be catching the stagecoach at ten fifteen. There being no time to ask Rachel's permission for him to use her Town House, he had written a letter and given it to Jacob to deliver, upon their arrival at Kiddsmere.

Seated in the full stagecoach, travelling towards London, Blue pondered over this uncanny feeling of his that the gold find by Brent was somehow connected with his father. Even though today was cold, his thoughts, at times, made him feel very uncomfortably hot under the collar. What a fool he would look in Francis' eyes if all this was a wild goose chase?

But I am a fool! He acknowledged and smiled to himself – a fool of a clown!

In an endeavour to ease those erratic feelings he tried conversing with his neighbouring travellers, but had no response. Prince lay quite content beneath the seat and by the time they arrived in London, it was too late by far to pay a visit to the solicitor, Mr Blizzard, so, they found their way to Coleville House.

He was accepted at Rachel's London home with open arms, and after sustenance and a comfortable night's sleep, he prepared to visit Mr Blizzard that morning.

The Solicitor made him most welcome, and after reading the newspaper article, regarding the gold find, apologised, stating he could give him no more information.

This came as a great disappointment to Blue.

"Are you desperate for money, Mr Blue? Or in trouble?" he seriously questioned, because of the unhappy look of his client.

Turning to a detailed page in an accountancy ledger, he added, "You have requested no money from your account, and a much larger sum was deposited some time ago," he said, telling him the sum deposited.

"Thousands?" Blue repeated, giving a look of disbelief. "You mean I have no need to wait for money? Joshua can have his respirator?"

"Respirator?" the Solicitor repeated, looking most bewildered.

"Yes. For Doctor Joshua's hospital at Cambsworth," he enlightened him, his face flushed with excitement, trying to explain the needs of the hospital to a very surprised solicitor.

"I am not in financial difficulties. My friend and I earned enough money while working in the circus to see us through the winter. Now where do I find a respirator?"

Mr Blizzard agreed to accompany him on his quest and seemed to have business contacts in every quarter. Blue certainly felt his luck was in!

Blue was first taken to a building attached to a large hospital, known for medical inventions. There, a Controller listened with interest to Blue's requests, making note of some things Joshua had listed and needed urgently. Giving them a copy of the items purchased, Mr Blizzard gave his name and address as surety for payment.

The Controller suggested they visit the Memorial Institute, where many pieces of up-to-date medical equipment were waiting to be tried. Because testing was a necessity, the total expenditure would be less, they were informed. With some items, they could be taken on a trial period. Nothing detrimental to the patient.

The two buyers found a young student doctor at the Institute very interested and helpful. He was also keen to see the respirator that they had purchased. This young man was willing to travel, even prepared to move, in order to try out the new techniques and equipment, in what he termed 'new technology to further the quality of life'.

He was given Doctor Joshua's address at Cambsworth, to ascertain his major requirements.

The morning had passed very quickly and most promisingly. Blue was very happy and as usual, hungry, so he suggested to Mr Blizzard that they call at the nearest tavern to have a meal before going back to the office, to discuss the pros and cons of this morning's achievements.

Much later, sitting comfortably in Coleville House, Blue recollected the happenings of the day. All he had to do now was to wait patiently for the equipment to be approved by Joshua and delivered to Cambsworth.

Deciding he would go in search of Leonardo, Blue walked to the busy main thoroughfare and hailed the first carriage which came along, asking the cabby if he knew of a Music Hall in town where a magician named Leonardo Crutch was performing.

Much to Blue's surprise, the man knew exactly where, and, delighted with this information, asked to be taken there.

The vehicle joined the busy throng of carriages and people.

It didn't seem long before they stopped in front of the large Hall, well in time for the commencement of the show. While Blue was paying the cab driver, he heard someone say, "I shall be ruined! Ruined!"

"Not you, Alfonso! Not you!" the cabby answered laughing.

Alfonso, the man who had spoken, a portly gent of Italian appearance, in great agitation, was standing by the stage door. Pulling a silver timepiece from his pocket, he consulted it, muttering loudly.

Blue walked towards him and asked if anyone was inside.

"Who you-a-wanta?" the distressed man asked, wiping his perspiring face with a silk handkerchief.

"Leonardo Crutch," Blue replied.

"Yes, go up. He will-a-tell you the muddle I am in!"

Alfonso waved his arms.

Blue found his friend practising his act. Delighted at meeting again so soon, Blue asked, "What's the matter? There's trouble downstairs. A man named Alfonso is very upset!"

Leonardo explained. "An artiste, Angelica, she sings like a nightingale, didn't show for her performance last night and she hasn't arrived yet for this evening's show. Yesterday evening, after a substitute singer gave her performance, poor old Alfonso was pelted with fruit. Pandemonium, it was. I must admit, they had cause to complain. As yet he has no stand-in."

A loud banging and Leonardo's door burst open, letting in an over-wrought Alfonso. Persuading him to take a seat and calm himself, Leonardo poured him a drink.

"What can-na I a-do, Leonardo, you-a tell-a me, my old friend?" he said, gulping down the drink.

Blue, quickly weighing up the situation, asked, "Care to take me on? With my dog? How much time do we have, Leonardo? Prince is at Rachel's villa. I must have him."

"Time enough if I fetch the dog, and Alf help you sort a costume."

Alfonso sat rooted in his chair, overcome and dejected.

"Come, come, Alf, my friend needs stilts and clown attire. Find! Find! Pronto! You have plenty of costumes in the closet."

Leonardo half-lifted him from his chair then quickly left to fetch Prince.

Searching through racks and boxes, no clown clothes could be found, only very large, black evening suits with long tails. Top hats, bowlers, cloth caps, many fancy bonnets, frilled lace pantaloons and parasols and a selection of other garments. From these Blue chose a very elegant blonde wig. He noticed a stockman's whip; Prince was accustomed to this back home and trained with hats, they would come in useful. Gathering his bundle, Blue set off for Leonardo's room, but Alfonso opened a door to another room, saying, "You have-a this room. I hope-a you-a know-a what you are doing?"

Both hands clasped the sides of his head in desperation.

"Find me some stilts, please, Alfonso, or get the stage hands to make some! Pronto!" requested Blue, sorting over the garments and fitting his costume.

Alfonso hurried away, returning in due course with two long poles onto which someone had nailed wooden blocks. Blue hopped onto these and began strutting around the room.

"Hunky-Dory!" shouted Blue.

"Santa Maria!" exclaimed Alfonso. Then began laughing. This young man was dressed in a grey top hat, pink shirt, long white pants and frilly lemon bloomers with dangling ribbons. Red and white striped woollen socks were pulled over his boots. Alfonso sat down. He laughed so much the tears rolled down his cheeks and his sides ached. Leonardo appeared with Prince, saw Blue, whose painted face and curly wig was a picture to behold, then he too began laughing.

Alfonso, now a much happier man, scurried away to complete other duties. Blue tried a few tricks, known to the dog, with the bowler hats. The whip jumps were also well remembered. They had an hour to put their act together.

Blue was to follow the magician on stage. Leonardo had promised to stay in the wings, and if necessary, be of assistance.

Alfonso was the Compere.

"Just send those bowler hats onto the stage, when I ask, please Alfonso," Blue gave him to understand.

At the appointed time: "The house is full! Jam-packed solid! You-a know why-a don't-a you? Come-a specially to-a make-a rumpus! Like-a yesterday, they will want-a their money back. You-a, young man, will-a soon-a know! Prepare-a to make-a run for it. Please-a make-a something good!"

He clasped his hands together and looked to the heavens.

In the wings a troupe of pretty young women waited for their cue. Some began laughing when Blue and Prince appeared.

With a flourish the orchestra struck up. The curtain rose and the girls danced. A man recited a monologue, another played a mouth organ, both well received. The show continued until it was Leonardo's turn. His act put the audience into good fettle. Blue felt apprehensive and hoped the audience would remain so. No back-up music from Matthew or well-known props for Prince, just an ordinary stool, two hats, the stockman's whip and some china plates.

Blue heard the Compere announce his act in a most elaborate manner, giving his correct title: "Blue the Kangaroo Clown and His Dog, Prince of Dogs."

Silence followed the announcement. Blue made his colourful, but spectacular, entrance. Someone laughed.

More laughter while clowning and juggling the two bowler hats. Prince waited at his side, watching every movement. Pre-arranged and miming, Blue encouraged Alfonso to throw him another hat. It rolled on the stage. Prince picked it up, took it to his master, who immediately juggled with it and the others. Two more came. Prince dropped these at Blue's feet. With a quick flip, Blue had all five hats circling. The Drummer took up the Clown's rhythmic movements with an occasional beat of his drum.

Squatting on hind legs, Prince waited for a hat to be thrown towards him.

"Well caught!" a member of the audience shouted, as the dog put the hat down, catching the others and laying them in a straight line. Blue bowed and pointed to his dog. The audience clapped. Jumping onto his stilts, he took up the stockman's whip, gave it an almighty crack, then gently swirled it for Prince to jump. As the thong passed under, back and forth, the dog jumped, not making a mistake. Another loud crack. A wooden frame was placed on stage, holding vivid silk scarves. Again, with whip-cracks, one-by-one the scarves were severed from their mooring. Blue was precision perfect. His act, gaining momentum, delighted the audience, as he swayed on his stilts and juggled plates.

Alfonso could hardly believe his eyes when he saw the dog stand on its hind legs and tap his front feet together, gave a jump and sat on the stool. Putting the plates to one side, Blue scooped Prince into his arms and on to his shoulders. By the tone of the audience, their act was a success. They left the stage, the dog holding one paw aloft. It looked quite comical.

This night, instead of fruit, one happy reveller threw some coins on to the stage, and more satisfied theatre-goers followed suit.

For the Master of Ceremonies to leave his rostrum between acts was very unusual. This evening, making an exception, he walked on to the stage to where Blue and one of the chorus girls were retrieving the coins, and asked Blue if he could manage another short performance; an encore.

After quietening the audience, he told them, "The money you-a have-a given, so-a generously, will-a-be sent to Cambsworth hospital. Our-a young-a friend has agreed to entertain-a you-a again later."

His announcement was received with great enthusiasm and applause. His face wreathed in smiles, he signalled the orchestra to play, and on with the show.

In the second half the Clown and his dog gave another unique, sensational performance, making Alfonso a very happy man. It was very unusual to have an animal performing on stage.

With a keen eye to business, and, with the promise of good payment, Alfonso persuaded Blue to perform his act again the following evening. Blue agreed. Overnight, the Theatre's show had become the talk of the town, with every available seat sold.

Now, on their way again to join the Music Hall entertainers, and in good time, Blue read on several hoardings, 'One man and his dog aids hospital charity'. On the pavement outside the Hall was a large placard that read, 'One Night Only: Blue The Kangaroo Clown and His Dog Prince'.

The price of admission had increased slightly, and, to the amazement of the other artistes, they had been offered an increase in wages.

The show commenced. Alfonso excelled himself, introducing every performer with entertaining vocabulary and wit, smoking an extra-large cigar, and banging his gavel with forceful emphasis. He, like the audience, was not disappointed. At the end of the evening's entertainment, all the artistes were given a standing ovation, some of whom were moving on the next day, scheduled to appear elsewhere.

Likewise, the following morning, Blue and Prince would be leaving London for Cambsworth.

Cheerfully, wishing one another a fond adieu, the artistes went their separate ways, with the exception of Leonardo and Blue who found a small eating house. There they enjoyed a pleasant meal and exchanged news, before finding their respective ways home.

With several passengers on board, the stagecoach rolled along the turnpike, stopping at local inns to discharge or take aboard passengers.

Blue sat, enjoying a feeling of elation, remembering with pleasure the Music Hall, especially the audience for their generosity, for above him on a rack was his large canvas bag containing a great deal of money. Doctor Stone would be delighted. Truly, on Blue's arrival, Joshua was overjoyed, and listened intently as to how Blue had acquired the money.

"Of course," Blue added, "You must thank Alfonso." Then he added, "Why not invite him here sometime?"

With so much to discuss with Joshua, Blue stayed at the hospital for a couple of nights. Before leaving for Kiddsmere, he reminded the doctor of his promise for himself and one of his associates to design an artificial limb suitable for Matthew.

"No need to remind me, it is on the drawing board already!"

Chapter 26

Late afternoon, arriving at the Kiddsmere Rectory, Blue found no one at home. Fresh from his journey and with so much to tell Matthew and Rachel, he went immediately to their home.

It had become a habit for Blue to enter the Hall via the kitchen, where he was always sure to find someone busy and who knew where to find Matthew or Rachel, still quite unaccustomed to the attributes of their butler.

Both were in the sitting room. Beside Rachel's feet stood a wicker basket. After exchanging a cheerful greeting, Blue peered into the basket.

"What have we here?"

He saw a small furry pup, identical in every way to Prince when he was very young. Prince was also nosing into the basket inquisitively.

Matthew chuckled. "You rascal dog," he said affectionately, patting Prince's head as Blue lifted the pup from the basket.

"Where did you get it, Matt?" he said, stroking and fondling the little mite.

"Our gamekeeper's bitch produced a litter. He noticed this one looked familiar and brought her to us. Her name is Patsy."

Prince, on hind legs and wagging his tail, made himself known to his offspring.

Blue put the fat little pup back into the basket, and Prince sat himself beside it, on guard, giving it an occasional lick.

"Blue, it is lovely to see you. Are you hungry?" Rachel inquired, never knowing him not to be, so gave a laugh as he nodded his head. "I will get Cook to send something. I will go and tell her."

After she had gone, Blue handed Matthew the article in

the *Gazette*. Taking a quick look, he suggested they talked in his study, as Blue could not understand how the person had procured the information.

Matthew told him of the newspaper correspondent's card, brought to him by the butler on the day of his wedding. Neither he nor Rachel had yet heard anything of Neville or the court case, only that their Solicitor was dealing with the matter on their behalf. Rachel returned. Nothing more was mentioned.

With so much to tell them concerning his latest trip, Blue talked while having his meal. The Music Hall show, money for the hospital and so forth, but saying nothing about the gold-find – well really he had nothing to tell.

"Thank you for the delicious meal and for the use of your London home. Matt tells me you are both making ready for the highways and byways. Springtime! Exciting and wonderful! A new beginning!" Blue declared, happily.

"Our first event will be at Cambsworth, on the big Green. Abdul, his troupe, other artistes and travellers, all congregate there every spring. Everyone looks forward to it, or so I have heard, it is a popular place."

Rachel looked at Blue wide-eyed, then glanced at her well-manicured nails and delicate hands.

"Matthew tells me I must cook and clean. I can only promise to try," she stated tentatively.

Blue laughed at her, "I will invite you both to dine with me, when and if you have a calamity."

"Oh Blue! You darling!" she said, blowing him a kiss.

"Matthew has vetted the clothes I had made ready and returned more than half to the closet!" Rachel said with pique.

"Sure did!" he agreed. "We had no room for five large trunks! Now the pup is coming!" he said with good humour. "She would take Kate if at all possible!"

Rachel pulled a face at him.

"Just you wait, Matthew Dere, my puddings will be the

envy of every traveller."

Blue said it was time to make for his wagon, leaving them to their happy banter. Walking to the rectory through the park under the millions of bright and twinkling stars, Blue thought of his home in Australia. Of his father and mother. Were they rich? Where had Brent found the gold? Had Justville hospital been completed? Was Jake in good shape? Blue smiled, remembering him. He taught me to crack the stockman's whip.

"Came in useful, my old pal!" he said aloud.

A party of geese, squawking and flapping, took flight. Prince gave an excited bark, bringing his master back from his reverie.

A dim light shone at the rectory as he passed. He would wait until morning to see Francis, remembering their late night sessions at Cambsworth Hospital.

"We will bed-down in our own bed tonight, Prince, old pal! It has been quite a day!"

Sadly, soon would come the parting of the ways with the Peake family. But, he vowed, as he opened his wagon door, he would keep in touch with the Rector and his wife, especially as Matthew would be living at the Hall, likewise with his association with the Cambsworth Orphanage and Hospital.

Blue recollected his promise made to Mr Dere, that he would return with Matthew to the Homestead. What chance of that happening now? Oh! Well! As his father always maintained, it will sort itself out – sleep on it!

Francis, sitting at his breakfast table the next morning, saw Blue coming towards the house heavily laden with neatly-wrapped parcels.

Blue carried these parcels into the sitting room, giving Peggy a package and telling her to inform Mrs Peake and Francis that he had returned from London.

Pleased to see him, they both came into the sitting room, eager to hear his news.

Blue said, "I will tell you my news later, but first, please

246

accept these."

Giving Mrs Peake a token kiss on her cheek, he handed them both a large parcel. Francis was first to undo his, and held before him a long black cape, made of thick woollen material. A row of shining hooks and eyes neatly clasped the front openings together. Blue began unhooking these clasps and placed the garment around the Rector's shoulders. It was a perfect fitting and as Francis put his hands into the two large, inner pockets, he found a pair of knitted gloves and soft felt and leather slippers. Francis was overwhelmed, his voice husky with emotion.

"I do not know how to thank you, Blue. You have given us great joy the short time you have been here. We miss our boys immensely..."

Hearing a gasp from his wife, he turned to look. She had taken longer to untie her parcel, diligently coiling the string into a tidy bundle for re-use. From the folds of the paper, she had lifted a red tartan-lined, navy blue wool coat to hold against her.

"It is lovely! Never have I had such a gift. How did you know what size to bring?"

Finally trying on the coat and doing up the buttons, it fitted her to a tee.

"Dear Blue, you are so kind. You have a heart of gold," she said, putting her arms around him.

"Hearts of gold belong to both of you!" Blue said, seeing her wipe a tear from her cheek. "You gave Matthew and me a place in which to stay. What is more, you trusted us and made us welcome. And brought great happiness to Rachel. 'He' giveth in most unusual ways, as well you know, Francis. I will be leaving soon, and of course Matthew and Rachel will return to the Hall, but I ..."

His voice trailed away, then quickly added, "Come, Mrs 'P', you have another package to undo!"

The next parcel contained a pair of long black button boots, in nearly the same style as those he had given to Peggy.

Bereft of words, so overwhelmed with such great goodness and kindness, unable to undergo the task of fitting the boots, Mrs Peake sat herself down in the dilapidated armchair. A sharp knock, and the door opened, and Peggy came forward carrying her pair of boots.

"Mister Blue, I do thank you kindly, sir, but …"

She was about to say she could not accept them when she saw her mistress with new boots on her lap. Her embarrassment left her and she thought to herself, 'No matter what the village folks might say, my boots will be jolly useful'.

Turning to Mrs Peake, she said, "Let me help you try on your boots," and knelt in front of her. She had not seen her mistress so lifeless before. Maybe she had had a bad turn! In a weepy voice, Mrs Peake said, "Thank you, Peggy. Aren't we the luckiest of people? Look at all these gifts! Bless you, Blue! My boots are also a perfect fit."

Peggy found another handkerchief, relieving her mistress of Blue's sopping wet one, saying "I'll go and fetch some tea. It will do us all good!"

Snowdrops began pushing green and white spikes through the soft moss and ivy covered ground in the rectory garden. Here and there, odd patches of yellow aconites had appeared overnight. Sticky horse-chestnut buds, brown and fat, waited for the moment to release their delicate green leaves and flowers, just as Blue waited for the time to come for them to be on the move.

His affairs concerning Cambsworth hospital were now placed in the capable hands of Francis and Mr Blizzard.

Unfortunately, Matthew and Rachel had encountered problems. Interviews to appoint a competent agent to run their estate, under Clinton Howard's supervision, had proved difficult.

Following those unsuccessful interviews came the court proceedings of her cousin, Neville Coleville-Grey. Earlier, it had been disclosed, Sir Chester Peggleton did offer to stand surety for Neville. But this had not been accepted.

Blue, Matthew and Jacob were forced to attend the trial, but luckily only Jacob was called to give evidence, having previously given the Inspector the name of the London herbalist, where, in the course of his duties as Coachman, he had collected various packages, prepared in Mr Neville's name. He had no idea what the packages contained.

The trial took but a few days. Mrs Crispe had given the relevant information asked of her, assisting the court most generously, emphasising the degradation and humiliation suffered from her employer, Neville Coleville-Grey, for failing to administer the poison. Thinking her own life to be in danger, she admitted to making two attempts to kill or frighten her mistress, by putting the poison, which Mr Neville had given her, into the milk. Vowing, on oath, there being no animosity between herself and dear Miss Rachel, Mrs Crispe accepted her need for alcohol was her undoing.

Listening to and accepting the Housekeeper's story, both Judge and Jury dealt with lenience, sentencing her to a three-year imprisonment.

As for Neville, enough information had been gathered supporting the evidence of the Housekeeper. He had procured and passed on the poison on every occasion, getting more and more aggressive towards the Housekeeper, when she failed to use the substance against his Cousin Rachel Coleville-Grey.

After the Judge announced Neville's long-term sentence, of fifteen years' penal servitude, for the attempted murder, and the abduction of the Housekeeper, a stunned, white-faced Neville was led away, handcuffed.

Chapter 27

March winds and April showers. After those two months, in her husband's words, his wife would begin to really live. Put the terrible past behind her.

Part of Reverend Peake's Sunday service, the day prior to the travellers leaving, had been dedicated to their safe journey, listing good deeds done by these two young gentlemen during their short stay, and offering prayers for their safe return.

This morning, Matthew was seated at the church organ, providing the music for the service.

On this occasion the Organist had consented to his playing. There had been some controversy after the Rector had told her Matthew would be playing the hymns for the Harvest Service. The Rector had subsequently relented. After all, organists were hard to come by!

His music vibrated through the oak rafters, encouraging the congregation to sing, and at the completion of the service to sit and listen.

Upon their leaving, well-wishers shook hands with the two young men, wondering if the Estate would revert to the old days.

The following morning as they left, some village folk watched the two caravans pass through the village, most of them women, as the men were working. A couple of women, inside the Butcher's shop, saw Blue leap from his seat and bid Sam the Blacksmith adieu. He had a liking for the elderly gentleman, because of his kindness to the young apprentice from the orphanage. After giving the lad a couple of coins, Blue jumped aboard his wagon again, gave his horse Silver a gentle slap and was away, with Matthew and Rachel following closely behind in their new caravan.

One of the two women commented to the Butcher, "Did you see that? Plenty of money to throw about! Wonder where he gets it? Bit of a mystery, if you ask me. Both of them!"

"No one's asking you, Ma'am," replied the Butcher. "I have no bones to pick with either of them. Hall owes me nothing since that rogue cousin was locked up. Miss … er … Mrs Rachel seems happy enough!"

"But," the woman carried on speaking, "married to a gypsy, a crippled one at that."

The talkative woman turned to her companion, who waited patiently to be served.

"Who's to know if they bump that poor girl off? That husband of hers will have done well for himself. I said to my man, yesterday, 'Where did they come from?' Makes you wonder! Don't it?" Tossing her head, had it not been for her large hat-pin, her hat would have fallen off.

The Butcher, chopping bones for his next customer said, "Parson is no fool. Got a special licence for them. He knows something we don't. Anyway, I can't see why you should complain, the other young gypsy fixed your brother-in-law's leg and hip for nothing!"

Without further ado, the talkative woman left the shop.

Travelling slowly along the byways was pleasurable. Rachel enjoyed every moment, putting names to many wild flowers and shrubs bursting forth in the hedgerows, and could tell Matthew, as they passed Halls and Mansions, the names of the occupiers. She felt secure in the fact no one would recognise her, as her well-kept long blonde curls had been neatly fashioned, pinned to the top of her head and covered by a black felt hat. Dressed in long black clothes, a multi-coloured shawl, she looked and felt very unlike her former self.

Slowly progressing each day towards their destination, the prepared food, which Kate insisted they took with them, had been eaten, with the exception of two large cured hams. Soon it would be her turn to prepare a meal. A wide grassy verge near a ford seemed the ideal place to stop for the night. Tomorrow, they should reach their destination, Cambsworth Fairground.

A good start, early next morning, in order to get as near to the circus ring as possible, was Blue's aim. Matthew pulled his horse onto the verge behind Blue's wagon. Rachel started to lay the fire, while the horses were taken to the water and then hobbled on the sweet grass.

After a meal of crisp pancakes, dressed with honey and vinegar, Rachel took her dirty laundry to the ford. Both dogs followed, making her laugh as they splashed and frolicked in the water. Matthew joined his wife, bringing back the wet load to peg on a rope attached to both wagons.

Rachel felt embarrassed as her undergarments could be scrutinised by any passer-by. Matthew laughed at her.

Blue, sitting by the fire, stitching something, didn't notice the wet dog until Prince shook himself with great force, splashing Blue with cold water.

"Oh! You Prince of Dogs!" he exclaimed, throwing a cloth over the dog, began to dry him. While doing so, he heard shrill shrieks from an animal. Dropping the cloth, he raced away in the direction of the noise, with Prince beside him. Experience had taught him that speed was essential.

In the nick of time, they spotted a small brown and white animal about to drag its capture undercover. All shrieking had ceased. Prince raced ahead. Realising its own danger, the stoat scuttled away, leaving behind a nice, fat rabbit.

With great pride, Prince carried his find back to the fireside.

"Poor creature!" Rachel uttered with remorse.

Blue picked it up and turned it over.

"It's a beaut. A stoat selects only the best, then mesmerises it. This one didn't have a chance. It'll make a sure good meal!"

Sitting beside glowing embers, twilight fading, the three of them saw the bright moon slowly rise above the hawthorn hedge.

"Tomorrow, Rachel!" said Blue, "you should meet Abdul and some of our friends. Some will be friendly. Others keep themselves to themselves. There are bound to be troublemakers, often in the audience."

Leaving the two sitting by the fire, Blue bid them "Goodnight" as it was his bedtime.

He awoke early the next morning, made the fire and went for a dip in the river. The water was very cold, but refreshing. A moment or so later, Matthew followed suit. It was then Blue noticed the red weal still on Matthew's leg and commented upon it. Matthew shrugged it off as nothing, "only the frame twisted slightly," and continued with his wash-down.

Blue returned to the fire in a pensive mood. The kettle full of water, now boiling, was poured over the tea leaves in the black enamelled tea pot. Taking a long forked stick, he toasted thick slices of bread over the hot ashes. Matthew spread orange marmalade over a slice of toast, filled a mug with tea and took it to his wife. He returned and placed a jug of clean water inside the wagon.

Within the hour they were ready to leave for Cambsworth. Looking at the sky, Blue questioned, "Sunshine and showers today, maybe? Right, Rachel?"

"One never can tell with our English weather, Blue. Have your umbrella ready!" she warned him and laughed, pushing her laundry well into the confines of their wagon.

Tremendous activity surrounded them as they travelled through the narrow cobbled streets of Cambsworth. Old buildings with ornate doors and gateways seemed to swallow gowned scholars carrying books. Barrow-boys shouting their wares for sale and men sitting on cart and carriage seats, trying to avoid collision, adding to the mayhem. A clock, chiming the hour, reminded Blue of the direction to take in order to find the large Green.

He found it without difficulty, and saw several caravans already in position. He also spotted Abdul with an assistant, looking for a suitable area on which to erect his large canvas tent.

Pleased to see them again, Abdul pointed to where Blue should park his wagon. Matthew, pulling alongside, proudly introduced his wife to Abdul.

Abdul remained silent, eyeing her up and down as if she were one of his prize elephants. They could almost hear his mind ticking over: 'This beauty is too delicate for the rough and tumble of circus life'.

Matthew, anticipating just such a remark, advised him, "Rachel is very strong, an excellent horse woman. She could ride an elephant!" Such a prospect, in reality, never occurring to him.

Abdul grinned, showing an array of gold-filled teeth. "May have to take you up on that," he replied. "My granddaughter is sick."

Rachel had little chance to answer. Someone shouted his name and he hurried away.

They had been with the circus folk for two days. The main work of erecting the tent and preparation of the seating and arena was complete.

Rachel, busy teaching Patsy to obey, saw Matthew hurrying towards her looking very worried.

"Rachel, my sweet," he began, "would you dare to sit on the back of an elephant? Rajah is not vicious, he is very gentle or I would not ask you. Abdul's granddaughter is still sick; you are both about the same size, so the costumes would fit."

Said with great haste, Rachel hardly had time to understand any of it.

"Me? On an elephant's back? But how?" she asked, bewildered. "Is there no other artiste or their child who could stand in?"

Matthew looked a little sheepish.

"I told him it was too much to ask of you, but Abdul has Rajah expertly trained. A wonderful performer. You would look like an Eastern Princess, seated on his back!"

She laughed, saying, "And like a limp ragdoll if I fell off!"

"You would not fall. Anyway," Matthew said assuredly, "Blue will teach you the art of falling and landing correctly and he would be by your side all the time. Come and see for yourself." Matthew held out his hand to her.

The magnificent Rajah, freshly washed, looked in a happy mood as Abdul put him through his routine. Rajah, remembering each move to perfection, knowing his next sequence without Abdul's instructions, curled and lifted his great trunk, expecting his young partner to join him. She was not there! He waited.

Rachel stared with great trepidation at the enormous elephant. Blue, who had joined them, asked, "Do you think he would lift me, Abdul?"

Abdul laughed, "Yes, of course Blue, no problem, but you don't look as beautiful or as delicate as a sweet young maid!"

They all laughed at Blue's reaction.

Summing up a little courage, Rachel asked, "Will he take to me? I feel very nervous, and some animals sense this. Another thing, could I learn enough for the first performance?"

Now, gently stroking the elephant's face, "Tell me, what do I do, Abdul?"

Abdul explained carefully after asking her to remove her boots. "Wait for him to coil his trunk for you to gently place one foot on it, hold on to his trunk as he lifts, and you will find your free leg helps you balance."

Blue saw her doubtful look and offered his services, carrying out Abdul's instructions with such ease that Rachel consented.

Her heart fluttered as the gigantic creature carefully lifted and lowered her, turning his head from side to side. Slightly unsteady, she stepped on to firm ground. Laughing, she patted Rajah as he began to lower himself, finally remaining in a sitting position. Blue, watching closely, had seen the action before with Abdul's granddaughter and an assistant, so he stood beside Rachel as Abdul issued the next command.

"Ready?" Blue asked her, lifting her with an easy movement onto Rajah's neck, her legs finding a place behind the
elephant's large ears, and holding tightly to his ornamental
headgear. Another command. The elephant rose and began
walking, with Rachel swaying easily to his rhythm.

Quite at ease now, she laughed with those who stood below.
Her lessons had begun. Now to find a costume.

Rummaging through Abdul's massive clothes basket,
because she wanted to wear something of her own choice and
style, Rachel found a blue silk, mandarin-type jacket trimmed
with multi-coloured glass sequins, a pair of matching voluminous pantaloons, sequined satin slippers and a yashmak.
A wide circular diamante band to encase her blonde top-knot
completed her ensemble.

Dressing in these, she presented herself to Matthew and
Blue for approval, before going to Abdul.

"A real Sheila, eh, Blue?" said Matthew, quoting a stockman's approval.

After gruelling lessons from Abdul and help from her
husband and Blue, she was about to make her debut.

Casually, she remarked, "When on Rajah's back, I feel I am
sitting on top of the world." Matthew, giving her a hug, said,
"My beautiful love, you look delightful and mysterious, like a
pea on a pumpkin!"

Quickly side-stepping, he avoided a box of the ears. Loving
every moment of their light-hearted banter, Blue laughed, his
large red painted mouth stretching from ear to ear, as happily,
the trio moved off towards the circus ring.

Blue hoped Joshua and his specialist friend had managed
to get to the Circus. A quick trip to the Cambsworth Hospital
during the morning had found Joshua busily attending his
patients. The Doctor, overjoyed at seeing 'The benefactor
Superb', as he had named him, promised he and his most

knowledgeable friend would meet Matthew at their wagon on the Green.

Blue's thoughts were quickly interrupted when trumpets and drums, in the large tent, gave a rousing fanfare. The evening performance was about to begin. Coloured lanterns gave the ring a most attractive appearance.

Blue, colourfully dressed, walking on stilts and juggling, leaned over to torment Matt as he played his accordion. Prince, wearing his neck ruffle, circled around both clowns, barking and jumping upright on hind legs, and generally, so it seemed, getting in the way. The children in the audience, encouraged by the two clowns, began to clap their hands. To the amazement of both children and adults, the dog stood on his hind legs, tapping his front feet together, causing shrieks and laughter.

A fast-moving show with horses and trapeze artists, it soon became the turn of Abdul and his well turned-out elephants.

A very nervous Rachel walked into the ring, close to Rajah's side. Abdul and his elephants began their performance. Matthew's heart pounded and yet with a feeling of great pride, watched his wife being lifted, in all her finery, to sit astride Rajah. Blue, on his stilts, was almost level with her. Concealed behind the yashmak, no one could recognise her.

Very carefully, she balanced on the elephant's broad back, circling the sawdust-covered ring at a steady pace, followed by another small elephant, Mimi, clutching Rajah's tail. All went well with the lifting and the commands from Abdul. They left the ring, followed by loud applause. Abdul's assistant handed her a glittering cloak, as the night air was chilly. The coolness had passed unnoticed by her, as she was bathed in perspiration and trembling.

She chatted with a brother and sister, whom she learned were Italian, both fire-eaters. After their act would come the grand parade and the show would be over for this evening.

So far, to the relief of all concerned, the first performance had gone very well, but her trembling remained.

Later, speaking of this to her husband, he said, "Come my love, a hot drink will steady your nerves. You did wonderfully well! Everyone suffers from nerves, especially on the first performance."

Prince, running on ahead, barked at the two well-dressed men waiting beside Blue's caravan. They were Joshua and his friend, Taggerty. Very pleased they had arrived, Blue introduced them to Matthew and Rachel.

In a short while, bereft of make-up and warmly clad, the three artistes had a kettle on the boil and a large pan of prepared oxtail and vegetables simmering over the fire.

Two candle lanterns, suspended on hooks on poles, gave them light. Taggerty was the Doctor researching artificial limb replacements, and, at the request of Blue, had come to meet Matthew in order to view his existing leg support.

Choosing what he thought to be the right moment, Taggerty asked Matthew about his leg support and if he could see it, as he was experimenting with artificial limbs and using different metals at the hospital.

Leaving her husband with the Doctor, Rachel moved away. Matthew never complained about his disability, but she knew he suffered and she had seen for herself the condition of his leg. Confidentially, Blue had told her of Joshua's friend, who designed more modern, shaped, artificial legs, complete with a foot.

It would be marvellous if Matt could wear both boots, Blue had enthused. Taking a jug of ale and tankards from her wagon, she returned to the party. Matthew and Taggerty were laughing together. A sigh of relief escaped her, overhearing her husband say, "Definitely tomorrow, at your place!"

With a smile on her face she passed the full tankards around, leaving bread and cheese for them to help themselves, and wished them a 'Goodnight'.

Both Doctors thanked her for her company and the most delicious meal. They would, no doubt, meet again.

Rachel, snug under a down-filled bed cover, as tired as she was, her body aching, could not find sleep. She relived the day's happenings, experiencing a certain pleasure in her achievements, wondering what her darling Kate would have to say when she knew her protégé rode an elephant! Her way of life had changed completely, but she was enjoying every moment.

Much later, Matthew came to bed. Careful not to disturb her, he was very surprised to find her awake.

Kissing her tenderly, he told her of Taggerty's conversation.

"I will try a new aid and be taught to walk correctly."

She slid her arms around him, overjoyed with his news. Her warm, scented body sent him into raptures.

"My lovely, lovely, Rachel. Dearest," he murmured, "I hope you never regret marrying me, a cripple!"

Burying his face in her silken hair, with great passion she pressed his hard, young body more closely to hers, gloriously sharing a most wondrous moment of joy and love, looking towards his future wellbeing and their happiness together.

As usual, Blue was the first about early the next morning. A pan of sizzling bacon and hot cocoa welcomed Matthew and Rachel. Both were dressed when they made their appearance, in readiness for their meeting with Taggerty.

The morning was dull and cloudy, with every likelihood of rain, so they were all eager to get to town and back quickly.

Upon meeting Doctor Taggerty, they were told Joshua was exceptionally busy. An epidemic in the hospital was causing him great concern.

Leaving them to discuss their affairs, Blue went in search of Joshua and found him with his other associates in the dining room, about to take some well-deserved refreshment. They invited Blue to join them, poured him some tea, pushing a plate of hard-looking biscuits towards him.

Their main topic of conversation was the epidemic among the children. Blue listened with interest, as each in turn sought an explanation for the outbreak of dysentery.

Not wanting to be critical or presumptuous, Blue spoke of his previous visit, when off-loading food to the kitchen and storehouse, and how he had noticed flies, cockroaches, traces of vermin, and water vessels in a state of uncleanliness, adding, "My father, a doctor, insisted on the highest standard of cleanliness, always using carbolic or soda wherever possible. Your ward cleaners are exemplary!"

"True," one doctor agreed, "But we rarely have cause or time to visit the kitchens. They are the jurisdiction of the Housekeeper. It could be the answer. I will investigate."

Eager to get back to their duties, Joshua's associates went their separate ways.

"Anything nice in your bag, Blue? There usually is!" quizzed Joshua. Blue opened it.

Peering in the bag he exclaimed, "Toffee brittle! May I sample a piece?"

Delving his hand into the bag, he selected a large lump and popped it into his mouth.

"I bet I know where you are taking that. You spoil those boys, Blue!"

With both jaws practically glued together with sticky toffee rendering him almost speechless, Joshua raised his hat and rushed away.

Blue went in search of the boys. He found them working. Wood chopping, sweeping, stable cleaning and one other job, most hated by them all; carting ash and clinker away from the giant boiler house.

Blue offered them chunks of toffee, passing various comments to each one, as they in turn gave him a smile of thanks. What a humdrum existence, he thought, as he watched two more boys at work. One boy was aged about ten, the other, at a guess, twelve to fourteen. He offered them toffee. Only one took a piece. The other, older boy, looked very serious. When asked what was wrong, the younger boy replied, "Take no notice, he's got picked to go and work for old Squire Bullock."

"Old Squire's a wrong'un, Mister Blue, beats the daylight out of you! None of the boys stop with him for long. They scarper!"

Blue asked the serious boy if this was true. With a glint of moisture in his eyes, he gave a nod in agreement and turned away.

"He wants to be a Doctor!" a lad shouted, pointing, laughing at the embarrassed lad as if it were a great joke.

"Is that so?" Blue asked. "Can you read and write?"

He nodded again. Blue took the boy's hands in his own, turning them over, noting calloused, but sensitive fingers.

"Tell me about yourself! I may be able to help – I cannot promise, mind!" Blue told him with a smile.

No knowledge of his parenthood; this boy, John Ware, could only say that he desperately wanted to study. To become a doctor. But with a shrug of his shoulders he declared he could never see that wish being fulfilled. Leaving the clown, he returned despondently to his job of filling the ash cart and to the prospect of work on a farm. Blue hurried back to Rachel and Matt. Time was limited; they had to get back to the showground to complete their share of the circus work.

Everything had gone well for Matthew. He had been measured and was most impressed with what he had seen and learned. After all these years – he would have another foot, albeit artificial.

Night after night with the other artistes, the trio worked tremendously hard in the ring. During the day, Blue and Prince travelled to the hospital, donning clown attire, to give impromptu performances to the children well enough to enjoy the entertainment. Hearing their laughter gave him immense pleasure. Needless to say, Prince was adored. Soon they would be moving on.

One morning, Abdul called his band of artistes together and gave them instructions as to when they would dismantle, and their next pitch. He had planned it to coincide with a lamb sale, several miles away near a large town. Blue called in at the hospital to say goodbye to his friends, taking with him a large box of goodies.

On arrival at the hospital, he found Joshua overjoyed. A much-wanted piece of hospital equipment had arrived from London. Joshua invited him to take a look, saying, "Blue, we cannot thank you enough. You were Heaven-sent!"

In front of them stood a large metal respirator, known as an iron lung. Joshua reverently walked around the machine in complete awe. Then gave an explanation of its working. It would help patients to breathe in time of recovery.

Afterwards, he said, "Come with me, Blue," escorting him into the large hall. "Take a look at this!"

Hanging on a wall before them was a painting of a laughing clown, identical in every way to Blue's laughing face, and beside the clown, a begging dog.

The inscription beneath read, 'Benefactor Blue Everest with Prince of Dogs'.

"Whoever painted it?" Blue exclaimed. "It is a work of art!"

"One of the stable lads. It is good, isn't it? I must go now. Blue, don't stay away too long."

On the point of leaving, Joshua added, "By the way, that boy, John Ware, the lad you were concerned about, who wants to become a doctor? Using part of your gift of money, we are sending him to a London School of Medicine. Give him a chance, yes? All the best!"

Always in a hurry, Joshua raised his top hat and was away before Blue could ask for more details.

Tonight's finale meant a great celebration before the rigours of dismantling and loading. Fires burned brightly, cooking pots and pans were full, sending aromatic, mouth-watering odours wafting over the Green. As Blue made his way to his caravan, pangs of hunger surged through his body. Matthew had arrived home first and had begun preparing the meal.

The evening light had not quite faded and the night was pleasant. Enquiring the whereabouts of Rachel, he was told she had called to see Abdul's granddaughter.

"Tripe and onions for you, Blue, or faggots and peas?" Matthew asked when the food was ready.

"Both. I am truly starving!" Blue laughed, patting his stomach. Matthew hesitated. Strange, Blue did not usually mix both, yet nevertheless filled Blue's plate.

Rachel joined them with a sad look on her face.

"My work is finished. Abdul's granddaughter will be well enough to take over again."

Then she said rather tearfully, "I shall miss Rajah and Mimi and the happy voices. I have loved every moment!"

"Never mind, my sweet, we need you," Matthew said, placing an arm around her waist. Smiling a watery smile, she kissed him. "Thank you darling!"

"Mr Blue, sir," a young voice was heard.

All three turned. A short distance away, cap in hand, stood a tall, rather nervous youth. Blue greeted him.

"Why! It is my friend, John Ware from the Orphanage! Come, sit down and join us. Meet my friends. Have some food. How did you manage to find us?"

"I followed this lady. Seen her at the hospital with you. I have come to thank you," the boy blurted out quickly.

They bade him take a seat, and placed a large plate of food before him. John Ware looked at the food apprehensively and said, "I haven't been able to eat for a day or so. You see, I'm going to London. Never been to a large town before."

Realising the nervous state of this young lad, Blue set about giving him some confidence, telling his friends how John had studied all the medical books he could lay his hands on. As Blue chatted, John began to eat. Matthew joined in with tales of the London he had seen. Rachel disappeared to their caravan, returning with her printed card.

"Should you ever find yourself in any trouble, go to this address. Someone there is sure to help. Have you any money?" she asked, giving him the card.

"I am to be fitted out with clothes and given some money when I leave, thank you Ma'am," John acknowledged, adding, "I must get back to the Home before I am missed. Thanks again, I feel much better. Oh, Sir, I have to tell you, no one else is being sent to Squire Bullock's place!"

Blue grinned and shook John by the hand.

"Well done. Our mutual friend, Dr Joshua, will inform me when you make top grade. You will!"

A fiddler, somewhere on the Green, began to play. John gave a little dance, smiled and waved, a degree or so more prepared for his gigantic step into a new world. Pensive, Blue sat, retracing his own life. Help and love from both parents. Enough money to stand on his own two feet. Those lads at the orphanage had no one, save the staff, to care for them. More than half the boys there could neither read nor write and their prospects were exceedingly poor for the finding of a good home and stability. Likewise, in the other section of the Home, young girls, barely in their teens, were sent out as servants to widowers, widows, shopkeepers or anyone needing cheap labour.

Some of the youngsters knew nothing but drudgery in their new homes. Young John had sense enough to push ahead, and taken it into his own hands to learn, often being caught out of bounds in the old library and punished many times. His lust for learning drove him on, not caring if punishment was deprivation of his meagre food. Food for him was medical literature.

"Come, Blue, you've been daydreaming long enough. Estelle and her family are calling us to join their party," said Rachel, who had changed into a very effective gown. She and Matthew were ready to leave.

Blue shook his head. "I will come later."

"Oh! Blue! Estelle will be so disappointed. I think she has taken a fancy to you. It is time you found yourself a wife!" Rachel tormented him.

Now, stretched on his bed, with Prince beside him and Patsy at his feet, as much as he loved a party, strangely, he sought solitude.

True, Estelle had shown great interest, often seeking his company, but for some inexplicable reason, he could not return her affection.

Blue slept fitfully, tossing and turning, pushing and pulling his bedcovers. One moment, a coldness swept through his body, the next he was consumed by burning heat. Returning at a late hour, Matthew heard Blue call out. He rushed into his wagon, letting out both dogs, turned up the lamp and found his friend bathed in perspiration. Fetching some tepid water he began bathing his forehead.

Groaning and holding his stomach, Blue opened his eyes and indicated to Matthew to fetch a bottle of medicine from his cupboard. Reading the instructions aloud and thinking it to be quinine, he saw Blue nod his head, so administered a dose accordingly. He stayed at the bedside, helping his friend as best he could.

Rachel, within calling distance, prodded the fire into life, making sure the kettle boiled, praying Blue had not caught that terrible dysentery from the hospital. The night slipped away. Her husband came out into the night air and she handed him a mug of tea, and prepared a bowl of disinfectant and water.

Blue seemed slightly better, well, more calm he told her, not talking as much rubbish. The medicine was having an effect.

Taking the bowl from her, he suggested she should get some sleep. Dawn was breaking. A sharp trill from a robin signalled commencement of the dawn chorus. Soon, dozens of birds began whistling, their voices trilling, sending messages across the Green and out over the fields, woods and gardens. Standing beside her wagon steps, Rachel listened and wondered what message each extolled. Perhaps, 'My young hatched during the night! Or we have four eggs in our nest!' Or it could be a message of sadness.

"What are they singing about? Your guess is as good as mine, Prince and Patsy, my darlings," Rachel said, patting the dogs. "You must come into my bed now, both of you." Prince cocked his head to one side, looked at her and wagged his tail.

She slept late. Matthew called her. He looked weary, but was pleased Blue's fever was shortlived and had subsided. He was now sleeping peacefully.

Rachel sought out Abdul, telling of their problem and began helping as best she could, until Matthew arrived.

By evening, everything was packed and loaded, ready for them to move off at first light the next day. Exhausted, Blue had remained in his bed all day with Matthew keeping an occasional eye on him.

Outside Blue's caravan, Abdul listened to Matthew's plans. He would drive Blue's caravan and look after him, as Rachel was quite capable to drive their own.

"Surprising as it may seem," he told Abdul. "Neither of us have had an illness, not so much as a cold."

A noise from within Blue's wagon sent Matthew hurriedly to his bedside. Although deep in sleep, Blue shouted again, uttering more gibberish nonsense. To Matthew, it reminded him of the guttural language of an Aborigine. Blue began twisting and pleading, holding out his hand for something to be given to him. Beads of perspiration accumulated on his forehead as he tugged at his undershirt.

Quietly speaking to him and wiping his brow, Matthew gave him another dose of the medicine. Blue opened his eyes, his face flushed, and placed his hand in the region of his heart.

"Fair dinkum, Blue! You have been dreaming! Easy does it, pal!"

Blue looked around in a vacant fashion, and asked, "Where am I?"

"In your wagon in England," Matthew answered.

Mumbling a weak, "Oh," he closed his eyes.

Quietly, Matthew withdrew from the wagon. Abdul, still waiting, listened as Matthew related what had just happened, saying to Rachel, "I cannot remember seeing him in this state before." Then a faint recollection came to mind of seeing Blue having a turn, similar to this, back home. "Maybe I should consult Joshua."

Matthew returned to the now-sleeping Blue. The quinine must be taking effect, he thought, as he sat by his bed. He must have dozed. A gentle tap on the shoulder awoke him. It was Joshua. Abdul had sent for him.

Quietly they spoke together, Matthew recounting the happenings, as Joshua placed his fingers on Blue's pulse. His touch roused Blue, but not enough to awaken him completely.

Watching his patient carefully, he saw a flicker of a smile cross his face, heard the groan as he asked for something, felt his pulse rate quicken, saw the perspiration forming, then heard the guttural gibberish as Matthew had said, finally the cry of, "Give them back!" as Blue pulled his arm away.

A sharp slap from Joshua's hand brought Blue back to his senses.

"Tell me, before you forget. What is it you want back, Blue?" Joshua questioned.

Blue moaned, "I don't know!"

"Yes you do! Tell me!" requested the Doctor in his most authoritative manner.

Very quietly he answered, "Matthew's sister, Ruth, has my beads. She will not give them back!"

His two friends looked at each other in wonderment.

"So?" enquired Joshua.

"Oh!" Blue groaned again, "That Old Fella said I would know. Oh, no it wasn't him, it was Madame Clare!"

Holding his head in his hands, he told them the story of the carved beads. How strange he had felt when Ruth wore them, back home. Quickly he swung his legs from his bed, stating in a matter-of-fact tone of voice, "I have to go home!"

Arguing, but too weak to stand, Blue collapsed on his bed.

Joshua mixed a concoction from bottles in his bag, bade him drink, telling him he would feel better in the morning. Within a few seconds, before the Doctor had left, he was asleep. Matthew, going back to Rachel, told her very little of the evening's events, except that Blue should sleep until morning. He had eaten nothing but had taken water.

With Rachel fast asleep beside him in bed, Matthew thought of his sister, Ruth. What age was she now, eighteen? Sparks always flew between her and Blue. Memories of home began returning. A vision of his father sitting in his rocking chair, a Bible on his lap, came before him. Dear God, Matthew prayed, may Blue be better by morning. With his father in mind, he fell asleep.

As soon as daylight appeared he awoke, dressed and took a quick look into Blue's wagon, found him still fast asleep, then stirred the fire.

All around he heard voices, and the smell of food cooking, reminding him of the early start. He began preparing breakfast, then saw his wife on the wagon steps, looking refreshed and beautiful. My! How he loved her.

He answered her questioning look as she gazed towards Blue's van.

"Still sleeping," he said, handing her a mug of tea. She also began helping with the preparation of breakfast. Estelle's father and Abdul came over, seeking news of Blue. Matthew could tell them very little. Rachel offered them food, which they accepted gratefully, and they stayed, eating and talking. To the surprise of everyone, Doctor Joshua appeared, wishing them a "Good morning," and let himself into the patient's wagon. Matthew followed him. They emerged from the wagon, the Doctor looking quite pleased, saying, "Our friend's pulse is good and the fever has gone. I know you are moving today, I have left more sedatives in case any are needed."

Matthew thanked him, offering a large piece of toast and bacon. Delightedly he accepted the food, but shook his head when offered money for his services.

"What can you make of it, Doctor? Is it dysentery?" Abdul asked, thinking what effect it could have on his performers.

"No," replied Joshua pensively, adding, "I am unable to diagnose it yet. I have heard tell of Witch-Doctors but …" His voice trailed away.

Abdul looked at him with great interest and asked, "What do you mean?"

Joshua gave a look in Matthew's direction, but asked Abdul, "You are a man of the world, have you any knowledge of tribal superstitions, or voodooism?"

Abdul, giving the question some thought, shook his head and said, "Whatever it is, I hope he is soon better." With that he left.

"What's cooking, Matt? Say! I am starving!"

All heads turned. Dressed in his everyday clothes, Blue stood at his caravan doorway. Slightly unsteady, he descended the steps, holding his head and saying, "I feel very strange."

No one spoke.

Joshua quickly stepped forward.

"You have been through a rough spell."

"Spell? Spell, did you say?" asked Blue, sitting himself down.

"Metaphorically speaking, of course," Joshua hastened to add.

To change the subject, Matthew quickly intervened, saying, "What would you like to eat? We are ready to leave. Joshua has just eaten toasted bread and bacon."

"Fine, fine, just fine," he agreed, "with a mug of tea, please."

Noticing Estelle's father, he said, "Sorry I missed your party last evening. I felt a little out of kilter." He rubbed his stomach.

"Well," said Estelle's father, not rectifying his loss of time, "tripe and onions, faggots and peas, all mixed together, enough to make any man sick!"

Blue grinned. "Oh, no! I only ate faggots and peas," he said, accepting his breakfast. Leaving him to his meal, they left to prepare for their journey.

Chapter 28

In an orderly fashion, the entertainers left the Green, with Blue insisting he was well enough to drive. Truthfully, he really did feel stronger every moment. But something deep within body or mind, and he was unable to determine which, bothered him greatly. Not being able to pinpoint his problem, he said nothing to Matthew.

Several days they travelled, heading east through very rural and sparsely populated areas, each day stopping well before sunset to rest, until, finally, they found the large Common of which Abdul had spoken.

Already a few shepherds with their flocks of sheep had taken up position, in and near the sheep-pens provided, eager to be first on the sale list.

Abdul issued instructions, knowing exactly where to place everything and direct every one. For countless number of years, he and his father before him had visited this place. Rich farmers and landowners came from all parts of the country to buy this special breed of sheep, always in great demand for its wool and meat. Money and animals changed hands freely.

By mid-afternoon, Abdul asked for a group of colourful entertainers to assemble in readiness for a small procession to the nearby town, leaving those remaining to finish assembling the Big Top.

Drummers and buglers to the fore were closely followed by himself and his two elephants, surrounded by the trapeze and other artistes. Four white ponies pulled a small but beautiful gilded carriage. The clowns and Prince added more colour and hilarity. Following the procession, children with smiling faces hopped and skipped, as folks in nearby fields and villages stopped work to watch the circus people go by, some never having seen an elephant. Many were not able to go to the circus.

One could almost hear them saying, "The Circus has arrived at Torsel Common!" This last day or so, joviality had begun to creep back into Blue's being. Joshua's potions had helped him to sleep, yet that strange feeling persisted within, a feeling that he could not explain, not even to himself. Increasingly, his thoughts dwelt on the Dere Homestead. Trying to find a reason for this, he concluded it had been his home for quite a long time. His mind was so preoccupied, that, walking on stilts, he failed to see an enormous pothole in the road, until someone gave a shout.

Rachel had decided not to join the procession, but stay behind to prepare the meal. Prettily dressed in a long red and white check gingham dress and black shawl, she picked up her wicker basket, pulled on a broad-brimmed hat, to take a walk with Patsy in search of deal-apples and twigs for the fire.

Estelle joined her. Both women, about the same age, had become good friends, and chatted happily together as they walked on this perfect, sunny afternoon.

Rachel removed her straw hat, and using it as a fan, cooled her warm face, letting her blonde curls cascade around her shoulders.

Estelle touched the silken ringlets rather enviously. Her own jet black hair was a mass of tight curls. Her father was Spanish and her mother Maltese.

"What nationality is Blue? He must be a relative of yours. You both have a similar complexion," asked Estelle, but received no answer as her friend darted off, collecting pieces of tinder-dry wood and cones.

Due to the many layers of pine needles, the two women had not heard the approach of two horse riders and were surprised by them. Coming face to face with them, Rachel pushed her hair under her hat. Blushing, she turned away quickly, hoping against hope she had not been recognised.

Rachel heard Estelle angrily speaking in a flourish of Spanish, ending in English, that she had six brothers!

"Gypsies!" one announced, then spurred their horses on.

"Oh! La-la! How handsome was that young man!" Estelle remarked, coquettishly, after they had gone. "I wish my tongue had not been so fiery, but one has to protect oneself."

Then, registering Rachel's deathly white face, she exclaimed, "Rachel, you look ill! Are you unwell?"

Desperately trying to smile, Rachel assured her friend she was fine, hugging her basket to her, and Patsy to her side, and started walking back towards their site.

Now, standing over her cooking pot, Rachel relived this afternoon's encounter. The elder of the two riders was the Duke of Barnham, an associate of her cousin, Neville. His wife, the Duchess, was always vindictive, remembering their last meeting at Sir Chester's house party. She never liked her. Surely, they did not pay a visit to the circus! It definitely was not her scene, one would have thought. Maybe he was here to buy sheep. Her heartbeat started to race again, wondering if he lived at Torsel.

Dropping pastry pieces into a boiling pan, she said aloud, "What mattered if the Duchess did visit the circus? It would only be out of sheer inquisitiveness, to spread a few rumours. The woman is like that."

Hearing the sound of the drums as the procession returned, she thought, what would Matt say when she told him of the encounter?

Seeing Blue coming her way, she pushed her own affairs to one side, and thought of his strange illness. She made some tea. Smiling, he looked much better, and gave her cooking pot a stir. Shouting at him to leave the pot alone, she saw her husband limping towards them.

Rachel, very concerned, gave him some tea and suggested

273

she should bathe and bandage his leg, which she did.

Joshua had promised to send the new limb by special messenger. She prayed, let it be soon. Everyone hoped this fine weather would stay, for tomorrow was the big day when the whole arena would come to life. With two performances daily, everyone would be extra busy.

The unceasing blaring and bleating of sheep, as more flocks arrived, would continue until every sheep or lamb was sold. Assembled around the circus encampment were vendors eagerly waiting to sell their wares of appetising sweets, various pies and pastries, silks, lace, pegs and artificial flowers. Some had already started to sell their refreshments.

Twilight came. At last Rachel was alone with her husband and able to tell of her encounter with the Duke of Barnham.

"Does it matter, my love? Neville is locked away. What if your grand Duchess tells her friends about you being here?" he asked. "You are happy, darling?"

Turning her face towards his, he placed his lips on hers. Holding her protectively, he whispered sweet endearments to calm her fears.

Blue, unable to rest in his wagon, had checked the horses, then wandered towards the river. Pens of sheep, rigorously watched over, no doubt, by Shepherds and dogs, were settling for the night.

Leaning on a hurdle, one foot resting on a rail, gazing into a clear, starlit night, his nostrils full of the aroma from sheep, nostalgia besieged him.

Hearing grunts, coughs and sneezes, his imagination transformed this scene into one of many experienced at the Australian Homestead, with Jake and his gang of men rounding-up, dipping and marking. Mouth organ music. Matt's flute, others with spoons or paper and comb, harmonising, around the glimmering firelight in the scrub-covered pasture. Good old Jake, good-on-ya, you taught us so much. He could visualise him sitting on the veranda steps, hat cocked against the sunlight. Other faces came to the fore. That of his own father, bending over someone – a patient?

Instantaneously a dark, weather-beaten, toothless grinning face seemed to appear. It was Nerimbo, he remembered him well, and, as if it was happening this very moment, the old man removed the necklace of wooden beads from over his grey head. Blue saw his father politely refuse the gift, although he knew pastures forever green and rest eternal awaited the old man very soon. The old Aborigine, now quite upset, pleading for one of them to take it, held the necklace for Blue to take, and, as he did so, each bead seemed to glow out of all proportion, turning into iridescent rays, piercing both eyes.

Blue, reaching forward, was about to take the beads from Nerimbo's hands, when a loud voice and a bright light shone into his eyes, bringing him to his senses. Prince growled.

"Hey! You! Up to no good, I'd dare say!" A man accused.

Blue, brought back to reality very quickly, answered, "No." Then with a forced laugh, said, "Enjoying a pleasant evening among friends."

"You get hung for sheep stealing, you had best get going before I call my mates," the man said, lowering his lantern.

Blue, not wanting to upset anyone or have a fight, asked this man, whom he assumed to be a Shepherd, "Will you be visiting the Circus?"

"I'd like to. Can't spare the money," came his quick reply.

"Well then, if you have the time, come along to the Big Top, bring a mate, and just ask for 'Blue'. You can remember that, can't you? You will both get in free of charge. That is a promise! And, by the way, I do not steal!"

The man was lost for words.

Wishing him a 'Goodnight', Blue walked away, Prince beside him, following the rough track back to their wagon.

The next day all was ready for the first performance.

"Matinee starts in ten minutes! Not to be missed! Step this way," Blue invited. "Yes, Sir, Lady, Ma'am."

From high above, as he walked about on his stilts, Blue looked down on an assortment of people of all ages. Some were neatly dressed, others he could tell had insufficient cash to enter, yet he did his best to entice them into the tent. He looked the picture of fun and frivolity with Prince perched high on his shoulders, the dog glancing suspiciously at two monkeys hopping up and down on a barrel organ, as their master, turning a handle, churned out melodious tunes.

Abdul emerged from the tent, carrying an enormous bell, which he shook vigorously. Many folks had already seated themselves inside, and more followed. Soon it was filled to capacity. The show commenced. Blue's man from the night had not appeared.

Evening came. Tirelessly, again the same ritual, enticing as many people as possible to part with their money.

This time, the 'man of the night' and his associate did appear.

Wearing long smocks over breeches, buskins and boots, the two men looked slightly bewildered and out of place. Both carried a heavy, knobbed cudgel. Blue saw them go towards Abdul at the tent doorway where he was busy shouting and ringing the bell. Abdul smiled, gave a wave, then bowed and ushered them inside, showing them to two of the better class bench-seats at the front.

Selling toffee apples for a friend, Rachel, disguised in a black wig and oriental gown acquired from Abdul's box, with her face colourfully painted, stopped beside Blue's guests, offering them each a toffee apple.

Both men shook their heads.

"Oh! But you must! These are free! Blue is giving you these," said Rachel, giving one of her prettiest smiles, handing the apples to them.

Furtively looking about, one man asked, "Who is this 'Blue'?" taking the luscious brown toffee-coated apples, both murmuring their thanks.

"You will see. He will come to shake hands with you. He is one of our most kind-hearted and generous performers," said Rachel, giving them two more toffee-apples.

Leaving them she moved away to sell her wares. The show would begin in about ten minutes.

Abdul made his appearance, announcing the commencement of the show. The musicians played. The athletic gymnasts filled the ring, somersaulting, vaulting and generally tossing each other hither and thither. In came the clowns, tormenting them with mock severity. One gymnast grabbed Blue, and with great strength and dexterity, held him aloft, only releasing him when Prince started barking and running around in circles, more often on two legs than on four. The dog, lifted high by Blue, patted his front paws together, encouraging applause.

Playing his accordion, Matthew, with the other musicians, rendered a foot-tapping tune. Abdul's Circus was in full swing with unbridled merriment. To loud applause the elephants performed perfectly with Lolita, Abdul's granddaughter a perfect picture, now well and performing movements, faultlessly, which Rachel would never have anticipated doing.

Walking, skipping, hopping, Blue The Kangaroo Clown, high on his stilts, gave of his best. Stooping forward, he pushed out an elongated wooden arm, complete with white-gloved hand, in the direction of his 'man of the night'.

Feeling embarrassed, not wishing to be made to look a fool, the man turned away, but Blue, with much face action and foolery persisted, until the false hand was taken and shaken.

The folks in the audience held their breath in awe as the brother and sister fire-eaters seemed to consume flame and deemed to roll the flaming torches on their bare skin. They were given a wonderful ovation as they left the ring.

White horses, trotting and tossing plume-bedecked heads, led the clowns into their final act – whip cracking and rope twirling.

To loud applause, the entire cast filled the sawdust-covered ring for the finale. The audience, well satisfied with a most thrilling and entertaining evening, began leaving in an orderly fashion. The Duke of Barnham, seeing the clown's two guests making their way towards the exit, accosted them.

"So, my snivelling peasants, don't come cap in hand for more pittance, when you squander your money on such tomfoolery as this! Who's minding my sheep while you go gallivanting, eh? Answer me, one of you, or have you lost your senses?" he bellowed.

One of the Shepherds answered, "No need for thee to worry. Sheep are well tended, Sir, and a friend paid for us to come here!"

They saw their Master's leering grin when hearing this.

"A likely story. I'm sure your missus will be pleased when you tell her your money's gone, her with six kids to look after!"

Having walked to the front to meet his 'Man of the Night' face to face, Blue had heard enough. Quietly speaking to the pompous man, he said, "What this man has told you is correct. Not a penny have they spent in here. Both are guests of mine!"

Astounded, the Duke looked at the clown. Blue, still dressed in his familiar attire, said to the two Shepherds, "Come my friends, let us away to Bella's food stall. No doubt you will be up at dawn tomorrow, and after the sale have to walk home." Blue bowed to the Duke.

Meekly, hats in hand, they followed the Clown to the stall. There Blue asked for slices of roast beef covered in horseradish, sandwiched between two large slices of bread, two pickled eggs and some of her special fried potatoes, enough for three hungry men. Joking with her, he tossed his money to Bella, who turned a large steaming mass of potatoes onto greased paper, wrapped them expertly in an old newspaper, and handed them to him.

"More of your lame ducks, my darling?" she quietly questioned Blue, giving him his change.

Sitting, eating their food this warm, light evening, backs propped against a stack of wooden boxes, Blue and the Shepherds watched Bella and her family toss more half-cooked potatoes into a large pot of hissing fat. A good thing Prince was secure on his lead or he may have gone to investigate.

A red glow of burning charcoal was encouraged into occasional flame and smoke by spits of hot fat splashing and sizzling from the suspended pot. Whipped by a gentle breeze, the smoke twirled and whirled into the faces of passers-by, the delicious aroma tickling their tastebuds into irresistible temptation. Trade was brisk. Her food delicious. With barely a word spoken between the three, so absorbed were they in the rudiments of eating, they had practically finished when suddenly, Blue jumped to his feet, for standing in front of them were Jacob and Matthew.

Blue flung his arms around Jacob in a fond embrace, so pleased was he to see him. Matthew, smiling happily, said, "It is a long story, Blue, but Jacob is our messenger from Doctor Joshua. He has brought my new leg. Kate is with Rachel at our wagon."

About to tell more, both heard Jacob exclaim, "Well! Bless my soul, if it ain't my brother, William!"

Jacob had just noticed one of the Shepherds Blue had befriended.

Jacob held out his hand, helping his brother to his feet, exchanging pleasantries, slapping each other on the shoulders and laughing together.

What a small world, thought Blue, quickly giving Bella a signal for four more large packages of food. They would all go to the wagons and meet Kate.

Blue, when he met Kate, picked her up in his arms and planted a kiss of paint on her cheek. He had no time to clean himself. With mock severity, she scolded him, asking to be released.

Now seated outside beside the fire, William couldn't grasp the fact it was Rachel who had given them toffee apples. Kate agreed with him.

"No more amazed than I. When I saw Mr Matthew holding hands with a foreign, black-haired woman, well ... until she spoke my name and removed her wig, I was fair flummoxed!"

William, looking at his sister-in-law, could see how devoted she was to the young woman and to find her and her husband as brother Jacob's boss was unbelievable! He thought:

One would expect complete ignorance when two clowns talked about sheep; but not on your life! They spoke of breeds unheard of by us two Shepherds. Quality of wool and suchlike, even suggested starting a flock on their estate; best of all, offering me the job as shepherd, by the recommendation of my brother, Jacob. Took his word for my character! Unbelievable!

When they arrive home to Kiddsmere before Michaelmas, they will send Jacob to fetch me and the family. That I had suspected the other young gentleman was contemplating stealing sheep turns me hot under my 'kerchief. Of course, I apologised to Mr Blue, who, with that mischievous grin of his told me I was only doing my duty and shook me by the hand, pleased to have met me! My mate, Jack, I feel sure, has enjoyed this evening as much as I have. Perhaps there will be room for him at Kiddsmere, if the flock is big enough.

"We had best get along now, eh, Jack? It is long past midnight. I will have something to tell my Sophie when I get home," William said, thanking everyone for their kind hospitality.

"What a wonderful, happy and exciting evening," declared Kate, "and we are staying the night!"

"Now, if Kate sleeps with me in our wagon, you or Jacob could rest with Blue, or in the carriage. Do you approve, Blue?" Rachel asked.

"Yes," Blue agreed, "there is room for three in my wagon."

Matthew laughingly said, "I will wager, you two talk for the remainder of the night. You agree, Jacob? You did say your wife has been like a fish out of water, since we left? Even with Helen and her family to look after!"

Rachel lightly boxed his ears.

Rachel picked up a lantern to show Kate to bed, leaving the menfolk to retire when ready. It would be another busy day, and they should be about early in the morning.

As it happened they were about early, enjoying breakfast, and, the most essential thing – fitting Matthew's new artificial leg.

To help him master his new aid, Jacob cut a hazelwood walking stick from the hedgerow.

For the first time in years, Matthew now had two feet, one of which was giving him quite a problem. Stumbling, he was falling around like a drunken person, so unaccustomed was he to the additional weight and protruding foot and boot.

The length and fitting of the limb was perfect and comfortable. Taggerty had briefly shown him the correct way in which to walk, by bending his knee. Now, sheer perseverance on his part was the only solution. No one could help. For all his circus performances, he would revert to his old device, which would not help matters. Jacob and Kate stayed with them for two days. They loved the elephants. Both behaving like children, they attended every performance, enjoying every moment, seeing the clowns working. They even loved living in the caravans and marvelled how well Rachel had taken to the travellers' life.

While Francis had been on one of his 'Do-Good' missions to Cambsworth, as Kate labelled them, he had suggested Annabel be taken to the hospital for a doctor to look at her back. The Doctor was studying manipulative treatments. Consequently, Kate and Jacob would be returning to Kiddsmere via Cambsworth, in order to convey Francis, Helen and Annabel home.

Time had come for them to say goodbye. The sheep sales finished, it had been a most happy interlude.

For the circus travellers, packing and moving to the next pitch was the order of the day. Work was hard and the days long, but thoroughly enjoyable as they moved from place to place.

Working as a team and in friendship was a great help. Sharing food and laughter around the campfire was a delight to all.

Gradually Matthew overcame his disability, treading carefully, suddenly having the confidence to enter the ring using his new aid. Rachel and Blue were delighted, as were all the other artistes who greatly admired his willpower. No shirker, he always pulled his weight.

The two clowns devised new tricks; their act took on a new momentum, loved by all who came to watch, especially the youngsters.

Daylight began to shorten, the year was slipping away. Soon everyone would go their separate ways, some resting for the winter, having to travel several miles back to their homes. This season, they agreed, had been very good and rewarding.

Polishing a pair of Matthew's boots, Rachel began thinking of her home, wondering if, after all this travelling, she would be able to settle, but she felt happy that wherever her husband went she would go with him. He had begun to smile again; his wound had healed. She remembered the time, not so long ago, he had clung to her in the depth of despair, the inability to walk immediately after all his waiting had nearly broken his heart.

In a day or so, the travellers would reach their final venue, a coastal seaside resort. On this late-summer day, after arriving at their last venue, and having completed as much work as possible, holding Matthew's hand, they walked together on the golden sand. Letting a gentle breeze blow through her hair, Rachel couldn't wish to be happier.

A soothing faint swish, as the ebb-tide lapped loose shingles, was punctuated by an occasional call from a passing gull.

"What a perfect ending to my lovely summer. I've never, ever, enjoyed myself so much. Thank you, Matthew, my dearest," she said with such sincerity that Matthew held her close and kissed her.

"Matthew!" she cried out, looking about them, "someone will see!"

Laughing, he deliberately kissed her again.

Coming upon a groyne, Matthew suggested they sat for a while. Resting against the damp wood, feeling the warmth of the sun on their faces, Matthew, apparently intent on throwing pebbles at a piece of seaweed-covered wood, suddenly said, "Blue has to go back home."

Answering him quite innocently, joining in the stone throwing, she said, "Oh! Isn't he coming home with us?"

"Well ... Yes ... but ..." He stopped throwing stones, his voice sombre. "Home is a long way from here. The other side of the world, in fact."

He heard her gasp. "But, you ... Matthew, you will stay?" she cried.

Seeing her stricken look, he quickly placed his hand over hers, saying, "Of course, my love." Gathering her close in his arms to still her trembling, he felt this was the right time to tell her of his life in Australia and the Homestead. He began his story. She listened without interrupting, hardly taking it all in.

Finally he said, "I let you think I had no money. You saw I was a cripple. If you could marry me under those circumstances, only then would I know you truly loved me, not as an escape from Sir Chester. Francis Peake had to know whom you were marrying. He promised secrecy. You are almost a daughter to them, they have your welfare at heart. But, when we left home, Blue and I made a promise to my father that we would return. I recollect you once saying, you were prepared to travel the world with me. My dearest one, is that still true?"

Placing a finger under her chin, he lifted her face, looking into her eyes, and waited for an answer.

"Yes, my dearest, darling. We will both travel the world with you." Spoken with love, her lips a fraction from his, her words suddenly registered.

"Do you mean ... you said ... 'we' ..." He looked at her.

She smiled, fingering his face. "That is right, I am with child! Practically certain!"

Holding her as if she were a piece of fragile china, he smothered her with rapturous kisses, making declarations of love, over and over again.

In a most joyous mood, taking his flute, he began playing Madame Clare's lullaby, the trill notes floating over the sea, like a Goddess walking on water.

Blue, preparing food, saw them returning. Both looked extremely happy. He doubted very much if Matthew had broached the subject of travelling home to Australia.

"Blue, we have something terribly important to tell you," said Rachel.

Blue looked at her flushed cheeks and listened to Matthew continuing, almost bursting with pride. "I am to be a father! Blue, a father!"

Blue tried his utmost to smile, but his heart sank into the bottom of his boots, thinking that there was no chance of Mathew going back home with him now.

"Well, cheer up! Aren't you going to congratulate us? Now you have to take three to the Dere Homestead!" Rachel said happily.

Matthew saw a flood of relief pass over his friend's face, and with great reverence saw him take Rachel's hand and press it to his heart.

"You truly are a most wonderful friend. I wish you both God's Blessing."

So full was Blue's heart, tears of joy and emotion ran unchecked onto his cheeks.

"Goodness me!" she reprimanded him, "There is a smell of burning fish!" Laughing, she chided him, "I thought I was the only one allowed to burn our dinner!"

Blue brushed an arm across his face, while Matthew took the well-cooked fish from the fire.

Luckily, superb weather stayed with them. Some said it was an Indian Summer. On the whole, the weather had not been bad. Yes, they had days of rain, but this did not inconvenience them overly much.

Abdul, very sad his clowns would not be joining him again the next season, wished them well on their travels. Most certainly, he would pay them a visit at Kiddsmere Hall when they returned, just to hear, again, Matthew's delightful music.

To mark their finale, and Matthew and Rachel's forthcoming parenthood, Blue arranged a gigantic party for the group of travellers.

The seaside town at which they were now performing had a large open air market. Visiting this, Blue purchased fruit, meat and savouries, lobster and crab, oriental food, bread and fancy cakes and any other delicacy needing minimal preparation, including wines and beers.

Feeling so happy, because a burden had been lifted from his shoulders, he could virtually 'jump over the moon' as the saying goes. He was going home, or rather they were going home.

Asking Abdul for the use of his tent, he gave invitations to all the artistes and their families to attend.

After the final performance, many helpers happily arranged the food on boxes and benches, or on any available space they could find. The party began. Music song and dance, the age-old adage, 'eat, drink and be merry', certainly applied. Rachel had never seen people enjoy themselves with such fervour. One had the feeling this party could go on forever, as everyone came to celebrate, even babes in arms.

Each family in turn gave a short, impromptu performance, their expertise exhilarating and thrilling.

Blue invited the children into the ring to try walking on stilts, and after an enormous amount of fun, gave a demonstration of his famous 'Kangaroo Hop'.

Gradually, energies spent and getting late into the night, the children becoming tired and unmanageable, some from Abdul's band and Matthew gave a rendition of 'Auld Lang Syne', the travellers joining hands to sing and cheer at this never-to-be-forgotten party.

The party over, Blue found Estelle beside him, helping to clear the remnants of food. When she asked where in Australia they were making for, Blue gave her a most colourful description of fruit trees, roses, blue-gum trees, spinifex and surrounded by red, craggy mountains, omitting to give her the description of a phantom woman on horseback, whose facial details always eluded him.

"Take me with you, Blue," pleaded Estelle, holding on to his arm.

Blue looked at her sympathetically, apologising.

"Sorry, Estelle, I do not wish to hurt you. My heart feels nothing. All the time I am searching for someone in my dreams. You are a beautiful young woman who will make some young man a wonderful wife, but ..." he was saved from further explanation by a young artiste who brought him a box of neatly packed fruit.

Accepting her battle was lost, a despondent Estelle said a sad goodbye as the clown turned away, talking with the young man.

Everything to do with the circus was packed, neat and tidy, by the middle of the following day. Abdul and a few travellers would soon be away, some making for their usual place of shelter in Devon. One by one, with cheery goodbyes they left. As the trio wended their way across the flat broadland, the windmills and waterways fascinated Blue.

Old, timbered dwellings and buildings, with plump, thatched roofs, colour-washed in a variety of pastel pinks and creams, and the numerous, round towered churches were magnificent. Then further inland, small fields of wheat and oats and tall hedgerows of bright berries and crab-apples.

Seeing a field of small shrubby plants, and noticing a delightful perfume, he stopped his horse, Silver, and shouted, "What is it?"

"Lavender," Rachel answered.

Why, of course, he thought, dear Harriet Green's Norfolk Lavender.

Seeing women busy working, Blue jumped from his wagon seat, looping the reins over a post, and set off across the field, intent on purchasing a bundle or two. Returning with an armful of short, stubby stems, he handed some to Rachel, who immediately rubbed the seed-head, then tied the seeds in the corner of her handkerchief.

During the several days spent travelling with the occasional stop to visit a church or two to view the organ, should it have one, Blue tried to make up his mind where to park his wagon. At Kiddsmere Hall or with Francis at the rectory? Eventually he decided it would be with Francis. They had much to discuss and little time. He did not think he would visit England again.

During the evenings, as they rested from their day's journey, the trio began to plan ahead. Matthew dearly wanted their child to be born at the Dere Homestead. Rachel had no preference. Calculating April as the possible arrival of their baby, they should leave England within the next month or so.

This suited Blue fine, but the affairs of the Kiddsmere Estate had to be settled and arranged for several months ahead, possibly over a year or two.

Nearing home, Blue thought, we have travelled full circle, when looking across the fields, with their stooks of golden corn on the outskirts of Kiddsmere village.

The next turning, he knew, would be Pound hill, then the Smithy, sheltered under leafy oaks, their pale golden acorns clipped onto cases like tobacco in a clay-pipe, waiting for the moment to drop to the ground, to be gathered for animal feed or used as 'shot' in a child's elderwood pop gun. Blue smiled to himself.

Sam the Smith stood at the half-opened shop doorway, a red-hot horseshoe gripped between tongs, and beside him stood his apprentice lad. Both looked happy and well and shouted a greeting.

Blue answered, raising his hat, but did not stop. So far, nothing seemed changed. I do believe it is the same bunch of women in the butcher's shop, he laughed, raising his hat as they stepped out to see the return of the Lady of the Manor and the clowns.

Singing, giving a wave and lift of the hat to other folk, they bet news of their arrival would travel like wildfire, and, before Rachel and Matt could cross the stone bridge, Kate would be halfway along the drive to meet them.

At the rectory entrance, Blue halted, gave a cheery wave as his friends, bubbling with excitement, passed by.

The iron tyres of the wheels crunched and rattled on the rectory's gravel driveway, as Silver pulled the wagon to within a few feet of the open door of the scullery. The air was filled with that wonderful aroma Blue associated with Mrs Peake and her kitchen; boiling jam.

He and Prince hurried in, calling as he went, finding her busy at the stove. In joyous greeting. Blue gathered her in his arms and twirled her around. Laughing, they collapsed on to the two chairs beside the kitchen table, then sat and chatted happily. Francis was out visiting in the village, but would be returning shortly.

Blackberry and apple jam stood on the table. Mrs Peake saw Blue look at the testing dish, and walking over to her bread pot, collected a thick crust, spread it with butter and handed it to him.

Smiling broadly, he spooned dollops of jam from the dish, spreading it on his bread, took a large bite, chewed, licked his lips, murmuring, "Delicious!"

"You are so like my eldest boy, Richard," Marjorie Peake said, giving a sigh. "Perhaps he will come home next year," she added wistfully.

Blue put his arms around her and gave her a hug.

"I have to leave you, sad to say, I must attend to Silver. I will be back soon."

Nearing the door, with Prince at his heels, he suddenly turned and remembered to give Rachel's invitation for her and Francis to join them at the Hall for supper.

"Just what I need," she said happily.

Francis had returned when Blue, all clean and tidy, made his appearance at the rectory door. Losing no time, he had paid a quick visit to the Smithy to book Silver for shoe repairs and have a congenial word with the lad apprentice.

Various documents had been placed on the rectory study table for Blue to see, with regard to the Orphanage. Francis was very pleased with the results and happenings at Cambsworth. The equipment and state of affairs.

A call from the Rector's wife, telling them Jacob had arrived, ended their talk of business, but a great deal had been accomplished.

Jacob smiled broadly and welcomed Blue home. "Pleasure to see them back, isn't it, Rector?" helping Mrs Peake and the Rector into the carriage.

"It is indeed, Jacob," she answered. "I have missed them!"

Jacob, driving his passengers to the Hall, agreed, like every other worker on the estate it was a blessing in disguise the day those two lads first came upon him and Mistress Rachel in distress, now a baby on the way, or so his Kate had informed him, confidential mind. He sat alone on his carriage driving seat, ruminating. And to top the lot, Kate and he had been asked to go with them to Australia! His stomach gave another somersault at the thought! Kate was over the moon.

The Boss was making plans already, and only been back five minutes, as the saying goes. Jacob stopped his cogitating to carefully manoeuvre his coach and passengers over the stone bridge.

After which, his mind began to mull over the recent events. From all accounts, things would be moving pretty fast. No grass grew under young Master's feet and the Agent for the Estate, Major Angus Browne, had turned out to be a pleasant, honest chap and capable of being left in charge, with the help of Clinton Howard.

After receiving young Matthew's letter, the Major soon arranged a cottage for brother William and his family. William would be leaving his present employer at Michaelmas. Jacob chuckled, bless my soul, before coming home, those boys had arranged for a flock of sheep to be delivered for his brother to look after, as soon as he gets moved in. And look after them, he will. Best Shepherd around for miles, even though he said it himself.

Stopping the carriage at the front steps, Burroughs appeared immediately, opening doors, ushering Francis and Mrs Peake inside.

They greeted Rachel affectionately, then stood and gazed at the walls and ceiling of the large hallway, now completely redecorated, with the floor polished until one could see one's face in it.

Rachel told them that Kate and the servants had thoroughly cleaned the whole place.

"They have done wonders while we have been away," she said, taking both her guests into the sitting room, where Matthew greeted them, apologising for his lateness.

"I must say, young man," Francis said, looking at Matthew, "You and your wife certainly look the picture of good health." He had observed the new limb, but made no comment.

Matthew, beaming with pride, drew his wife into the circle of his arm, and announced they were to become parents.

The Rector and his wife were both delighted and could talk of little else, until supper was announced.

Champagne stood by the crystal glasses. Tureens with vegetables and soup and a joint of meat had been placed on a side table. Unused to this elaborate setting, Blue made a remark: "Smoked ham, pea and potato soup, served with burned toast? Is that correct, Rachel Dere?" as he lifted the lids inquisitively.

The three travellers laughed and begun telling of their experiences, as they ate their delicious supper, not forgetting to mention the number of village churches they had visited, especially one with a beautifully carved altar.

An intricately carved, wooden font cover, five to six feet in height, raised and lowered by chain and pulley, something which Rachel remembered vividly.

Francis and his wife listened avidly, sometimes adding information, especially when Blue spoke of a church with pews and mangers, troughs and metal rings secured to inside walls.

"I am unable to remember if the heads of the Angels were missing from the woodwork in that one; they were in some we visited," Blue remarked.

"Oh, yes, quite true, I expect it seems quite strange to you, but horses were taken inside," agreed Francis. "There are many unhappy years in the history of our Church."

The subject of returning to Australia arose.

"Rachel now knows I am no roving, penniless, Minstrel," Matthew said, adding, "We would like our baby born at the

Dere Homestead."

He did not add the urgency of their going home was due to Blue or his mysterious illness.

"Thank you, Francis, for investigating Matthew's background on my behalf. Of course, no matter what anyone said, I would have married him anyway," Rachel said, smiling at her husband.

The Peakes and Blue were ready to leave for the rectory, when Marjorie said, "You must dine with us before you set sail for Australia."

"And you shall have blackberry and apple roly-poly pudding!" Blue announced, laughing. "I have already sampled the jam!"

He gave Mrs Peake a wink. "It is Matthew's favourite!"

A week passed. Plans for their journey began to fall into place. After calling upon Helen and her family to say goodbye, Blue would continue to Cambsworth. From there he would travel to London and make contact with Mr Blizzard.

Taking with him all the relevant documents, it was his duty to make all the arrangements for their passage to Australia. He would then stay and wait for them at their London home.

Blue, with his dog, left Kiddsmere village early one autumn morning, on the first leg of their journey. After great deliberation, he had decided his faithful friend, Prince, should accompany them home to his place of birth. In any case, now, looking at his dog sitting beside him on the seat, and giving him an unexpected pat, he couldn't bear the thought of leaving him in England.

After this cool climate, he hoped the heat back home would not affect the old fella too much, but by the time they reached Australia, winter would not be far away. Making a leisurely journey, he arrived at Wethergate and was met by Annabel running down the garden path. Gathering her in his arms, he carried her into the house, amazed and very pleased with her progress. She now had plump, rosy cheeks and her body was developing healthily.

"Where is Princess Rachel?" she asked.

He explained Rachel was waiting for them to join her at the Hall, before leaving to visit a new country.

Helen bade him welcome, as he stood Annabel down, and listened as her daughter told her, in a tearful voice, that Rachel was going away again.

"Have you forgotten? Jacob is coming to collect you, next week. Your friend, Elsie, is waiting to take care of you, for months!" Blue tried to paint a brighter picture.

Blue then told her of Rachel's performance on Abdul's elephants, and making the children in the Big Top laugh.

Annabel's recovery was Helen's tonic. She looked a different person as she poured tea and handed round some biscuits. But a morose quietness settled over them when Blue told them this was his last visit.

Sadly, Annabel placed her arms round his neck, pleading, "Boy Blue, you will return, won't you?"

"Possibly. Matthew and Rachel will come home. One day I may return," he said, giving her a hug. "How about you coming to Australia to see me?" he suggested, telling her what a great country it was.

Time came for him to leave. Promising he would keep in touch, he leapt on to his wagon seat, and with a quick smile and wave, urged his horse forward, casually turning, raising his hand, seeing them at the garden gate, waving farewell. Tears blinded his eyes.

Parting had been equally as difficult with Francis and his wife. To go in such haste! "Stay for Christmas at least," they had pleaded.

Blue's thoughts meandered, a lovely couple ... whatever would the Kiddsmere parishioners do without Francis?

He drove on towards Cambsworth to spend a few days with Joshua and his friends. Then it would be time for him to travel to London.

Something or someone urged him on. 'Do not dally', it seemed to say. He felt elated at the prospect of returning home. An urgency for his journey was always uppermost in his mind, but he could not pinpoint the reason.

His farewells said, he was now in London. The days had passed very quickly.

Having completed the tasks he had undertaken most satis-factorily, he now stood patiently beside a window, waiting for the Kiddsmere carriage to appear.

He did not have long to wait, and raced to the front door, opened it before Maslin came, just as Jacob eased his horses to a halt.

It was pandemonium for a while, everyone talking and laughing, pleased to have arrived safely.

Jacob began unloading the neatly labelled boxes and trunks, helped by Maslin and the stable lad, Johnson, from Kiddsmere.

Leonardo had agreed to accompany Johnson with the Kiddsmere coach and horses, taking with them Blue's horse, Silver. It would be a rather slow journey, but Silver would then spend the remainder of his life in retirement, at Kiddsmere.

In a few days' time I will be re-loading these boxes and heading for the Docks, ready for embarkation, Jacob thought to himself, stopping to look around.

He removed his hat, scratched his head, fanned his face with the hat, thinking about the sea voyage. His stomach lurched again. Replacing his hat, he passed down more luggage.

"Don't do to stand and think!" he murmured.

Rachel rested for the remainder of the day. The next day she enjoyed visiting shops with Kate, making elegant purchases, gifts for her father and mother-in-law, and Matt's sisters. Having no close relatives of her own, she became excited at the prospect of meeting them.

Dress lengths of pretty materials, beads and lace. When confronted with so many parcels, Matthew threw up his hands in mock despair, telling them they would sink the ship.

The last few days in London had moved at an even faster pace.

The previous day Blue's wagon had been manhandled and securely fixed on board ship. Boxes and trunks were loaded. Soon they would be sailing.

"Do you really mean, Matthew, your father owns this ship?" Rachel asked, sitting with her husband on a comfortable bunk bed, after boarding the ship.

"Well, not exactly, my love. With others. A company affair," he answered truthfully. "My poor, wandering Minstrel!" she laughed at the look of guilt on his face.

"Yes, my father is quite wealthy." Quickly kissing her, he said, "I am also rich, for I have you, my treasure. Come sweetheart, let us go to watch the cast-off," steadying her up the ladder to where Blue, Kate and Jacob were watching the deckhands making ready for sail.

With a look of alarm on his face, as distance grew between ship and jetty, Jacob moved away from the ship's railings, holding Kate's arm, and sat himself down on the first available object, which happened to be a large coil of rope.

Blue and Kate managed to help Jacob down below deck, assuring him he was not going to die, and would feel better in a few days' time. This being only the beginning of the voyage, they wondered as to his reaction out on the ocean.

Back on deck with Prince, Blue looked about him as the ship made its escorted way down the River Thames, trying hard to imprint the sights and sounds in his mind, as somehow, a strange feeling gave him to believe, he would not set foot on English soil again.

Chapter 29

In Justville, Australia, Martha Everest glanced across the road and saw several mailbags being unloaded and carried inside the sorting office. The weekly mail had arrived. I don't suppose for one moment, she thought, as she had many times before, there would be any correspondence from that son of ours. If it wasn't for letters received from Mr Blizzard – true, the details originally came from both boys – one would think they were dead. Giving a sigh, Martha turned away, trying to concentrate on her work ahead, it being duty-day for her at the hospital, but for some unaccountable reason, she was unable to take her mind off her son. What would he think of the new hospital building? Longer wards to accommodate even more patients. Spacious rooms as living quarters for young people training to nurse, and no finer bunch of doctors to be found in the whole state; their reputation gathering momentum for the excellent surgery and treatment of ailments.

Because of the hospital, the town of Justville had become considerably larger, with a more prosperous community. Two new hotels, with pleasant rooms and facilities, enabling folks from the Outback to come and stay over, catch up with the gossip and visit the stores. Some of the shops, including the bakehouse, butcher and laundry, were commissioned to supply the hospital.

Martha could not believe how dramatically her lifestyle had changed. Their travelling days were over. Duke seemed to be quite settled and happy. The Everest and Jackson families, now looked upon as guardian angels, and highly respected.

Her thoughts were broken by a light tap on the door and Rebekah came into the room.

"Duke is busy at the moment," she said, "so I have brought this to you." Rebekah handed a package to Martha.

Martha, with excitement, exclaimed, "It's from England! 'Bekah wait, don't go! Maybe Blue is coming home! Please sit down a moment."

Quickly tearing open the package, her face aglow with anticipation, she unfolded a large sheet of paper, saying, with great disappointment, "It is from Mr Blizzard," looking at a full, neatly handwritten page.

Then with an exclamation of delight, making Rebekah jump from her chair and cross the room to her, she cried, "They are coming home!"

Reading on, she said, "Matthew and his wife, Rachel, Blue and Prince, and Kate and Jacob, leaving London …"

Rebekah glanced over Martha's shoulder, noticed the date of the letter.

"Martha, look at the date, they will soon be arriving! We haven't long to wait!"

Duke made an appearance.

"I heard excited voices. What is it about? Sounds like a party," he ventured a guess.

"Duke, darling! Blue is coming home!" Martha rushed to him, put her arms around his neck, and began to cry.

Unobtrusively, Rebekah left them, wondering if Matthew had sent a similar message to Papa and Mama. Her brother, married!

Glancing at her timepiece, there was no time to dawdle. Being a Senior Nurse in charge, her duty today finished at midday, unless any emergency arose, and so far, all appeared well.

Rebekah walked towards her small bungalow, set in the hospital grounds, planning her free afternoon and evening, her duties finished until six o'clock the next morning. Firstly, her hair needed washing. To sit on the veranda with a book, letting her hair dry, she thought, would be absolute bliss.

Casually lifting the lid of her mailbox, she took out a long envelope.

Looking at the bold writing and letting herself into her neat home, she wondered how the letter had arrived, as it had no duty stamp.

Her bungalow consisted of a large, light, kitchen-cum-dining area, equipped with a small, solid fuel stove for cooking and heating, when required. A wash-up area, spacious, comfortable sitting room and a medium size bedroom, the bungalow was her pride and joy. As much as she had enjoyed living with Duke and Martha, she was delighted when told she would have a place of her own. Her nursing salary enabled her to add a touch of homeliness. With Abigail's wonderful needlework, soft cushions enhanced the comfortable divan and easy chairs, with curtains to match. Rebekah valued her independence and privacy, but being a workaholic, often spent her off-time working in the hospital.

Abigail still found time for her needlework, even though she and James had twin baby girls, Primrose and Patience.

Opening the envelope, she first looked at the signature.

Brent Gordon! Her husband!

Her heart skipped a beat. Sitting herself down, she began reading: 'Dear Rebekah, for the first time in several years, I am in Justville. I have a small matter to discuss with you. Meet me at the Lucky Slipper Saloon, tonight, six thirty, for supper. I know you have this evening off duty. Yours, Brent Gordon.'

Her heart raced. She felt unable to move. After re-reading his letter, many questions sped through her mind. What did he want? Where had he been all this time? She had nearly forgotten his features. From the day of their wedding, she had not seen him. His name was constantly mentioned by Martha and Duke, because of the gold find on a claim registered by them. No personal contact, ever, always from a Hobart Office.

With an effort, she began washing her hair and body, drying

herself and tying a towel around her head. She opened her wardrobe, wondering what she should wear. The evening could be quite cool.

Having very few clothes, this required no great decision, and so she chose a full-length red velvet dress, which had three-quarter-length sleeves, so no need for a jacket or coat. To complete her outfit, she added black lace mittens and black leather boots. Everything ready, she continued drying her hair.

Six o'clock. Dressed and in a complete state of nervous apprehension, she glanced in her dressing table mirror for the umpteenth time, making sure no strand of hair had escaped from its tight clasp. Flinging a black shawl around her shoulders, she made her way towards the saloon, a few hundred yards or so from the bungalow.

A well-dressed man, quite a distance away, walked towards her. She knew instantly it was Brent, and that he had seen her.

Passing a few remarks to people walking by, she casually gazed into a store window, giving the impression she was in no hurry to meet him, but in reality, her heart was beating madly, and she felt a dreadful urge to rush forward and put her arms around him. Instead, with a fixed smile on her face, she hardly spoke a word when he greeted her, quietly saying, "Hello, Mrs Gordon, I trust you are well?"

His eyes took in her immaculate appearance and on his handsome face he wore a daring look, as if he were about to enfold her in his arms and kiss her.

Together they entered the Lucky Slipper Saloon, where he propelled her to the seclusion of a small back room and a table neatly set for two. This reminded her so poignantly of their last meeting.

The jovial proprietor brought a bottle of wine, telling them food would be ready in five minutes, leaving the two alone.

Brent gave her a glass of wine, pouring some for himself, noting the fact she wore no wedding ring.

"Have you eaten today?" he asked, smiling.

Seeing her blush, sipping wine, taking in her every feature, he suggested she drank some.

"Yes. I have eaten, thank you," she said and asked, "When did you arrive? Are you staying in this place?" meaning the Saloon.

"Yesterday – late evening. I have a clean, pleasant room here," he answered as a young person brought in a tray laden with dishes filled with chicken and freshly cooked vegetables, which he had ordered beforehand, undoubtedly assuming his invitation would be accepted.

This assumption rankled with her. She had vowed to get even with him, one way or the other, but, to date, she had had no chance. She could have refused this invitation, but her heart gave her to understand otherwise.

After their meal, with barely a word spoken between them, Brent, without hesitation, said, "The reason why I have asked you to meet me, is I want you to consider an annulment of our marriage. I realise my mistake, blackmailing you. I regret it, and apologise most sincerely. It will not be difficult, our marriage not having been … consummated."

Instantly she felt outraged. So, the tables had turned. He had no idea of the pain and heartache he had caused. He was the one who had suffered, supposedly from guilt! A woman somewhere? Well, he could jolly well wait!

She laughed, contemptuously.

"So, the biter has been bitten. A woman in the wings, no doubt, eagerly waiting for you to marry her?" Rebekah accused sarcastically, yet felt appalled at the prospect.

His face paled at her outburst.

"Why wait so long before confronting me? Is it because you now have no hold? Martha and Duke have enough money to build six hospitals, without your help!" she shouted furiously.

"Never will I give my consent to an annulment! Never!"

Jumping to her feet, she pushed the table towards him, ran out onto the sidewalk and raced to the sanctity of her bungalow.

Breathless, she flung herself onto her bed in the darkness, sobbing into her pillow, wishing she could die, feeling as if her heart would break. After all this time, deep down, she had hoped against hope that something would be forthcoming from this foolhardy marriage.

She did not hear the door open and close, or see Brent cross to her bedside, only heard his voice trying to calm her.

Her body, racked by sobs, was his undoing.

"Rebekah, my darling, I love you, oh, so desperately!" he said as he cradled her in his arms.

"You … cannot … possibly …" she answered between sobs, struggling to gain release from his arms, to no avail.

"I do. I have loved you and wanted you from the moment I saw you. That was why I blackmailed you. I could see no other way of you marrying me. I was jealous of both Seth and Teddy Jackson."

Still not releasing her, softly stroking her hair, her crying gradually ceased.

"I love you, please believe me, my darling," he pleaded.

"This evening … why did you ask for …?"

Placing a finger over her lips, the rest of her sentence remained unspoken.

"I will tell you another time. What I want to know, my beautiful Rebekah, is will you consent to my calling upon you in the traditional manner of a beau? Do I stand a chance of gaining your affection, or do you hate me?"

With bated breath, Brent waited for her answer, which to him seemed an eternity.

Held close to his chest, she could hear the rapid beating of his heart and could feel her own heart beating just as madly. At this moment, she relived the many times a blanket-covered miner or construction worker had been brought into the hospital after an accident, fear clutching her heart, until she had seen the face and found it was not Brent. She loved this man. Her husband.

Much to his despair, before giving him an answer, she released herself from his hold. In darkness, in fear of breaking the magic of this moment, she opened a bedside drawer, found her wedding ring and slipped it on her finger. Returning to him, she gently touched his face, placing his hand over her hand, so he felt the ring on her finger.

"I love you, Brent," she whispered shyly. "How soon do you wish to start calling? Remember, I am a married woman!"

She heard him gasp and felt his lips on hers. Passionate, demanding kisses, as they clung to each other.

Brent left her bungalow before daylight. Together, they had made plans for their future, and to see her father at the Homestead as soon as possible. Brent was intent on making his confession.

Rebekah's duties started at six, and, during the morning, she asked for a few days' leave from the hospital, giving no reason.

Her request granted, Brent met her with a hired wagon to convey them to the Homestead.

Her mother and father were overjoyed at this unexpected visit by their daughter and, with their usual courtesy, welcomed her escort.

Beth Dere, looking from one to the other, thought something was amiss. Brent, in his forthright manner, came straight to the point. He had a confession to make to them, and hoped they would forgive him, as Rebekah had forgiven him. In the comfort of Beth's kitchen, Brent divulged their secret marriage in Sydney, painting a bad picture of himself, his love for Rebekah and his jealousy, and finally the blackmail.

Her father surveyed his daughter across the table, saying gravely, "You did this for the hospital? You do not wish to

302

release him? You must love him, your … husband!"

Rebekah blushed, hung her head, and uttered a quiet, "Yes, Father."

"Good for you, my girl, you have my blessing!"

Turning to Brent, he said, "So, after all this time, I am meeting the benefactor of the Justville Hospital! My … Our … Son-in-law!"

Giving a smile in his wife's direction, he then inquired of the couple, "Have you enlightened Duke and Martha Everest?"

Rebekah spoke, "Definitely not, Father! No one knows, but you and Mama!"

Ruth rushed into the kitchen, interrupting them, planted a kiss on her father's head.

"I wondered who was visiting. Thought it was my prodigal brother."

"No, Ruth, your prodigal sister and her husband, Brent Gordon," Rebekah enlightened her proudly. "This is my sister Ruth, Brent."

"Saints Alive! The Brent Gordon, your husband?" Ruth repeated, openly admiring Brent's handsome looks, holding onto his outstretched hand and uttering another inaudible, crude remark.

Her mother, distressed by Ruth's abominable behaviour, quickly said to Rebekah, "Show Brent to the new guest room, 'Bekah dear. You must need to refresh yourselves. I will get some refreshment."

With a great deal to discuss, the couple stayed at the Homestead for two days, Brent appreciating every moment. For the first time in his whole life, he felt part of a real family, giving them a brief description of his childhood, his upbringing by his grandparents. They considered his education of the utmost importance, and consequently were very strict.

He told them little of his father. Occasionally he saw him, when he visited Hobart, but they seemed to have very little in common. After his grandparents and his father died, he was left to care for his young half-brother, Seth. Sadly bitterness had entered into his life, against women, because of the trauma caused when Seth's mother left his father, leaving them penniless.

When it was time for them to leave the warmth and comfort of the Homestead, Brent was quite sad.

Arriving back in Justville came the task of telling Abigail, Martha and Duke of their marriage. That he was the benefactor of the hospital, and that she would be leaving to live with her husband in Hobart, after Matthew's return home.

After the first initial shock, news of their marriage became equal to a nine-day wonder. Everyone who knew her gave their blessings and congratulations for a long and happy life together, hoping they would return occasionally to Justville. Great appreciation was shown to the man who had given them this wonderful hospital. Justville folks would always be proud of him.

Abigail hoped her mother and father would come to stay with her and James, to await Matthew's arrival.

"You know how much Mama and Papa adore the twins. James and I do not expect Ruth will condescend to come," said Abigail, when talking to Martha.

They were making sure they had enough accommodation arranged for everyone.

"No. Your sister, Ruth, has become a strange young woman," Martha agreed, remembering the sarcastic remark she had made – "An aristocratic frump, no doubt!" – after learning of the marriage of her brother.

Satisfied with their arrangements, Abigail departed, having left her twins in the care of their Grandmama Jackson.

In Martha's estimation, Ruth had grown into a beautiful, wild, tomboy, but very temperamental. Adored and spoiled by her father, Ben. He was putty in her hands, as the saying goes, letting her run the Homestead, which she did, expertly, nothing escaping her eyes.

Jake was once heard to remark, 'That gal knows if a new blade of grass shoots up overnight!'

Martha's thoughts ran on … it is a pity Ben allows that young lad, Jason, around the place, always seeking Ruth's company, upsetting the regular workers.

Martha remembered the young man had first visited the homestead when firefighting, a night or so after Abigail's wedding, reappearing about a year ago with a shearing gang. Although a handsome fellow, he seemed of doubtful character.

It was possible Ruth would come to Justville to meet her brother and his wife, but it was very difficult to predict her actions, being a law unto herself.

At one of Beth's family gatherings, which she and Duke attended, Ruth dressed herself as an Hawaiian girl, flowers in her hair and Lei decorously hung around her neck, to become the life and soul of the party.

Jason could not take his eyes off her, as she danced, Hawaiian style, to music provided by a group of stockmen and their friends.

When the garland began to wilt, Jason made fun of her. Grimacing at him, she left the barn hurriedly, going towards the bungalow, Jason following.

Martha remembered the moment well. Jake was sitting on the veranda steps as she and Duke had walked towards the brightly lit bungalow. They stopped as Ruth came from within, bereft of the garland. Holding hands with Jason, the young couple returned to the party.

They heard Jake muttering. Both knew Jake had no time for young Jason. The old man had become very wizened, but still very observant and had his wits about him, although one had the feeling he was hanging on to life, waiting for the return of Matthew and Blue.

While talking with Jake, they had heard someone shouting for the doctor. Quickly returning to the shed, she and Duke were told Ruth had suddenly become very ill. Duke had taken command, carrying Ruth to her bedroom. Ruth was clutching her necklace and became violently sick. With a glazed look in her eyes, the young girl looked around the room as if she was searching for someone, then, placing a hand over her heart, sank lower into the bed, moaning and talking nonsense.

Duke had ascertained she had received no venomous bite.

She had noticed her husband release the necklace from Ruth's grasp, remove and pocket the beads.

A very distraught Ben asked if his daughter was about to die, pleading for Duke to do something. Praying aloud.

After giving Ruth a sedative, which she drank with reluctance, it had taken them quite a time to pacify him, assuring him his daughter was not about to die.

Leaving them in the room, Duke had gone in search of Jason.

Later, when she and Duke were alone, her husband told her, that, while mixing the sedative, he had asked himself, 'Had the strange necklace something to do with Ruth's illness? He felt sure it had. To whom did it belong? Jason? Had he given it to Ruth?' He had seen his old Aborigine friend, Nerimbo, wearing similar beads, and, if his supposition was correct, this was the tribal necklace given to Blue by Nerimbo. If this was the case, she would recover in a day or so.

Duke had found Jason leaning against a wagon close to the bungalow. The young man, quite concerned, had asked after Ruth. After enlightening him as to her condition, Duke had carefully questioned him, showing him the strange, wooden beads. Jason had not seen them before that evening.

Satisfied he was telling the truth, Duke felt his suspicion was correct. This carved necklace, an Aboriginal tribal love token, was the one given to Blue by old Nerimbo. At some time or other, Blue had given it to Ruth!

As Duke told this to her, she could not believe it, and at the same time had said to her husband, "But they were like cat and dog! Are you sure? These" – handling the wooden necklace – "a love token? Ruth and our son? Do you believe in such things, Duke?"

Her husband had only shrugged his shoulders and would not commit himself, mentioning he would return the necklace to Ruth.

Much to the relief of everyone, Ruth made a fine recovery in a matter of days. But what had happened to cause her to completely ignore Jason, they had no idea. This soon became obvious to those around her, pleasing no one more than Jake. At last, she had, in some way, seen through the young stranger.

Jake, when asked by Duke, what he knew about Aboriginal tribal beliefs and customs, had retreated into his shell as if in fear, and glossed over the question by saying he had little to do with them.

"Didn't do to meddle. Live and let live. But, he added, now, that Clare woman ... twiddle-twaddle ... those two boys mixed up ..."

Martha gave a laugh; daydreaming again, she chided herself, gathering a bundle of neatly rolled bandages, and declared happily, "Blue will soon be home!"

Chapter 30

Blue was waiting at the Justville railhead for Matthew and the others to arrive by passenger train from Adelaide. Earlier he had travelled from Adelaide by freight train with his dog, horse and wagon. His horse was in superb condition, as he knew it would be, at Albert's stables.

After arriving at the Port, they had spent a short time with Albert and his family, but, as Rachel, although withstanding the sea voyage quite well, was becoming travel-weary, everyone agreed they would like to get to their destination as soon as possible. So, with luck, in a few days' time, they would be in Justville.

Blue heard a shrill 'toot', the thunder of metal wheels, then saw the train, amidst steam and smoke, ease its way to the well-worn stopping place, where several people had gathered. Doors flung open from the many carriages and Blue finally spotted his friends, instructing the baggage handler to collect their luggage, directing them to his wagon. Both ladies looked hot and in need of refreshment, but in good spirits, their journey being delayed some hours by a rock fall.

For the night, Blue had booked them in to a newly-built hotel. The busy junction was fast becoming a popular place, and new shops and dwellings lined the dusty, Justville road, vastly different from Blue's memories.

Leaving the ladies and Matthew in the hotel, Blue and Jacob went to buy a couple of horses. Leaning on the wooden rails of a corral, letting their eyes roam over a few horses, they could not see one to their liking.

A stout, short man waddled forward to greet them, eyeing them up and down, trying, no doubt, to assess their means and knowledge of horse flesh.

After asking their requirements, he told them to follow him to the barn.

What Jacob saw, when the owner opened the barn door, almost made him weep. Five scraggy creatures stood deep in dung. Disgusted, Jacob turned on the man, stating in no uncertain terms he should be horse-whipped for keeping animals in such conditions.

The dealer, leering, stated as a matter of fact that city folk knew nothing, began cursing and told them to leave.

Calmly, Blue informed the ranting man to expect a visit from the Government Inspector, and with that they left.

At a newly-built establishment, they purchased two horses of a reasonable age, but in good condition and temperament, suitable for Blue and Matthew to ride to Justville. Jacob would drive the wagon with Kate and Rachel.

"Can't get over the fact how big and blue the sky looks," Kate said looking about her. "So different from England."

"I haven't seen a drop of rain! It is very hot, isn't it?" Rachel said, fanning herself as they left the hotel.

"Wait until we have a storm, my love, then it really does rain," Matthew told her.

All their arrangements seemed to be falling into place and they had been journeying a couple of days in the wagon. With great excitement Matthew announced, "Another hour and we will be in Justville!"

Rachel looked around, smiling, quite liking the vast country, pointing to a host of vivid coloured birds. Out in the open last evening, under the millions of stars, listening to strange, animal night calls, which gave her an eerie feeling, she had nestled closer to her husband, before retiring with Kate inside the wagon, but, by daylight, everything looked wonderful and beautiful.

Soon, very soon, she would be meeting Matthew's family. But before that, a much-needed rest.

Next day, placing her hand in the crook of Matthew's arm, she walked a short distance with him to view the waterhole, while Blue deftly cooked slices of meat over a fire. Kate and Jacob, happily talking, seemed to be enjoying every moment of this strange lifestyle.

Hardly had they finished eating when Blue pointed in the direction of a ball of dust. It was time for them to push on, so they quickly gathered their things together away from the dust.

Along this wide track, cattle and riders had met and passed them. Some riders waved; others had no time, busy urging their cattle forward.

Nearer to Justville, Blue thought how much busier the cattle road had become, and laughed to himself, recollecting the first time he travelled this way and the episode of the chilli paste. Ruth must be a young woman. Tempestuous as ever, no doubt. Could not possibly be married.

"Married? No!" Blue said aloud, pulling up his horse.

Matthew, riding close beside him, asked, "You feeling ill? I have spoken to you several times."

"I am fine thanks," Blue gave a brief reply.

Matthew gave a sigh of relief. Blue's ghostly white face had quite frightened him. Thank God they were nearly home.

"Justville!" Both shouted, pointing and laughing, throwing their hats in the air. Through the shimmering heat they could see the town.

"You are grown men!" Rachel laughed with them. "You behave like boys!"

The town had developed beyond their recognition. Fashionable large houses vied with small shacks, their shining tin roofs reflecting the sunlight. They could not believe their eyes. Past the large hospital building, stores, a saloon, then on to the much older houses.

On the familiar veranda steps of the Everest house stood Blue's mother. Someone must have told her of their progress.

Blue jumped from his horse, kissed her, picked her up in his arms and twirled her around. Then, taking a look at her face, he gathered the corner of her white apron, and dabbed at the tears running unheeded down her cheeks. Making fun of her, he told her Matthew's wife and their friends from the other side of the world were waiting.

Rachel liked Blue's mother the moment they met, as did Kate and Jacob.

Matthew looked around for his parents, disappointed they were not here to greet his wife, then spotted his sister, Abigail, hurrying along the sidewalk, two babies in her arms. Quickly walking to meet her, relieved her of one of the babies, and learned of their father's fall at the Homestead and the abandonment of their celebrations in Justville.

Still holding his niece and with his arm around his wife, he proudly made the introductions. Abigail looked amazed; a maid and manservant.

"Tell us the names of your babies."

"Primrose and Patience," she replied as Rachel took the other baby from her. Saying. "I hope our infant will be as beautiful as your babies."

Nothing could have pleased Abigail more, as they made their way into the cool of Martha's house.

Rachel and Kate had just returned to the sitting room when Rebekah rushed in.

"I have just heard you've arrived! Matt, you have changed, but you look wonderful. Is this your wife?" They kissed.

Rachel noticed Rebekah's wedding ring.

"Matthew, you didn't tell me Rebekah was married."

"Is she?" he asked innocently.

"Yes, Matt. To Brent Gordon."

Happy now it was no longer a secret.

Cool drinks were handed around and a selection of cakes placed for the now-weary folk to enjoy. Everyone began talking, asking and answering questions. The room was a babble of happy voices.

Duke presented himself, apologising for being unable to be there on their arrival.

"Let me look at you, son." The Doctor's piercing eyes searching his son's face. "You've been unwell?" he queried.

"If I am, I cannot afford to pay for a cure. I spent my last cent buying two horses."

Blue laughed.

"Father, meet Matt's lovely wife, Rachel, and our good friends, Kate and Jacob."

Leaving his father, Blue followed his mother into the kitchen.

"Not quite the same old place," he said to her, opening neat, fitted cupboard doors.

"Well nearly. We do have a refrigerator, run by an engine outside. Keeps things fresh and cool. Take a look," his mother suggested.

From inside the cool-box he chose a jug of lemonade. Giving him a glassful, she watched as he drank, her eyes fixed on his face, remembering the wooden beads and his father's theory.

He told of some escapades, the circus, and the friends they met. Rachel's lovely home.

Then quite out of the blue his mother asked, "You did not find yourself a nice young English wife?!"

Her son, for an unguarded moment, gave an absent look. Then he laughed in his same old way.

"Not on your life!"

Quickly he changed the subject, suggesting they join the others.

Looking towards and around his feet, he said, "Anyone seen Prince?"

Kate answered him. "He became so excited, so we tied him in the wagon. Tried to jump off, he did."

Blue fetched the dog in. Talking to him as if he were a child,

312

he gave him a tit-bit from one of the plates and a drink of water. Martha petted him, and gave him more scraps.

"Prince of Dogs, you haven't changed at all, except for a few grey whiskers!"

"He has some offspring at Kiddsmere. Patsy! Eh, boy, Patsy!" Blue spoke to him. Prince cocked his head to one side knowingly and wagged his tail.

"I have never seen such an intelligent animal. His circus performances nearly brought the house down. Everyone loved him," said Rachel. The dog pricked up his ears and wagged his tail all the more, as Rachel continued, "Paid for your dinners, haven't you, my boy?"

Blue snapped his fingers. Prince stood on his hind legs and tapped his front paws together. This amused everyone, causing them to laugh. The babies wanted to get to him.

"Were you a performer, Rachel?" Rebekah asked.

"Yes. With elephants. Not for long though. Rajah and Mimi, two lovely, gentle creatures. Completely ignorant I was, Matthew and Blue helped me so much," she said, looking at them both lovingly.

Abigail was sorry to leave them, but James would soon be home.

"Lunch at our place tomorrow, Matthew," his sister stated, picking up her babies, who had begun to get rather irritable.

It had been planned they would all stay with Martha and Duke for a couple of nights, and she was now showing every-one their rooms. She could not take her eyes off her son, as he helped bring a few boxes of their essential needs upstairs. A handsome young man. The image of his father!

Sitting talking with his father the next morning, Blue learned of the gold and mineral finds on land that had been registered in their name.

"On the advice of Ben Dere, several years ago, when he visited Adelaide, his solicitor did all the transactions for us," said Duke. "You remember when desperately sick folk gave us seemingly worthless documents as payment for my services? The others who had found nothing, had they stayed, would have been exceedingly rich. But the going was tough and some died."

"Just as well, Father; when I learned of a gold find and Blizzard gave me my statement of account, I made financial promises and purchases of apparatus for a hospital in England, Cambsworth hospital, and cash to help an institution for poor and needy children. Gee-Oh! Some were sick!"

Blue talked to his father for some considerable time, telling of his friends, Joshua and Taggerty, and Francis Peake, as well as the making of Matthew's new artificial limb.

Thoughtfully, Duke looked at his son and asked, "What happened to the necklace Nerimbo gave you, when you were very young?"

As if it was of no importance, Blue answered, "Oh, that old thing. Why do you ask?"

"Curiosity, maybe. I saw one not so long ago. Have you given it away?"

Blue shook his head, unable to tell on Ruth, but was saved by a timely interruption from his mother that his father was urgently needed at the hospital.

Sitting alone with his thoughts, he wondered about his future. Matt and Rachel would return to England in the course of time, and his faithful Prince would not be around forever. If he searched the world over, he would never find another dog like him. What of himself? His future? Join a band of Circus travellers? Without his two companions, his act had little meaning. Rich enough to idle away his time; that thought made him shudder.

Rachel found him on the veranda, shoulders drooping, bereft of his usual jubilance, feeling sorry for himself, very unlike the Blue she had come to know.

Enquiring what was wrong, he explained, making quite certain not to make her feel guilty.

Trying to cheer him, she said, "You will find yourself a most attractive wife and together you will travel far and wide. Your gift of laughter and merriment is infectious. It works wonders for rich and poor alike. Just you wait and see!"

"I only hope you are right. I feel abysmal," he stated dejectedly.

"Come with me to the store, Blue," she said, trying to change his mood. "I would like to see as much of your town as possible. We will be leaving for Matthew's home tomorrow, and remember we are lunching with Abigail and possibly meeting my brother-in-law. Kate and Jacob will join us. At this moment, Matthew is showing off his new artificial limb to a doctor friend of Rebekah's."

Chapter 31

Early in the cool of the following morning, the travellers were ready to leave on the final stage of their journey. The short stay at Justville had been wonderful.

Upon reaching the Dere Homestead, Blue's duty would be accomplished, after which he would return to his parents' home to decide his future.

Now, in the saddle again and mentally pulling himself together, he became the life and soul of the party, enjoying the freedom and joy around their campfire.

On the second day, when Matthew's home boundary was in sight, he sang and whistled, just as he and his father had done in years gone by. He even persuaded Matt to play 'The Magic Flute'.

They stopped on a slight incline, the shrill notes of Madam Clare's lullaby echoing across the heat-hazed pastures.

Jacob pointed forward. Someone on horseback was riding towards them.

Matthew continued playing his flute. No one spoke. For some apparent reason the whole area seemed electrified, charged with supernatural powers. Strange was not the word for it!

Blue sat transfixed, his eyes on the rider. Perspiration formed on his forehead. Erratic heartbeats drummed in his ears like those thudding hooves he had encountered in his dreams. He shivered. The rider was closer now; he could see a sheath of red hair streaming in the wind.

At last, he had found his phantom rider – Ruth! He gave a groan and heard Matthew shouting, "Reckless woman! You will kill yourself and the horse as well, riding like that!"

He looked at his sister through the dust, her hat hanging loosely around her neck.

"How do you do? So pleased to meet you," she said in an affected, mocking voice. Ruth was imitating English High Society, without a doubt, for the benefit of Rachel.

Her brother looked at her with disgust and contempt, saying, "I now realise what a spoilt brat you are. Your manners are atrocious!"

Rachel looked at the pretty young girl, summing her up. A chip on her shoulder, no doubt. Given time, she was sure to find out why, but for the moment, because she knew this exhibition was for her benefit, she calmly held out her hand, repeating in an identical tone of voice, "How do you do? I am most pleased to meet my … er … sister-in-law, Ruth. Am I correct? The weather here is quite unsuitable for removing one's hat, I suggest you put it back on, or would you like to borrow my old bonnet?"

Matthew, hearing the retort from his wife, started to laugh. Blue also laughed, which did not help matters.

Ruth turned her horse, never once glancing in the direction of Blue, and rode away at great speed.

"Wow!" exclaimed Matthew. "What a reception! So sorry my love!" he said apologetically.

"That filly will take some handling. Wouldn't like the task of breaking that one in!" Jacob remarked to no one in particular.

Their happiness evaporated. In near silence they covered the remainder of the journey over pastures dotted here and there with sheep, until the Homestead came into sight. Getting closer, Matthew remarked that a new wing had been added to the Homestead. More sheds had been built and three windmills supplied power. His mother could be seen waving. His father stood beside her, a walking cane taking his weight, his arm cradled in a white sling.

Alighting from his horse, Matthew crossed to the wagon and helped an exquisitely dressed Rachel to the ground. She had purposely saved this gown in which to greet her father and mother-in-law, having slipped into it on their last stop.

With great seriousness, Matthew said, "Father, Mom, my wife, Rachel."

Ben placed his lips to Rachel's offered hand, smiling as he did so. Beth kissed the young girl's cheek, desperately wanting to give her a hug, then turned to her son, unable to hold back the tears, hugging him. She then noticed he was wearing both boots. This really was too much for her and she drew her daughter-in-law into their embrace. Only then did she realise that Rachel was with child.

With Matthew otherwise engaged, Blue took over the introduction of Kate and Jacob. "Rachel's faithful servants! In other words, Mr Dere, Kate is Rachel's second mother!"

Blue greeted Mrs Dere with an enormous kiss, laughing, telling her, "I have kept my promise. Brought home three instead of one! Fair dinkum?"

Matthew, with Rachel at his side, had walked to where Jake was sitting.

"Rachel Dere, meet my 'Godfather'."

Jake, so overcome by emotion, just held each by the hand.

Rachel stooped and kissed him, saying, "I have heard so much about you."

Sitting down, one on either side of him, she gave him her wisp of lace handkerchief to wipe away his tears.

Eventually, gaining control of his emotions, he grinned, showing well-spaced, brown teeth, and told them, "No one has kissed me since I was a baby. I will sleep well tonight, this under my pillow," waving the delicate piece of lace and calling to Blue, "Thanks for bringing him safely home."

"He also brought my wife, Jake, and our little one to come."

This was nearly too much for the old man, who began shedding a few more tears, eventually rambling on about the day Matthew was born. He hoped he would be around to see this 'un come into the world too. Both assured him he would, helping him to his feet, and heard him say over and over as he walked towards his bunk-house, "Something to live for again, a young'un. Whoopee!"

If his old buckled legs had let him, he would have danced or performed a side-kick.

Now, well and truly refreshed, Rachel and Kate sat talking with Beth. This was a most pleasurable treat for her, who of late had only Ruth and Ben for companions.

Ruth had become most difficult and, since her illness, strange.

Waiting to start supper, where was Ruth? she wondered. Excusing herself, she went in search of her daughter. Feeling uneasy, she opened Ruth's bedroom door.

The room was in semi-darkness. About to close the door, Beth thought she heard a sound. "Ruth?" she called and switched on the light.

Her daughter sat by the window. Beth went to her, asking no questions.

"Jason has asked me to marry him," Ruth blurted out.

Calmly, Beth asked, "Have you given him an answer?"

Ruth turned and looked at her mother. Large, sad eyes dominated her pale, lovely face.

"Something strange has happened to me. I do not even like him anymore! He was so angry with me, vile in fact! I have told him to leave. He will not go! Said he will ask me again tomorrow!"

Beth placed her arm around her daughter's shoulder, choosing her words very carefully.

"We travel life's path but once. Our life is tremendously short. Guided, we most certainly are, but the final choice of partnership is left to the individual. I have the feeling you have already made your choice. Darling, I came to tell you supper is ready," she said, giving her daughter an extra big hug. "Would you rather have your supper here?"

Ruth shook her head.

"No. I was rude to Matthew today. I must say I am sorry."

Beth could not believe she had heard correctly. So used now to tantrums, and very rarely apologies, she gave her the news of Rachel and Matthew's baby.

Hearing laughter coming from the library, Beth said, "Oh, Ruth, how wonderful, your father is laughing again. Blue is with him."

Matthew was sitting on a chaise-lounge, his arm around his wife, looking at an album of portraits, when his mother and Ruth appeared.

Kate, busy with some crochet, saw Ruth go to her brother and sister-in-law and heard her calmly apologise for her appalling behaviour.

At first Matthew looked bewildered, then jumped up, gave his sister a quick kiss and hug. In quite a jovial manner, he said, "In England, when things are not quite as they should be, they blame the weather. That so, Rachel? Well, meet my sister Ruth, everyone." He said this as if they had not met before. "Always a little nuisance, but I love her."

Jacob, who was standing, said, "Pleased to meet you. You can certainly handle a horse, I give you that!"

Rachel moved along the chaise, making room for her. Ruth sat down and turned a page of the album, telling who it was in the picture.

"Have you thought of a name for your baby? A family name? Grandfather was Benjamin, same as Papa," Ruth enlightened her, turning over another page.

"Well," replied Rachel, "if it is a boy we have agreed on my late father's name, Augustus, followed by Benjamin Coleville. Marie Elizabeth for a girl. My father died in an accident, shooting game," she added.

"We have thought of putting Benjamin before Augustus, but, poor little thing would be nicknamed 'BAD'! We could not have that, could we?" Rachel said, giving a laugh.

New portraits had been added since Matthew left, and Rachel, wanting to know so much about his family, asked question after question, until Beth insisted they have supper.

Seated around the large polished dining table, conversation ranged from Kiddsmere Estate to the Dere Homestead.

"Do you ride, Rachel?" Ruth asked.

Matthew answered for her. "She could out-ride me!" Then he told of their early morning rides, with quite often only Jacob having the knowledge where they could be found.

His mother looked horrified. Matthew teased her by saying, "A rich old gent was trying to catch my lovely wife for his bride, so I had to work fast."

They all laughed when Blue added, "Breakfast was regularly served for them in the rectory garden, even Reverend Francis Peake and his wife nipped up to enjoy bacon and eggs, smoky tea and toast, after the lovebirds had flown."

"Did they really?" Rachel asked him, giving a giggle. "How wonderful!"

"I demonstrated my expertise on them one lunch time, by introducing them to our sauerkraut. Our friend, Hans, made a delicious meal using it, serving it with sausages, when we were on tour. That's right, isn't it, Matt?"

"For a moment, Blue, I thought you were about to say 'Freddy Darling'," quipped Matthew. "What did they think of it – Francis and Marjorie?"

"Not a lot!" Blue remarked.

Apart from this, Blue's contribution to the conversation had been minimal.

Seating arrangements were so that, as yet, Ruth and he had not spoken a word to each other. He was, however, acutely aware of her presence, as an unusual sensation spasmodically travelled up and down his spine.

After supper, Ben rose from his chair and invited everyone into the lounge.

The room was pleasantly cool. A large fan, suspended from the ceiling, slowly rotated. Relaxing in comfortable chairs, as the evening passed, Rachel and Kate had difficulty staying awake. Matthew noticed this, and, in a protective manner, suggested it was time for them to retire, as it had been a long day.

Sun-up next morning. Blue asked a few workmen to help unload his wagon, carefully handling two chests of crockery, wrapped rolls of material and bed linen, small packages and an assortment of luggage. Looking at the quantity neatly arranged on the veranda, it was a marvel how it had all been packed into the wagon. A good thing their horse was stalwart.

Giving his wagon a thorough clean, whistling and scrubbing noisily, Ruth had to hammer several times on the side of the wagon in order to make him hear.

Wiping his hands on some rough towelling, he peered out to see who it was.

Ruth stood in front of him, dressed in a suede riding suit, looking a bit dust-covered, but otherwise immaculate.

"Breakfast is ready," she announced, pulling off her leather gloves. "I have been to Devil's Ditch. Do you remember it?"

"Yes." Then asked her, "Did Matt go with you?" because he had heard two horses leave the yard very early.

Her face crimsoned slightly.

"It was not Matt. It was a friend of mine, Jason, one of the hands," she said, leaving him and going towards the bungalow.

Blue quickly hopped from his wagon and walked with her, reaching out to open the kitchen door. Ruth flinched, as if he was about to touch her. Saying nothing, he stepped back, allowing her more room to pass.

Blue loved sitting at Beth's kitchen table. It gave him a wonderful 'at home' feeling.

"The dining room table is set, but everyone wanted to have breakfast in the kitchen," a flushed and happy Beth announced.

With Kate helping, Matthew flipped fried eggs onto hot plates, neatly piled with ham and bacon.

As was always the custom, Ben said prayers.

Ruth seated herself beside her father, occasionally helping him cut his food. Reporting her visit to Devil's Ditch, he became angry, saying, "You know I do not like you going there alone, someone would have driven you there. Matt or Blue perhaps. Now we have some help around the place for a while, why not take a break? Go to Justville or a trip to Adelaide? You deserve a break, I think you have been over-burdened of late!"

Ruth jumped up, knocking over a cup, and shouted, "So, now your pets are home, I'm not wanted!"

Flinging her table napkin on to her vacant chair, she rushed away.

Ben apologised to everyone.

"That is not what I meant at all!"

Deeply perturbed, he excused himself and left the room.

A hush descended over everyone. Beth broke the silence by telling of Ruth's illness.

"Until then, she was always a wild one, but never spoke with disrespect to her father," Beth concluded.

"What illness did she have?" Rachel asked.

Giving a few details, she said, "It came upon her quite suddenly. One moment, laughing and happy, then in no time, sick and trance-like. Ill for two or three days. From then on, she became a totally different daughter. I cannot understand why."

Rachel saw her husband shake his head and decided not to pursue the subject in front of Blue.

Earlier that morning, Matthew had asked for a covered wagon to be made ready. This glorious morning, he wanted to show his wife, Kate and Jacob one of his favourite parts of the Homestead.

Kate asked not to be included, anticipating Beth needed some help.

Finally, Ben chose to join his son and daughter-in-law on the tour, and began talking amicably with Jacob.

Blue, left to his own devices, finished his cleaning. Opening his 'traveller' box, he picked out some packages. One of these he placed on Jake's lap, as his old friend sat dozing on the half-shaded veranda and waited while he opened the long, black leather case. Inside the case rested a tobacco-pipe, with the shape of the head of a horse for the bowl, delicately carved with silver finishing.

The old man lifted it reverently from its blue velvet niche, exclaiming, "Boy! Oh! Boy! That is a beaut!" turning it over, looking at the silver patterns, as Blue dropped another smaller packet on his lap.

"Matches and bacca, or baccy! That is what some English folk say," Blue told him.

"You're a good, kind and thoughtful lad, Blue. May God Bless you. Thanks a million."

Jake patted Prince on the rump. "Good to see ya both back home."

Looking across to the paddock, Jake asked suddenly, "My old hos, Conker, needs a ride. Care to take him out?"

Blue looked at Jake in amazement. No one ever rode Jake's horse.

"Do you think I could handle him?"

"Sure you can, boy, docile as a dolphin!" Jake said, laughing.

"Thanks. Any special place you want me to visit?" he asked, suddenly suspecting a reason for this request.

"Well ..." Jake thought carefully. "You know that far rock 'neath the Douglas Pine – my favourite look-out spot – remember?"

Seeing Blue's acknowledgement, he continued, "I have not been able to get there lately ..."

Blue quickly interrupted him. "Want me to take you there in my wagon?"

"Not yet lad. You go there. Maybe one day …"

Jake quit talking, closing his eyes, then opened them quickly as Beth brought him a glass of drink.

Following Beth into the kitchen, Blue placed a long package, addressed to Mrs Dere, on the table. Accepting a drink from Kate, Blue said, "I bet you are thoroughly enjoying yourselves."

Kate agreed, waiting as Beth opened the package.

Inside the box, covered with layers of protective paper, lay two silver-framed pictures, one with Matthew and Rachel dressed in their circus costumes, the other with Blue and Prince in clown attire.

"How lovely!" she exclaimed, as she passed one for Kate to see, looking at the other with admiration.

For Ben's present, Blue had chosen a more sombre picture of Matthew and Rachel taken in their drawing room at the Hall. With this, a pocket-size prayer book, gold cut and bound in leather. Both of these he left on the desk in Ben's study.

Having not seen Ruth since the breakfast tantrum, he left her boxed gift, a china figurine, against her room door. It was duly marked, 'Fragile – A memento from the Prince of Dogs'.

Outside again, Blue set off to saddle-up Conker. Jake hobbled over, leaned on the railings, placing fingers between his lips, and gave a piercing whistle.

Conker, his beautiful Chestnut horse, heard the call, trotted over and nuzzled into Jake's chest. Both men talked to the horse as they slipped on the halter and saddle and rearranged its silken mane.

Complete with gun, food and water, Blue leapt onto a rail and into the saddle, gently giving the horse the go-ahead.

"That boy has power to charm the Devil," Jake declared, as he watched his horse ridden away. "Come, old pal, you stay with me today," he said to Prince, as they ambled across to the veranda.

Blue followed a string of fences deep into the lush pasture. A small herd of cattle were grazing contentedly, while their young calves trotted and galloped towards horse and rider inquisitively. These animals were kept solely for the Homestead use.

"Cattle and sheep don't mix," Ben had told him. Now, this new breed of sheep in which Ben had invested were more profitable.

Kangaroo quickly raced away in great leaps and bounds, Blue laughed, he had forgotten how fast they moved. Taking his time, it was well after lunch before he reached the river.

Tying Conker at the riverside, the horse waded into the fresh water to drink, while he, himself, sat on a large boulder, undid his bag and began to eat, realising he was hungry. Past the bend in the river and along the swampy track and they would be there.

He looked around. Nothing seemed unduly changed, more growth perhaps, taking in the scraggy bushes. For a while he sat deep in thought, his heart heavy. Unable to make up his mind as to when to leave the Homestead. With no reason to stay now, he should move on quickly. But, move on to where? What to do, or rather, what to make of his life now? If he were in England, his aim in life would be to ease some of the pain of those in the Institution; give them a promising start in life. It would be a joy to see them well and happy in this wonderful country of ours! Are there needs for such Institutions here? He had no idea.

For a moment or two he studied his hands. Had he healing powers within, as Matthew had suggested?

His thoughts centred on Annabel and his manipulation; he certainly had no wish to be referred to, as some are in that profession, a Quack Doctor, even if he did have such a gift. Should he follow in his father's profession? No answer seemed forthcoming. He had sat long enough. The tall Douglas, high on the mound, its branches giving shelter to vivid parrots and parakeets, beckoned him. He could discern the accumulation of rock through the undergrowth. Someone had set new saplings, leaving a clear space in the centre, save for natural rock scattered here and there in the seared grass.

Taking his gun, field glasses slung over his shoulder, and leaving his horse grazing contentedly, he climbed higher and on to the topmost rock. No wonder Jake had a special affection for this place, taking in the magnificent panoramic view. One could see for several miles.

He scanned his surroundings. There was very little movement at this time of day, with the birds and animals tucked away in the shade, coming out to feed before nightfall.

Suddenly, in the distance, a sharp glint of sunlight on metal caught his attention. Focusing his glasses, he saw what looked to be a cattle wagon. That is strange. When helping him unload his wagon this morning, a stockman told him they were all going to Devil's Ditch.

Watching attentively, he counted four riders bring a small flock of sheep forward, pen them, turn and ride away to fetch more sheep, penning a possible dozen or so. The tailboard of the wagon lowered, and the sheep were herded inside.

The makeshift pen was dismantled in a great deal of hurry, the hurdles loaded on board and everyone moved away quickly.

It all looked very suspicious, especially when one of the riders left the gang to go in the opposite direction.

Noticing the position of the sun, he scrambled back to his tethered horse. No shilly-shally, it was time he left for the Homestead.

Letting the powerful horse have his head, he felt exhilarated as they galloped over the turf, then eased the horse to a slower pace, getting his breath back to jog along quite happily.

Something about the vast area made him want to sing. It was a strange feeling, when only a short while ago his heart was heavy. Nearing the Homestead, he wondered what the menu was for supper. Then, without any warning, he experienced a most nauseating pain in his stomach, and a weakness of his legs. He could not believe it! No faggots and peas this time! Again, he put the horse to a gallop, with only one thought in mind, to get home quickly!

Galloping along, the wind cooling his face helping to ease the nausea, he began to feel slightly better.

The nausea had been replaced by a most strange, uncanny feeling, affecting both his heart and mind. Something that he could not explain, the same peculiar feeling he had encountered in England.

Jake and a young lad were in the yard when he arrived home. The boy took the horse, as Blue sank on to a seat beside Jake, thankful to be home. Saying nothing to Jake of his strange feeling, he began to relate the events of his day.

The old stockman listened intently, squinting at Blue through half-closed eyes, occasionally uttering an expletive, showing more and more anger, not at Blue but towards his trusted stockman.

"You mean, your headman is stealing sheep?" Blue asked in a hushed voice.

"No! No!" Jake replied angrily. "For missing that damned culprit. Told him last week something was amiss."

Jake sat pensive for a moment.

"We will get the hobo. Thought it was you and Miss Ruth out riding early, 'til I saw you unloading your wagon."

Blue laughed. "She won't ride with me! Doesn't like me, in fact."

"Why she keep your picture handy then? Tell me that?" Jake snapped.

Mulling over Jake's words he said, "Jake, Ruth would never steal her own sheep?"

Their conversation ceased abruptly. Rachel came from within the bungalow, Prince following her. Seeing his master, the dog chased to him and into his arms, licking his face in an affectionate greeting. Ruth watched from the doorway.

"Suppose I had better get cleaned up for supper, eh, Jake?"

Taking his gun and glasses, he started walking with Prince towards his wagon.

"I have tried re-arranging my hairstyle, Rachel. Would you please be so kind and come to my room ..." Blue heard Ruth say, until their conversation became inaudible.

Thinking to himself, how strange; Ruth so rude one moment, then issuing an invitation as if nothing untoward had happened.

Minutes after collecting his toiletry, he heard Rachel shout a long, drawn-out "Blue!"

He raced to the bungalow, and with an enormous bound leaped the veranda steps, thinking only of Rachel and her baby. Where was Matt? Had Ruth done something drastic? Surely not!

Not knowing what to expect, because Rachel was now calling for her husband, he hurried along the passage. Ruth's bedroom door stood wide open.

He entered and saw Ruth sitting in front of a large dressing table mirror. He could see her reflection and noticed her eyes transfixed.

Rachel, now very agitated, put out a hand to Blue, just as Matthew came rushing into the room. Blue, taking no notice of either, walked over to Ruth.

"What insult has my sister inflicted now, my love?" Matthew asked, gently encircling his wife in his arms.

Assuring him nothing was the matter with her, only that she had become frightened, she directed his attention towards his sister.

Blue, at Ruth's side, stooped and kissed her cheek, taking from her head the circlet of wooden beads into which, at Ruth's request, Rachel was endeavouring to roll and clip her mass of silken red hair.

Blue pocketed the beads, now knowing the reason for his dilemma regarding his future. His heart was bound to this young woman – the horse-woman of his dreams! Still in her trance-like state, he gently lifted her from the stool and placed her on a sofa, murmuring something inaudible, kissed her again, then turned away.

Matthew and his wife looked on, spell-bound, unable to believe their eyes. Saying nothing, they moved to one side to let Blue pass.

Blue, with a quaint smile on his face, said, "No need to tell your Mama. She will be fine now Matt."

Picking up his bag of toiletry, he walked away.

He had no idea how he should know Ruth would be fine; was it because the beads were safely in his pocket?

Matthew and Rachel had been sitting in the room for quite some time before Ruth noticed them. Ruth, putting a hand to her forehead, asked how she came to be on the sofa.

"You became unwell while Rachel was arranging your hair. You spoke to her strangely. Do you not remember? Do you feel better?" he asked, noticing the colour returning to her cheeks and that she no longer had that peculiar, vacant look about her.

"I am fine, I think, thank you," she said, putting her feet to the floor and sitting herself upright.

"Which dress are you wearing this evening? Remember, your Mama has arranged a supper dance. Can I get it ready for you?" Rachel enquired. "It will be supper soon."

"Well, I had planned to dress Hawaiian style, but now I will wear the new green one I have been saving for Matt's homecoming. Will you arrange my hair for me, please?" Ruth asked her, and, with no sign of distress or giddiness, walked to her dressing table.

The men were in the music room, waiting for the ladies to appear. Ben had smiled to himself when his wife suggested a supper-dance, remembering their children dressing for the occasion and he and Beth teaching them to dance. It had been great fun and a long time ago.

Looking at his son now, he felt very proud. Neatly attired, his handicap hardly noticeable and married to a most beautiful young woman.

Jacob, with whom he liked talking, was very spic and span. But Blue, well, in the matter of hours, his entire appearance had changed dramatically!

The jacket of his black suit had reveres, matching a green silk shirt, but not only was he dressed in such a magnificent way, his old joviality and humour had returned. Rachel came and sat down. A very subdued Ruth followed. She was dressed in a long gown of emerald green, edged and trimmed with black lace, her red hair secured by a green, velvet band and pinned into a loose roll at the nape of her neck. Blue was enchanted by her beauty.

Beth and Kate were last to arrive, chatting to each other nineteen-to-the-dozen, having put the final touch to the evening meal.

Beth stopped in her tracks, looking firstly at her daughter, then to Blue, their outfits bringing to mind a coincidence of similar choice in the past.

"How elegant everyone looks this evening," Beth stated happily. "Supper is ready."

She helped her husband to the dining room, with Matthew positioning his chair.

"You will have to let Blue look at that arm for you, Father. He has rare healing powers in his hands."

Ruth sat opposite to Blue, which pleased him greatly. On her best behaviour, she smiled and chatted amicably to everyone.

A stockman's wife, Ellen, who came to help Beth at busy times, served their meal of roast beef, Yorkshire pudding and an array of vegetables – a traditional English meal.

Matthew tormented Kate, "No need to wonder who had a finger in the pie! Yorkshire pudding!"

"But I am keeping you all guessing as to the pudding," Kate

blithely answered.

"Spotted Dick" Blue laughingly suggested.

Kate, shaking a finger at him, said, "No! I am not telling."

Beth did so love her family suppers. In a few days' time all her family should be here. Sworn to secrecy, only Kate and her helpers knew, because of the extra activity in the kitchen. Lost in her own thoughts, she missed out on the conversation, smiling when she heard the last of the puddings mentioned.

The guessing ceased, when, piled high on a large silver dish and brought in by Ellen, a monument of various coloured vanilla creams appeared, and a crystal bowl of Gooseberry Fool.

"Dearest Kate," exclaimed Rachel, "you have excelled yourself!"

"Definitely no fool!" Blue laughed at the pun, as Ellen carefully served from the top of the pudding, as Kate suggested, to avoid mishap.

Kate's puddings were delicious.

Taking their drinks into the music room, Ruth, full of life, asked Matthew to play some music.

"I always loved the Gavotte. Remember Mama, you and Papa taught us the steps? Do you dance, Rachel?"

"Yes, Ruth, but I prefer to sit and watch you," she replied, making herself comfortable. Matthew played his accordion.

Ben agreed to try a few steps with his wife, it being a very sedate dance. Kate stood to dance with her husband, leaving Ruth and Blue to dance together.

The first time around the polished floor, stepping and pointing in the wrong sequence caused hilarity. Gradually, memories refreshed, they stepped, pointed and swayed in perfect rhythm, Blue wishing the dance would last forever.

My! Now so aware he loved this young woman! The feeling was painful!

He had encountered nothing like it, ever! No wonder Matt moaned around in England like a lovesick dog.

Ruth teased him when his step faltered.

"I am lost in your beauty!" he tormented. "Shush!" Ruth blushed. "Mama will hear!"

This statement was in complete contrast to her past behaviour – then it would not have mattered who had heard!

The dance almost over, he dared to suggest she meet him on the veranda. Ruth smiled at her mother, hoping she had not heard Blue's request.

Amid the laughter as the dance ended, Ruth's very rosy-cheeked mother asked, "Be a darling Ruth, and fetch my fan. It is on my bed."

Determined not to miss this heaven-sent opportunity, Blue walked with Ruth. Once in the passageway, he turned Ruth towards him, saying, "Time is very short. If you slap my face now, heaven forbid!"

Giving her no chance to resist, he closed his arms around her, and planted his lips firmly on hers.

Slowly her arms reached up to touch his mass of blond, curly hair, returning his kiss.

"Ruth, I have waited so long to find my dream. My heart has been locked. You are my dream, the person to whom I have given my heart!"

He kissed her again with great passion. Never had he felt the urge to kiss any young woman.

"Blue, I must get back," she said, feebly trying to free herself.

"Before we return, please Ruth, do I stand a chance that one day you could care for me, love me? Could you share your life with me? I am a fool. It would not be easy! I love you Ruth! If you say no, then I will go and not bother you again."

"If this is love," Ruth whispered, "then I am in love with a fool."

"My beautiful love. I adore you!" He kissed her again and again.

She pulled away. "Blue, I must go. Mama!"

She raced to her mother's room, but could not find the fan any place.

Blue had taken a quick look into the music room and saw Beth using an Ostrich feather fan, totally engrossed in conversation with Rachel.

Ruth saw her own pale reflection in her mother's table mirror and Blue leaning against the doorpost. Remembering the wooden necklace, she put her hands to her throat.

"We have a lot do discuss, my dearest," Blue said, opening wide his arms.

"Come, no need to look further, your mama has her fan, and the necklace is in safe keeping."

Ruth went to him. Strains of music from Matthew's flute reached them. Between kisses, he murmured, "Madam Clare!"

"Who is Madame Clare?"

"One day you will meet her."

With a sigh, he looked into her lovely green eyes.

"May I ask your father for your hand in marriage? Ours, like your brother Matthew and Rachel's courtship, will be short, if you agree."

Frightened by the suddenness, she asked, "So soon, Blue?"

"Of course, why not?"

Cupping her face in his hands, he said, "No need to be afraid," kissing her tenderly.

Noticing her furtive glances towards the music room, he said, "It is a shame, but we had best return to the party. Promise you will ride with me in the morning and no one else, my darling." He held her until she answered.

"I would love to," spoken softly against his lips.

Ruth found her mother still talking with Rachel.

"I could not find the fan, Mama."

Beth looked at her daughter closely and said innocently, "No. Look, I found it. Sorry to send you on a fool's errand."

Blue left the party quickly and raced across to his wagon.

"Strike while the iron is hot," someone had once told him. Picking up a jewel case, he slipped it into his inside pocket.

Jake, outside his quarters, sat smoking his new pipe. Blue spoke to him, and told him he was in a hurry.

"Ruth has accepted!"

Jake's crackling laugh ended with a fit of coughing as he said, "I told you so!"

Blue hurried away.

"Good luck!" Jake shouted. "Hope you will be able to handle her."

Out of earshot, Blue didn't hear his last sentence.

Ben was leafing through some music sheets when Blue approached him.

"Please Mr Dere, may I have your permission to marry your daughter, Ruth?"

To Ben this request came as a great surprise. Most unexpected. Looking at Blue's serious face and then to his daughter on the other side of the room, he was lost for words.

He had no idea!

It seemed to Blue an eternity before Ben gave an answer. Looking puzzled but pleased, he said, "If that is what you both want, of course. Blue – are you sure? The pair of you have always been …"

Taking note of the relief in his face and his smile, he forgot the rest of his sentence.

Blue's face was wreathed in smiles and he had a look of sheer happiness.

"Thank you. I promise to take great care of her for the rest of my life."

He crossed the room to where Ruth was sitting. On bended knee, in front of her and those present, he proposed marriage. Taking her left hand in his, he slipped a diamond and emerald ring on her third finger.

"Oh! Blue!" Her cheeks turned scarlet.

Thinking she would run away, he held her in a vice-like grip, then shouted happily, "Ruth has promised to marry me! Matthew – music please!"

Gathering his fiancée into his arms, he danced around the room, grinning from ear to ear.

The first tune to come to Matthew's mind was the Wedding March. Ruth began to laugh, accepting hugs and kisses, her embarrassment over, and said to her family, "Look at this lovable fool whom I have promised to marry!"

Rachel answered most sincerely, "Yes, Ruth, but underneath that foolery you will find a heart of gold!"

Blue, laughing, pulled an idiotic face and calmly informed Matthew and his wife, mimicking Burroughs from Kiddsmere Hall, "Have breakfast of bacon and crisp new rolls ready when my fiancée and I return from our early morning ride!"

Matthew, Rachel, Kate and Jacob laughed, explaining that the impersonation of their Butler was perfect.

Taught by their friend, Hans, and one of Blue's favourite pieces, Matthew played a rousing Bavarian melody, ending with the tune neither would ever forget, least of all the person whose voice they had first heard singing it – Madam Clare's lullaby. As the following day progressed, the Dere and Jackson families began to arrive. Rebekah, Brent and Duke and Martha came together, taking what each said was a well-deserved holiday from their work.

They were all quite surprised to hear of the betrothal between Ruth and Blue.

The glorious party at the Homestead to welcome Matthew and his wife had turned into a double celebration.

Everyone thought Ruth and Blue's courtship, and even marriage, would not be without traumatic events, but plans were made for their marriage to take place in June.

Duke and Martha, at first apprehensive, wondering if their

son would be able to settle, consulted him as to his future, suggesting the building of a dwelling on a piece of land on the other side of the river, adjacent to the Dere land.

The idea suited Ruth amicably. She would be close to her parents, and her beloved Homestead, having agreed with Blue that while Matthew and Rachel stayed in Australia, she and her husband would travel. They would journey around their country; after all she had seen very little, save for the local townships.

Blue had not completely given up the idea of Clowning. In fact, in Adelaide he had acquired a trumpet. With Matthew's help and his own perseverance, he was able to create a noise with a semblance of tune.

Prince was no help at these sessions, his howling very off-putting, and was discouraged from attending. Age was beginning to have its effect on him, and he encountered difficulty when walking but, determined not to be left behind, was often lifted into the wagon.

Very sadly, one morning, Blue awoke to find his faithful old pet had passed away. Many tears were shed as 'The Prince of Dogs' was laid to rest beneath the Walnut tree, planted by Blue and Matt several years ago. With him, they had laid his clown attire and hat.

Plans had been put in place to try and catch the sheep-stealing culprits.

Orders were given in advance for the stockmen to make ready for a certain destination in order to cut an extensive fire barrier, and to be prepared to stay overnight. Ruth was in ignorance of the plan.

Jake was not a man to accuse, unless he found it to be the truth. He had two stockmen whom he knew he could trust implicitly, and both were in on the plan.

Just before the men were ready to leave, Ben called those two to one side.

"Will you stay back for a while, we need help to check the cattle? You can join the others later."

The trap was set.

A short time after the others had left, the two stockmen rode away towards the Dere boundary and concealed themselves close to the river.

Patiently they waited and were not disappointed, when, in the distance, they saw a covered wagon and two riders. A lone horseman appeared to meet them and then all disappeared from sight.

The two Homestead stockmen realised the gang were about to round-up sheep from the neighbour's flock.

Jumping on their horses, they made for the boundary and there they found four men in the act of rounding up the sheep, one of the fellas being Jason.

Jason spotted the men and made a dash for the thick bush alongside the river and was lost.

The other three gave the stockmen some 'cock and bull' story, but the Homestead lads were having none of it, confiscated their guns and horses, and made them sit in the wagon back to the Dere Homestead.

Jake saw the wagon approaching and called the Boss.

Ben's stockmen gave them the details of what they had seen and that Jason had galloped away towards the river.

Ben decided it would be up to his neighbour, Raymond Weston, to deal with this, as they were on his land.

"Take these men to him. You have a couple of hours before dark. Leave their guns and horses here," Ben told them.

Jake was fuming because Jason had got away.

"I must say, Ben, I have had my doubts about him from the moment I set eyes on him!"

When Blue's mother and father came to stay for the birth of Rachel's baby, which they had planned they would, Ruth and Blue had decided it was only right that he should spend some time with his parents, so would return with them to Justville. Jacob and Ruth became very good friends, horses their main topic of conversation, and he found himself riding around the vast sheep-station, thoroughly enjoying himself with her and Blue.

Jake soon overcame his disappointment of not catching Jason in the act of sheep rustling, because on the 23rd of April, Rachel was delivered of a son. He was overjoyed, as were the whole family.

Matthew gazed at his dark-haired son, cradled in Rachel's arms. His wife smiled. Tenderly he kissed her and gathered them both in his arms, words and tears of joy mingling with relief.

After a while, Matthew took his baby son to where Jake had taken up his position, and with reverence and awe the old man held the baby in his arms, too full of emotion even to speak.

On the first Saturday in June, at the Dere Homestead, Ruth and Blue made their wedding vows.

Family and friends had gathered for this double celebration, for, following the wedding ceremony came the christening of Matthew and Rachel's son.

Augustus Benjamin Coleville Dere.

Ruth and Blue were his godparents, and Matthew their Best Man.

With tears glistening in his eyes, Ben's gaze rested on his lovely, newly-married daughter, holding her brother's baby.

Still very strong-willed, no frills or frippery, her wedding outfit consisted of a cream suede suit and hat, trim leather boots and a bouquet of green orchids, cream ribbon and two silver horse-shoes.

Abigail's twin girls, suitably attired in pink and white organza dresses, were her only attendants. Blue also wore a cream suit and pink shirt with a tie to match, sporting a green orchid button-hole, the orchids brought to them by Rebekah and Brent.

A large spread had been prepared in the flower bedecked barn, after which Ruth and Blue would begin their months of travelling. The wagon had been well stocked and was ready and waiting.

Blue went to his father-in-law's side.

"I promise we will return," he stated gravely.

"I know I can trust you to take great care of her, my boy!" Ben told him, wiping away a tear. "Strange how sorrows have been woven with delights. Yes, trust is one of the greatest things of all time, Blue. May you both receive many blessings!"

The End